*D*AVID pu  rned
to her. "Oh, ... ay at The
Willows without you?"

They came together with quiet intensity, his arms folding her in to him, his mouth reaching for hers. Tender, eager, unlearned. She could feel his heart, pounding against her breast.

"Eulalie?" It was a painful, urgent question, his eye beseeching her, needing no words.

"There be time," she said with quiet dignity. He was askin'—not takin'. Nobody ever lay with David before. She be his first woman. An unfamiliar, startling desire took root in her. "David, pull the wagon off the road."

Under the pine trees, with the lush Southern grass as their bed, David took her.

What happens between a man and a woman can be beautiful, Eulalie realized with a sense of awe. With David, it was beautiful. With his father— but she would never remember that, ever again! David cleansed her body, washed away all the ugliness. He made her whole again. . . .

EULALIE

Julie Ellis

A FAWCETT CREST BOOK • NEW YORK

For Irving

EULALIE

Published by Fawcett Crest Books, a unit of CBS
Publications, the Consumer Publishing Division of CBS
Inc., by arrangement with the author.

Copyright © 1970 by Julie M. Ellis

ISBN: 0-449-23550-5

Printed in the United States of America

10 9 8 7 6 5 4 3 2 1

1

The house stood, tall and stately among magnificent oaks, on a rise beside the Chattahoochee River. The plantation grounds spread for hundreds of acres on the Georgia side of the river. The Willows had been owned by the Woodstocks since George Woodstock's grandfather—a former saddler in Sussex, England—went into business, prospered, and decided to try the New World. It was one of the largest and richest plantations in the South, with over four hundred slaves at the latest count. Pristine white against the lush June foliage, the mansion—its tall, narrow windows shuttered against the early-afternoon sun—appeared cool despite the ugly heat.

The river was a sickly trickle across the red-clay bed that had been nearly drained dry by the sun; it gave no inkling that it would, in another season, rise and spill over its banks and threaten the cotton crop. Everywhere was the sweet, heavy perfume of the honeysuckle vines, the fragrance of the magnolia blossoms, blooming dramatically, in the splendor of satiny green leaves, on trees that soared higher than the house itself

On the shaded back porch, young David Woodstock, his face white and miserable, tried to focus on the book open before him Eulalie, usually so still, living in a small world of her own, moved restlessly in the cane-seated maple chair, her thin, cotton hand-me-down clinging to the nubile, thirteen-year-old body, perspiration beading the golden forehead, rolling down the slender, golden column of her throat Both David and she were excruciatingly conscious of the drama being played in the elegant front bedroom belonging to David's seventeen-year-old sister, Lucinda—and in the far-from-elegant slave quarters to the west of the house

"Really, Master David," Ashley Bradford, the most recently imported tutor, said sharply. "I know it's terribly hot—but you can do better than that " Bradford, late of London, himself looked wilted despite his impeccable attire which so impressed neighboring young ladies

"I'm sorry," David mumbled, his blue eyes fastened to the book before him He frowned, making an effort to concentrate.

"Masta David, you think slowly,' Eulalie coaxed compassionately, in that liquid velvet voice of hers "You can git it."

Eulalie started—as did the other two at the table— when the crying upstairs rose again to an hysterical crescendo that ricocheted through the mansion, filtering outdoors, chilling everyone within earshot No use pretendin' they didn't *know* what was goin' on, Eulalie thought. This be a day to remember forever. Eulalie's heart pounded as she contemplated the happenings of the last hour. Missy Cindy up in that big, beautiful bedroom, lyin' across the fourposter bed that her Mama brought down all the way from Philadelphia, and Missis lacin' into her somethin' awful Down below, in the slave quarters, Massa Woodstock be whuppin' Alexander.

Eulalie's amber eyes were wide, fearful. Missy kept sayin' over and over again that nothin' happened with her and Alexander, but Missis Margaret be carryin' on like

Missy done been raped. Missis and the Massa believe nothin', till the doctor gits here and say she not be teched.

David cleared his throat self-consciously.

"I think I've got the answer, Mr. Bradford." He felt shamed because Eulalie—always bright and quick—had already solved the problem. Since he was seven and Eulalie was six, she had been sharing his lessons because of a whim of his mother's. "Is this it?"

With adoring eyes, Eulalie watched him anxiously. In Eulalie's dreaming mind, David was the prince in the fairy tale, the knight on the white charger. She was forever grateful that Margaret Woodstock had decreed that she share David's lessons under the stream of tutors who came to The Willows through the years.

Missis Margaret might be queer, Eulalie considered, the way folks said behind her back, but she was good—when she wasn't havin' one of her bad spells. The other slaves said Maw and herself was uppity, the way Maw worked in the house always and the way she sort of growed up in the kitchen and on the back porch with David and Missy. The others Eulalie's age was workin' in the fields already.

"Cindy, stop that screaming!" Missis Margaret's voice soared in anguish. "Do you hear me, young lady? You stop it this minute!"

Here came Maw now, out of the kitchen onto the back porch, totin' a pitcher of lemonade, tryin' to pretend nothin' awful had happened. Maw looked gray about the face. Cindy was her baby, almost as much as Eulalie was. When Cindy be so sick with the fever, it was Maw who took care of her, slept on the floor by her bed. Missy Cindy's own Maw and Paw be afraid to go into the bedroom, afraid of the malaria. For black folks, it wasn't so bad, Missis said. But plenty black folks die, that time.

"You bes' be havin' somethin' to cool you'all off," Maw said quietly, her head high, still pretendin' the earth wasn't turnin' upside down.

Seraphina—Eulalie's Maw—put the pitcher down on the pinewood table. Her big brown eyes were sorrowful. Her satin-smooth skin—almost as light as Eulalie's—

glistened with perspiration. The full mouth was working nervously.

"Thank you," Mr. Bradford said with reluctant politeness.

It rubbed him the wrong way, Eulalie thought, havin' Maw queen it in the kitchen and herself settin' here like she be white folks. But learnin' meant she could be with David—and nothin' in this whole world she wanted more than bein' with David. Sometimes, Missy said mean things —and lied, too—but David was somethin' else.

From down below, from the slave quarters, came a high, anguished wail—which all of them at the house had been steeling themselves against hearing.

"A-h-h!" It reverberated through the hot, sultry day; it repeated, over and over again, in towering pain. "A-h-h-h! A-h-h-h!"

Eulalie gritted her teeth. That be Massa George floggin' that black nigger that Missy say don't tech her. Mista Bradford look real sick, like the way she be feelin'. He looked green, like he was ready to run out to the bushes and throw up his insides.

They didn't know—Massa George and Missis—about how Mista Bradford kept runnin' after Alexander, too. Like Mista Bradford be one of the black gals always hangin' round Alexander. Mista Bradford, he took one look at that big, black buck, and after that, he was always wanderin' round, tryin' to be close to Alexander.

Mista Bradford didn't know—and Alexander didn't let on he knew—how David and she be playin' by the river, and she be chasin' after a ball. There, in the bushes, was Mista Bradford, down on his knees, pleadin' with Alexander to let him feel him up. Mista Bradford had his hand right there, on his thing.

Eulalie felt her golden skin turn pink as she remembered, visualized vividly, the stark tableau in the bushes that afternoon. Alexander—six feet two, glistening black, the most handsome buck on the plantation—standing there with his feet firmly planted, wide apart, on the ground, and pale, skinny, white Mista Bradford there on his knees. It wasn't Alexander's fault, about Missy chasin' after him that way. She bet he tole Missy to keep away, that she be beggin' for trouble.

The screaming upstairs subsided into muffled sobs. The cries below, in the slave quarters, rent the air. Eulalie shut her eyes against the vision of Alexander hanging with his wrists fastened to a beam, his feet just missing the floor so he could offer no resistance when the leather thong laid open his skin. She tried not to think about how that leather would cut into his black skin, how the red blood would be pouring out of the cuts ripped into Alexander's bared body. She shivered. Alexander be raw meat afore Massa George be done!

David frowned, trying to pretend to be concentrating on the arithmetic problem before him. Perspiration stained his shirt, darkened the thick blond hair. His hand was unsteady when he poured himself a glass of lemonade. Eulalie's eyes moved compulsively to David. Massa George say he be givin' Alexander one hundred lashes! No nigger stand up under that. Not even Alexander!

Eulalie's heart pounded as she unconsciously counted the wails from down below. There was a long, thin, seemingly endless wail that deepened into an animal gurgle. Eulalie's nails dug into her palms. David shut his eyes tightly, slammed a fist on the pinewood table. Mr. Bradford rose shakily to his feet.

"Excuse me." Mr. Bradford staggered away from the table, across the wide porch, seeking solitude for his humiliation in a clump of evergreens close by. Sitting there on the porch, Eulalie and David heard the sounds of his discomfort.

"Seraphina!" Margaret Woodstock's voice was agitated as she called loudly on her way down the impressive circular staircase. "Seraphina, didn't Dr. Cooper arrive yet?"

"No'm," Maw called back, her voice heavy with misery. "Not yet, Missis."

The doctor be able to tell them if Missy been teched. But Alexander done got his, one way t'other. Massa wanna show the other niggers how you don't meddle with white folks. But it wasn't Alexander's doin'. It wasn't right, givin'

Alexander that floggin'. For the first time in her thirteen years, rebellion seeded itself in Eulalie.

Margaret Woodstock was in the kitchen now, moving about with languid grace, switching on her southern charm for Seraphina's benefit.

"Seraphina, I'm so thirsty," Mrs. Woodstock wheedled. "And you know how I'm near distraction today."

"Now, Missis Margaret," Seraphina reproached softly, "You *know* it ain't good for you. And you been feelin' so well. If I give you it, Massa done tan my hide." And out on the back porch, Eulalie flinched, remembering Alexander's hide.

They played that game, Maw and Miss Margaret, about how Missis Margaret not be well sometimes. Everybody at The Willows knowed how the Missis liked bourbon. She musta been real pretty oncet. Even now, when she was all fixed up for the balls they had here at the house, three, four times a year, Missis Margaret be somethin' to see.

It was Missis Margaret who took her on, like a little pet, when she was no more than a year old. Keepin' her in her own room, talkin' to her when she had one of her spells, havin' her sleep there on a pillow right beside her own bed—Eulalie didn't remember that—Maw told her about it. She hated goin' back to their cabin at night, after bein' up here at the big house all day.

"Seraphina, I have to have it," Margaret Woodstock was saying urgently. "Listen to him. Oh, listen to him!" And then, quite suddenly, it was over, in a thin, high wail that carried the flogged slave into unconsciousness. "Thank God for that," Mrs. Woodstock said, her voice thick with emotion. "My husband—" Contempt crept in now. "My husband feels he's such a man when he stands there with a whip in his hand! That's the only time he truly feels he's the Master!"

"Missis, he be sendin' Missy away?" Seraphina asked fearfully. "Missis, you know nothin' done happen to that beautiful, precious li'l' baby."

"Well, it isn't because she hasn't tried," Margaret Woodstock said in a brutal burst of candor. For a moment, her eyes fluttered shut. "Seraphina, you and I know. Maybe it's better that we do send her to England for a while."

"Oh, my li'l' Missy—" Seraphina's voice broke. "I don't know how we stand it here, without that li'l' baby."

"Have some more cold lemonade," Eulalie urged David, out on the back porch where they sat tense in their chairs, before open books neither of them saw.

"Papa shouldn't whip Alexander," David said tensely, clenching and unclenching one hand. "He's got no right. Nobody's got that right."

"Sssh," Eulalie warned uneasily, because David was echoing the rebellion taking root in her. "Sssh." Every time somebody was whupped, she got these strange feelin's inside. Like she wanted to take up the whip and hit right back herself.

Alexander didn't tech Missy—he knowed better 'n that. But Missy couldn't keep them soft, pretty white hands off that fine black body. Massa George said, "All the black wenches on the plantation have the hots for Alexander." And a seventeen-year-old white one, too.

"Seraphina, I hear a carriage," Mrs. Woodstock said, her voice deepening. "That must be Dr. Cooper now."

Eulalie sat at attention, listening to the sounds in the house. With Seraphina at her heels, Mrs. Woodstock was hurrying towards the front door, complaining mightily because Chloe was never around when somebody arrived.

Massa George kept sayin' he was goin' send Chloe out to the fields again, Eulalie remembered. But he didn't. Chloe be his bed slave. Maw was sure Chloe be knocked up, but Chloe not be talkin' none. Once Massa George knew, he wouldn't be havin' nothin' to do with her no more. That was the way it always was with the Massa and his bed wenches.

Eulalie listened carefully to the goings-on at the front door. Dr. Cooper be arrivin', all right. My, the carryin'-on between white folks, all that polite talk that don't mean nothin', when what Missis wanted was for him to go up there and look at Missy and say she wasn't damaged none by that Alexander.

What good it do Alexander? Eulalie shivered. She'd seen a man who'd been whupped by Massa George. Afterward, she'd seen him. She heard him screamin' in the hospital down a piece from their cabin. Screamin' all night long when they fix his cuts. Massa George made sure they fix him up. That nigger had to be back in the fields, pickin' cotton again.

Dr. Cooper and Mrs. Woodstock were walking up the stairs, talking in low tones that didn't reach out to the back porch. Then they were in Cindy Woodstock's pink and white bedroom, and Cindy was screaming at her mother and Dr. Cooper.

"Get out!" Cindy screamed. "I don't want you in here! Get out!"

There was the sound of something smashing against the wall. Mrs. Woodstock's voice rose imperiously. Dr. Cooper intervened with masculine authority. David got up and walked off to the side of the porch, staring down at the red-mud trickle that was the Chattahoochee in the summer. There was quiet upstairs, except for a shriek from Cindy, who quickly subsided into silence.

Eulalie waited. By and by, when he was ready, David would talk to her. David was her only friend. She was his only friend. David kept correctin' the way she talked, kept tellin' her she had a fine mind and ought to use it. All right, she was *goin'* to watch the way she talked. Let the other niggers think she was uppity—it didn't mean nothin' to her. They thought that already, anyhow.

She hated the cabin Maw and she shared with the others. She loved this big house with all the fine furniture in it—some that Massa George's grandmaw brought all the way over from England, some sent from that furniture-maker up no'th in Philadelphia. She loved the way the furniture shone from all the polishin', and the fine curtains at the window, and the thick rugs that were softer than the bed she shared with Maw. Sometimes, at night, she'd lay there and think about how it'd be to live in a house like this— and be a fine lady with all those clothes like Missy had.

Truant thoughts were creeping into Eulalie's head, and

they were nurtured by the strange stories that were circulating among the slaves. About how some slaves were running away, making it to freedom up North. Some of them going all the way up to Canada. It was 1851, and Eulalie was dreaming of freedom.

Upstairs, Dr. Cooper and Mrs. Woodstock were talking quietly to a chastened Cindy. Seraphina had discovered Chloe dozing in a pantry, and she was scolding her vociferously. Mr. Bradford, white and weak and ashamed, had skulked upstairs to his room. In low, heated whispers, David was talking to Eulalie about how he thought a plantation ought to be run, the way he'd do it when his time came. David and Eulalie stiffened into silence when they heard the sound of heavy boots stomping into the huge foyer.

"Margaret?" The Massa's voice thundered through the lower floor of the mansion. "Is that Doc Cooper's carriage settin' out front?"

"I'll be there directly, George," Mrs. Woodstock called down, sounding less distraught than earlier. Eulalie guessed she'd had a nip from the bottle.

"You be here right now!" he yelled back nastily, yet with relish.

"I hate him," David whispered, his face taut. "He's an animal."

"You don't talk like that about your Paw!" Eulalie was shocked.

"Someday," David promised, "things will be different around here. You'll see, Eulalie! They'll all see. It's a sin against nature, to hold black people the way we do."

"Sssh."

Eulalie was scared. Sometimes, exhilaration lighted her up when she listened to David talk the way he did, knowing he meant it, believing—with him—that he was right. But now, with George Woodstock in the house, she was terrified.

"All right, what did Doc say?" Woodstock was demanding of his wife.

"She—she's intact," Mrs. Woodstock said coldly. "You went down there, and you flogged that poor Alexander for nothing, George."

"It wasn't for nothing," he snapped back. "Didn't our own overseer come and tell me he saw them together in the fields?" His anger was rising again as he remembered.

"George, nothing happened!" Impatience overwhelmed Margaret Woodstock. "You whipped the best stud on the plantation—for nothing." A bitter triumph undercoated her voice, because her husband prided himself on his business sense. "God knows, how long Alexander's going to be lying in the hospital."

"One thing, I can tell you, Margaret. He won't be lying with no wench—black, yellow, or white! I lashed him till he was broken—and then, Margaret, then I cut off his big, black nuts!"

"Oh, George—" She sounded sick. "You're disgusting."

"You think I'm going to let him go around with that big thing ready for action, after Jim saw him in the fields with my daughter? You've got to show those niggers, Margaret —you've got to show them who's the master."

"You enjoy whipping a slave," Margaret Woodstock taunted. "You stand there, with that whip in your hand, swinging out at bare black flesh—and you get pleasure out of it. *That* kind of pleasure!"

"I didn't get any pleasure out of you," George Woodstock shot back. "You were no better than a dead log in bed!"

"I was a lady," she retaliated with pride. "Not one of your black bed-wenches."

"What's Doc doing, still up there with Cindy?" he demanded suspiciously. "If everything's all right, what's he sticking around with Cindy for? You cooking up a story for me, Margaret?"

"Go up and talk to him yourself," she ordered vindictively. "He's up there giving Cindy something to calm her down. She's not taking too well to being sent over to England for a year."

"She'd rather take it from some black buck, flat on her

back," George Woodstock snorted. "I'm going upstairs and talk to Dr. Cooper myself."

Mr. Bradford came out on the porch to join his pupils again. His eyes were veiled. He was pale. But he was ready for the lessons. Conscientiously, Eulalie concentrated on the day's learning.

Eulalie was so engrossed in the studies that she didn't hear Margaret Woodstock walk out into the kitchen, pour herself a tumbler of bourbon—because Seraphina was upstairs with her "precious baby" and couldn't stop her mistress—and now come out to the door to watch Eulalie and David, both listening intently to Mr. Bradford.

"Eulalie," Mrs. Woodstock ordered suddenly. "Come here."

Startled, sensing something of grave portent was about to happen, Eulalie rose to her feet, walked slowly towards Mrs. Woodstock.

"Yes'm?" A chill brushed her when she saw the peculiar glint in Mrs. Woodstock's eyes as they moved from her to David, back to her again. Saw, comprehended, and trembled.

"We'll go into the kitchen, Eulalie," Mrs. Woodstock said peremptorily.

For a frightened instant, Eulalie's eyes moved to meet David's, read the unease in his. What Missis be after? Her heart pounding, she followed Margaret Woodstock down the long corridor into the kitchen. Just inside the door, Mrs. Woodstock stopped dead, took a deep breath. Eulalie was aware that Chloe stood off to one side, watching avidly, dawdling as usual over a household task.

"Eulalie—" There was an unfamiliar coldness in Mrs. Woodstock's voice. "It's time we put a stop to this ridiculous business of the lessons. You're thirteen already. It's terribly wrong to be putting false notions into your head. You understand that, Eulalie?"

"Yes'm." Her voice was barely a whisper. No more lessons, Missis be sayin'.

"It just starts up trouble, making a pet of a slave. Mr. Woodstock's been telling me that for a long time," Mrs.

Woodstock went on with an aggrieved air, as though Eulalie had been leading her astray. "Your Maw's needing help in the kitchen since Samantha's been sent back to the fields. Starting right now, Eulalie, you work in the kitchen. And mind your ways, or the Master will ship you out to the fields!"

Off in a corner, Chloe giggled.

2

Nine o'clock. The foreman had made his rounds, accounted for every slave in every cabin. The day was done.

Rain poured outside, leaked in through the many crevices in the makeshift cabins. Eulalie lay huddled at the edge of the bedstead, which she shared with her Maw, and watched the clay-stained rivulets creep beneath the outer wall of the cabin, across the earth floor.

Maw got up, went across to the window, hung a piece of flannel on nails to mask the unglazed opening.

"There, that be better," Maw said with satisfaction.

It would be soaked through in a minute. Eulalie thought fretfully. In the next cubicle set off from the main, communal room of the cabin, the five inhabitants, who sprawled crosswise over the bed, were complaining about the density of bodies. Tonight, nobody could sleep on the floor.

Since Eulalie had become a house maid, each day was agonizingly like the one before. Maw kept her busy in the kitchen, about the house, so she wouldn't have time to brood, Eulalie realized. She was exhausted at the end of the long day, which began at sunup and ended at sundown. Her back ached, her feet pained—but nothing was as bad as the mental anguish of coming face to face with her status at The Willows. She was a house slave, who—at the slightest infraction—could be banished to the fields.

"Eulalie, you be awake?" Maw asked softly, when they had been lying in silence for twenty minutes.

"I be awake," Eulalie conceded.

"Baby, it not be good for we to fret over what we not change," Maw chided. "Not right for we get fancy ideas in our haids. You be well off, workin' in the house, not in the fields."

"I know," Eulalie lied. She knew nothing of the sort.

"Not right for slave to learn like white folks," Maw went on sorrowfully. "First, you be Missis's pet, then Mista David's pet." She wasn't David's pet, Eulalie thought rebelliously. His friend! "I knowed it be wrong," Maw continued dolefully, "for you to get book larnin'. For what good, Eulalie?"

How long since Missis took her away from the lessons, away from bein' David's friend? Six weeks! Seemed more'n six years. Mista Bradford gone now two weeks, and the new tutor comin' in tomorrow. Missy Cindy in England, writin' home about the beautiful gowns she buy and the fine balls her cousin Lydia, once removed, be givin' in their fine house close to London.

"You go sleep, Eulalie honey," Maw exhorted and turned over on the hard bed; she began to snore in seconds.

Eulalie lay on her back and stared at the planks that made up the ceiling. The rainfall was accentuating the heavy sweetness of the flowers outside, blending it with the body scents of the crowded, insufficiently washed cabin members. In her mind, she went over the contents of the book David slipped to her yesterday. She read in a cupboard near the kitchen, or off in the woods. If Chloe saw her reading, or any of the other slaves, they'd make life miserable for her.

Eulalie reached for the piece of cloth she kept in lieu of

a handkerchief, mopped the perspiration away from her forehead, tugged at the cotton garment that served as dress by day and nightgown by night. Despite the rain, the weather was oppressively hot. She felt self-conscious, remembering how Hector—the new slave Mr. Woodstock had bought to replace the incapacitated Alexander—had looked at her when he brought wood into the house to feed the kitchen stove. Like he could see right through her dress, Eulalie thought with rising distaste. She didn't want Hector touching her. *Nobody* touching her.

David said, when the new tutor be arrivin', he share his lessons with her, anyway. When nobody see, he himself show her and she study. She learn to talk like white folks, Eulalie reminded herself resolutely. No talk like other slaves. She be different. She make herself different.

Eulalie lay still, so as not to disturb her mother. Go to sleep! By the time the sun began to rise over the cotton fields, she be scurryin' to the big house to begin the day's work. Fifteen hours of workin', fetchin', runnin'. But it be better, Eulalie acknowledged with honesty, than pickin' cotton in the fields.

Eulalie moved quietly about the dining room, ever conscious of the beauty of the room, the elegance of the mahogany table, the inlaid sideboard, the exquisitely upholstered chairs, the crystal chandelier that hung above the table. Only Mrs. Woodstock and David were at breakfast this morning. Earlier, Seraphina had served Mr. Woodstock, who was en route to the fields to talk with the headman about a cotton problem. Later, one of the male slaves would take the carriage into town to bring out the new tutor.

Now that she was serving, Eulalie wore the neat, white uniform which Mrs. Woodstock declared more suitable and which made Eulalie—filling out physically—appear older than her thirteen years. David made a point of never looking directly at Eulalie when she served. There was a sullen defiance in his eyes that said he resented seeing Eulalie in this servile capacity for which she had been bred and born.

The white uniform showed off Eulalie's tiny waist, the swelling of her breasts, highlighted the satiny gold of her skin, the auburn tints of her brown hair that had none of the kinky qualities associated with Negroid hair. She walked, like all Negro females, tall and proudly.

Eulalie placed the hot platters of eggs, sausages, fresh biscuits, the bowl of grits, the steaming cups of coffee, before Mrs. Woodstock and David. Eyes cast down, she fled—in relief—to the kitchen. She *hated* this morning routine.

In the kitchen, Chloe was in a corner, taking her time over shelling peas. Maw was standing by the pinewood worktable, finishing off what breakfast George Woodstock had left on his plate. She knew, of course, to transfer the scraps to her own plate. Eulalie, unobserved, spooned out the grits that remained in the pot for herself, before soaking the pot to clean it. She helped herself sparingly to the butter. George Woodstock was known to go into a tantrum over the heavy consumption of butter, which he attributed to the house slaves.

Eulalie went to the window nearest to the hallway that led back to the dining room—not admitting, even to herself, that she longed to hear the discussion at the breakfast table. Eulalie was beginning her private learning.

"You speak like white folks," she told herself sternly, "you *be* like white folks."

She leaned forward intently, spooning the grits between the full, pale lips as she listened.

"I'm sure Mr. Jefferson is going to be a fine tutor," Mrs. Woodstock was saying lightly. "You'll like him, David."

"Maybe," David said grudgingly.

"David, it's important you do well with your studies," his mother pursued. "Someday, you'll be master of The Willows. You'll have to run the plantation."

"It's no fun, studying by myself," David shot back. "Why can't Eulalie—"

"Now stop it!" Mrs. Woodstock cut in sharply. "I wouldn't be surprised if that wasn't one of the reasons

Mr. Bradford left us. I didn't believe that story at all, about how he just couldn't stand the heat. It was the way we pushed Eulalie onto him; that's what it was."

It was the way Massa beat up Alexander, Eulalie corrected with inner defiance. Mista Bradford went right down to the hospital oncet, to take somethin' to Alexander. Now, the Massa be sellin' Alexander for bein' a troublesome nigger, if Alexander don't watch hisself. Alexander wasn't gonna make no more slaves for the Massa— wasn't *going* to make any more slaves, Eulalie corrected herself, with a flush of pride.

"Eulalie made it fun to learn," David said stubbornly. "It was like a race to see who could finish a problem first. Lots of times, she did," he wound up with a touch of sardonic humor.

"It was my mistake." Missis gettin' all worked up, Eulalie decided. "I declare, I never expected it to become a major issue in this house. David, it was wrong of me to take that child and treat her like she was white. It won't do any good for a nigger to learn to read and write—it just makes them restless, dissatisfied with what God meant their lives to be."

"God?" David demanded. "Or Southern plantation owners?"

"That is enough, David! I won't have any more of that kind of talk!" Margaret Woodstock tinkled the small bell at her right hand, continuing impatiently until Seraphina herself answered. Only Seraphina was allowed to respond to this summons. It meant, usually, that the mistress of the house was intent on lacing her coffee with bourbon.

Eulalie began washing the breakfast pots. Smiling dreamily, Chloe was looking out the window. Chloe was big-boned—she was just beginning to show. Chloe felt important because the Massa gave her a baby, Eulalie thought with contempt. What good did it do? That baby would grow up in the slave quarters, a slave, like its Maw. It didn't matter none about the Paw. And Chloe wouldn't be Massa Woodstock's bed wench no more. He be findin' hisself a new gal. Maw said he was lookin'. Maybe that black Venus that had such big ideas. Venus, near sixteen, wouldn't let nobody tech her yet. Maw said she was savin' it for the Massa. Didn't it turn Missis Margaret's stomach, the way he took a gal to bed right in the next room from her?

Recurrently, Eulalie thought about her own Paw. Maw was sold when she be pregnant. Her Paw was white—Maw be proud of that. Maw said she be the spittin' image of her Paw. At The Willows, everybody knew about who was who's Paw—exceptin' for her, because Maw got her seed a piece away from The Willows. Maw said it was nobody's business who her Paw be. Who her Paw *was*.

Maw got sent out to the fields, no more house slave, when she be—when she was—knocked up. She worked in the fields right up to the time Massa Woodstock bought her—two months before she dropped the baby—to be maid for his mother. The field slaves say Maw and she be so lucky to work in the big house. Not plantin' cotton, hoein' cotton, pickin' cotton. What was so lucky about bein' a slave—anywhere?

Eulalie looked up as Maw came back into the kitchen, went off into the pantry where Missis's private bottle of bourbon was kept. Maw came out of the pantry lookin' sorrowful, the way she did when Missis started goin' too much to that bottle.

"Eulalie, you polish them pots good," Maw exhorted, en route to the dining room again. "Chloe, don't set there all day shellin' them peas. We wants 'em for dinnah."

Eulalie's long, slim fingers fought with the grits that stuck to the pot. Her hands were beautiful, large but delicately shaped. Unconsciously, a faint smile touched her oval face because Chloe had begun to sing—softly, melodiously—and the music soothed the resentment in her.

Frowning, Maw came back into the kitchen. Right away, she yelled at Chloe for taking too long with the peas.

"Eulalie, you go outside and fetch Henry," Maw ordered. "It's time for he go to pick up the new teacher. Missis want for talk to he."

Eulalie went out of the kitchen by the back door. Henry

would be workin' on the flower beds at the west side of the house. Massa grumbled about the way Missis kept a good field hand messin' around with her flowers, but he was right proud of how folks praised up what Henry could do with the flowers.

"Henry," Eulalie called to him—conscious that Henry was tall and brawny and good-looking, even though Maw called him a lazy, no-count nigger. More than once, Eulalie saw Cindy hangin' out the window, lookin' at him. Not as handsome as Alexander—but handsome enough to make the black gals wiggle their asses for him. "Henry, Missis want for you—want you to come inside the house. You gotta go take the carriage into town."

"Ah reckon ah kin do that," Henry drawled, rising to his full six feet, enjoying the sight of Eulalie standing there in the sun with her lissome slimness outlined beneath the uniform. His eyes fastened themselves to her breasts.

"Well, hurry up," she said spiritedly, self-conscious before that passionate stare, and turned to flee.

Too often now, she felt male eyes stripping away her clothes, down to the dusky nipples set atop the richly swelling breasts. Almost like she was pregnant, Eulalie thought guiltily, seeing the way her breasts stood out, like they were filling with milk. But she not yet fourteen, she thought defensively. No buck touch her yet. She lifted her head proudly. No buck ever touch her.

She ran back around the house, feeling Henry's eyes following her. At the slave quarters, she knew they looked at her that way—Henry's way—the young black men, and some not so young. Nobody goin' to tech her, she reiterated with determination. She work in the kitchen, stay away from everybody. No slave's woman, no white man's wench.

Aaron Jefferson arrived and settled down among the residents of The Willows. He had obviously taken this job because he relished the leisurely living on a Georgia plantation. David studied diligently, surreptitiously passing his lessons on to Eulalie. Maw knew what was going on, Eulalie guessed, but kept silent, out of fear of starting

23

trouble for either Eulalie or David. But Maw looked fearful, Eulalie thought uneasily, like she was scared what Massa George would do if he found out. Missis was drinkin' more than ever, with Cindy away. Missis didn't know much of nothin' that was goin' on.

The summer pased into the glorious Southern autumn, with flowers and birds in rich abundance, and less of the tiredness brought on by the heat afflicting the residents of The Willows. But there was another heat in Aaron Jefferson. The new tutor had a way of standing and watching her, Eulalie knew, whenever they chanced to encounter each other.

Mista Jefferson was goin' out of his way to see her, Eulalie guessed nervously. She didn't want nothin' to do with that white man. It was bad enough, the way she was fendin' off the black boys.

After supper, one late-September evening, Eulalie was about to leave the big house to go down to the slave quarters when Mrs. Woodstock summoned her to bring coffee into the drawing room. There had been a long, newsy letter from Cindy that day, and Mrs. Woodstock was feeling happy. In the drawing room with her husband and Mr. Jefferson, Mrs. Woodstock was boasting to Mr. Jefferson about her beautiful young daughter in England when Eulalie brought in the coffee.

"Mr. Jefferson, I'm hoping my husband changes his mind and brings our darlin' home soon." Margaret Woodstock was carrying on in the charmingly flirtatious manner that is part of the Southern woman from childhood to the grave. "She is just the prettiest li'l' thing you ever saw."

Eulalie moved quietly about the drawing room. She served coffee first to Mrs. Woodstock, who sat elegantly gowned on the Directoire sofa, then to Mr. Woodstock, who was sprawled in a chair that flanked the fireplace, and finally to Mr. Jefferson, who stood at the marble-faced fireplace. Mr. Jefferson had a polite smile for Mrs. Woodstock, but his eyes followed Eulalie's young, undulating figure.

"How long you been down here at The Willows, Aaron?" Mr. Woodstock drawled, his eyes sardonic.

"Close to six weeks, sir," Aaron Jefferson said politely. He always seemed slightly wary of conversation with his employer.

"Well, that's a long time without a wench in your bed!" Woodstock slapped his thigh in amusement.

"George!" Margaret Woodstock colored, her voice showing her distaste for this line of conversation.

"Or has it been without?" George prodded, while Eulalie hurried down the hall, back to the kitchen.

Eulalie stood there, washing up the dishes in the kitchen and waiting for the three in the drawing room to be done, so she could wash up the rest. The ribald laughter in the drawing room echoed down the hallway to the kitchen. When Missis got mad at the Massa, she called him coarse and vulgar. He liked makin' her mad that way.

"Eulalie—" Missis stood at the entrance, her cheeks twin spots of red, her eyes flashing. "You send somebody down to the quarters to fetch Chloe. When she comes, you send her upstairs, to Mr. Jefferson, you hear?" She sounded self-conscious, ashamed.

For a minute, they weren't slave and mistress. They were two women.

"Missis Margaret," Eulalie stammered. "Chloe, she be pregnant."

"I know." Margaret Woodstock's smile was dry. "The men discussed that quite fully. Mr. Jefferson, it seems, has a preference for this. He—he was quite elated."

"I'll send for Chloe," Eulalie said softly, amber eyes wide. She'd heard Maw talk about men like that, who liked to take their pleasure with women who were pregnant. Maw said there was all kinds of men, with all kinds of likes.

Eulalie slipped out of the house. She found a boy close by, sent him off to fetch Chloe. How was Chloe going to take this? she wondered curiously. Chloe so proud because the Massa give her a baby. And now the Massa give her to Mista Jefferson. But Chloe have no say.

Mrs. Woodstock left the gentlemen alone and retired to her own large, ostentatiously furnished bedroom at the head of the mahogany circular staircase that, at times, was the pride of her life. The two men were smoking and drinking as Eulalie, moving about the drawing room, collected the dishes. She felt, rather than saw, Mr. Jefferson's eyes lingering on her.

Eulalie felt her face grow warm. Not from the logs blazing in the fireplace. With the first cool nights, Mrs. Woodstock was one to order a fire started in the drawing room and the bedrooms. Eulalie remembered the discomfort of cold nights in the slave quarters—with the earth floors and only a framework of wood—the windows unglazed and haphazardly shuttered to offer a pretense of protection against the cold that, even in Georgia, could be wretched in the midst of winter.

"Now Aaron," Mr. Woodstock chortled in high good humor, only partially bourbon-induced. "I sent for this black bitch to come bring you pleasure. Just the way you like it, boy—so don't you go lookin' round the house!"

Her face hot, trembling, Eulalie scurried out of the drawing room, down the corridor to the kitchen, where Maw was scolding the kitchen boy for not being neat enough.

"Me run down for that Chloe," he was saying aggrievedly and pointed to Eulalie. "Ask she."

Seraphina's questioning eyes shot directly to Eulalie.

"I sent him to bring Chloe," Eulalie concurred. "For Mista Jefferson." Her voice was a whisper. "He like woman that way."

"All right, clean up this mess," Seraphina ordered Eulalie brusquely. "It's time we be gittin' to the quarters. You, you no good nigger, you mop up this floor before I break youh haid in!"

Eulalie tried to concentrate on cleaning the dishes, but she heard Chloe singing softly to herself in that faintly off-key fashion that made Eulalie feel good inside. Chloe walked into the kitchen, holding herself proudly, the swell of her belly lending a strange grace to her posture.

"Where be Mista Jefferson's room?" Chloe asked, white teeth suddenly flashing in a broad smile.

"You go down to the fourth door from the haid of the

stairs," Seraphina said disapprovingly. "And mind your manners, gal. You do like he says. He don't mind you be knocked up."

"He don't min', I don't min'," Chloe giggled. And then, suddenly, the giggling stopped. "What he wanna do, Seraphina? He wanna come up to me from behind? Me no like that, Seraphina," she objected vigorously.

"You do what Mista Jefferson say do," Seraphina ordered. "You be his bed wench."

Feeling dirtied by all this talk, Eulalie lowered her eyes. She didn't want to think about Chloe, upstairs with Mr. Jefferson, doing whatever Mr. Jefferson asked of her. She didn't want to remember the way Mr. Jefferson looked at *her*. Chloe strutted out of the room, mollified—for now— by the knowledge that she was inside the big house.

Eulalie dried the good china that Mrs. Woodstock always like to use for coffee in the drawing room, carefully put it away because Mrs. Woodstock said you couldn't buy china like this any more. She didn't hear the footsteps coming into the kitchen. The heavy, masculine voice startled her.

"Eulalie!" Mr. Woodstock, imperious and loud, shot terror into Eulalie. "Eulalie, I'm goin' up to my room. You bring me up a hot toddy."

"Yessuh." Eulalie's voice was a whisper, her eyes wide with shock. Mr. Woodstock's message was clear. He never have nobody bring up his hot toddy, except Chloe. Her eyes wavered before his heated gaze. He stood before her, mentally shucking away the neat, white uniform, seeing her naked and golden before him. His eyes moved avidly over the slender length of her. In his mind, he was already thrusting his impatient maleness into the golden body that had never known a man.

"You make that toddy good and hot, you hear?" George Woodstock repeated. "And you bring it straight up to my bedroom." He spun on his heels, stalked from the kitchen, whistling under his breath.

Eulalie stood frozen into immobility, staring after the husky, retreating figure. No! She wouldn't! She wouldn't let him!

"All right, Eulalie," Seraphina lashed out, after a heavy, stunned moment of silence. "You do like the Massa say. You fix that hot toddy, and you take it right up to the Massa's bedroom. Move fast, gal."

But Seraphina's eyes were sick when they met Eulalie's. Sick and sorrowful—and resigned.

3

The bedroom was large, square, high-ceilinged, its wide-board floor covered with a rug designed to duplicate an Aubusson. The furniture—chosen painstakingly by Margaret Woodstock as a bride—was incongruously elegant, considering the earthy qualities of the master of the house. A mahogany fourposter bed, ornately carved, dominated the room.

The walls, which looked like masonry blocks, were, in reality, long-leaf pine beveled and painted with a sand finish. George Woodstock's mother, in her time, had proudly pointed out that this had been copied from the late President Washington's home, Mount Vernon.

Right now, a fire blazed in the tall fireplace, sent splashes of color across the room—at this moment otherwise unlit. Stripped to the waist, George Woodstock stood before the fireplace, scratching his massive, hairy chest and the roll of belly that spilled out over his trousers; he was relishing the freedom from clothes.

The fire was not needed tonight, he thought with good-humored contempt, even while he enjoyed its warmth. That was Margaret, always ordering a fire for every room in the house, at the first cold wind. With the bourbon she consumed, how could she feel the cold? Where was that hot toddy? Why didn't that black bitch get up here with it? Not black, he corrected himself with a stir of anticipation. High yaller. Seraphina had herself a white stud for that one, for sure.

His eyes glowed as he thought about the girl. He'd been looking at that bitch a lot lately. All of a sudden, she was a woman. A pair of tits like he hadn't seen in a long time. Better than Chloe. And that small, rounded ass—that gave him the feeling, down there in his groin. Hell, she must be fourteen. That was the age! He cleared his throat, passion rising in him as he thought about breaking in a new wench.

That Jefferson fellow had the hots for her. For a while tonight, when Eulalie was sashaying around the drawing room, he thought that damned tutor was going to pop right out of his pants every time the wench got within touching distance. Anyhow, this tutor was a man. Crazy, the way Margaret was already getting ideas about bringing Cindy home. Did Margaret think he was letting Cindy marry somebody with no more prospects than a tutor? Even if the little filly was hot as a pistol.

His arrogant, going-to-dissipation face softened as he thought about his daughter. Cindy would stay out of trouble, over in England. She would be kept busy with buying clothes and going to balls and all. She wasn't going to be left alone long enough for any man to get in. No need for Margaret to be so nervous.

"David!" Margaret Woodstock called out sharply in the hall. "Where are you going at this hour of the night?"

Margaret disliked having David witness her night-walking downstairs, George thought drily. She didn't like him knowing how many trips she made to the liquor cabinet. One of these days, he'd put a lock on that cabinet.

"I'm just going downstairs, Mama," David explained patiently. "I left a book down there—I want to finish it before I go to sleep."

What was the matter with that boy, George asked himself with recurrent frustration. Almost fifteen—but they still couldn't sit down and talk like a real father and son. Like he'd done with his own Papa when he was fifteen. Usually, Papa was calling him down for too much fooling around with the black wenches. If David wasn't his son, he'd be worrying about the boy's manhood. When was David going to start taking his due?

"You get that book and take yourself right to bed, young man. Do you hear?" Margaret was ordering firmly.

"I'll be right up, Mama," David reassured her. He was already on his way downstairs, his voice moving away. "You don't need to wait for me."

Annoyed at the mother-son exchange in the hall—because to him it sounded unmanly—George strode to the door, pulled it wide.

"Margaret, for God's sake, stop nagging at the boy!" George began and then stopped dead. His gaze followed his wife's.

David was halfway down the long staircase. Eulalie, tray clutched in her slim, golden hands, was about to ascend. Margaret's gaze swung from Eulalie to her husband—with disbelief, contempt, hate, etched on her face. She crossed to the door of her own room, making a point of not looking at her husband, slammed the door shut. Down below, on the staircase, David stood aside, to allow Eulalie to pass.

Christ! He hadn't expected Eulalie for another ten minutes, at least. Chloe always dawdled that long. Why was David standing there, staring at him like that? Lord, he was ash-white, with one hand balled into a fist. Couldn't a man have any privacy in his own house?

What was so special about Seraphina's wench, that Margaret and David looked like that? She was just another bitch, to give him pleasure—for all the high-and-mighty ways Margaret tried to give her for a while. It was nobody's business, who he took into his bed!

He stood there at his door, feet wide apart, eyes stony, watching Eulalie, in her thin poplin uniform, head down, careful not to spill the hot toddy on the tray as she slowly mounted the long staircase. So his wife and his son knew the gal was coming to his bed. They both knew about the other wenches, before Eulalie. Even the boy knew. Hell, David should be taking his own already! He was going to have to sit down and talk to that boy.

Was the young whelp getting ideas about Eulalie himself? Now, there was a thought. Satisfaction stirred in him as he considered this possibility. Didn't David know enough to help himself to any piece that he wanted about the plantation? None of the bitches would turn him down. Hell, he was the master's son and would be the master himself one of these days.

Why didn't the boy pick himself one of those sassy young ones working in the fields? He knew what to do, didn't he? They talked plain enough in the house. Margaret was forever carrying on about that. His wife, who was as respectable under the blankets as she was in a church pew on Sunday morning.

"All right, girl!" George said loudly, malicious in his wish for his wife to hear. "Get up here with that."

David was down in the library, stalling until they were back inside the room. The boy knew, George thought again, with ribald satisfaction. He cleared his throat in heated anticipation as Eulalie—head down—walked past him, at his direction, into the bedroom. In his mind, he was already driving into that young golden, early adolescent body.

She'd never been in this room—he could tell that she felt uneasy. Did Chloe—and the others—talk about what happened here? Did they brag about how much he had to give them? That Chloe carried on like a wild one. He bore bite marks from her even now.

"Put it down there, on the table," he ordered brusquely. His fingers tingled as he imagined the dusky nipples between their short, stubby length. "Don't leave!" His voice was sharp because there was the look of a hunted doe about her when she turned away from the pedestal table.

"No, Massa."

Her eyes sought the floor, pinkness staining the satin gold of her skin. God, she was a beautiful piece!

"Eulalie, you're fourteen," he said, his voice mellow. "What black buck's been messing around with you, that I don't know about?"

"Nobody, Massa," she whispered, but this time she raised her head, a rebellion in her eyes that raised desire in his loins. Spirit. He liked a gal with spirit.

"You're old enough," he said as he reached for the hot toddy. He was greedy in his gulping as his mind raced on.

He'd seen that new stud—that Hector that set him back eleven hundred—looking at Eulalie, like he couldn't wait another minute. Damn, it was a shame he had to cut off that Alexander's big black balls—he was the best stud on the plantation. With the crops being so poor, it was the breeding that was keeping them above water, paying for Cindy's staying over in Europe, all the fancy clothes Margaret was always ordering sent down from New York City. Prices in New Orleans were rising every day. This one would bring a pretty price out there in New Orleans —a bitch who could pass for white was a prize. But he couldn't—Seraphina wouldn't be worth a damn in the house, if he sold her child.

George put down the cup, reached for her. She was trembling.

"Come over near the fire, girl," he said. "Warm you up." His eyes lighted. "Then I'll give you another kind of warming up." What was she scared about? Listening to some of the stories the old cows threw around? Seraphina hadn't been bad in bed ten years ago. Till she started spreading that way. She was all ass now and going to fat because Margaret was always spoiling her. Blackstrap molasses and corn pone weren't good enough according to his wife.

"Chloe show up yet?" he asked, releasing her unexpectedly, to sit down in the horsehair chair that flanked the fireplace. "I sent for her to pleasure Mr. Jefferson. You think Chloe can satisfy him?"

"Yes, Massa." Eulalie's voice was barely audible. She was still trembling. Waiting. "Chloe be in the house. She do what Mista Jefferson ask."

These bitches knew everything from the time they were

five, he thought complacently. Eulalie knew all about Mr. Jefferson's special delights. It was there, right in her eyes. He had some special delights of his own.

"All right, girl." All at once, he was impatient with the byplay. "Take off your clothes."

For a heated instant, their eyes clashed. For an electric moment, he thought she was going to defy him. No slave ever defied him yet. They knew better! His eyes darkened with anticipation as he watched her pull the uniform over her head, then fold it neatly, nervously, and drape it over her arm.

"Put the lamp on," he ordered thickly, pulling the uniform away, tossing it on the floor. "I want to see."

With the grace of a finely bred kitten, head high, ignoring her nakedness, Eulalie moved to do his bidding. George Woodstock's eyes lingered on the small, high breasts, the slim waist, the faint, sensuous swell of her belly. Again, he cleared his throat, crossed the room to grab at her wrist.

For a tense pause, they were not master and slave. They were man and woman, he aggressive in passion, she defiant, contemptuous in rejection. But this was no match —this was master and slave. Inexorably, Eulalie knew, he would win. She shut her eyes, clenched her teeth, dug her nails into the palms of her large, delicate hands. Then he thrust her across the wide, already turned-down feather bed.

George Woodstock walked across to the washstand, splashed cold water on his face, masculine pride bringing a faint smile to his libertine mouth. This was a piece worth waiting for. No reaction—dead as a lightning-struck magnolia. Like Margaret in that, he thought with dry humor. Yet beneath that tense rejection, he was conscious of a startled, frightened, secretive response. Once he was there. She'd been virgin, all right. But like he thought, passionate, once she'd let go. You mix the breeds, and every time you get a passionate bitch.

"Don't go back to the quarters, girl," he ordered brusquely, yet his eyes told her she had pleased him. "Bed down in the kitchen, near the fireplace." He walked across to the bed, beside which she was awkwardly climbing into her uniform again. "Take this." He swept the top quilt from his bed. His eyes were mocking. "Well?" he challenged. "Don't I even get a thankee?" She had a certain status now. Her master had broken her in.

"Thank you, Massa," she said, her voice colorless, amber eyes veiled. Hiding defiance, because showing defiance could bring a leather strap across that golden body.

Not the familiar *thankee* that any other slave gal would have uttered, even a high yaller like this one. That came of Margaret's babying her with the lessons. Christ, it was against the law now, to teach a slave to read! But when Margaret made up her mind to something, that was it.

He watched the slim body undulating gracefully as she moved to the door. He recognized with astonishment—and pride—the fresh arousal making itself known within him.

"Wait," he ordered imperiously.

This wench was something, even when resistant. How many years since the urge came on him twice in one night? This one was special. Rough, he reached for her—he was clamorous to make passion come alive in her. He knew it would be a long while before another slave bitch could make him feel this way—like sixteen again.

4

Margaret Woodstock, in a lace-trimmed wrapper that Cindy had sent her from London, stood at the tall, narrow window and stared past the green brocade drapes into the late-September night. A moonless sky above wrapped the landscape in shadows. It was unseasonably cool, too, for this time of year. Flames licked about the piled-up logs in the fireplace, which failed, however, to send its warmth beyond six or seven feet.

Margaret told herself, head held high, that she did not want to hear the sounds that came from the bedroom on her left. The Master's bedroom. But, perversely, she listened. How many painful nights had she stood this way, clothed in degradation? Why did George have to take the next bedroom for himself? Why not somewhere else, where she could be spared the humiliation of overhearing his passion. Dear God, this house! On nights like this, she felt as though she were living in some fancy woman's house. George, next door—and down the hall, Mr. Jefferson, satisfying himself with Chloe.

Why did George take that child into his room? Seraphina would not take kindly to his using Eulalie that way. First, the mother, now the child. George was so coarse, so vulgar—there was no sensitivity in him at all. He was at home in boots, with a whip in his hand. The male animal. That was all he thought about. It was the symbol that ruled his life—his manhood.

Margaret's hand clutched at the green brocade drape as the gush of ribald laughter blending with excitement emerged from the other room. That child, pretty young Eulalie! Margaret felt sick, smitten with the vision of the incongruous pair stretched across the Master's feather bed. Down in the slave quarters, Seraphina must be looking out into the night this way. Knowing what was happening in the Master's bedroom up at the big house.

Eulalie wasn't like the others. Her Papa had to be quality. It was there, in the child. She was so bright, so pretty. Had it been wrong, spoiling Eulalie the way she had? But all these weeks now, Margaret Woodstock reminded herself righteously, she'd had Eulalie working in the kitchen. The learning, the being company for David, was all over. She hadn't realized, until that awful day with Cindy, that the children were getting to that age. No point in having David get ideas. Bad enough, with his father like that.

Margaret brought the glass in her hand up to her pale lips. The contents had been drained. She moved back to the fireplace, reaching for the bottle that waited on the mantel. Avidly, she poured more bourbon into the glass that was inevitably in her hand these long night hours before she succumbed to sleep. She frowned in annoyance. Not a drop left. George was so nasty—deliberately nasty —the way he made sure she didn't keep more than one bottle on hand. Sometimes, she fooled him—fooled Seraphina, who was commissioned to carry out his petty orders.

With a sense of urgency, Margaret crossed the room to the door, intent on going downstairs to the liquor cabinet, which was never locked. George simply found an ugly amusement in forcing her to go seeking a fresh bottle—as though the sight of her fleeing towards replacement gave him a savage satisfaction.

The lamps spilled mellow light on the thick carpeting that, in the first two years of her marriage, had been Margaret Woodstock's pride—before she came face to face with the cold knowledge that her chief attraction for the then-dashing George Woodstock had been Papa's money, which had been so essential in building up The Willows to its present glory.

Walking past her husband's room, she averted her face from the thick oak door that separated her from the coupling pair on the Master's bed. Damn, George should have thought before he took Eulalie! Seraphina practically ran the house. With Seraphina upset, there would be domestic difficulties for sure. Why couldn't George understand that the slaves had feelings, too? Maybe they knew enough not to show them, but they had ugly thoughts, rebellious thoughts, envious thoughts. You couldn't pick up a newspaper these days without reading about some runaway slave being sought.

Margaret Woodstock clung to the balustrade as she descended the circular staircase. The familiar tightness in her throat, in the pit of her stomach, was part of her being overwrought. Why couldn't she grow used to things? After all these years, why couldn't she stop feeling humiliated because her husband preferred the black wenches to his wife? She was glad, *glad,* she'd told herself, when George moved into the other bedroom. The night that David was born. He had his son, his heir—he had no more use for her.

David was *her* child; Cindy belonged to her father. She would not let David grow up to be like his father, no matter what the cost! Not to treat his wife the way his father treated her. Sometimes, she was fearful for Cindy. Cindy had her father's passion. Even as a little girl, Cindy would look at the big, black bucks—and in those lovely green eyes, Cindy's mother saw the woman that Cindy could become.

Margaret moved, with a sense of urgency, into the drawing room, to the cabinet that held the liquor supplies.

With the fresh bottle of bourbon in hand, she felt less insecure, more equipped to cope with the night. She started at the sound of footsteps—heavy, bare feet coming down on the wide-planked corridor that led to the back door.

"Chloe," she called out softly as the girl moved, with the awkward grace of her pregnancy, past the drawing-room door.

"Yes, Missis." Chloe halted demurely, her dark eyes secretive yet smug. Obviously, Mr. Jefferson had been pleased with her favors. Chloe clutched something in her hand—a coin or a trinket.

"Chloe, you send Amelia up to the house," Margaret ordered on impulse. She hadn't thought about that until this minute. "I won't ever get to sleep tonight without soaking in a hot tub."

"Yes'm, me send," Chloe promised, eyes down.

What did the slaves think about the relationship between the master and the mistress? Once, years ago it was, she went down to the infirmary when one of the house slaves was sick. A black buck with a frozen foot had been lying there, on the ground, on a blanket. It was a hot morning—he lay there half-naked. For one startled moment, her eyes met his, and passion rippled through her, because she knew he was seeing her as a woman—in his mind, he was using her as a woman. But that was ten years ago, before her body thickened at the middle, before her breasts began to sag and lines crept inexorably about her eyes and mouth and throat.

Amelia would bring in the tub and fill it with hot water before the fireplace and massage the tense nerves at the back of her neck. Eventually, she'd fall asleep. Half a dozen times, George had tried to breed Amelia. It was useless. After the first try, the doctor had told George it was useless.

Margaret sympathized with the silent hatred for males that Amelia harbored and that showed through at unguarded moments. Last year, George tried to sell Amelia. It was the one time she'd stood up to him, she remembered with pride. Amelia's mother had been her maid. She had promised Amelia's mother to keep the girl here at The Willows.

Clutching the bottle to her breast, Margaret climbed the stairs to her room. Eulalie was still in there with him. She knew because she heard the murmur of his voice as he talked to the girl. He had talked to her on their wedding night, she remembered. Ugly, dirty talk. As though she were one of the black wenches. The first night, she had stopped loving her husband. The second night, he had not come to her bed at all.

And he'd tried to do ugly, dirty, unnatural things. She had never told anybody about that. Not even Mama. She had loved him before that. He was handsome, muscular, young—and nurturing inchoate ideas about the wonder of being taken by your husband she had discounted all Mama had told her.

Mama had told her a wife had to submit. It was her duty. But Mama had not told her about a man like George Woodstock. Once, he had taken a strap to her. She had lain there, naked, across the bed—and the strap had laid ugly welts across her buttocks. Just once. Her mouth tightened in remembrance. That was something Papa wouldn't stand for—hitting his child.

Again, passing her husband's room, Margaret averted her eyes from the ornate oak door. She went inside her own room, moved close to the fire. In a few minutes, Amelia would be coming up to the big house. She'd go into the kitchen and put up kettles of water, bring them upstairs to pour into the galvanized tub.

Already, Margaret could feel the limpid comfort of the hot water. Amelia's large, strong hands kneading her tense flesh. Why should she care that her husband took his pleasure with the black wenches? Men were animals. And yet, in Margaret Woodstock, there lingered a furtive, wistful wish that she could find for herself the kind of pleasure a girl from the slave quarters could find with a man.

Amelia came quietly into the room after a gentle knock on the door. She brought the galvanized tub, set it down before the fireplace. She leaned forward now, a handsome, *café au lait* girl, with the spare body of an early adolescent, to heap logs onto the crackling fire.

"De water be ready presently," Amelia said, gentle hands urging Margaret into the rocker that flanked the fireplace.

"Thank you, Amelia." She settled herself in the rocker, closed her eyes. It was good to feel Amelia's hand stroking her hair, that was like early-morning sunlight—the one feature that had remained unchanged from girlhood.

Without asking, Amelia refilled the glass from the fresh bottle waiting on the mantel. Her poor baby, her David, Margaret thought sentimentally. What was going to happen to him in this insane household? Cindy would take care of herself. What about David? Why had she felt such a sense of foreboding that day when she'd seen David looking at Eulalie on the porch? The day he'd stopped looking like a child. It would be natural for David to take his will from a slave. Why did it turn her sick when everybody thought it was just natural?

The bourbon was easing away some of the tensions. She leaned back in the rocker while Amelia brushed the sunlit hair. Then Amelia was going downstairs, on the endless trips to fill the tub. She waited, expectantly, for Amelia to say the tub was ready for her.

Amelia kneeled before the tub, a slender hand cautiously testing.

"The water be all right, Missis."

Margaret stood before the waves of warmth spreading forth from the fireplace, slipped out of her clothes, allowed Amelia to help her into the tub. She remembered when her waist could be tied into a seventeen-inch corset; she thought, with pride, of the time when her body was beautiful enough to please any man. But why did she think about that, when her body was so ugly?

Margaret clumsily jackknifed herself into the soothing water, closed her eyes as Amelia's hands settled at the back of her neck.

"Pretty child," Amelia crooned. "So pretty."

In a few minutes, Amelia's hands would leave the back of her neck to stroke her shoulders, to fondle her breasts.

Amelia loved her fine, white skin. Amelia's mouth would kiss the white skin ever so gently. A faint smile touched Margaret Woodstock's mouth. In a little while, she would feel so good. She would go to sleep. She would not care that her husband never came to her bed.

Margaret Woodstock slept late, as she always did after a night when Amelia came to her. She came awake slowly, conscious first of the slaves singing in the fields, then of sunlight seeping through the drawn drapes to lay across the rug like a golden ribbon, and finally of the soft morning sounds downstairs in the big house.

With a tight look about her mouth and secretive eyes, Seraphina brought her a breakfast tray. Poor Seraphina, upset about her baby. But in a little while, Seraphina would forget. It was always this way in the big houses on the plantations. Seraphina knew.

"I have some cloth for you, Seraphina," Margaret said on impulse. "It will make you a pretty dress."

"Thankee, Missis." Seraphina's voice was polite enough, but her eyes were evasive. This morning, Seraphina was not in a mood to be cajoled with a gift.

"What's all the excitement downstairs?" Margaret asked, frowning slightly as she listened to the high-pitched chatter. "Seraphina, go see why on earth they're carrying on that way."

She listened intently while she dug into the fluffy omelet Seraphina had prepared for her, then split open a hot, golden biscuit. The coffee was strong, black. David was down there, she realized. She could hear his voice, which had been growing unfamiliarly deep this last year. Running up the stairs now, he was talking to Seraphina.

Her face lighted as she thought about David. From the beginning, after the difficult birth, David had been a joy to her. Sometimes, she feared for the relationship between his father and him. Sometimes, she caught the look of naked rage on David's face—it was always elicited by some action of his father's. David was gentle, fine—like the men on her side of the family.

"Mama, Mama!" David burst into the bedroom, his

face alive with interest. "Look!" He held a letter aloft in his hand. It bore the new glued postage stamp the government had voted in four years ago, in 1847.

"Massa David, you knock 'fore you be goin' to a lady's bedroom," Seraphina scolded. But Seraphina loved David, almost as much as she loved Cindy.

"Is it from Cindy?" Margaret's face lighted as she reached out for the envelope that had been brought back from town this morning.

"I don't think so," David said, craning his neck for another look at the stamp before the envelope was out of view. Mr. Jefferson had suggested he start a stamp collection since they were receiving mail from England as well as from up North. "It's President Washington's picture— that means it's a two-page letter. Mr. Ben Franklin's picture is on the one-page letters."

With David and Seraphina hovering over the bed, Margaret ripped open the envelope, pulled out the two sheets covered with a spidery handwriting.

"My goodness!" Her voice was suddenly soft, girlish. "Cousin Madeline is coming down to visit us, all the way from New York City! I declare, she ought to be arriving in another day or so. Look, David, when the letter was mailed out. She'll be following right behind."

"How long will she be staying?" David asked. "Is she coming by herself?" Caution was in his eyes because the last time a cousin had come from New York, she had come with two giggling daughters scarcely older than David. They had just about driven David crazy, Margaret remembered, her face soft with affection. The way they'd carried on about their handsome young cousin! But last year David had been too young to tolerate girls. Except Eulalie. Discomfort invaded her again. Always Eulalie coming into her mind. George was right about one thing. She was overly sentimental.

"Cousin Madeline will be staying a month or two." An unplanned sharpness crept into her voice. "That's the least, considering the trip," Margaret admonished her son. "She doesn't say anything about bringing the girls," she added, scanning the letter again. "She'll be taking the railroad to Baltimore. From there she'll take a boat to Portsmouth. At Portsmouth, she'll board a railroad car again. My goodness, she ought to be arriving in Atlanta by day after tomorrow? She should be here the following day." Margaret Woodstock's eyes glowed with anticipation. "Seraphina, we'll have to polish all the silver, wash down all the best china. You put Eulalie and Chloe on that right away. Bring Venus in to help them. I'll talk to Mr. Woodstock about our giving a party to introduce Cousin Madeline to the folks around." At moments like this, she almost felt like a girl again. "David, you run find your Papa. Tell him I have to talk to him."

Times like this, they were almost a family. If only Cindy were home. Her eyes were wistful. Maybe—just maybe—George would relent and let her bring Cindy back from London. It seemed so terrible, to have your only daughter—a child like that—living with cousins in a foreign city. It wasn't like anything really happened that time. Cindy was always just so full of vitality, so friendly. Folks misunderstood. Even her Papa. All Cindy wanted to do, that time, was to talk to Alexander.

Ten minutes later, while Seraphina was brushing Margaret's hair, George stalked into her room. Margaret was starkly conscious that he never entered this room unless summoned. The last time he'd entered on his own volition she was giving birth to David.

Dr. Cooper had been downright shocked when George insisted on being there in the room. He had said it was his son and he wanted to be there when the boy came into the world. He was dead certain the second one would be a boy. George had stood there, frowning, one hand clutched about a bedpost, perspiration lining his forehead as it lined hers. He watched while Dr. Cooper hovered above her and she, in her agony, bore down at the doctor's exhortation. He had the same look on his face that he had when he hovered above her in their marriage bed.

"All right, Margaret," her husband's voice destroyed her introspection. "What's all this nonsense?" He was annoyed at being summoned to the house.

"Cousin Madeline is coming," she explained, handing

the letter to him. "The way I figure, she ought to be arriving in Atlanta day after tomorrow. She'll be here the following day. We ought to give a party for her early next week."

"I suppose," he conceded grudgingly. He enjoyed showing off The Willows. "Only it comes at a bad time. I've got a slave trader coming in to talk business."

"George, he's not going to stay here at the house!" Margaret's eyes dilated in distaste. "Not with my cousin staying here."

"I want to do business with the man," George shot back, irritated. "I don't have to tell you the last crop was bad. I don't know what's happening to the earth. Every year, it's a little worse. I'll do business with the man, Margaret," he reiterated grimly. "Some wenches are beginning to show already—that brings a better price."

"George, you don't break up the families," Margaret said self-consciously. "That was one thing Papa could never abide."

"I'm considering selling that Alexander." His eyes narrowed in anger. "That one's looking to be a troublemaker, the way I see it."

"How do you mean?" Unease brushed Margaret Woodstock. You heard about such things of course—and George was a rough master. But nothing was going to happen here, was it?

"Just a rumbling," George admitted. "But I mean to stop that right now. You'd think that nigger had learned his lesson!"

Margaret sighed. No use trying to persuade George to bring Cindy home. He still didn't trust his darling baby, with all those big black bucks moving about the plantation. Maybe he knew Cindy better than she did—they were so much alike. Dr. Cooper hadn't lied to her, had he? Cindy hadn't let Alexander do anything to her, had she? Her mind anxiously considered dates. No, nothing had happened—Cindy would be screaming her head off by now if she were pregnant.

"Well, let's don't make it unpleasant for Madeline,"

Margaret warned softly. "You know how some Northern-ers feel about the slave trade."

"I'll put the trader up for one night," he compromised. "Maybe he'll be here and gone before your cousin Madeline arrives. Who knows?" he chuckled cynically. "Maybe Madeline's just spoiling to see a dealer in action."

"Stop that, George." Margaret lifted her head proudly, the nostrils slightly dilated. "Madeline comes from my side of the family."

For a heated instant, their eyes clashed. Then George was striding from the room, and Seraphina—at a look from Margaret—was bringing over the bourbon bottle.

5

The big kitchen was overwarm, with the kettles of water boiling on the stove and steaming up the windows. Eulalie, eyes downcast, stood before the basin filled with soapy water; she was seemingly absorbed in washing the best china to a sparkling cleanliness. At a table near Eulalie, Chloe stood polishing the silver, all the while humming to herself.

Seraphina, busy now with breakfast for Mister Jefferson and David, turned to look at the fire.

"No more wood for de fire," Seraphina ordered. "The Massa no like waste." Her eyes moved to Eulalie, softened. "Them dishes bes' be shinin'," she exhorted. Her eyes said much more than she dared to put into words.

"I know, Maw," Eulalie said, rebellion coating her voice.

Maw looked worried. Didn't it turn her sick, knowin' about last night? It bothered Maw, the way she be tryin' to make herself over. The way she be tryin' to talk like white folks.

Last night told her she *wasn't* like white folks. She hated the Massa. Slaves wasn't supposed to have feelin's. You be a slave, you just lie down and let that man do anything he want. He knew she hated him, Eulalie realized with meager triumph—he knew she didn't want him doin' that to her, even if he be white. She had a knife last night, maybe she kill him.

What about David? Pinkness stained the gold of her high cheekbones. David knew. He stood there, lookin' at her walk up them steps with that hot toddy, and he knew. She felt shamed before him. Now he be disgusted with her. Not have anything more to do with her. He say—he *said*, she be doin' so good. Not just the lessons, the way she speak.

No matter what Missis say, David shared his lessons with her. Every day he hide the papers in a book in the cupboard on the backporch, and she find it. Right now, David say she know more than Missy Cindy. Pride brought her head erect, lent a glow to her eyes. What you know, nobody take away from you.

But now—how it gonna be *now*? David be disgusted with her? Nothin' goin' to be the same, no more. Now, she sleep in the kitchen, by the fireplace. Waitin' till the Massa call for her. Some day, she get away from here. Go up North. Alexander be talkin' strange-like about slaves goin' to a place called Canada. Be free there. The law say so.

Eulalie remained silent, ignoring the good-humored jibes from Chloe, who considered Eulalie raised in status, now that she had lain in the Masters' bed. She didn't want to be carryin' the Massa's baby in her belly, Eulalie thought, sickened at the prospect. It didn't happen, the first time like, did it? If it did, she promised herself with furious determination she make Maw take the baby away.

Chloe, glancing about cautiously, pulled a chair over to where she worked, knowing that, when Seraphina returned, she would be chastised for taking this liberty. But when Seraphina returned to the kitchen, she was full of talk about the cousin arriving from New York City and about the party to be given next week.

Eulalie strained her ears. She was trying to hear, beyond Maw's talk with Chloe, the conversation between
David and Mr. Jefferson at the breakftst table. She knew
they'd be going into the library for the lessons soon.
Would David leave the new lessons with the corrected
ones from yesterday for her? Her heart pounded. She die
if David not be her friend no more. She die without the
lessons!

Margaret Woodstock joined her son and Mr. Jefferson
for coffee in the dining room. The Missis be feelin' good
this mornin', Eulalie noted, hearing the girlish, high-
spirited chatter around the dining table. The Missis like
somebody else, when company comes once or twice each
year. But ever since that time with Missy and Alexander,
Missis not be the same with she. With *her*. What the
cousin from New York like, Eulalie wondered with her
voracious curiosity.

Eulalie was in the cupboard off the kitchen, stealthily
studying the lesons David had left for her—just as though
nothing had happened between his Paw and her, Eulalie
reiterated self-consciously—when she heard the convivial
voices in the huge foyer. The welcoming sounds told her
the guest had arrived. Absorbed as she was in the lesson,
she hadn't heard the carriage drive up before the portico.

"Madeline Henderson, do you mean to stand there and
tell me you made that whole trip with just your maid?"
Margaret Woodstock was disclaiming with disbelief.
"Your husband allowed this?"

"Margaret, you women down here in the South live in
such a vacuum." Her voice was warm, brisk, vital. "Women are beginning to fight for their rights. Why, I almost
postponed my trip because there's going to be a convention of women advocating suffrage, up in Seneca Falls.
Two days of convention," she elaborated with relish. "But
I knew if I postponed coming down to see you, dear
Margaret, I might just never get down here. And I so
wanted to see The Willows."

Eulalie listened avidly to the goings-on out in the foyer;
she was intrigued with the vibrant personality of Margaret

Woodstock's house guest. What did she mean, suffrage? That be a word to look up in Mr. Webster's book. The Missis was takin' her cousin and the maid—a white lady, Maw just reported—upstairs to their rooms.

"You take up hot chocolate, Eulalie," Maw ordered importantly, obviously impressed with the new arrivals. "Them fancy cups, Missis say. And me fix cake plate. You take."

When Seraphina was content with the festive tray, Eulalie hurried upstairs to the guest rooms. She was eager to see the owner of the authoritative feminine voice that spoke about women fighting for their rights. *She* was a woman, Eulalie thought with defiant pride. She not be a slave always. Lying in the kitchen last night, wrapped in the comforter the Master had given her with a gesture of magnanimity, Eulalie knew she would not always be a slave.

Eulalie knocked lightly, entered at the Missis's invitation.

"Bring the tray over here, to this table, Eulalie," Margaret Woodstock ordered gaily. "Oh, and tell Seraphina to give you one of the small fruit-cakes to bring up. I'm sure my cousin will like that."

Eulalie was conscious of Madeline Henderson's friendly interest as she moved about the table, serving the hot chocolate and laying first the plates for the cake, then the exquisitely polished silver. Mrs. Henderson was a short, round, bright-eyed woman who bristled with energy—not one of the languid, Southern ladies who came to The Willows to talk about their flower gardens and their new clothes and the parties being given at the other plantations.

Hurrying out of the room, Eulalie was conscious of the white lady's maid in the bedroom already hanging away the fancy dresses Madeline Henderson had brought with her—she also seemed brisk and efficient. Eulalie went down the stairs, out the corridor to the kitchen, for the small fruit cake Margaret Woodstock had ordered brought up. When she was coming up the wide circular staircase again, she could hear the animated voices inside the guest rooms.

"Madeline, that personal-liberty law was all wrong," Margaret Woodstock was saying emphatically. "You just don't understand our colored folk. Why, it would be a moral disaster to free the slaves!"

"They did it in England," Madeline Henderson reminded her triumphantly. " 'Way back, eighteen years ago, I think it was. That's right, 1833. Of course, England reimbursed every slave owner," she reported conscientiously.

"Thank goodness, Congress had the sense last year to pass the Fugitive Slave Bill," Margaret Woodstock pointed out virtuously.

"Why, Margaret," her cousin gibed good-humoredly. "I never suspected you followed what was happening up there in Washington."

"That's a law that's important to our tradition," Margaret said, bridling slightly. "George talked to me about it at great length."

"But you still have runaway slaves in the South," Madeline pointed out softly. "You can't stop what has to be—"

Eulalie entered with the fruit cake. At a sharp look from her cousin, Madeline fell silent.

"What about the new singer you were telling me about, Madeline?" Margaret asked, brimming over with effervescent charm. Seein' her now, Eulalie thought, you could believe the Missis had once been a beauty. You never think she could be so sad sometimes. Once, Maw say, she try to kill herself. "What's her name?" Margaret Woodstock squinted in thought.

"Jenny Lind," Madeline picked up. "The Swedish Nightingale."

Somehow, Madeline Henderson's presence in the big house was an impetus for study, Eulalie discovered. She threw herself with religious fervor into absorbing the lessons David left for her. Maw knew, she suspected, but Maw was afraid to say anything, for fear of starting trouble for David and her. Mr. Jefferson was a harder taskmaster than his predecessor. Eulalie relished the challenge.

With her towering determination to make herself over, Eulalie was increasingly conscious that her covert studying was possible only as long as she remained a house slave. Let the Master become angry with her, and she would be banished to the fields, put to picking cotton. Night after night, he summoned her to his room. She submitted to his will, yet found satisfaction in his knowing that she gave him her body only.

Eulalie made excuses to be around Madeline Henderson, to listen to the heresy their guest spouted with increasing abandon under the Master's roof. Now, they hardly bothered that she was about when they talked.

"Madeline, I think it's unladylike for you to go running around the slave quarters the way you do," Margaret Woodstock reproached. "Even if Mary does accompany you." Mary was the apple-cheeeked Irish maid. "Sometimes, I think the only reason you came down here was to run us down."

Eulalie intercepted the guarded look that passed between Madeline Henderson and her maid. Her cousin, unthinkingly, really, had hit upon the truth. Mrs. Henderson had come down here, to The Willows, to see slavery for herself! More and more people up North were saying it was wrong to hold other humans in slavery. She didn't get to the slave quarters much, but the word was sifting through. Alexander said that someday there would be war, that the North would fight the South and all slaves would be set free.

"Margaret, honey, maybe you're too close to see it as it really is." Madeline was gentle, sweet, determined to speak her mind without offending her cousin. "Now, I'm not saying things are as bad here as they are at the other plantations, mind you—but yesterday, I went visiting, you know—and Mrs. Butler was kind enough, knowing my interest, to show me all about her plantation."

"Now that was downright silly," Margaret Woodstock bridled. "Some things a lady does not expose herself to, Madeline."

"I saw the huts where those poor souls live." Madeline's voice rose indignantly. "Ten humans shoved together in two closets not big enough for one person—but they call this home. Moss for mattresses, rags for blankets, with the wind and the rain and the cold free to come in as they please! And the women pushed back to the fields, soon as they drop their young!"

"It's not that way at The Willows," Margaret said, tight-lipped with anger. "We're kind to our slaves. I told you before, we have a moral responsibility to them. Why, left on their own, they would probably starve to death."

"Margaret!" George Woodstock's voice thundered through the house as he strode into the foyer. "Margaret —"

"We're in the drawing room," she called out, trying to make her voice casual and unconcerned, as though she didn't mind when he blasted that way. "And George, why must you come raging into the house that way? One of these days, you'll have a stroke."

"Call the house slaves together," he ordered brusquely, coming into view. A vein hammered away in his forehead. "Hector's disappeared. We can't find him anywhere. We locate that nigger before nightfall, or there's going to be a flogging at The Willows!"

No trace was found of Hector, that day or afterwards, though the men were out with the dogs far into the night. Again, Alexander was flogged, for aiding Hector's escape. Hector's woman was flogged until she lost the baby she was carrying.

The other slaves moved about in fear, dreading more reprisals. Even the house slaves were cowed. And Madeline Henderson became more outspoken. On her knees polishing a floor, Eulalie heard one of her outbursts.

"Margaret, how can you expect the slaves not to run away, not to resort to revolt?" she demanded righteously. "This is only the beginning, I tell you."

"Madeline, you don't understand," her cousin retorted. "Every plantation has some bad niggers like Hector. We're good to our blacks. There's none of them flogged without reason. They eat regularly. When the women give birth, they don't have to go back to the fields for three weeks after their confinement."

"They work fourteen or fifteen hours a day, Margaret! They live in hovels. They eat worse than pigs. They own nothing, not even the right to think! And you expect them not to revolt?"

"You Northerners make me sick," Margaret flared. "You don't know the situation at all. The slaves are not like us—they're an inferior race. They don't have feelings like us, desires like us. You treat them the way you would a pet cat or a dog, and they're happy."

"Margaret, the day is coming when there will be no more slaves in America," Madeline prophesied. "Think ahead, plan—you'll have to run The Willows with freed, paid labor."

It was a relief to the Missis, Eulalie realized, when Mrs. Henderson and her Irish maid packed their belongings and began the long, arduous trip back to New York. The Massa was in evil temper. The floggings increased. Eulalie would hide herself in a cupboard, try to shut her ears to the cries as leather drove into naked flesh. The Massa brought in a new driver because he was beset with the conviction that more slaves plotted to run away. Chloe, Venus, the other slaves who worked in the big house, wore uneasy faces.

The winter was cold, this far north in Georgia. Eulalie knew she should be glad for sleeping by the dying embers of the fire in the kitchen, but she could never banish from her mind the knowledge that, many nights, one of the two small niggers who did for the Massa would come down, solemn-faced, fighting giggles, to say she was wanted in his room.

It seemed to Eulalie that this winter would never pass. Other winters, she had been David's companion, his friend. Now, their relationhip was furtive, unspoken. A look now and then, the secret exchanges of books and lessons, an occasional penciled note of approval. She worked in the kitchen from sunup till sundown. And then there were the nights.

Margaret Woodstock read aloud, frequently within Eulalie's hearing, the extravagant letters Cindy wrote home about the beautiful gowns she'd bought, the parties, the city entertainment for which, quite obviously, her mother pined. George Woodstock grumbled about the expensive tastes of his daughter, yet felt a great pride in her becoming a lady of fashion in London. She even talked about a trip to Paris in the spring.

Mr. Jefferson, late in the winter, announced his decision to relinquish his position. He longed for a return to Philadelphia, where life offered so much more diversion. He had discarded Chloe by now, for Venus, who was also pregnant—some claimed, pregnant by the Massa. It was no secret that the Massa was eager for mulatto girl babies, who brought a high price on the market.

It had become an obsessive fear of Eulalie's that she, too, would become pregnant. She wanted no child of the Massa in her belly! She wanted no child of hers to grow up a slave. Soon—her mind refused to grope with actual, specific timetable—she would run away from The Willows. All the time now, she heard about the cars that ran runaway slaves to freedom.

The Massa carried on so about the crops being bad; but the crops that interested George Woodstock, Eulalie knew, were the slaves being born in the spring. Regularly now, he was selling off the slaves that could not do a day's work in the fields or that showed promise of being troublesome niggers or young mulatto girls that would bring pretty prices in New Orleans.

Eulalie knew Maw worried that one day—angry at her—the Massa might sell her to some trader going West. Even though the Missis promised Seraphina never to sell her baby, he might do that. There was such anger in him, you never knew what he might do next.

Mr. Jefferson left. His replacement was an elderly ex-actor who relished the lazy life on the plantation. David hated him violently. Margaret Woodstock, intrigued by his rhetoric, made him her confidant. Like Mrs. Woodstock, he had a taste for bourbon. His employer treated him with veiled disdain.

George Woodstock was making efforts to encourage David's interest in females. Margaret took to inviting ingenuous young neighbors to tea, along with their mothers, with the hopes of their finding favor in David's eyes. David was fifteen. He was polite, but bored.

David's father joined his mother after one of these social gatherings. He was outspoken in his disgust, under the persuasion of a few shots of rye.

"By the time I was fifteen," George Woodstock bellowed, "I knew what it was to throw a wench across her back. I'd had my taste of half a dozen of the best black bitches about the place—with and without my Pa's permission." His face glistened with complacency. "Only once did my Pa flog me. That was for taking his new, high-yaller gal before he had a chance to break her in himself. She was fourteen and hot!" His eyes beamed in reminiscence. "She near about bit me to pieces before I was through with her."

"David is my son," Margaret told her husband, between clenched teeth. "He won't run to wallowing in the dirt with slave wenches."

"Let him prove himself a man," George insisted. "What are we rearing here? Male or female?"

"Must you talk so loud?" Exasperation edged her voice. "Must every slave in the house know our personal problems?"

"They probably know more about that boy than we do," his father said grimly. "Margaret, you think he might have a taste for the lads?"

"George." Her voice rose in outrage. "You are a depraved man. Suspecting everyone else of sinking to your level."

"I never had a thing to do with a man," he said smugly. "What about you, Margaret?" The dryness in his tone should have alerted his wife. "Have you never looked at a black buck and wondered how it would be with him?"

Margaret rose in fury, flounced from the drawing room, and went upstairs to her own room. George roamed through the house, in search of David. Hastily, Eulalie retreated out of sight. She knew David was in the library. Let his father find David himself. She wasn't going to tell him.

The night was warm, with the first hint of spring. Eulalie put away the supper dishes and the silver while Chloe scrubbed down the floor. She was humming softly to herself, awkward in her advanced pregnancy, but strangely satisfied. Why did Chloe feel so good because her baby was part white? Didn't Chloe know if the baby looked too white, like the Massa, both she and the baby be sold quick? The Massa didn't want no half-brother or half-sister of David's and Cindy's bein' around the slave quarters. Least, not one that David might have his suspicions about. David be funny, that way.

Chloe finished the floor, straightened up, looking tired. It was close to her time.

"Time me go," she said to Eulalie. "Before head man come check." She stared curiously at Eulalie. Wondering, no doubt, how she felt about sharing the Massa's bed. Her eyes rested, for an instant, on Eulalie's small, flat belly, wondering if the Massa's seed was growing there.

"Me do de silver," Eulalie said carelessly. Don't talk like white folks around Chloe, around the others. Do that all by herself. Soon she'd be talking good as Missis herself, she thought with pride. Up North, nobody would be thinking Eulalie was a slave. But up North she would not be a slave. Fourteen now. Time, oh time, to get away! Yet, no plan formed in her mind. Not yet. Only inchoate determination.

Chloe left. Seraphina was already gone, along with the others. Eulalie liked these moments alone in the kitchen, at night, when she could feel almost free. Almost. She walked to the door, opened it, gazed out into the night, sniffed the fragrant fresh air. The hyacinths were in bloom, disturbingly sweet in the night. The moon was near full, she noted. A bad night for a runaway slave.

"Eulalie!" George Woodstock called imperiously from the entrance to the kitchen. "You put yourself in the tub, scrub yourself down good, then come up to me. Bring me a hot toddy, when you come up, girl. Mind you, make it a stiff one."

"Yes, suh." Instantly, the veiled eyes, the flat tones, that marked her the obedient slave, though hardly the responsive one he kept hoping to find her.

He left her. She dragged out the galvanized tub—it had been utilized by Chloe before her, and how many others? —brought it into the middle of the kitchen, close to the dying fire. Despite the warmth of the night, Eulalie dropped another log onto the dying fire. Put up the kettles of water. Scrub down for the Massa. Nobody comin' into the kitchen this hour of the night. Still, she closed the back door.

Eulalie sat in the tub, letting the warmth of the water embrace her, trying not to think about these nights when her body was used for the Massa's passion. He was pleased that she didn't get pregnant. As soon as she did, he'd be lookin' for another. Before that happened, she had to run away. More and more, running away from The Willows bore upon her mind. Hector got away. Nobody ever caught up with him, even with the ads running in all the newspapers. The Massa was fit to bust about Hector—because now, others, like Hector, would have the same idea.

Eulalie stalled in the tub as long as she dared. Then she spilled the water out in the back, hung away the tub, made the Massa's hot toddy, and reluctantly walked through the silent house to the wide circular staircase. A knot tightened in her stomach as she began the ascent.

"Come in, come in," George Woodstock called gruffly in response to her light knock.

He stood there, barefoot, in his winter drawers. The lamps were burning bright. He had a fire struck in the fireplace. One window was slightly open, bringing in the heady sweetness of the hyacinths that bloomed below the bedrooms.

Eyes down, Eulalie walked to the table in the center of the room to put down the hot toddy beside the bottle of rye sitting there. He'd been drinkin' already, but not so much as to put him out of action, Eulalie thought dryly.

Her face was an impassive mask, as it always was in these moments.

"You cold with the window open?" he asked, his eyes already shucking away her poplin uniform, beneath which there was only Eulalie.

"No, suh." Her eyes remained on the rug. She steeled herself for the ordeal. Maybe he would have his will, but there would be no response from her. She took savage pride in that.

"Man, you'd bring a pretty price on the New Orleans market," he drawled.

Her eyes widened in alarm. The pale, full mouth, set in the perfect oval of her face, dropped open. He promised Maw he would never sell her. Now he was thinkin' about that! Panic closed in about her. She'd heard about fancy yaller wenches in New Orleans!

"Don't you worry your head, Eulalie," he crooned, his face lighting in satisfaction at this reaction from her. "I'm not selling you. Not as long as you bring me pleasure. You been awful cold, girl, and I've been telling myself it's because you're young. But fourteen's old enough to prove you're a woman." He was reaching for the hot toddy, his face already flushed from drinking. His eyes remaining on her, he walked across the room, picked up his riding corp, which lay across the dresser. "Tonight, Eulalie, you show me you're alive—or maybe I'll have to find out for myself. Other ways."

She flinched as the crop whipped through the air, missing her by inches. The Massa never hit her. Not once. Not yet. Suddenly, she was trembling. There was something menacing in the room. Tonight was different.

"Here, girl," he ordered, striding back to the bottle of rye, pouring a shot into the glass, hnding the glass to her. "Drink it down. I said, drink!" His voice thundered when she hesitated.

The rye was bitter, scalding to her throat. But she drank it down. Her eyes stung for an instant. Then the rye settled warmly in her belly, making her head light. He moved in to her, rippled his hands about the slender body, his eyes dark, enigmatic.

She watched the odd, sadistic smile settle about his mouth while her heart pounded. This was something new, and she was afraid.

"You stay right here, Eulalie," he said quietly. "I'll be right back."

George Woodstock stalked out into the hall, walked down the carpeted area towards the other bedrooms. She waited, her mouth going dry, knowing tonight would be unlike the others. Where was he goin'? For the new tutor? Was the Massa tired of her, givin' her over to the tutor? Venus been goin' to him, now and then, not regular-like. She thought him too old for that. Hot color flooded her face. Maybe it be better to be a field nigger than this.

She listened to the voices in the hallway, turned cold. David. The Massa be bringin' in David! Her eyes were dark with pain. What the Massa up to now, bringin' David in here? *To watch?*

"David, I'm tired of all the babying your Mama gives you," George Woodstock was saying heatedly when the two of them walked into the bedroom. "You need a father to take over, to make you prove yourself a man."

"Papa—" David's eyes went sick when he saw Eulalie.

"Don't you Papa me," his father flashed back.

"I'm going," David said, swerving towards the door.

"Not yet, you're not," his father said with relish. George Woodstock walked to the door, locked it, shoved the key beneath the feather mattress. David stared at his father, his face whitened. "I'm tired of watching your mother make a woman-man out of you. I'll bet you never pushed your manhood into a wench yet, and here you are fifteen years old."

"Papa—" David's voice was a shamed whisper. "Papa, please—"

"We're father and son, David. You have to learn what it is to be a man, to feel like a man, to take your pleasure like a man. Tonight, you learn." George Woodstock's eyes flashed with half-drunken triumph.

Eulalie shut her eyes when George Woodstock crossed the room and hovered before her. She didn't move when he ripped the uniform down the front, from neck to hem.

She clenched her fist as his short, stubby fingers moved greedily about the slender gold of her body. David! Oh, why did he do this to David? Sickness rose in her in threatening waves as George Woodstock fondled her nakedness, trying, as always, to elicit signs of arousal in her. As always, failing.

"Don't worry, David," his father was promising thickly. "You'll have your turn, boy!"

The feather mattress hit at the back of her knees. He swept aside the torn uniform, thrust her roughly across the width of the bed. She bit at her lips to keep from crying out at the roughness of his hands. She bit until the lips were crimson with blood when he took his pleasure in her.

His breathing was labored, his eyes triumphant as he raised himself from her.

"All right, Davey, boy," he chuckled with satisfaction. "You can have her now!"

But David didn't hear his father. He hung over the washstand in the corner, retching into the basin.

6

Spring was the time of the year that Eulalie normally loved most. New hope came alive in her each spring, as life came to the winter-dead earth, filling the plantation with the glory of floral scents, the splashes of color, the lushness of the newly green trees. This spring was unlike all the others. Eulalie was weighed down with humiliation that never withdrew its ugly tentacles. David had seen her, like *that,* with his Paw.

Early-May warmth caressed her this morning as she stood behind the big house, leaning over the tub, scrubbing the white lace curtains soon to be hung in the drawing room. Lilacs bloomed in lavender splendor, blending their fragrance with that of the heady honeysuckle, the more delicate sweet peas, jasmine. But this year, Eulalie was aware of nothing—except the material beneath her fingers as she scrubbed.

The lessons had stopped. With a shattering, agonizing suddenness, Eulalie was cut off from all that made her life endurable. David avoided her. If she were in the room, he looked elsewhere. He was washing her out of his existence. Four weeks now. Four weeks since she'd gone to the back-porch cupboard, with her heart pounding, and reached inside for what wasn't there. Would never be there again.

"Eulalie." Maw's voice broke into her somber introspection. "Eulalie, you hurry. Time we gettin' breakfas' on de table. Soon, Missis ring."

"I be right there," Eulalie promised, her sullenness unveiled before her mother. She avoided her mother's eyes. She knew the concern, the misery, in them.

"Baby—" Maw's voice was rich with anguish. "Baby, what me say to you? No good, way you fret. We no change things. The Lawd made it so."

Maw didn't know about what happened up in the Massa's room—with David locked in that way. Nobody knew, 'ceptin' David and the Massa and she. Yet the house was filled with the ugliness of that night. Maw make her mad sometimes. Maw bow her head and take everything. You be a slave, you have no feelin's, Maw pretended. But it wasn't that way. You hurt, inside, just like white folks!

"Don't bother 'bout me, Maw," Eulalie said, lifting her her head proudly. "I be all right." But the liquid amber eyes were angry, resentful.

"You be right in de kitchen," Maw reiterated, her voice reproachful. Not because she was concerned that Eulalie would be late in serving breakfast, but because she felt, without understanding, the ominous undercurrents at The Willows.

Why did the Massa say that she had to serve at the breakfast table every morning. Eulalie asked herself, with the ever-simmering rebellion. He came right out to the kitchen hisself and tol' Maw. But Eulalie knew why. To punish David. To make David look at her every morning and remember what happened on that bed—and his own shame.

Eulalie took out her anger on the delicate lace curtains by scrubbing them until the golden knuckles were scraped, sore. Once in a while, before the head man made his nightly check, she got down to the slave quarters, on various pretexts, to listen to the whispered eloquence of

Alexander, who swore revenge on the Massa. The time was comin', Alexander kept sayin', when they'd all be free. When? Could she wait that long? How to get away? She churned inside with the need to break away from the ugliness that hung over The Willows.

"Eulalie!" Maw stood in the spill of sunlight at the back door. Her voice was sharp, masking her anxiety. "You git yo'self inside de house, girl. Breakfas' be ready. They's waitin'!"

A swath of gold poured through the tall casement-windows, across the immaculate linen that covered the elegant dining table. Flanked by his wife and his son, George Woodstock sat at the head of the table. He appeared in a jubilant mood this morning, sitting at the table with pen in hand, writing a letter, ignoring his family, who —Eulalie guessed—were happy to be ignored.

"Well, that does it," George said, sliding the sheet of paper into the envelope in readiness. His arrogant eyes moved from his wife to his son with sly satisfaction. "Once I make up my mind to do something. I do it."

"What is it this time, George?" Margaret refused to display any sign of curiosity. It annoyed him when she didn't grab at verbal bait.

"Bringing the little queen home, that's what," he announced triumphantly. "I wrote Cindy. Her cousins can make arrangements for her to ship out on the next boat home. I'll go up to Charleston to meet her myself."

"Oh, George!" Margaret Woodstock sparkled with vivacity. "You're really bringing her home? You're not teasing me?" Now caution crept in. Her husband's sense of humor could take a cruel turn when the mood suited him. He knew how desperately she wanted her baby home.

"She's coming, all right," he announced with relish. Everybody knew Cindy could twist him 'round her little pinkie mos' of the time, Eulalie thought, moving about the breakfast table. Only time he got outraged with his little darlin' was when he thought she'd been violated. He wasn't goin' to take kindly to any man havin' anything to do with his baby. Even in the marriage bed. "Reckon it's about time, too." He glanced at David with a look of secretive amusement. "I figure, when we have Cindy home, she'll be bringing some other young ladies into the house —before her brother gets the idea he's a young lady, too."

"George!" Color stained Margaret's face. "Can't you ever stop being vulgar?"

"I'd like to see the boy being vulgar, as you call it," her husband mimicked contemptuously. "What's he think he's got that thing for, anyhow?"

The cream pitcher slipped through Eulalie's nervous fingers, crashed on the oriental rug.

"Oh, Eulalie," Margaret moaned impatiently. "Whatever made you do a thing like that?"

"Sorry, Missis," Eulalie whispered, scarlet. "I sorry!" She fell to her knees, ineffectually trying to mop up the mess with the skirt of her uniform.

"Don't bother about that, girl," George Woodstock ordered briskly. "Send in Jason to clean up the slop. You fetch more hot biscuits." Eulalie caught the undertone of sardonic amusement in his voice. The Massa knew why she dropped the pitcher of cream. Most of the time, the Massa and Missis think slaves don't hear good—but he knowed she hear. "And tell Seraphina to send in more of the sausages—'less she's been giving them all away down in the quarters."

Eulalie fled to the kitchen. He knew Maw wasn't givin' away food. The Massa knew every pound of butter be in the kitchen, every bit of first-run molasses and meal. But, dutifully, she reported the Massa's exhortation.

"He knowed better'n dat." Seraphina bridled good-humoredly. "He take right out my hide." But her eyes were anxious, aware of confusion in Eulalie. "What bother you, baby?"

"I spill the cream," she admitted, her voice low. "Massa wants Jason in, to clean up. Send Jason quick."

Seraphina yelled out the back door. Jason was on his haunches before the petunia beds. He came swiftly, in reply to the summons, scraping his bare feet at the back steps because he knew Seraphina would tan his hide if he brought dirt into her kitchen.

"Go clean de dinin' room," Seraphina ordered vigorously. "Be quick or Massa sen' you to de fields again."

Eulalie moved on noiseless feet into the dining room again, bearing a fresh platter of hot biscuits neatly covered with one of the linen napkins that had been a gift from Madeline Henderson. George Woodstock was talking with obvious relish about his daughter's imminent homecoming. There was no complaining, now, about the costly trip to London. He was eager to show off the elegant young lady she had become—in his eyes—during those long months in London.

"We'll give a party that they'll remember all over the state," he boasted. "Everybody will come, from all the way up at Atlanta, from down in Macon and Augusta." His eyes went opaque. "Time Cindy started meeting the right kind of young men."

"George, that kind of party is going to be awful expensive," Margaret pointed out cautiously. "You're always complaining about how we spend money like water."

"We'll manage the party," he shot back pugnaciously. "There'll be a trader coming through in a couple weeks— I'll be doing some business with him." He smiled dryly. He knew it always upset Margaret when he brought a trader into The Willows.

"Again?" Margaret frowned.

"I know these fellows upset your delicate sensibilities," George mocked with sarcasm. "The only thing you have in common is a mutual appreciation for my best bourbon. But it's easier for me to trade with him than to go wasting time at the market myself when I'll only be selling three or four slaves." He chuckled reminiscently. "Last time I went to New Orleans, it was an unpropitious occasion. That was when I came down with the clap."

"George, even you should understand there are some things you don't discuss at the table." She was tight-lipped with anger, the knuckles on her clenched hand showing white. "Some things a gentleman doesn't discuss anywhere." She gazed anxiously at Eulalie, who was coming back into the dining room with a platter of neatly browned sausages. Missis be wondering, Eulalie knew, if she'd heard the Massa. She had.

Everybody on the plantation knew last year, when the Massa came back with a dose from the New Orleans whores. Dr. Cooper had kept him in quarantine for almost a whole month. All the bedclothes had to be washed separate—all his clothes. He didn't go near Chloe, near anybody.

"I tell you right now," George Woodstock said emphatically. "I wouldn't care if that young fellow there—" He turned scornfully to David. "I wouldn't care if he came down with the clap himself, just to prove to me he's shown himself a man!"

"George," Margaret began, cutting her mind off from the distasteful discussion with a strength that showed itself only in moments such as this, "who're you planning on selling this time?"

It always upset Margaret Woodstock, when slaves were sold. She disappeared into her room, with Amelia in constant attendance, until the deals were consummated and she was certain none of the families were split up. It was a source of pride in her that they followed her Papa's dictates along these lines.

"Let's see what the trader's aspiring for, Margaret," George said, bored now with the conversation. "I was thinking about getting shed of Alexander, but he won't bring too good a price now that he's useless for breeding. Besides, I think it's a good idea to keep that nigger around." His face tightened in remembrance. "Helps to keep the others in their places."

"You like having Alexander around." Margaret bristled with contempt. "It does your heart good, knowing what you did to that poor negra." Her eyes said, did for no reason at all.

"We can use Alexander for a house nigger," George said calmly, only his narrowed eyes giving away that he was baiting his wife. "Now that I don't have to worry about what he might be trying to do."

"I'm not having Alexander in this house," his wife said intensely, one hand clenching and unclenching. "You make sure of that, Mr. Woodstock." She never called him that, except when she was livid.

David hadn't said a word all through breakfast, Eulalie thought with compassion. He hadn't eaten much either. He just sat there with that stricken look on his face.

The mansion resounded with the preparations for the party that was to welcome Cindy home. All the drapes and the curtains had to come down. The rugs had to be taken out and beaten. The extra china and the silver had to be brought out of the cupboards, the floors and the furniture polished till they shone. Extra help was brought into the house. The tutor, caught up in the excitement of the imminent occasion, took upon himself to arrange entertainment, utilizing singers he chose from the slave quarters.

The tutor brought into the house, with Margaret Woodstock's approval, an ebony-black stripling of eleven, to care for his needs. "His little pet," Margaret affectionately labeled the boy, but the boy's eyes were bold with freshly acquired knowledge. The tutor might be too old to take himself a wench regularly, Eulalie decided with cynicism, but a young boy could service his needs on a steady basis.

Still David made a stubborn point of avoiding any contact with Eulalie. Covertly, she borrowed books from the library, hid them away in the backporch cupboard, to read in the moments of privacy she managed to filch. In her was a gnawing need to talk to David about what she read, yet he made this impossible. It was over, she thought sadly. Poor David. Poor, lonely David. She was able to feel for David's loss as well as her own.

Eulalie, curled on her comforter on the kitchen floor, came awake earlier each morning as the sun rose earlier. This morning, she woke with a nasty taste in her mouth, because last night had been one of those when the Master summoned her to his room. For the first time, last night, he had laid a rough hand on her. He slapped her, first across the mouth, then across the rump, when she showed some reluctance to acquiesce to his esoteric desires. It was growing increasingly difficult not to show her contempt. And ever-present was the fear that she would carry his seed in her belly. Though not from what happened between them last night.

The sun hid behind clouds this morning. Grayness invaded the kitchen, carrying a message of somber foreboding. Eulalie shivered despite the warmth of the morning.

Maw was scared, knowin' somethin' had to happen, know-in' Eulalie was filled to her gullet with bein' the Massa's bed wench, knowin' she lissened, ever' chance she got, to Alexander. Maw didn't want to know what Alexander was sayin'. It scared Maw somethin' fearful.

Eulalie rose from the comforter that served as a pallet, stretched in her nakedness, then reached for the uniform that lay in readiness for another day's work about the big house. She drew the thin poplin about her slim, golden body, her mind rejecting another day like all the others before it. And yet, there was in her this morning a strange excitement, a prescient awareness that today would not be like the others before it.

Maw came early to the kitchen, a contented little smile on her round face.

"Chloe drop de young'un," Maw said complacently. "He be right black."

"We be needin' somebody in the kitchen," Eulalie warned. "With all the cleanin' and polishin' to be done before missy get here."

"Chloe be back by suppah time," Maw said calmly, moving over to start up the fire in the cook stove. "We do till den without."

The early-morning hours rolled past quietly. Then Margaret Woodstock came down for breakfast with the mincing steps that told the house slaves she had laced her coffee, which had been taken to her in bed by Seraphina, with liberal amounts of bourbon. Moments after she was seated at the dining table. David joined her. At the same time, his father came in from a quick early-morning turn about the fields. The tutor never emerged in time for this first meal of the day. It was tactitly assumed he drank his breakfast.

"The trader spent last night over at the Ashley plantation," George announced between noisy gulps of steaming-hot coffee. "I expect he'll be arriving over here sometime this morning."

"To stay the night?" Distaste spread over Margaret's fading features.

"Just one night," George replied with sardonic humor. "You enjoy spending the money the man leaves here at

The Willows. I reckon you can put up with his company at supper one night."

"I'll be visiting Mary Butler for most of the day," Margaret said with a sweet, set smile. "I'll be sure to be home in time for supper."

"I expect he'll survive without your company, Margaret. It's the slaves he's coming to see."

Margaret hesitated, the blue eyes cloudy.

"George, you won't be splitting up any of the families? You promised."

"God, woman, you have an infernal complex about the slave families! The next thing, you'll be asking me to treat them like they were white folks!"

"Papa always said the one thing he would never condone was to break up the families," Margaret insisted self-righteously. "We can abide by his wishes." She hesitated. "Considering—"

A heavy, menacing silence fell over the dining room. Even Eulalie, serving a fresh platter of sausages, was conscious of this.

"Considering what?" George's voice was dangerously calm, his eyes glinting with anger.

"Considering that Papa did so much to help us put The Willows on its feet," Margaret said, color climbing up her throat.

"Don't you be spending your life throwing your Papa in my face!" His own face was florid, the pulse in his temple throbbing violently. "Ever since you set foot in this house, I've been hearing about your Papa's money. The Willows existed before him, and it'll exist after him. *I* run this plantation! The way I see fit!" George Woodstock drained his coffee cup, threw his napkin upon the table, and strode from the room.

Margaret Woodstock sat quietly for a moment. When she spoke, her voice was high and strained.

"David, honey, do pass me that platter of sausages. They look so appetizing."

The house was unnaturally quiet. Hours ago, Margaret Woodstock had driven off in the carriage to seek the comfort of female companionship on the Butler plantation. Shortly after that, George Woodstock had received the trader and gone off with him into the fields to look over the slaves about whom they were bargaining almost from the instant the trader crossed the threshold. This was the time of day when David was usually closeted with the tutor, who was apt to digress into lengthy monologues about his career on the stage, where he claimed to have appeared with Fanny Kemble.

Alone in the kitchen Eulalie worked on the fine English silver that had been Margaret Woodstock's wedding gift from her father, who had—years past—taken his slaves and moved West in search of better earth to grow the crops. A man's capital was his slaves—not his acreage. Only Seraphina's voice punctured the stillness of The Willows this May afternoon. She was upstairs, calling down the cluster of slaves supposedly washing down bedroom windows.

"Yo no-'count niggers," Seraphina was scolding righteously. "Stop loafin'—you be here to work! Git them windows sparklin', or the Massa'll hang you up an' flog you till you raw meat!"

In the distance, Eulalie heard the rich Negro voices of the field slaves raised in melodic folk songs. She smiled, in the sympathy of the house slave for the field slave. Lissenin' to the singin', nobody know how tired they be at the end of the day. Work, always work—whether be frost on the ground or sweat ridin' over their bodies. Nothin' for doin' good, punishment for doin' bad. Never knowin' what the next day bring, but sho' it won't be good. Better for the house slaves, so long as the Massa be pleased.

The silver beneath Eulalie's hands shone. Reverently, with long, slender fingers, she touched the ornately designed sugar bowl, the creamer, the teapot. A look of admiration showed on the beautifully molded face. She saw her reflection in the shining silver. Just her face, unbetrayed by the tawdry uniform. And in her mind, she saw herself in one of Missy's ball gowns, her silken hair—auburn-glinted—piled high upon her head. She saw herself a great lady, moving with pride, yet nurturing compassion.

Frustration ripped through her as her mind dashed

ahead. What chance? What chance for her? Suddenly, the kitchen was overbearingly hot, without air. She couldn't breathe. Eulalie hurried out of the kitchen into the back-yard, moving, without seeing, towards the clump of woods behind the house, towards the trees, that George Wood-stock was always saying ought to be cut down, but which his wife wanted left alone because they were a sanctuary for the birds she loved.

Already, the woods were lush with greenness. The black birds, the mockingbirds, carried on exuberantly above Eulalie's heard as she walked along. They were undisturbed by her presence and almost seemed to welcome her. *More free than she,* they seemed to be saying as they sang and twitted and swooped from tree to tree.

Then she saw David lying on the velvet grass, his blond hair spilling over the cradle of his arms. His eyes stared at the patch of blue sky, yet Eulalie knew instinctively that he saw nothing. Her bare foot snapped a twig. She gasped, turned to go. David turned, saw her.

"Wait," David called out, a tone of urgency in his voice.

She stood there, trembling, all at once terrified of these strange new emotions that enveloped her. He rose, stood before her, his eyes accusing.

"You hate me," he whispered. "You hate us all!"

Her eyes were wide. For an instant, she couldn't speak.

"Not you," she denied. "How I hate you?"

"How *can* I hate you?" he corrected automatically. "Can't you, Eulalie? Don't you?" he persisted, his eyes dark with pain. "I want to kill my father. Night after night, I want to kill him."

"No!" The rejection was wrenched from her mouth. "David, he is your father. He is a white man." Her large, slender hands gestured in a poignant eloquence that made David flinch.

"He has no right. Other white men don't behave as he does. Not all white men, even in the South, rule planta-tions, take their will as they like!" He was shaking now, white. "He uses you, like you're an inanimate thing and not human. And you have nothing to say about this!"

"I be a slave, David," she reminded simply, her face

taut. "I have no rights. I do what the Massa tell me to do."

"He prides himself on being such a man," David lashed out in contempt. "He's an animal. It wouldn't make me a man, to do what he says." David's face was a dark red as he remembered, but there was in him a resolution to talk. "How many slaves down in the quarters have my father's blood in them? How can he walk among them and not know how terribly wrong this is? Some day, Eulalie, I'll be the master here—and everything will be different."

"You're different," Eulalie said softly, her eyes luminous.

Their eyes met, clung. Eulalie trembled. She saw the arousal of manhood coming to life in David. She saw his eyes caress the delicate swell of her breasts beneath the thin poplin, then move to the slender hips. She knew his eyes dwelt on her in passion.

"Eulalie, you must get away from here," he said intensely. He did not touch her. But in their minds, they were together. "If you stay here, I'll kill him. I'll have to kill him!"

"David, don't talk that way." Terror turned her to ice.

"Somehow, you have to get away from The Willows," he reiterated. His hand reached for hers, held it. The towering emotions in him—the first coming into being of his manhood—was transmitted to her by the pressure of his hands. It was almost as though she could feel herself filled with his passion. A strangled sound escaped him. "Eulalie, somehow, we'll find a way. We'll watch. The time will come—we'll be ready."

"David, how?" The words were soundless.

"Eulalie—Eulalie, where you be?" Seraphina's voice called from the backporch. "Eulalie, you get yo'self here. Be work to do!"

7

David lay stretched on the hammock on the shaded backporch, a book opened at the middle, lying face down across his flat young belly. Unread. Ignored. He stirred with this newness in him, this awareness of his manhood, of fresh desires that exhilarated and alarmed him simultaneously. Shame rose in him because, involuntarily, he understood some of which his father had tried to tell him about the nature of being male.

Eulalie. He felt like *that* about Eulalie. What Papa did with Eulalie, his body wished to do with her. His face grew hot with dark color. He was conscious of the unfamiliar reaction of his body, the response that came of its own and which now discomforted him. Self-consciously, he gazed about. If any of the slaves walked in on him now, this minute, the way he was, they'd know, right off, what he was thinking about. His hand moved to cover his shame, leaped away instantly, as though burned.

When he was ten and Cindy was thirteen, Cindy used to like to play that she was the lady of the plantation and he was the prime buck. Then she'd make him strip down to the skin and she would walk around him, pretending she was the white-trash trader bargaining for the buck. She'd feel him all over, getting pink in the face when she squeezed him there. Mama got awful mad when she walked in that time. But she hadn't told Papa because Mama didn't want to set off his temper.

David stiffened to attention. He heard voices in the distance. Papa and the trader coming back to the house. Papa was with him a long time. That meant they were doing business. Otherwise, Papa wouldn't bother.

Papa wouldn't sell Eulalie, would he? Fear struggled with defiance in him. Maybe it would be better if Papa did sell her. Then she wouldn't be going up to his room any more.

No! Quickly, he brushed aside the unrealistic solution. Changing one master for another wouldn't do. Eulalie should be free. Eulalie had to run away. If Papa got mad enough, he'd sell her, even though Seraphina would be spoiled as a house slave. And one night, Eulalie would rebel. He could read that in her eyes. Papa would get mad and sell her. His mouth went dry, thinking about Eulalie on the auction block out in New Orleans. Thinking about men going over to her, touching her—anywhere they liked. A slave wasn't a person. No soul. A thing. That was what *they* thought.

Eulalie shouldn't be a slave—she was too bright. Brighter than Cindy, any day, he remembered with pride. Even Mr. Bradford and Mr. Jefferson said Eulalie was real good with the books. Papa said she was probably a quadroon—one-quarter black.

Papa and the trader had come into the house. David could hear his father bellowing to Seraphina to bring ice into the library. It was one of Papa's niceties, not to take the trader into the drawing room. David listened attentively. Papa was bringing out the liquor now. With the warm weather here, all the doors and windows were kept wide—you could hear everything, clear through the house.

"Seraphina," George Woodstock yelled again. "Hop to it with that ice."

"Me bring, Massa," Seraphina called back in her rich, melodic voice, which was undisturbed by his tones.

Mama said, last week she read in the newspaper about an ice-making machine somebody built at Apalachicola. It would be nice to have something like that at The Willows. But they'd be the last to have it, David guessed scornfully. Papa didn't like seeing things change—everything had to go on the way it had for the last hundred years.

That time when Grandpa came here from Louisiana to visit, he and Papa had a real battle about how Southerners don't understand how they are mistreating the land. The soil was poor, right in the beginning, nowhere as good as in the North. There were the long, hot summers baking the earth, and the rains and the floods that came to wash away the topsoil.

"We'll keep on making the same mistakes our fathers made," Grandpa proclaimed contemptuously, in that stentorian voice of his. "Up North, in Europe, the farmers are learning. Why can't we in the South learn? Cotton! All the time, cotton. Can't even raise enough food to set a decent table. *Won't* raise it," he corrected himself disgustedly.

Mama wouldn't drink the way she did, if Papa wasn't always so angry at everything—and everybody. His face grew tender in contemplation of his mother. He remembered Mama when she was beautiful, sometimes gay and playful. It was awful, for Mama's pride, the way Papa kept bringing the black wenches into his bed. Thinking about this, David colored—for the memory of Eulalie, for the recognition of the new desires evincing themselves in him. Grandpa was right when he said the South had a lot of learning to do.

Why did Papa hate the way he did? Why was he happy only when he was hurting? There were hard times when he was a boy growing up at The Willows, and he was the youngest—he always talked about that, about being the one who got the short end of things. But the others grew up and moved away. When his Papa died, The Willows was his. With Mama's money, they made it one of the finest plantations in the whole state. Why couldn't Papa be satisfied?

"You did a fine piece of trading, Mr. Woodstock," the trader was complimenting artfully. "I never expected to part with this much—cash on the barrel—the way I'm doin' this minute."

"You're getting your money's worth, or you wouldn't be buying," George shot back, but David was conscious of his father's satisfaction with the trading. "I never sell a wench when she's open. Let them begin to show, and you've got a better deal. You're putting two on the block instead of one."

"Sure you wouldn't be wantin' to sell more than the two wenches?" the trader was wheedling. "I'm pressed for cash, but I could handle another pair, if the price was right."

"You come back in the fall," George Woodstock ordered in high good humor. "We'll talk then."

Papa sold two pregnant wenches, David interpreted, frowning. He didn't say anything about selling their bucks. Unease stirred in him. Mama was going to be fit to be tied if Papa was breaking up families. Grandpa said that was something no gentleman ever did. Of course, his father laid no claims to being a gentleman, David thought wryly. Papa seemed to take pride in not being a gentleman.

Restless now, David rose from the hammock and went into the house. He walked with cautious quietness past the library on his way upstairs because he had no wish to encounter his father and the trader. The day was warm, humid. He'd been excused from further lessons. He'd go upstairs and take a nap.

In his room, David stretched across the fourposter bed, ordered himself to sleep. Sleep would be a way to cleanse his mind of the troublesome images that insisted on dwelling in his mind. But sleep was elusive. He tossed about the feather bed, his body a traitor. This was what Papa meant about being a man.

Eulalie's skin would be satin-soft, cool. Her breasts were high and small. In his mind's eye, he saw them prodding beneath the poplin uniform. Involuntarily, his hands cupped, feeling themselves closing in about the pointed rise of her.

He swung over on his stomach, buried his face in the bedspread. It was awful, living here, seeing Eulalie every day, feeling this pain in his gut. Not for just anybody. He wasn't like Papa, he thought with pride. Only for Eulalie, this feeling in him. He wanted to do that with Eulalie. Not everything that Papa did, he stipulated, recoiling from memory. But he wanted to refresh himself in the sweetness of that golden body.

Papa would be proud if he knew. But he wasn't going to know, David promised himself savagely. Papa would bring up a wench from the quarters for him to take to bed. No matter how Mama might carry on about it. For an instant—a potent, heated instant—David thought about bringing one of the wenches up to his bed. No! Not son, like father. Not this son.

The late afternoon sounds downstairs told him supper was in preparation. Once, he heard Eulalie's voice; she was talking to one of the other house slaves. Hearing her, his body reacted, because his mind moved swiftly beyond more hearing. How did you stop it, he asked himself in shamed frenzy? What happened if Papa looked at him and knew? If Mama looked at him when he was like this? Self-consciousness, unhappiness, rolled over him in waves, even while there was a subtle joy in his body because he was no longer a child. He was a man.

"I don't know why you don't spend the night," David heard his father say expansively. Papa must have got a good price if he was behaving this way. Which two wenches? David wondered uneasily. There were so many. *What about the males?* "We set about the best table anywhere in this state," George Woodstock boasted. "My wife doesn't believe in stinting when it comes to the table."

"Well, now, I would be right pleased to stay for suppah," the trader offered genially. "But right after, I'll be takin' the wenches and headin' west. I want to be close by my next callin' place, in the mornin'."

The two men downstairs were swapping stories now about other trading, each intent on embellishing on the truth. They'd sit there, talking over their drinks, until supper time, David guessed.

David rose from the bed, went over to the washstand to splash cold water on his face, to clean his hands. Mama would be coming home any minute now. She was going to be awful displeased that Papa invited the trader to stay for supper. Most times, the trader ate at the head man's table, slept in his house. At least he wasn't staying the night.

When he was descending the sairs, David heard his mother leaving the carriage before the portico. When she'd been away all day this way, she'd go straight up to her bedroom and call for Seraphina to bring her tea. For a long time, David had known about the bourbon that laced the tea.

"David, baby," his mother greeted him with dramatic warmth when they met at the foot of the staircase. "I feel as though I've been away for weeks, not seeing you since breakfast this way."

"Papa's in the library with the trader," David said, his voice low. His mother winced. "He's staying for supper, but leaving right afterwards."

"Supper here in the house?" Margaret asked distastefully. She was outspoken in her valuation of slave traders as *white trash*.

"Papa sold him two slaves," he confided unhappily. "Two who are having young."

"What about their bucks?" his mother asked sharply.

"I don't think so," he admitted, his eyes troubled. It was a terrible deed, to take a man's wife and baby away from him, David realized with fresh understanding. Just to send them away, like they were pieces of furniture.

His mother's face tightened. Her eyes glinted angrily. "We'll see about that, David. We'll see." Laying one finely veined hand on the balustrade, she brushed past him. "Send Seraphina to me, darling. It's been such a long day. Mrs. Butler is a sweet lady, but she does talk so much."

"I'll tell Seraphina," David promised and turned to walk back down the corridor.

Eulalie was in the kitchen, her back towards him. For

a moment, he stiffened, then pretending to ignore Eulalie, he swung to face Seraphina.

"Seraphina, Mama would like her tea," he said gently. "Up in her room."

"Yessuh, me bring. Right away," Seraphina crooned.

The "yessuh" startled David. Only recently had Seraphina elevated him to this status. He squinted—he was uneasy. Seraphina knew an awful lot. Did she know about him, how he was feeling? But she didn't know he felt this way about Eulalie. He shouldn't, he thought, furious with himself. It was dirty, to feel that way about Eulalie. She was his friend. His only friend. But he wished, with painful intensity, that she were more than that.

David waited patiently for Mama to come back downstairs. Perversely, he dreaded a confrontation between his parents, yet craved it. He walked restlessly about the lower floor of the house, conscious of the pleasing aromas filtering from the kitchen, aware of his own hunger. Mama hadn't come down yet. Twice, Seraphina had gone upstairs with the tea.

David heard Seraphina padding into the library. Now she was talking to Papa.

"Missis be feelin' tiuhed, aftuh visit. Not be down fo' suppuh."

"Then get it on the table right now," George ordered, mildly annoyed. "That's the trouble with the womenfolk," he grumbled to the trader. "They can't wait to go gallivanting all over the countryside, visiting first this plantation, then that one. But they come home *tiuhed*," he drawled, mimicking Seraphina. "Too tired to be worth much to their menfolk."

David flushed, balled one hand into a fist. Papa shouldn't talk that way. Mama was right when she said he wasn't a gentleman.

David was summoned to join his father and the trader at the supper table. He sat there, stiffly erect, his eyes on his plate as Eulalie moved about the table, serving the chicken, the rice, the black-eyed peas, the fresh cornbread, the bread pudding floating in yellow-rich sweet cream. He contributed little to the table talk, speaking only when spoken to directly.

"Jason!" George bellowed when coffee had been served and he'd noisily drained his first cup of what was usually a four-cup quota at supper. "Jason, get your black self into the dining room." He relished his departure from his wife's more ladylike method of summoning the house slaves. Tonight, the bell sat idle.

Jason sidled into the dining room, with the respect due the Master—but not the speed the Master preferred.

"Me here, Massa." He smiled broadly, displaying the absence of several front teeth. His father was responsible for the loss, David remembered.

"Go down to the head man's house," George ordered. "And move like you're alive! Tell him to bring those two wenches I sold today up to the stables. They'll be leaving shortly." The trader was taken aback by the note of dismissal. He was obviously enjoying himself at The Willows' elegant dining table. He would have preferred to linger, but was acquiescent since he was pleased with his purchases.

"That younger one's a mighty purty piece," the trader said with a lascivious grin. "I don't mind sayin' I might be doin' some samplin' tonight. If it's cold out there where we camp in the wagon, I might be warmin' myself with the two of 'em."

"Take it easy with that young one," George cautioned. "It's her first. She's showing early. You don't want her to lose that sucker, just to give yourself a night's pleasure. That would be mighty expensive, sir. This is the time, right at the beginning, where you have to be careful." He pushed back his chair, his eyes restless. Bored now with the trader, David interpreted. He was anxious to have the visit over. "Let's go sit out on the portico for a spell. The stable will send over your wagon with the wenches when they're ready."

David was about to break away, intent on returning to his room, when his father stopped him.

"Don't stay in the house on a night like this. Come on out on the portico with us," his father commanded. With the trader's money in his pocket, he was in a mellow mood tognight. "Time you learned to spend a few hours with menfolk. It's no good, always hanging around your Mama. And soon, my little girl will be back," he said to the trader with gusto. "Cindy's the prettiest little thing in this whole Southland." Pride lent him a deceptive gentleness—for a moment.

The two men and David sat down in wide, cane-seated rockers that lined the two-storied, white-pillared portico. Night moved in with caressing warmth, bringing the May scents of lilac, wisteria, honeysuckle. Fireflies moving across the grounds before the house. The breath of pine from the woods to the rear mingled with the delicious, spicy aroma of the magnolias that grew tall across the front lawns and were just now coming into luxuriant bloom. It was a moment to impress the trader, David realized. Here was the storybook view of the Deep South, with Seraphina, even now, moving her graceful bulk out onto the portico, a tray of mint juleps in her sturdy hands.

"Mister Woodstock!" The urgent voice, laden with anxiety, came from the west of the house, jarring the quietness of the night. "Mister Woodstock!" The voice was coming closer as the man ran towards the portico.

George leaned forward in his rocker, scowling, his eyes fastened to the approaching figure of his overseer, a massive man chosen for the job because of his reputation for handling troublesome slaves.

"All right!" George demanded in irritation. "What is it?" David sat hunched in his chair, feeling himself part of an unreal, imminent drama. "Dammit, out with it, man!"

"Them two black bitches," the overseer said, charged with agitation. "The ones you sold. They lit out! I can't find them no place. They're gone!"

George leaped to his feet, eyes shooting off sparks of rage, hands clenched.

"What about the bucks?" he spit out the words. "You check them?"

"Gone," the overseer admitted, not meeting his employer's eyes. "It wasn't my fault, Mr. Woodstock. They lit out, the minute my back was turned. You can't be watchin' them every minute."

"Bring out the dogs!" George bellowed.

"They'll be headin' for the river, sir," the overseer pointed out cautiously. "Dogs won't be much good."

"The falls will drive them off the river before they're five miles north. We'll go straight up there. You send somebody over to the Butlers, tell them to go looking on the other side of the river." His eyes scanned the night sky; it was clear but moonless. "Not much chance they're heading south, but tell Butler to head that way if he don't see them on the other side." He turned to the trader in apology, his face florid. "Sorry about this, but we'll get those black bitches back for you before this night is over!"

It was easy for David to slip into the house again. In all the excitement, the rounding up of the slave-hunters, the yipping of the hounds, nobody noticed that he had gone. David knew what he must do tonight. His heart pounded, and there was fear deep inside because his father was a rough, intemperate man—but David knew what must be done.

David moved noiselessly down the carpeted corridor to the large, high-ceilinged library, from which vantage point he could watch the imminent departure of the search party. Without lighting a lamp and pleased with the cloak of darkness tonight, David stood behind the drapes, staring out into the night through the faint opening he'd made for himself by pinching the elegant material between his fingers.

George Woodstock, the overseer, and a crew of drivers emerged from the stable with horses. As the slave-hunters mounted, the hounds yipped raucously, joyous for an opportunity to hunt. Impatient to be on the way, George shouted orders.

His pulse racing, David watched the men gallop away. He saw Seraphina and Venus scurrying down to the slave quarters to be there before the head man made his nightly check. But tonight, he wouldn't be going around, opening doors, looking in, counting heads. Tonight, he was slave-hunting. From the way the two women moved, David sensed, with compassion, that they were fearful about what had happened. Papa, they knew from past experience, would mete out reprisals.

All right, now! Go find Eulalie. Now, while the men of the plantation were off trying to track down the two desperate slave couples who risked their lives rather than be separated. It was rough, escaping from Georgia. One of the hardest states. Cousin Madeline had made that plain. But it happened.

David moved with compulsive swiftness. A nerve hammered away in his eyelid. His mind was surprisingly clear. Eulalie wasn't in the kitchen. He was upset. Had she got frightened, run off to the slave quarters? He gazed about, auxious now because the moon was beginning to come from behind the clouds and pierce the darkness. A bad night for runaways, if the moon stayed out.

"Eulalie," he called out softly, certain that he was alone in the big house, except for his mother closeted in her own room upstairs since her return from the Butlers' plantation. "Eulalie."

Then he spied the faint glow of a candle emerging from beneath the door of a cupboard. He reached for the knob, pulled the door wide. Eulalie's eyes shot from the book held in her hands to his face. For an instant, the eyes dilated in alarm, until she realized this was David.

"Eulalie—" He reached urgently for her arm. "The time is here. Tonight! You have to run away tonight!"

"David!" She was terrified. Suddenly she was merely a fourteen-year-old girl who was bewildered at what had monopolized her thoughts for months without actually becoming real. Now it was real. "David, how can I?" Her eyes searched his.

"Papa sold two wenches who're carrying young. They ran away with their husbands. They'll be going up the Chattahoochee, until they hit the falls—or across the river into Alabama. All the hunting's going to be over that way—" He gestured strongly. "You'll have to go the other way, up into the hills."

"Oh, David, I'm powerful scared," she whispered, but already freedom touched her. "Where do I go? How?"

"You heard Cousin Madeline talking. She said slaves were escaping, even from Georgia. She said lots of white folks are helping them." He clutched at her arm. "Eulalie, think hard. Who down in the quarters might know somebody like that? Somebody around here who'll help you along the way to the North?" His eyes searched hers.

"I don't know." She lied, and color suffused her face. Why should she lie to David? Yet her loyalty to the other slaves stood between them.

"Eulalie, some slave must have said something. The word goes around. You know it does." His eyes clung desperately to her, pleading with her to trust him.

"Alexander," Eulalie whispered. "Sometimes he talks about—about sech things."

"Go down to the quarters. Ask Alexander," David instructed. "Find out who helps in this territory. I'll take you in a wagon."

"David!" Her eyes widened in shock. "Your father—"

"He won't know," David insisted. "They'll be out all night tracking down the others. Go to Alexander. Meet me in the stables. I'll have food in the wagon, and money. Eulalie, hurry!" Do it quickly, she interpreted, before he became too frightened to go ahead.

"I be right back. Meet you in the stables." She rushed past him towards the back door.

How small, how slight she was! Newly growing into his full height, he felt himself a towering man concerned about protecting her. But all he could do was to drive her away, to the edge of freedom—or, perhaps, death.

Tenderness blended with fear in him as he moved into the kitchen, found a bag, loaded it with provisions. Bread, cold pork, molasses. Enough to last a few days, though the pork might go bad in this warm weather. Clothes, his mind pinpointed. Eulalie was light. Dressed in Cindy's clothes, she could pass for one of the tenant farmers' women who had worked long under the sun in the fields— except that her features were finer. There was a delicacy about her bone structure.

All right, a dress. He darted out to the corridor that led to the staircase, bolted upward, taking the steps two at a time in his haste. Fleetingly, anguished for his mother, he halted before her door. She was crying into her pillow, with the helplessness of a woman who is sure life can never be better. She'd said she wouldn't let Papa separate the couples. Had he honestly expected her to stand up to Papa? Tonight, not even bourbon was lessening her pain.

In Cindy's room, he riffled through her closet, looking for the plainest, the least attention-attracting dress Cindy had left behind. No need to worry about shoes. Most of the tenant farmers' women went barefoot, except to church. But still, he bent low to inspect the row of shoes. Eulalie's foot was long and slender, not apt to fit into his sister's small shoes. A cloak, a hat, though it was already May-warm.

With the clothes over his arm, the bag of provisions in one hand, David stopped off at his room to pick up what little money he had. To Eulalie it would be a lot. He was at the door when he remembered the book of poems. The book Eulalie had particularly liked. Poems by Percy Bysshe Shelley. He picked up the leather-bound volume. His mother had given it to him for his fifteenth birthday. He wrote on the flyleaf, "For Eulalie, from David."

Now David sped from the room, down the corridor, conscious of the rending, hopeless sobs of his mother behind the heavy oak door. He hurried down the stairs, around the corridor to the rear, out the back door, towards the stables. The moon was playing an in-and-out game with the clouds. Right now, darkness enveloped the grounds. Far off in the distance, the hounds yipped.

He passed a woman in the dark. She was half-running, her head bent low. Amelia. Going to his mother.

In the stable, which was totally deserted now, David hitched up the wagon. No one would suspect him, the Master's son, of helping Eulalie to escape. His father thought he was soft, a baby, yet here he was, turning on his family. *Against my whole tradition*, David thought— yet he was filled with a strange exultation.

8

Conscious of the heavy silence on every side, Eulalie moved cautiously among the rows of huts. Except for the runaways, there would not be a slave outside the huts tonight. The word must have spread right away. Everything was like that on the plantation. The house slave whispered to the field slave, or the field slave passed the word along to the ones in the big house. This was the silken underground that spread the word about everything —how the Massa felt about the crops, why the driver had been flogged, why Missy was shipped away to London. They might be illiterate, but they were well-informed about everything that happened on the plantation. This contributed some color to the monotony of their daily lives.

Eulalie hesitated before the rundown hut that she and her mother shared with a family of nine. Her heart pounded. She wished desperately to go into the cubicle that held the sagging double bed where she had slept with Maw—but would not, ever again. She could remember the cozy body warmth of her mother on cold nights, the comfort of her mother's bulk when her world seemed intolerable. Maw wouldn't find out till tomorrow morning. By then she would be miles away. She *had* to be miles away.

Reluctant to move away, Eulalie bit at her lip. Just to see Maw once more. But she couldn't. She hovered at the open window—open to the wind and the rain and the cold, and the mosquitos during the hot months—and peered inside. Maw was lyin' there, but not sleepin'. Quickly, Eulalie moved away, watching where she walked, till she came to the hut where Alexander lived. She looked into a window. It was the wrong one. Nervously, she moved to the other side of the hut, which was hardly the size of a decent kitchen. She stared into the window.

Alexander lay stretched on the bed, which he shared with two other field hands. They snored in slumber now after fifteen hours in the fields. Alexander, his massive arms folded beneath his head, frowned into space.

"Alexander," she called softly, then watched him stiffen. He knew about the others. Prob'ly, he helped them. "Alexander," she tried again, with greater urgency.

Alexander shot upright, his dark eyes glowing in the darkness. He swung his legs to the dirt floor, paused an instant before he rose to his feet, then strode across to the window.

"What yo' do here, girl?" Alexander demanded, his voice a reproachful whisper.

"I hafta know," Eulalie said, fighting for calm. "Where I go from here on the way to the No'th? Who around here help me get away?"

"You crazy, Eulalie?" Shocked, he was already climbing out the window to stand beside her. "You heah about dem others, an' you get bad ideas in your haid!"

"I bes' be dead than stay here," Eulalie said quietly. "You tell me, or no, I leave. This minute David be fetchin' me food from the kitchen. He drive me in the wagon where you say go—" Her eyes searched his anxiously. "You talk, Alexander. You talk about runnin' to freedom.

Tell me how. Tell me!" Her amber eyes, dark with intensity, beseeched him. She couldn't turn back now.

"You say David take you?" Alexander asked brusquely. "How come you trust?"

"David be my friend." There was beautiful dignity in her voice. "I trust him."

"Seraphina know?" Alexander pushed.

"I can't tell." Eulalie lowered her eyes to the ground. "You know I can't."

"Massa catch you, he near kill you," Alexander warned.

"He catch, I don't care," Eulalie said defiantly. "I don't want no more what goes on in his room at night. I don't want him usin' me. I want be free, or dead!"

Their eyes met. Alexander, who had been castrated without reason, and Eulalie, who was violated at the Master's whim. Alexander gave a deep, shuddering sigh.

"Be a farmuh in de hills eleven miles pas' de Butler plantation. "They hide, take yo' further. Eleven miles, to the no'th and east, into the hills," Alexander said slowly, distinctly. His eyes were grave, compassionate. "Yo' young, Eulalie, be makin' de trip."

"I old enough." Rebellion was in her eyes. "I make it, Alexander. You tell Maw, I make it! Someday, I come back for her."

Alexander climbed back through the window. Eulalie moved through the darkness towards the stables. She hesitated at the stables, then walked to the door, peered inside. David was there, at the hitched-up wagon. She wouldn't be seein' David no more. Shock, unhappy comprehension, played havoc with her determination, yet she knew she must go. This was the time. There might not be another. Oh, it be awful not to see David every day!

"David," she whispered. He hadn't seen her.

David swung about. In the faint moonlight that filtered into the stables, Eulalie saw his somber face. He didn't want her to leave, she realized. An odd gladness surged through her.

"I brought you a dress," he said gruffly, reaching into the wagon. "Cindy won't miss it. Put it on."

David handed her the dress, turned his back on her.

Eulalie stripped away the uniform, pulled Cindy's dress over the delicately golden body. She was conscious of the delicacy of the material; such fineness had never caressed her skin before. For a moment, her fingers brushed—with awe—the softness of the fine cotton.

"I be dressed, David," she whispered. It fit her perfectly. Even without one of Cindy's corsets, her waist was tiny enough for the dress.

David swung about. His eyes moved over the gowned length of her and back to her face again. She was piling her hair atop her head in a facsimile of one of Cindy's less ornate hairstyles.

"You're beautiful," he said, his voice thick with emotion, his eyes eloquent as they lingered on her.

Eulalie's eyes shone. For that precious moment, they were two very young people on the threshold of discovery. David wished her for his woman, Eulalie realized, and the knowledge lifted her to heady ecstasy. The way he wanted her was not the way his Papa wanted her.

It couldn't happen—Eulalie knew this—but it was enough for now to know that David loved her. As she loved David. I always have, Eulalie thought defiantly as she lifted her head high. I was just too scared to put it into words.

"Alexander say we go to a farmer in the hills eleven miles pas' the Butler plantation." She was making a supreme effort to speak properly, to leave this memory of her with David. "It's no'theast. There be a red barn behind the house—that's how we know."

"Up in the hills." David nodded. "I've ridden up that way a few times." He reached into the wagon, brought something forth, and held it in the palm of his hand. "Here's a piece of paper with Cousin Madeline's address in New York. You try to get there—she'll help you. I know she will!"

"I won't lose," Eulalie promised, folding the paper into a small square, sliding it down into the protection of her bosom. David's eyes followed her hand.

"Here's money. Not much, but it'll help. Now, we'd best start," David wound up nervously. "Get down in the back of the wagon. Cover up with Cindy's cloak." He reached to help her into the wagon. She felt the tremor that rode through him when their bodies collided. "Cover up!" he reiterated sharply, to hide his confusion.

"David, suppose your Paw find out?" she asked David anxiously. What would the Massa do? Flog him? No, Missis wouldn't let him.

"He won't find out," David reassured her. "None of them will be back before daybreak. They'll be going up the river and across the river into Alabama. They're not looking for you, Eulalie. That's where we're ahead." He reached to pull the cloak more completely over her jack-knifed frame. Then he walked back to the head of the wagon, climbed up on the buckboard, and urged the horses on.

Eulalie huddled beneath Cindy's cloak in the bottom of the wagon. Everything was quiet about the plantation. Only the crickets broke the heavy blanket of silence. In the quarters, the slaves were exhausted from the long day in the fields under the May sun. They slept. The ones, like Alexander, who didn't sleep prayed for those who were trying to escape to freedom.

Eulalie lay still, tense, hearing the clatter of the horses' hoofs. She was conscious of the nighttime scent of the pines brought down from the mountains by the winds from the north. She knew that she would be hiding for many days in those mountains and traveling only by night. She listened to David, coaxing the horses to greater speed in his anxiety to put the plantation acreage behind them.

She knew when they were off the plantation. David stopped driving the horses so frenziedly. Far in the distance, they could hear the dogs. Nobody knew she had gone. Eulalie reminded herself. Nobody would know till morning. By then her tracks would be cold. The dogs would pick up nothing.

David pulled up sharply. The horses whinnied, came to a halt. "Come sit up front with me," David called back to her, his voice sounding unnaturally loud in the quietness.

Bewildered by his command, Eulalie pushed aside the cloak. He stood at the foot of the wagon.

"There's nobody around," he said, holding up his arms to help her down. "Sit with me."

This time, it was she who trembled as their bodies touched. She was going away from everything she'd ever known, just when she was discovering this wonderous thing between David and her that, up till now, had hid behind the guise of friendship. The wonderous thing that would be beaten to death if she had stayed, Eulalie guessed.

David helped her up onto the buckboard, sat so close beside her that their bodies touched. Pale moonlight bathed them as they drove through the night. Her eyes devoured David's handsome profile. When would she see David again? Would she ever see him again?

They drove into the pine-laden mountains, with David voicing nervousness about taking a wrong turn in the road. They couldn't hear the dogs any longer, only an occasional hound howling in the mountains above them. Eulalie laid her head on David's shoulder, cherishing the reassurance of his closeness. They drove that way in poignant silence, each aware of the separation ahead.

"It's not much further," David judged. "We've covered about ten miles. Eulalie. I—" He pulled the horses to a stop and turned to her. "Oh, Eulalie, how will I stay at The Willows without you?"

They came together with quiet intensity. His arms folding her in to him, his mouth reaching for hers. Tender, eager, unlearned. She could feel his heart, pounding against her breast.

"Eulalie?" It was a painful, urgent question, his eye beseeching her, needing no words.

"There be time," she said with quiet dignity. He was askin'—not takin'. Nobody ever lay with David before. She be his first woman. An unfamiliar, startling desire took root in her. "David, pull the wagon off the road."

Under the pine trees, with the lush Southern grass as their bed. David took her. She relished his passion; for the first time she lay neither supine nor hating beneath the weight of a male body intent on penetration. She raised herself to meet him, answering passion with passion. Glad

96

that she knew how to please him, help him. And then, David was fully the master. Clinging to him, she bit the pale, full mouth to silence the cry of climax that threatened to rend the night.

What happens between a man and a woman can be beautiful, Eulalie realized with a sense of awe. With David, it was beautiful. With his father—but she would never remember that, ever again! David cleansed her body, washed away all the ugliness. He made her whole again.

"We'd better get back to the wagon," David said. His eyes were reluctant, unhappy. "The moon's coming out awful clear." He scrambled to his feet, extended a hand to help her. Forever, she told herself, she would remember David, especially the way he looked at this moment.

They rode in silence, her shoulder brushing his, her head high. A farmhouse—small, extremely modest—lay silhouetted ahead of them.

"That's the farm," David decided. "See, there's a barn to the rear." He squinted, trying to make out the color. "It's red, Eulalie. This is the place."

David and Eulalie sat for a few, pregnant moments, with the horses at a standstill. The moment was here. What would they say to each other? How could they say it?

David cleared his throat in discomfort.

"Try to get to New York City. Go to Cousin Madeline. Someday, I'll be there, Eulalie. I'll come for you."

How could he come for her? He was white and she was black. But for now, Eulalie could push the realization out of her mind because so much lay ahead of her.

The door to the small farmhouse opened. A tall, gaunt, shirtless man in bare feet stood there with a shotgun in hand. He must have heard the wagon approach. If Alexander spoke the truth, then the man was expecting—some night—such an intruder as she.

"I'll go with you," David said.

"No," she objected quickly—for his sake and the man's. "Turn around and ride back to The Willows. It be better that way. They—" She nodded towards the man, standing immobile in the doorway, the shotgun in hand. "They like it better that way."

Eulalie pulled the cloak around her, reached for the bag of provisions, the bonnet, hopped down from the wagon.

"Thankee, David."

Then she was scurrying over red dust towards the man with the shotgun.

"Who you be?" the man demanded when she was a few feet before him. David was slowly driving away, looking backwards, anxious to make sure she was received.

"I be lookin' for freedom," she said. "In the quarters, a man tol' me—he say, come here."

"Inside, girl," he ordered harshly, looking out across the dark horizon. Only David and his wagon were in sight.

Eulalie moved quickly into the house. In the darkness, she could see a woman's form.

"Douglas, it be one of them?" the woman asked, a zealous quality in her voice.

"It be," he said, closing the door behind him. He walked in the darkness to a table, lit a candle. "You know, girl," he warned her, his eyes seeming to burn into hers. "It be a long piece to get you to freedom. You sho' you wan' to take that chance?"

"I want," Eulalie insisted. "I want make free."

"Wife, you know what we do," he said calmly. "She's a light one. We'll be travelin' two, three days. Put up plenty of provisions."

"I bring bread and cold pork," Eulalie said, her heart pounding. She came here, and these folks asked no questions. To Eulalie, a miracle was taking place in the small farmhouse. They'd come forth from sleep to take a black wench to freedom. Part of the way towards freedom. "I have some money." Eagerly, she reached to demonstrate.

"You holt on to that," the farmer's wife said tersely. "Don't give it away, leastways you have to." Unexpectedly, she smiled. A gentle, compassionate smile. "Come with me."

In the next room, the bedroom, the woman brought forth a box of rice powder. She squinted at Eulalie in the candlelight.

"You so light we don't rightly need this—but anyhow, let's play safe."

Obediently, Eulalie stood while the woman powdered down her face, stood back to inspect the results, smiled in approval.

"Anybody see us," the woman said complacently, "you pass for white. No troubles."

Out behind the house, the farmer was hitching up his wagon. His wife was talking quietly, as though she enjoyed having another female about—as though she considered Eulalie her equal. For Eulalie, it was a refreshing experience.

"Douglas and me, we don't have no children," the woman said calmly. "We feel God wants us to be helpin' those less fortunate. It be a sin against God to hold humans as slaves." Her eyes flashed. "Doin' God's biddin' gives us some reason for livin'."

"You help others?" Eulalie asked, seeking reassurance that others had made it before her.

"Five, so far," the woman said with pride. "You be the sixth. We don't stop until there's no call to keep it up."

The woman packed the provisions, reached for her cloak because the night air was cool, and gestured to Eulalie to follow her out the back. Eulalie froze, her blood turning to ice when she saw what Douglas was lifting into the back of the wagon. A coffin! Was she goin' to have to lie in that?

"We ride up front," the woman explained, her eyes showing that she saw—and understood—Eulalie's consternation. "You in the middle. Anybody asks questions, we be takin' the body of your husband back to his folks for burial."

"All right, we ready to be leavin'," Douglas announced crisply. "Climb aboard."

It was difficult to assimilate. She was on her way to freedom. Eulalie sat stiffly erect on the buckboard between the farmer and his wife. Unreality imprisoning her. Maw would find out in the mornin'. Maw would cry a while, but then she would understand.

Wonder filled her that folks whom she had never laid

eyes on before—without askin' questions—would take themselves out of their houses and travel more miles than she could imagine, to help her. She, who be nothin' for so long. For all her life. To help her make free.

Never again would she set foot on The Willows plantation, Eulalie swore to herself. Not unless it be in her coffin. She shivered—but not from the night chill. If she be catched, she kill herself. Not go back to The Willows!

9

George Woodstock reined in his horse, took a deep, shuddering breath. All this exertion, this hour of the night, was too much for his lungs. Forty-six, almost. Not a stripling like David. He frowned, thinking about David, while his eyes automatically scanned the forest of evergreens ahead of them and beside them. Thick, lush pines, perfect for concealment.

David ought to be with them tonight learning what it was like to track down a slave, to protect what was yours. Sometimes, the way the boy acted, he felt as though his own son was like those fellows up North who carried on about abolishing slavery. They could talk that way. It wasn't their life's blood at stake.

"Mr. Woodstock." Uneasily, the overseer rode over beside him. "You think we ought to go further into the hills? We won't be catchin' sight of 'em up here tonight, not even with the dogs."

George's gaze swept about, taking in the cluster of hunters.

"We'll go back," he decided brusquely. Why did old West, the tutor, come along? For the drama of it, he guessed dryly—the actor playing a role again. "All right," he called out in the bellowing tones known so well about the plantation. "It's useless to push any further tonight. Round up the hounds. Let's go back."

The first pink-gray streaks of dawn were rising into the sky when the search party swung into the lane that led up to the big house. The overseer herded the slaves who'd been part of the hunt, along with the dogs, towards the slave quarters to be checked in. In a scant hour, they'd be rising, going out to work in the fields again. George and Evan West rode back towards the stables.

"Company," West commented, an eyebrow lifted, as they passed in view of the house en route to the stables.

"Some of the Butlers," George surmised, his face grim. "They must have had no luck, either. Dammit, man, how can four slaves just get up and walk off that way? And not so long ago, it was Hector. My prize stud! That's a fat loss, if we don't catch up with them!"

George and the tutor dismounted, stabled the horses, strode towards the house. Now, approaching the portico, George could recognize Jack Butler and three of his sons sprawled in rockers.

"We couldn't find hide or hair of 'em," he called out. "Vanished into the night. Come on into the library. Let's have a drink. We need it after all that riding."

He'd run some ads in the newspapers. Plenty of ads with substantial rewards. It would cost him money, but he wanted those blacks back. Show the others they couldn't get away with this. Start looking around for a new overseer, a new slave-breaker. He needed hired hands who could teach the slaves who was Master at The Willows!

"We crossed the river," the elder Butler explained unhappily. "We went on for close to twenty miles. No trace of them. The dogs picked up nothing."

"They'll be holed up in the woods somewhere," the youngest of the three Butler sons prophesied. "They couldn't stay on the river too far up. Let's rest up a while, go out again." His eyes were zealous. That one would enjoy tanning the hide of a black, George guessed with approval. Why couldn't his son be a little like Butler's? What was going to happen to this plantation when he was gone? He was going to have to stop letting Margaret have her way, take that boy in hand, make a man out of him.

"They'll be hiding out till night, boy," Butler reminded his son. "You sure have a hard time—catching a nigger in the dark." He chuckled, briefly amused at his stale humor.

"You could find them," George shot back, "if some fools weren't helping them escape. You know those tenant farmers, how they feel," he reminded with contempt. "The varmints don't have anything, can't stand that we have something. They don't like slaves, but they like us less."

The men settled themselves in the library. George poured straight bourbon into tumblers, passed the drinks around. With his own glass in hand, he dropped into a deep armchair and sprawled with booted feet stretched out before him.

"George, we're living in troubled times," the elder Butler intoned. "I'm telling you, it's going to be a lot worse before it gets better. I go to sleep some nights—and I wager there's not a plantation owner in the South who don't feel the same way—and I wonder if I'm going to be alive when morning comes. It makes for fresh trouble, every time a black makes off this way."

"Well, you should have heard my wife's cousin Madeline when she was down here," George drawled. "To listen to her, slaves are every bit as good as we are. She couldn't understand why we don't have schools for them. Couldn't understand that when a slave is ignorant, he's happy. You start teaching them, comes the trouble."

"Why, I heard tell that up North they're establishing a college for niggers! What do you think of that?" the elder Butler demanded contemptuously. "And all these white folks—North and South—helping our niggers escape, taking the money they're worth right out of our pockets. It's a real mortal sin, acting against their own kind that way!"

George leaned forward, his eyes glinting with anger.

"What about that woman? What's her name? Harriet something or other. I was up in Baltimore on business last year, and I hear how this slave—an escaped slave, mind you—keeps coming back into the South to help other slaves escape. There's a big price on her head—somebody's going to help themselves to that easy money." George lifted his glass to his mouth, gulped the bourbon. He had five thousand dollars running out on him tonight—no matter how you looked at it, that was tough to take.

The elder Butler rose to his feet, beckoned to his sons. "Boys, we best be getting home. George, we'll ride out again tomorrow. I don't know how much good it's going to be, with the trail this dead; but let's give it a try. I'm passing the word around my plantation—flogging for the slightest infractions! We've got to teach those black bastards, George. We've got to show them who's the master!"

Butler's eyes looked uneasy, George noted dryly. The old man pissed up a storm in words, but he never even did his own flogging. Left that to the drivers, the overseers. That was wrong. You had to take the whip into your own hand, put the fear of God into them yourself. Pride suffused him. He was a man who wasn't afraid to mete out punishment when it was due.

The Butler menfolk left the house. George half-filled his tumbler again, walked to the staircase, ascended with an effort. No way for a gentleman to be spending his night, riding off to catch up with runaway slaves. His eyes narrowed secretively. Better ways for a man to be wasting his energy. At the head of the stairs finally, he paused, winded from the climb, taking deep gulps of air into his lungs.

He hesitated at his own door, on impulse moved ahead along the corridor past his wife's door to David's, reached to swing it wide. David was asleep, the feather pillow bundled up beneath him. Like a damn little kid—his father thought scornfully—hanging on to a rag doll for comfort in the night. Better he be hanging on to a well-built black bitch!

George quietly closed the door to David's room and returned to his own. Opening the door, he almost stumbled over the inert form of Othello, the older of the two brothers who had been brought into the house to help him dress in the morning, undress at night, run his errands. The boy was fattening up since he'd come into the house, George noted dryly. Must be stealing butter, stealing meat. They got spoiled with the easy living, once you brought them into the house. Got a headful of fancy ideas.

"Wake up, you no-account young nigger!" He kicked Othello sharply in the ribs. Most nights, Othello and his brother slept out on the backporch. Tonight, he must have been scared, knowing what happened. Ran up here.

"Me wake, Massah!" Eagerness churned with fear in Othello as he jumped awkwardly to his feet. "Undress yo', suh?"

"Just pull off the boots," George ordered as he lowered his bulk onto the bed. "I won't be getting much sleep this night." Hell, it was morning already.

He stretched, yawned, ran his large, stubby hands about his chest. He was tired from the hours of riding, yet oddly stimulated. No chance of his falling asleep, the way he felt right now.

Eulalie. His mind fastened with pleasure on her golden, slim body. Bring that pretty piece up to his bed. Time he taught that bitch a few things. Last time, he had to slap her, right across her mouth, her ass too, he remembered as renewed passion already took root in his groin.

"Othello, you run down to the kitchen, and you send Eulalie up here, you hear? Do it fast!"

"Yessuh." The big, black eyes were wide and knowing. "Me fetch, pretty quick!" And he knew what for, George thought with smug amusement. Another two years and that young whelp would be hiding in the hay himself.

Othello ran from the room, gently closed the door. George rose from the bed, anticipation stirring in him. He never flogged that little Eulalie. Some of them liked it. Some bitches never got really hot until you hit them with the leather.

He crossed to the closet, looked about inside for a crop that suited his fancy. This one here! Satisfaction in his smile, he brought out the crop, swung the leather through the air. He visualized the strip of leather cutting against the golden nakedness of Eulalie; he heard her cry out. He felt his manhood swell in response.

Why didn't Othello hurry? What was keeping that girl? He crossed to the door, swung it wide, stood there, heavy legs apart, the crop in his hand. His manhood ready to burst. He couldn't wait to push himself into that satin-gold body. She'd be different, once she tasted the whip. She wouldn't lie there like a dead log. She'd respond.

"Othello!" he yelled, ignoring the tender hour of the morning. "You dumb nigger, get up here!"

Othello's face appeared at the foot of the staircase. He looked terrified. There was an odd cast to his skin.

"Massuh, she not be there," Othello stammered, his voice shrill with alarm. "Me look. Me look all through de house."

"What do you mean, she's not in the house?" George thundered, striding forward in his bare feet. "You go back in the kitchen, and you look good. You find her, Othello, if you know what's good for you!"

George stood there, watching the boy scurry towards the rear of the house. Lust made him restless. He rarely felt this hot without a lot of doing first. Where was that yaller gal, when he was panting to pour himself into her? She wasn't going to lie there like a log tonight.

He waited a few moments, straining his ears for sounds downstairs. Only silence. Impatiently, he started down the wide circular staircase. Eulalie must have got upset, with all the clamor about the runaways. She must have run home to her Maw. He'd ship that black scalawag, Othello, down to the quarters to fetch her.

"Othello!" he bellowed again en route to the kitchen. "You go down to the quarters, and you tell Eulalie to get herself right up here."

At the entrance to the kitchen, George stopped dead. Seraphina stood in the middle of the room, her dark eyes frightened; she was listening to Othello dramatically relating his difficulties in locating Eulalie.

"Seraphina." His voice was ominous. "Where's that Eulalie?" If she wasn't in the kitchen and she wasn't with Seraphina, where could she be? Lying with one of the black bucks? Playing dead with him—but not half so dead with some big black buck just itching to use that thing between his legs.

"Massa, me not know where she be," Seraphina gasped, terror shining in her eyes. "Me think she heah."

"You go search for her, Seraphina!" Anger distended a vein in his throat. "You bring her right back to this house. I won't have this kind of gallivanting! When I call, I expect to be answered!"

George stamped out of the kitchen and strode down the long corridor that led to the library. In the library, he helped himself to a fresh shot of bourbon. Why did that slut have to be hiding somewhere in the hay when he was all heated up this way? When he got hold of her, he wasn't going to stop until she was a limp rag. She'd know what a white man could give her.

With glass in hand and still bootless, George dropped his bulk into an armchair again. He stuck his feet far out before him while his rancor built up. No matter how good you were to the niggers, it was never enough. They were always expecting more.

George was half-dozing from the night's exertion, and from the bourbon when he came awake to the noisy crying in the kitchen, the frenzied wailing. He leaped to his feet and stalked impatiently to the rear of the house.

"All right, what's going on here?" His loud, angry voice brought instantaneous silence.

Seraphina trembled before him, her face streaked with tears, the eyes red. Venus cowered by the stove, her hands clutching her pregnant belly. Othello stepped behind a chair as though this fragile piece of furniture might afford some protection against the Master's wrath.

"No find Eulalie," Seraphina whispered. "No find mah baby. Me look. All places, me look."

Outside, the bright morning sunlight poured across the flower beds, across the line of clothes hanging in the summer breeze. He must have slept two or three hours, George guessed. The knowledge infuriated him.

"You trying to tell me Eulalie's run away?" His face turned florid, the vein in his forehead throbbing furiously.

"What kind of a night has this been? Who's stirring up trouble down there in the quarters?"

Seraphina dropped her head, eyes fastened to the floor. One trembling hand caught at the other. Slowly, she shook her head.

"Me not know where she be." Seraphina's voice was barely audible. "Nobody talk in de quartahs."

"We'll find that bitch!" His voice soared in rage. The knuckles on one clenched hand were white. "First Hector runs off. No reason at all! Then those four last night—" His eyes grew guarded. He knew why those took off. Like Margaret said—splitting up the families, with the suckers on the way. It angered him to realize Margaret had been right. "Now you stand before me and you say you don't know where Eulalie is—when she should have been here in the kitchen all night. We'll find her, Seraphina, and when we do, she'll be flogged till she's raw meat!" He struggled now to gain control of his voice, which threatened to soar perilously, while the three slaves trembled before his rage. "Seraphina, she's your child. You go out there and you look for her. And if you don't bring her back, I'll lay this across your back till it's cut to ribbons!" He whipped the air with his riding crop. "Nobody's going to make a monkey out of George Woodstock!" He swung the crop through the air again, missing Seraphina's face by inches.

"George, stop that!" His wife's voice was shrill.

George swerved about, raised his hand again, but kept the whip slack. Margaret hovered in the doorway, her face white but determined. Her eyes flashed with contempt. With one hand she gestured to the slaves to leave her alone with her husband.

"What are you doing in the kitchen, at this hour of the morning, Mrs. Woodstock?" he demanded with razor-sharp sarcasm. "What do you care, that our property runs off, making us poorer by the day? I intend to teach every slave on this plantation a lesson. They're going to learn that they do what I say, or they'll be too sick to move! If Seraphina don't turn up with that Eulalie, I'm flogging her myself. You spoil them rotten, Margaret, all of them!"

"You lay a finger on Seraphina, George Woodstock," his wife said with a dangerous calm, "and I leave this plantation. I take David and Cindy, and I go right to Papa out in Louisiana. And nobody—not even you with your whip—is going to stop me!"

For a few pregnant moments, George and Margaret Woodstock hung before each other in silence, each evaluating the other. He hadn't suspected Margaret had it in her, he conceded inwardly, and yet right now, looking at her this way, he knew she meant every word. He couldn't have his wife walking out on him. How would he look before the other plantation owners? Pride lent him caution.

"I'm going to send out ads to every newspaper in the country," he yelled with a show of defiance, but he carefully avoided the issue of flogging. "I don't care what it costs. We're going to find those slaves and bring them back! Even if it costs me more than they're worth! When that Eulalie comes back, she goes into the fields! You had to teach her to read and write," he threw at his wife derisively. "Why I could have sold that yaller bitch in New Orleans for two thousand dollars! That would have bought a lot of pretty clothes for Missy Cindy!"

10

Rolling along at a swift pace over the sandy soil, the wagon wheels made a noisy clatter, disturbing the silence of the night. Eulalie was conscious that the woman beside her sat hunched over with cold and that she was fighting to stay awake. How long had they been here in the wagon? Eulalie looked up at the sky, which was showing a barely perceptible lightening, the first hint of dawn. Hours. They must be ridin' at least five hours.

The dank chill of the mountain air discomforted Eulalie not at all. She was too keyed up to be troubled by a need for sleep. The body warmth of the two, one on either side of her, lent comfort and a recurrent sense of wonder that white folks could treat her as though she were one of them.

"We bes' be stoppin' for a while," the man decided, tugging at the reins. "Don't do no good to keep goin' when you're tuckered out. The mind ain't keen then—you make mistakes. We rest a piece, because it's a while till we git you to the next station."

"Station?" Eulalie was alert with curiosity.

"That's right, girl." Pride touched the man's gaunt face. "You travelin' on the underground railroad. It's a lot of travelin', to a lot of stations, but we git you to where you goin', girl. Where you make free."

"Light as she be, she'll be fine in one of the big cities up North. Like Philadelphia or New York," the woman said calmly.

Eulalie's heart pounded at the mention of New York. Cousin Madeline's address in New York still hovered in its hiding place between her breasts along with the money David gave her. David say, go to New York, Cousin Madeline help you.

"Come on down," the man commanded, reaching to help first his wife, then Eulalie.

"Over there, in the bushes," he said, squinting thoughtfully. "I'll stay here with the corpse. Looks more respectful that way, case anybody comes nosin' around. They got a powerful lot of patrols roamin' around these nights, what with all the colored folks runnin' off." His smile was laced with relish; he was pleased to be part of helping them run off.

Eulalie and the woman obediently moved off into the bushes, laid their blankets side by side, then wrapped their prone bodies with the left-over segment of blanket. For the first time tonight, Eulalie was conscious of being cold. She was trembling now, but not solely because of the cold. In half an hour, it would be daybreak. She'd felt protected in the night, Now, when they climbed back on the buckboard again, she'd be riding up there in broad daylight for all the world to see.

Remember everythin' she larned with David. Talk *right*. Talk like white folks. Quality white folks. Don't let on she be scared. Hold her head high—she be—she *was* as good as anybody.

Despite her certainty that she would not sleep, Eulalie drifted off into troubled slumber in moments. Two hours later, she came awake reluctantly at the gentle prodding of the woman crouched beside her.

"We have to be on our way now," the woman explained,

her eyes moving about the sky. "It's full day already. We got another six hours of ridin' to do before we git you to the next station."

The man had a rough fire going. He'd made strong, black coffee, whose aroma brought forth from Eulalie a fleeting homesickness. The woman went over to the bag of provisions, brought out slabs of cornbread to go with the coffee. The three of them settled in silence to consume their morning meal. Back at the plantation, Eulalie was thinking, the house slaves didn't eat till they saw what was left over on the breakfast table to be scraped off onto their own plates. The field hands wouldn't be eating one of their two daily meals until hours after they started working the field. Six hours, maybe, of bending over the red-clay earth.

Eulalie felt heartened by the hot coffee—a luxury occasionally savored by house slaves—and the fresh cornbread in her small, flat belly. By now Maw was up, she thought, and in the kitchen in the big house. Maw knew she be— she was gone. Soon they'd all know. She shuddered. The Massa take it out on Maw? No, Missis wouldn't let him. Missis knew she needed Maw. Maw take care of her.

"Let's move," the man said briskly, beginning to tidy up. "It don't do to hang around no place too long."

They climbed aboard the wagon again and continued north through the pine-topped mountains. Pine trees. Everywhere you looked, pine trees. Eulalie was grateful not to be making her way through these mountains on her own. It would be a long ways yet before she was safe.

They passed through a stretch of mountain to the north, then began to descend into a valley. In the distance Eulalie saw a cluster of buildings that told her this was a small town. Her heart pounded. Her eyes brightened, avid with curiosity. She'd never seen a town. The Massa frowned on slaves leavin' the plantation. Once a year Missis take Maw into town to help her carry packages when she shopped. Maw used to wait all year for that day.

"We cut away from the town," the man said, disappointing Eulalie. "Less folks we run into, the happier I be."

They said, with the rice powder on her face and her hair up this way, she almost passed for white. Eulalie pondered. Self-consciously, covertly, her eyes moved to inspect the sun-browned face of the woman beside her. As brown as she, Eulalie confirmed. Still, it don't <u>do</u> no good to take chances, she exhorted herself. Besides, she wasn't worryin' about passin' for white folks. She worried about *makin' free.*

They rode through an area of small tenant farms where whole families labored in the fields putting in the cotton crop. The soil had long been misused and was presently uttering increasing complaints, by way of poor crops. Alexander tol' them there was lots more tenant farmers than plantation owners, Eulalie recalled. Maybe no more than a thousand plantations in the whole South—but they was the ones who ruled. Men like George Woodstock, who think they belong with God!

Eulalie concentrated now on the scenery before her. The houses were small, mean, yet infinitely better than the hovels that housed the slaves on the plantation. Eulalie looked upon the houses with respect, even while she was surprised to see white folks bent over the field that way, putting in cotton like they was slaves.

At a turn in the road, the horses made a switch in direction without any instruction from their drivers. The man chuckled good-humoredly.

"Becky, how you like these critters?" he chortled. "They make this trip so many times, they know the road good as I do!"

From the look on the man's face, Eulalie sensed that they were nearing their destination. They were approaching another small farm. The family, as usual, was out under the sun, laboring in the field. The wagon swung off the road, followed the lane that led up towards the house.

In the field, work had ceased. Three grown-ups and a cluster of children stood still, watching their approach. Now, the grown-up were striding towards the wagon. Walking rapidly, purposefully, as though they were fully cognizant of the meaning of this visit.

"Howdy," the young woman said with a friendly smile.

She was walking with quick, small steps ahead of the others. She was only a girl, Eulalie realized in astonishment, scarcely older than herself.

"We won't be stayin'," Becky said with a slow, meaningful smile. "We bring you a traveler." She turned to Eulalie. "Hop down, girl, you be at the next station."

Her eyes full of the gratitude she was too shy to put into words, Eulalie did as she was bidden. The other girl was viewing Eulalie with puppylike interest. Her parents, gazing about cautiously, prodded Eulalie into the house. They had only sparse words of farewell for the couple in the wagon. This was time for business to be done—no time to engage in small talk.

"We'll hide you up in the attic till night," the woman said brusquely, yet Eulalie was certain this was only a cover. "You climb up there and lay quiet, mind you. Never know when we be havin' visitors in these times. Looks like they suspect everybody of carryin' off slaves." Unexpectedly, she smiled. Eulalie relaxed a bit, smiled back.

"You hungry?" the girl asked eagerly.

"I ate this mornin'," Eulalie explained respectfully.

"This mornin'!" the woman hooted. "Well, that be a long time ago. You git up there in the attic." The man moved to help Eulalie. "Elizabeth here will bring you up a plate of ham and eggs in a few minutes."

Eulalie clambered into the low attic, careful not to bang her head on the eaves. At one end was a pile of hay. That would be for hidin' in, in case patrol folks came snoopin' around, Eulalie decided. She hoped nobody would come snoopin'.

It was hot in the attic, with the noonday sun beating down on the roof. She took off her bonnet, the cloak, pulled her dress high above her feet. She stared unhappily at the bareness of her feet. She wished—oh, she wished she had shoes.

A few minutes later Elizabeth climbed up through the opening.

"Dinnuh," the pert-faced girl announced, enjoying the circumstances. "I thought maybe you'd like some apple pie too. Maw cooks powerful good." She handed over a plate of ham and eggs, another with a generous wedge of apple pie.

"Thank you," Eulalie said softly, her eyes thanking for far more than the meal. "It looks real good."

Elizabeth climbed down, closed off the attic from view, but not before Eulalie caught a glimpse of the family taking its place about the table. Maw always wished they had a table and maybe two chairs. But if they had, where they put them? Place only for the bed.

Here she'd be stayin' until dark, Eulalie realized. The food claimed her attention now. She approached the meal with a healthy young appetite. Eatin' on their plates, she realized with satisfaction. They wasn't worried about that at all.

She finished her meal, stretched out against a mound of hay. She knew she would sleep again. The brief hours in the mountain bushes had been hardly enough. Now, thoughts of David invaded her mind. She was glad he'd asked her that way. It wasn't wrong, with David. Almost like bein' his wife. She drifted off to sleep, feeling David's arms holding her, feeling David's body close to hers.

Eulalie came awake with a jolt, a sense of falling through space. Startled, she pulled herself into a sitting position, the events of the past twenty-four hours running in kaleidoscopic swiftness through her mind. Soon it would be night again. Darkness was gathering outside. Soon she would be running again.

She listened attentively to the voices that were seeping up from downstairs. It was too late to be working in the fields—the family had returned to the house. Cooking odors assailed her nostrils. She listened to the reassuring sounds of the young children frolicking with one another, their voices raised now in indignant battle.

"Now you be quiet, all of you!" Their mother's voice rose authoritatively above the clamor. "Elizabeth, you go tell the girl to come on down here to supper. This time of night, the patrol's too busy fillin' their bellies to come botherin' folks like us."

Shyly, Eulalie joined the family at the supper table,

respectfully lowered her head while the father said grace. These be white folks, and they treated her like one of the family. Something good had to come when folks like this cared about folks like she. Like her, Eulalie conscientiously corrected herself. Now was the time to remember every bit of learnin' she pick up from the tutors. It could be the difference between makin' free and hangin'.

The family spoke little at the meal. They ate with relish, grateful that another day was past. Mainly, the children talked and the parents good-humoredly reprimanded. These were folks who worked hard in the fields. They'd eat their food, and then they would go to sleep to prepare for another day's labor.

When these folks worked in the fields, though, Eulalie thought somberly, nobody was standin' over them with a whip. Nobody floggin' them because maybe he be in a bad humor, or because somebody too sick to be workin' and he not believin'. They have this nice house and good food on the table and somethin' to wear beside one dress or one pair of pants all year—till it fall off your back. These folks work in the fields, but *they be free*.

Someday, she'd buy Maw her own house. Maw just cook for the two of them. She'd buy Maw pretty dresses and one of them pianos like Missis have in the music room. Maw jus' crazy about that piano music. Maw picked out songs when nobody was around. Pretty!

"I guess you're wonderin', girl, about gettin' to the next stop," the woman said briskly. Eulalie was aware that names were avoided—both ways.

"Yes'm," Eulalie said expectantly.

"We been thinkin' all afternoon about the bes' way to git you on your way. You travel tonight with the peddler-man who'll be comin' soon—" She stopped dead, listened sharply, her eyes swinging to her husband.

He rose from the table, crossed to gaze out the window into the darkness. A bright night unfortunately. The moon spilled light with rich generosity.

"It be the peddler," he said, nodding his head. "Eat up, girl. You'll be leavin' soon."

He walked to the door, pulled it open, waited for the

peddler to hitch up his horses, to walk into the house. A hush had fallen over the room. Even the children were silent, watching wide-eyed for the new arrival.

"Howdy, sir," Eulalie's host said pleasantly to the man approaching the door. He was not yet visible to those inside. "We'd be right proud if you'd have a bite to eat with us."

"Thank you, no." The heavily accented voice, low and melodious, captured Eulalie's attention. An old man, she thought, surprised—yet one in whom there was yet much vitality.

The stranger walked into the room. Eulalie's eyes were riveted on the figure of the peddler. He was a small, faintly stooped man, well on in years, with enormous brown eyes. A sardonic smiled belied by an air of infinite compassion. What beautiful hands for a man!

"I know why you won't eat with us," Elizabeth giggled good-naturedly, and Eulalie guessed there was much affection between their visitor and the children. "You scared we put pork on the table."

"Ssah—" He gently reproached her. "I think it wisest we go on our way before we have company asking many stupid questions."

"You expectin' trouble?" the man demanded uneasily.

"Patrols out early tonight. There was a fire last night at a plantation just across the state line. A slave is missing." He nodded his head significantly. "Come, we hide the merchandise, hah?" He chuckled with tender humor.

"The peddler has a box under all his goods," the woman explained. "It ain't the most comfortable way of travelin', but it's the safest. Even if they poke in there with their guns, all they'll feel is goods. You just lay there and stay quiet."

Eulalie battled waves of suffocation when she lay in the box and watched the lid coming down. She knew about the holes in the sides all around that would provide air for her to breathe, yet that door shutting down on her set her heart to pounding, brought anguished tightness to her throat. The peddler said it would be a long trip. Lyin', all the time, in this box, Eulalie's mind taunted.

She strained to hear the voices around the wagon. The peddler was doin' some business with the lady. Out there in the night, they were bargainin' about the price for a piece of cloth to make a dress for Elizabeth. That was to make it look good, Eulalie guessed, in case anybody came around askin' questions. The lady could show the cloth she'd bought from the peddler. That was all he was doin', she could say, sellin' his goods and movin' on his way.

Eulalie felt the motion of the wagon as the horses began to pull at their owner's urging. They were on their way. Minutes later, she heard the peddler calling out to the horses, exhorting them to pick up speed. There was much distance to cover tonight. She was embarked on another night of running. How many more, she asked herself? How many more?

She lay still, uneasy in the stuffiness of the box, wincing at the roughness of the ride. The bumps jarred her tender body with dogged repetition. Think about somethin' else, Eulalie ordered herself. About outside. What was it like outside?

The stars was comin' out in shinin' clusters—they was startin' to come out when she came into the box. David loved the stars. He taught her how to read the sky—the No'th Star, the Big Dipper, the Little Dipper, the Milky Way. How many nights she lay there in the kitchen at the big house, lookin' out the window, up there at the stars, knowin' David was at his window, lookin' up, too. It always made her feel close to him, that way. When she looked up, she'd made promises to the No'th Star. That was what she'd follow some day, all the way till she make free!

They were making a turn, Eulalie noted. She was instantly alert. Onto a new kind of road. It would be a corduroy road made of logs of wood. Oh! She winced with the roughness of it, the unevenness of the logs jolting her with every roll of the wheels.

She tried to sleep. She had dozed in the attic back at the farm house, and now sleep refused to come. Cramped by the narrowness of the box, she tried to adjust her position to a more comfortable one. It was futile. In this dark prison, she listened with painful intensity for sounds outside. She prayed she would hear none. So far, there was only the clatter of the horses' hoofs on the uneven corduroy road and the sound of the peddler's voice singing a plaintive, high-pitched chant that was strangely melodious.

She was travelin' alone with a man, Eulalie thought. An aura of tender amazement enfolded her; she no longer had any fear that he would try to take her in the rough man's way. Why was he helpin' her? Why did all of them, these white wolks that made up the underground railroad—and Alexander said there was blacks helpin' too—why did they bother, the way they did, with makin' slaves free? Because they knew that in God's eyes slavery be wrong. Alexander right—someday all slaves be free. She lay there, in the darkness of the box and exulted in the thought.

Eulalie stiffened, her ears sharpened by her confinement. More horses! She was sure. More horses comin' towards them! Her hands tightened into fists, the short nails digging into the pink of her palms. Trouble! Here be trouble!

"All right, ol' man," a harsh masculine voice ordered. "Pull that wagon over! We'll be lookin' to see what you're carryin' there!"

Eulalie bit at her lip, rigid with fear as she listened. Suppose they scared the old man? Suppose they threatened to kill him? He'd tell! He'd hafta! But she wasn't goin' back to The Willows! No matter what, she wasn't goin' back!

The men were dismounting from their horses. They were talking obscenely about runaway slaves. Eulalie shivered. They were looking for a man, but if they found a girl hiding in the box, they'd be pleased to grab hold of her, Eulalie knew.

They sen' her back, Eulalie thought in terror. The Massa always run ads in the papers when a slave run away. He always give a big reward for returnin' him. Sometimes, they be brought back. Sometimes, not. They be strung up to show the others not to run away. She could feel sweat forming between her breasts, beading her forehead.

"There was a fire last night!" a man was shouting menacingly. "One of them varmints escaped from the plantation—we aim to catch him!"

"You cooperate," another voice jumped in, "and you won't get hurt—"

"Gentlemen, gentlemen," the peddler pleaded softly. "I come from across the state line. I know nothing about a fire—"

"Never know who's hidin' one of them!" somebody shouted derisively. "Hop down from there, old man! We're going to take this wagon apart before we get done!"

11

Eulalie trembled. She was sick at her stomach and conscious of the men tearing at the merchandise above and around her. She was terrified that they would dig down to the box—which presumably held merchandise—and insist upon opening it.

"Gentlemen, gentlemen," the old man was mildly reproaching in his rich, melodious voice with its heavy accent. "Buy something to make your lady happy. This is not a night to be riding around on patrols! Look, I bring such beautiful cloth. Here, feel this, soft as a fine lady's skin. Take her a present, and you'll have a wonderful night," he insinuated.

"Soft as a wench's ass," a man laughed, and the others joined in with descriptive contributions.

"Here, gentlemen, this comes straight from England." The peddler's voice was coated with pride. "It is worth a king's ransom, but for you I sell cheap. I am sentimental. No lady of my own, so I dream of clothing others in beauty. Look," he pleaded. "What would she do for you for a dress-length of this?"

"Lie on her back spread-eagled," a man chuckled raucously. "But I don't be talkin' about my old lady."

The tone of the voices about the wagon changed. The night air resounded with raw, ribald humor as the men exchanged stories about their nights of passion.

"Lissen, with what I got," one bragged, "there ain't a woman that's goin' to throw me out of her bed!"

"There ain't one big enough to let you in!" somebody else taunted good-humoredly. "You need a cow to take you on!"

"All right, give the Jew what he wants," one of the men commanded. "We don't need to spend the whole night out on the roads. Not tonight," he wound up meaningfully.

Eulalie heard the horses riding away from the wagon. The old man was humming softly to himself while he rearranged the jumble of merchandise about the box. She started at the gentle tap on the lid, then realized this was meant to reassure her. The old man wouldn't dare talk, even with the patrol riding away.

The peddler climbed on the buckboard again, then urged the horses on over the rough corduroy road. Eulalie drew a deep sigh of relief. For a while she had been terrified. Now, from the exhaustion brought on by the emotions spent, Eulalie began to doze.

At first, the faint scratching on the box threatened to throw Eulalie into panic. The wagon had stopped! What was happening?

"It is all right, girl." The peddler's voice was deep with reassurance. "We will stop here for a while to refresh ourselves."

The old man lifted the lid from the box as he spoke. The fresh night air assailed Eulalie's nostrils. She gulped greedily. Oh, the sweetness of the pines, the fragrance of the blossoms, after the hours of narrow confinement! The sky was brightening into first dawn, she noted with relish while the old man helped her from her place of concealment. Another day on the road to freedom.

"I will prepare us a meal," he said, with a courtly bow.

"Nearby—there—" he pointed, "is a spring. You can wash there."

With a smile of gratitude, Eulalie headed for the secluded area by the spring; she was conscious of the peddler's determination to turn his back upon her to provide some privacy. When she was returned to the small fire he had made, she saw that the coffee was beginning to boil already.

"Were you frightened?" he asked compassionately, "when the patrol stopped us?"

"Yes," she admitted, accepting the bread he offered.

"We have learned how to deal with these people," he said simply. "We do what must be done." He turned his dark, piercing eyes on her and for a moment appeared almost ferocious. "Tell me, why do you want to be free? What does freedom mean to you?"

Eulalie sat quite still.

"It means I belong to me—to think for me, to feel for me, to work for me. It means I fly like the birds. I be afraid of no man." Her head was high. Her eyes glowed. "I be a human."

"I was a slave once." There was a faint, singsong quality in the peddler's voice, a look of turning-backward in his eyes.

"You?" Eulalie stammered. White slaves?

"In Russia, under the Czar. In 1825, Nicholas became the Czar. Was bad before then." He shook his head ominously. "To be a serf in Russia is to be a slave. A serf has a small house, his field, but the labors from his field must be paid to the lord—and the serf must work the lord's lands as well as his own. And if a serf be a Jew, he lives his life in fear of the pogroms." The peddler's eyes clouded. "I was away, working on the lord's lands, when the pogrom came to my people. They burned the house, the fields. Where there was a family—a wife, three fine sons, two beautiful daughters—there was nothing. So I ran, hiding in the fields through the day, running by night. And I escaped. I made free." He lifted his head with remembered triumph.

Eulalie and the peddler wasted no time in consuming

their meal. She returned to the safety of the box. She felt less suffocated this time as her mind turned over the story the peddler had told her.

She not know any other Jew, Eulalie realized—except, sometimes, the Massa say a slave dealer be a Jew, but not often. Jesus—our Lord, Jesus Christ—was a Jew, Eulalie remembered, finding pleasure in this. *Her* savior was a Jew. It would be a long road ahead, but she would be less fearful.

Eulalie and the peddler were to travel three more days and two nights, he told her. Each time they stopped for food and personal comforts, he talked to her about his past in a way that Eulalie understood was meant to offer solace. He told her about the people who made up the underground railroad. The unknown, not particularly literate, inarticulate people who felt deeply about the South's sin against God and humanity in handling humans as less than cattle.

He told her about the secret routes to safety, about the thousands of slaves who were finding refuge in Canada where slavery did not exist. He told her about a book that had just been printed up North—a book by a lady named Harriet Beecher Stowe, called *Uncle Tom's Cabin*.

They were crossing huge swaths of the South, Eulalie comprehended, marveling at the distances that made up the nation. The peddler was taking her, Eulalie now knew, into the state of Virginia—to the next station on the underground railroad.

When the peddler slowed down the horses, Eulalie assumed they were arriving at their destination. It was too early to be stopping for a meal. She was learning to tell the passage of time in her dark tomb. They ate at daybreak—which couldn't be more than a few hours behind— or at dusk, the least dangerous times of the day. She lay there, tense, eager for the next stage to freedom.

The lid to the box lifted up. The peddler's familiar lined face hovered above her.

"We are almost there," he said quietly, helping her, as

always, in his courtly fashion. Almost as though she was a white missy, Eulalie thought with pride.

It was a dreary day, threatening rain. She looked about uncertainly at the barren stretches of earth. No house, no folks in sight. She turned to him, her eyes questioning. For a fraction of time, suspicion rising in her that the peddler was, after all, but a man—with a man's common desires.

"I'd like to make you a present." He smiled self-consciously. "Please, from my stock of shoes I wish you to choose a pair."

"For me?" The amber eyes were childlike in their pleasure. Oh, she had been wrong!

"Please, pick," he coaxed, pleased with her delight.

Soberly, as though she were about to hand over her life savings, Eulalie handled first one shoe, then another, deliberating seriously before she made her choice.

"Them," she said, her smile broad. She never wore a pair of shoes. How they feel? She not care, she thought exuberantly—she, a slave, wearin' shoes!

"I congratulate you," he said with satisfaction. "You picked the best, exactly what I would have chosen for you. Go on," he ordered grandly. "Put them on. You must learn to walk in them.

Shyly, Eulalie looked at her feet, then hesitated.

"Please," she said, poining toward a folded-over bit of brown paper. "I take?"

"Wait," he said with an air of abandon and snipped off a length of cheesecloth to hand her despite her beginning protest. "You take it," he instructed. "Use it well."

Eulalie glanced about. There was a narrow, half-dry brook winding in the nearby field. With the cheesecloth tucked inside one shoe and both shoes in the crook of one arm, Eulalie darted, her skirt lifted above her ankles, across the summer-dry field to the faint trickle that was the brook. Carefully, she wet the cheesecloth, then industriously scrubbed at the feet that had never known shoes.

She worked until she was satisfied her feet were fresh; she dried them on the lush greenness of the grass and stepped into the shoes. The peddler was smiling when she rejoined him at the wagon.

"We will be at the station in half a mile," he said, his accent deepening in his anticipation. "One last present," he said formally and held out a pair of dainty white gloves. "It is nice that a lady keep her hands covered."

"Thank you," she said, remembering to say it as though she were Cindy or Missis. "I wear."

Slowly, with great deliberation, she pulled on the gloves. She understood why he gave them to her. She might almost pass for white—but almost was not quite good enough. A white man might look at her hands and guess her black ancestry. The peddler was a fine gentleman—he would not say this to her. He gave her, instead, a pair of white gloves.

Eulalie sat beside the peddler on the buckboard. Wearing the elegant white gloves and the new shoes, she felt uneasy, cast furtive glances about the wagon as the horses carried her over the last lap of the journey with the old man.

"You are nervous," he chided. "You have no need to be. Believe me."

"Maybe somebody passes," she whispered self-consciously. "Maybe they guess." Her eyes were eloquently fearful.

"No one," he pronounced with complacent certainty. "No one would suspect that a runaway slave would have the gall to sit up in public this way. With gloves on her hands and shoes on her feet," he added with a twinkle in his dark eyes. "You are safe. Do not worry." His voice deepened with authority. "I have made this journey before."

They were approaching the house now. It was small and modest, and it was built close to the road because in the winter snow fell in Virginia. Again, those in the fields became aware of guests. Two of them—a man and a woman—separated themselves from the others and went into the house.

"Come," the peddler said quietly. "You are with the Friends."

"We welcome thee," the man greeted them with a soft smile and an air of humility about his slender body.

"Come into the house," the woman invited the peddler. It was clear he was not a stranger here. "We will be happy to give thee dinner."

"I do not like those clouds up there." The peddler gestured towards the sky. "I thank you for your good offer, but I will go."

As though fearful that Eulalie would try to thank him, the peddler hurried back to his wagon, lifted the reins into his hands, and urged the horses on. A sense of loss rolled over Eulalie as she watched him go.

"Come, child," the woman said firmly. "It is better for thee to be hidden by day."

12

The house was neat, clean, pleasant. White curtains hung at the windows. The walls were plastered. The wide-planked floors shone. A huge table surrounded by chairs dominated the main room. A rocker flanked the fireplace. Another table was stationed by the window; it bore books neatly stacked along the length adjacent to the window. Eulalie was too ill-at-ease to stare, yet her eyes were drawn compulsively to the row of books on the table. These were folks who respected learning, she was certain.

"Prepare a meal for the child," the man told his wife. "I will go back to the field—there is yet much to be done. Thee can help her into the attic when she is done with the meal."

"I will," his wife said tranquilly. "Thee can return to the field."

Eulalie was intrigued by the manner of their speech, the modesty of their attire. What did the old man mean when he say, "you are with the Friends"?

"We are Quakers," the woman said casually as though she read Eulalie's mind. "We belong to the Society of

Friends. There have been times when we had to run also. Have thee never heard about the Quakers?"

"No ma'am." Eulalie's eyes were wide with interest, yet involuntarily they returned to the stack of books on the table by the window. At the door, the man stopped, halted by that look of avid curiosity in her eyes.

"I am the schoolmaster also," he explained gently. "Now, school is over for the year. We must work in the field. Thee like to look at the pictures in books?"

"I like to read," Eulalie said, her voice low, eyes cast down. "More than anythin', I like to read."

"Rachel did thee hear the child?" His voice crackled with excitement. He moved back into the room and towards Eulalie. "Thee can read?"

"Yessuh." Eulalie lifter her eyes to meet his.

"Where did thee learn?"

"On—on the plantation." No names, she remembered. "The Missis let me learn, with her boy—be company for him. I know the law say no, but Missis not care." She hesitated. Had she talked too much? Her eyes were anxious.

"Rachel, hear the child!" The man's voice was rich with discovery. "She learned to read. Given a chance, she learned to read! Thee can see how wrong they are who say the black man is an inferior race incapable of learning —that they are dull-witted, incapable of improving themsleves. Here is proof of what I have maintained all along." He swung about to Eulalie, his face glowing with zeal. "Will thee read for me, girl?"

"Yessuh." Her heart pounded. Oh, don't be makin' no mistakes—not when she bragged so about her learnin'.

The man and Eulalie sat down at the table. Her hands were unsteady when she took a book from him and began to read at the place he indicated. She read fluidly, with no mistakes. She read for him from one book, then another, and another, rejoicing in his approval, his mounting excitement because here was proof of his theory that the black man was capable of learning.

"Rachel, they are afraid to let them learn," he said with religious fervor. "Because when a man learns, he thinks, he asks questions, he wants to better his circumstances. He doesn't want to be a wretched chattel!"

"Someday—thee will see—all schools will teach all races of people. It will come to pass, husband."

"What else do you know?" he prodded Eulalie with avid curiosity. "Have thee learned to spell, to count sums, to take away?"

"Yes," Eulalie admitted, her voice an abashed whisper.

"Husband!" Alarm laced the woman's voice. "Horses! Someone is coming!"

Swiftly, Eulalie was guided into the shadowed safety of the attic. The woman was moving about in the kitchen, clanging pots and pans, to make a great show of preparing a meal. Eulalie huddled tensely, fearful of possible intruders. The horses were drawing closer. Would they stop? Had they seen the peddler leave her off here? She was so close to freedom now. Oh, let them not find her here!

The horses were riding past; they were beyond the house now. Still, the pair below continued their activities in the kitchen. They were taking no chances that the riders would return. Eulalie took off the white gloves, smoothed them, folded them neatly and deposited them in the bodice of her dress. And waited. She had long ago learned to wait.

She heard a movement at the door that led to the attic. The man was pulling it down.

"It is wisest thee eat thy meal up there," he said kindly. "When it is dark, thee will come down."

He gave her the plate of pork and greens his wife had heated up for her and a glass of milk; soon he returned with a small lamp and a book—to make the waiting less dull.

Eulalie guessed night was approaching when she heard the jumble of voices down below. The evening meal was being prepared. It was impossible for her to read any more, with her awareness of the family's return to the house. Soon she would be moving further into freedom, further away from everything that had been part of her life up until now.

One of the older children, faintly shy in the presence of

a stranger—though such arrivals were not unknown to her, Eulalie realized—came to invite her down to the supper they were about to share.

"The book your father give me to read," Eulalie said, smiling as she extended the book. The girl took the lamp as well to free Eulalie's hands for the descent from the attic.

"Papa is the schoolmaster," the girl said proudly. "Did thee know?"

"Yes." Eulalie's eyes were admiring. "He tell me." She looked about at the somberly dressed yet happy family scene. The children, like their parents, were dressed in muted grays, their clothes replicas of those their parents wore. Friends, the old man had called them. Eulalie liked that.

"Come to the table," the woman commanded. She was friendly but firm as she gestured her brood to their places.

Again, Eulalie was conscious of sitting down at a table —a luxury in itself for a slave—alongside of white folks. Eating what they ate, from their dishes. But first, they bowed their heads while the father said grace.

"We must be very careful about thee," the man said matter-of-factly. "Of late, there has been much trouble at the plantations. Nightly, the patrols are out. We have decided—" His smile took in his wife as co-adviser, "that the safest way is to be flagrantly bold. We will take thee into Portsmouth and put thee on the night boat to Baltimore. Thee will be a young lady going to Baltimore to a job."

"I pass?" Eulalie asked uncertainly. Suddenly, she was afraid.

The man's eyes were unhappy. They moved to his wife, then back to Eulalie.

"We must try," he said compassionately. "To go out at night, with thee hidden in the wagon, is to court disaster. Do you wish to try it?" he probed. "If it fails," he warned, "thee could be apprehended . . . sent back."

For an instant Eulalie flinched as though a whip had lashed across her back. But then her face tightened. Her eyes glistened with determination.

"I try. You tell me what do?" Baltimore, he said. She

be arrivin' in Baltimore. Alone. "Baltimore?" she asked hesitantly. "It a free state?"

"No," he acknowledged. "There are slaves in Maryland. But thee will find Friends who will help thee if thee go to them. From Baltimore thee will go to Philadelphia. In Philadelphia, there are schools for black children," he told her with satisfaction. "Philadelphia is a good city."

"Tonight?" Eulalie asked. "I go on the boat tonight?"

She never be on a real boat. Just canoe. Never *see* one. Missis talk about the fine steamboats that go up and down the rivers, about big boat that take Cindy to Lindon, all the way across the ocean. A knot tightened in the pit of her stomach when she considered going on the boat. Alone.

"There won't be a boat leaving Portsmouth until tomorrow night. Thee will stay here for the night. For an emergency, I will prepare Free Papers for thee—sometimes, they are accepted without question." His eyes left Eulalie to confer with his wife's. She nodded slightly. "After supper, it will be best for thee to go up to the attic again—it is safer. We never know who comes knocking in the night." He smiled slightly. "I will give thee another book to read, one I think thee will enjoy."

When Eulalie was finished with her supper, he went to the table by the window to forage through the books. Eulalie thought of the small book of poems that—since she had disposed of her bag of provisions—lay beneath her breast, held to her body by the tight bodice of her dress. Now, the Friend was giving her another book. She waited, expectantly, proud that he was making this gesture, that she was able to participate.

"Keep this with thee," the man said gently, putting the book into her hands. "It is yours."

In the attic, Eulalie adjusted the lamp so that she could read. She opened the book. It was a school book of famous orations. Reverently, Eulalie turned the pages. Liberty. These writers talked about liberty! Color rose in Eulalie's cheeks. Exhilaration filled her soul. *She* was on her way to liberty.

The time in the attic of the Friends' house passed more

quickly than Eulalie had thought possible. The family kept her supplied with reading matter. She slept, in voracious segments, from the exhaustion of these days and nights of flight. Now it was late afternoon, and the man and woman had stopped their work in the fields to prepare her for the ordeal ahead.

Her own dress—Cindy's dress—lay in a neat, small carpetbag supplied by the woman, and Eulalie, humiliated at first when the woman discovered she wore no undergarments, stood clothed in the modest Quaker frock that the woman had painstakingly fitted after providing her with proper undergarments. In the carpetbag also were the Free Papers Eulalie was to use only if cornered, because they could be proved false. In addition, the bag contained the book of poetry and the one of orations on liberty. In her white-gloved hand, Eulalie gripped another slim volume to impress any curious onlooker with her intellectuality—a trait hardly associated with a runaway slave.

"It's time we drove into town to be ready for the boat," the man decided. He then issued orders to the older children to ship the younger ones to bed at an early hour because they would have to be up at daybreak to go out into the fields.

Again the skies looked dreary when the three of them mounted the wagon. The wagon was covered, though—if rain came, she and the woman could go inside, Eulalie realized. But she hoped to be able to sit up here in the freshness of the night. So much of these past days and nights had of necessity been spent enclosed.

The horses carried them along at a steady gait for almost an hour before they approached the town. Eulalie stared eagerly ahead. She had never seen a town close up before. Her eyes greedily drank in the sights while one hand clutched tightly at the book and the other to the borrowed carpetbag.

"Thee look fine," the woman whispered reassuringly, inspecting with satisfaction the application of rice powder, which had softened the golden tones of Eulalie's skin. "Remember, read thy book until it is time to go to thy berth. Thee will be sharing it with another lady. Talk as little as thee can, pretend to be tired," the woman encouraged. "In the morning, thee will be in Baltimore. Leave the boat straightway when thee are in dock. Thee remember the address we gave thee?"

"Yes, Missis," Eulalie said quickly.

"Yes, Ma'am," the woman corrected, a gentle twinkle in her eyes. "Repeat it to me."

Carefully, Eulalie repeated the name and address, both of which were written down on the scrap of paper concealed in her carpetbag, but committed to memory by Eulalie in the event the paper should be lost.

"Good." Eulalie's companion was pleased.

They were arriving at the boat now. Eulalie stared with awe upon the paddle-wheel steamer tied up at the wharf. She was to travel on the boat alone. Her pulse raced. For the first time, all on her own. Nobody to help her, once she climbed up the gangplank, Eulalie realized.

"I never been on a boat," Eulalie whispered, her throat dry. "Just on a rowboat up the Chattahoochee—" She stopped dead, her eyes wide. Wrong, talk about the Chattahoochee. That tell where she come from. The Quaker couple, however, ignored the disclosure.

"This boat runs by steam," the schoolmaster explained. "Have you ever heard about Robert Fulton?"

"Yessuh," Eulalie acknowledged, taking pride in his recognition of her learning. "He the man who made the first steamboat."

"That's right."

Eulalie inspected the boat with fresh interest. Somehow, she realized, she had to tie it in with her learning. Seriously, she studied the paddle wheel and the tall smokestack that would be emitting black smoke when they put out to sea. With relief, she noted that sails were rigged in the event that the steam should fail. It was terrifying, yet fascinating, to know that she would soon be aboard that glorious monster of progress.

"Father will buy thy ticket." The woman dropped an arm about Eulalie's shoulder, as though in final farewell to a loved one. "The gangplanks are down—we can go aboard. In a very little while, the boat will be leaving." Her voice was rich with encouragement.

Eulalie allowed herself to be maneuvered by the Quaker woman. She was grateful for her efforts, her warmth, her presence. It seemed to Eulalie that everyone must be looking at her—suspicious of her antecedents—despite the rice powder. With both white-gloved hands, she clung to her carpetbag.

"Tea will be served soon after the boat leaves the dock. About six o'clock." The woman spoke softly. "It's really a meal. It's paid for by thy ticket, so don't hesitate to eat. It'll fortify thee until thee reach thy next destination. After that, thee will be assigned to thy berth."

"I'll remember," Eulalie promised, trembling with the newness of the boat journey.

"Thee will be all right," the woman encouraged. "No one will suspect."

In a flurry of affectionate leave-taking, the Quaker couple kissed her good-bye and talked loudly enough to establish an identity for Eulalie in the minds of her fellow passengers.

"Tell thy Aunt Dorothy we hope she can come down to visit with us soon," the woman said firmly. "And thee be a good girl and do thy job well, thee hear?"

"Yes ma'am." Eulalie said demurely, falling into the spirit of the moment. "I'll tell Aunt Dorothy you're just pinin' to see her."

Eulalie watched the nonvoyagers disembark. She was conscious of a tightness in her chest, perspiration moistening her forehead beneath the bonnet she wore. She was aware too of the covert glances from a tall, barrel-chested man with a loud mouth, who was boasting to a companion about the blacksmith shop he was about to open in Baltimore. He was making Eulalie nervous.

She made a point of sitting close to a coterie of women, each of whom seemed to withdraw from associating with fellow companions yet took refuge in feminine kinship. The steamship tea was announced. Her eyes cast down, Eulalie trailed the others into the room where the meal was to be served.

She knew how to eat and drink like a lady, she reminded herself. She'd practiced that in her daydreams. Still, the teaspoon fell from her uncertain fingers when she reached towards the sugar bowl. The barrel-chested man, his beady, dark eyes always seeming to dwell on her though he sat several chairs below, rose to his feet to retrieve the spoon for her.

"Thank you," she said, her voice barely audible. His eyes were bold, riveted to her breasts, snug beneath the dress that had been designed for one of flatter dimensions.

Did he expect her to use the spoon after it was on the floor? A slave do this. Missis wouldn't hear of such a thing though the Massa wouldn't have a second thought. Eulalie hesitated, sensing the man's eye were focused on her, waiting for her move. She took the spoon between her slim fingers, fastidiously wiped it on the hem of her skirt, then used it to stir her tea. She felt heartened by the way she'd handled this situation.

After the tea, came the ceremony of being assigned to their berths. Eulalie was to share her room with a broad-bosomed, broad-hipped, coarse-featured blonde who appeared about thirty.

"You don't mind me takin' the lower berth?" the woman asked good-humoredly. "You're spry enough to be climbin' up there without breakin' your back."

"I don't mind," Eulalie said, eager to please.

"Come on, honey, let's go get fixed up for the night." Obviously, she was intent on adopting Eulalie for the trip. "This is my first time on a steamship. Kinda excitin', ain't it?"

"Yes. My first time too." Eulalie was emboldened by the confidence.

"Let's go to the washroom." The woman's eyes were bright. "After we get cleaned up, maybe we can take a turn around the deck. I'm not one for goin' to bed early—I like to have a little life goin' on around me." She winked broadly.

Eulalie and the buxom blonde went into the washroom assigned to *Women*. No *White Only* sign, Eulalie noted— but maybe that was because no blacks were expected to be riding a steamboat in Southern territory. Eulalie and the blonde waited their turn to go into the inner washroom. Meanwhile, Eulalie glanced about, trying not to show how impressed she was with the elegant mirrors, the fancy lamps, the generous dimensions of the area.

Two women emerged from the inner dressing-room area. Eulalie hesitated, looking at her companion.

The stewardess—small, elderly, black, with a glint of humor in her eyes—cackled at Eulalie's uncertainty.

"Go on, honey, plenty room fo' two ladies in theah. Nice towel waitin', too," she added with pride. "We don't forgit nothin' on dis boat." Eulalie realized with satisfaction that the black stewardess had accepted her as white without question. The dim lights, the rice powder.

Eulalie and her newly found friend went together into the washing area. The meager towel obviously was meant to serve all the ladies on the boat. The blonde good-naturedly ignored this seeming lack of abundance. Eulalie, abashed but determined, washed her hands carefully—she didn't dare wash away the rice powder that coated her face—and dried them on the beautifully white petticoat provided her along with her frock. She noted that the blonde admired this fastidious touch.

"Let's take a turn around the boat," the blonde repeated firmly, linking her arm through Eulalie's, when they were out of the washroom.

"All right," Eulalie accepted, scared to do otherwise. Also, it was hot and stuffy in the cabin assigned to them. The air would clear her head.

"I hope it don't get rough," the blonde giggled. "I'd just die of mortification if I got seasick. But it's not like we was on the ocean. This is just Chesapeake Bay."

"This time of year, it'll be calm," Eulalie soothed.

Now Eulalie's mind was moving back to the minutes in the washroom. Was she just imaginin' it, Eulalie asked herself, or did the stewardess look at her in a funny way, when they was leavin'? The light was not bright down there. But maybe she gave herself away. Her heart pounded. She felt her face grow hot. If anybody guessed she be runnin' away, she never get off this boat. Not with the big rewards the Massa must be offerin' for her return. She wasn't goin' to be catched. No matter what, she wasn't goin' back there!

Dusk was edging into night as Eulalie and her companion sauntered about the deck. Eulalie was astonished to see how close they were to shore. The houses—sparse though they were—shone like beacon lights at wide intervals. The blonde was talking in a lively fashion about inconsequential incidents in her traveling experience. The talk was obviously aimed at attracting unattached males.

They swung around the bend and nearly collided with the barrel-chested man who'd looked at her with furtive glances in the dining room. Now, his eyes were overly bold, swaggering. They moved from Eulalie to the blonde and seemed to communicate without speaking.

It was a matter of another turn about the boat, and the contact was made between the other two. They were instantly absorbed in a sort of mutual conquest. Eulalie, feeling superfluous and relieved at an excuse to withdraw, stammered quietly and left them alone. Yet, retreating towards her cabin, Eulalie was conscious of the man's narrowed eyes following her in the deepening dusk.

Eulalie promptly went to bed, seeking safety in the darkness of the cabin. The boat rocked gently. If she were less unnerved, she would have dropped off to sleep. There was a stillness about the boat that told her most of the passengers had retired to their bunks.

The stillness was disturbed by the raucous giggling and the overloud tones of her roommate and the male conquest. Somebody called out a sharp complaint. The giggling became more subdued, the voices of a low murmur. Then there was only quiet. Eulalie guessed her roommate was coupling in a dark corner with the male passenger they had encountered on deck.

Eulalie lay still in her berth though there was no one here to gaze upon her with suspicious or accusing eyes. Troubled, she thought about disembarking tomorrow in the bright daylight of morning. The stewardess looked that way at everybody, Eulalie tried to reassure herself. And that man—he was just a animal thinkin' about those things, she told herself. That's all he was thinkin' about.

Eulalie stiffened to attention. Her roommate was being escorted back to the cabin. They were talking softly in deference to the other passengers. She had to strain to hear what they were saying.

"Now you know better than that," the blonde was giggling softly. "You can't come into a ladies' cabin and spend the night. They'd throw you off the boat!"

"Not in the middle of the night," he reproached. "They wouldn't find out till morning."

"No," the blonde was firm. "But I don't hafta go inside yet." It was a throaty invitation that Eulalie suspected wasn't going to be turned down.

"You know that girl in there with you," he began, and Eulalie tensed in terror. "Somethin' queer about that one."

"She's too young for a fella like you." She was giggling again, but was on guard because, Eulalie suspected, she was annoyed that he was interested in somebody other than herself. But what did he mean, somethin' queer about her? Eulalie's heart hammered.

"She's scared to death," the man said smugly. "You look, and she's ready to fly. Why?"

"Oh, come off it," the blonde expostulated. "She's never been on a boat before. She's going off to her first job. Sure, she's scared."

"The skin," the man said knowingly. "That one's not all white. Quadroon, I'd say. I'll bet you that's a runaway slave. The Quakers are like that, helpin' slaves make it to free states because they don't believe in slavery. For a pretty piece like that, I'll bet there's a juicy reward waitin' for whoever brings her back!"

"Joe, you can't just grab hold of her!" The blonde sounded intrigued at the financial possibilities, though.

"There's gotta be a way," he said. "That reward might be a hundred dollars! For doin' nothin' but holdin' on to her till the courts say she goes back. You know they passed that law last year," he reminded her.

"How you handle it?" the blonde asked doubtfully.

"Before we land, I'll figure this out. I'll have to go ashore in a skiff first, pick up the newspapers, row back and climb aboard. The Cap'n can be bought," he said with satisfaction. "Ten dollars will go a long way. I'll tell him what we think, and he'll play along. When you go in, take a look at her fingernails. Lots of times, that's a real giveaway."

"I will," the woman promised, her voice deepening

now. "But I don't hafta go into the cabin now." Insinuation laced her voice. "Why don't we go back up on deck and walk around some more?"

"I don't know about the walkin'," he gibed. Their voices were beginning to fade. They were moving away from the cabin.

Eulalie lay motionless, terror running through her, her mind struggling to cope with this newest obstacle to freedom. The massa would advertise for her. He be mad, with five of them runnin' off at one time. That was a powe'ful lot of money he was losin'. Maybe they catched the others—but it was her hide she be worryin' about now.

Her mind grew crystal clear with her need. She could not wait till morning, till daylight. She had to get off the boat before it reached Baltimore. In a while, the woman would return from her carousing. She would fall asleep. While her roommate slept, she would have to get off the boat. Eulalie shivered. She could swim well, from all the summers in the Chattahoochee—but this was a long stretch to shore. Could she make it? She had no choice. She had to make it.

Every minute dragged painfully, until the blonde was stealthily creeping back into the cabin. Eulalie tried not to blink when the blonde brought the lamp over to the berths, turned it on, held it so that the light spilled on Eulalie's hands. The woman grunted, turned off the lamp. Eulalie heard the buxom body settling itself in the berth below. In a matter of minutes, the woman was snoring.

All right, Eulalie exhorted herself. She sat up carefully in order not to hit her head. She had come this far; she wasn't going to be caught this close to freedom! Cautiously, nerves on edge, she lowered herself from the berth, bringing along with her the carpetbag she had taken up earlier. This was her dowry, and she had not left it in the community area of the cabin.

Watching the shadowed face of the woman for any sign of awakening, Eulalie began to undress. She took off the gray frock and the petticoat, rolled them up, and stuffed them inside the meagerly filled carpetbag. In pantaloons and camisole, the carpetbag clutched tightly in her hands, Eulalie stealthily left the cabin, climbed up the stairs to the deck. She was terrified at every sound. At this hour of the night, the crew—except for those essential to the movement of the boat—were sleeping in their berths, she encouraged herself.

She spied a shadow coming towards her. She flattened into a dark corner, frightened that her labored breathing would give her away. The man strode past, unaware of her presence, and Eulalie said a silent prayer. The deck on this side was clear. She moved to the railing. How dark the water looked! How terrifying!

The nearly full moon, which had been shining brightly earlier in the evening, had taken refuge behind the clouds. Her throat tight, Eulalie approached the pile of logs used to feed the engine. She clutched at one log, lifted it in her slim, strong arms, walked to the railing, thrust the log into the water.

Eulalie froze at the splashing sound. Her eyes darted about nervously. Nobody had noticed, not with the paddle wheels cutting through the water. No one came to investigate. Now, Eulalie told herself. Now she must follow that log into the water! Feeling queasy, she stared at the paddle wheels. She knew that would happen if she jumped within the reach of those paddle wheels. No, don't think about that. Jump!

Eulalie hit the water. For a moment, she was startled by its iciness. She lifted her head, the hair plastered wetly about her face, and looked about for the log. There it was. Holding firmly to the carpetbag, she swam towards the log, grabbed hold of it, pushed it ahead of her.

One final look at the boat, as she drove towards shore, told her that her absence had not been noted. It would not be discovered until the boat arrived at the wharf in Baltimore. Too late for the pair of conspirators to catch up with her.

She swam till she was near exhaustion, then turned on her back to float. It was a long haul to shore, but Eulalie aimed to make it. Yet she realized, with somber misgivings, that she was not yet in a free state. Yonder, along the shore, was the state of Virginia. A slave state.

13

Eulalie felt the sand beneath her feet. She could stand now, walk to shore. Relief encircled her with comforting warmth. She clung to the carpetbag and allowed the log to go its own way while she struggled through the remaining feet of water.

On the sandy beach, she fell to her knees. Exhausted, grateful, suddenly overcome with a need for sleep. With the carpetbag for a pillow to cradle her head, with the edge of the water safely distant, Eulalie curled up on the pale sand and slept.

She came awake slowly, with a subconscious caution developed in these last days of running. Gradually, the events of last night infiltrated her mind. She opened her eyes to the first rays of morning sunlight. Alarm spiraled in her. Daylight was dangerous. But the strip of beach was deserted. Beyond was a wilderness. Eulalie lifted herself to her feet, reached for her carpetbag, moved with quick, small steps towards the protection of the woods.

Inside her carpetbag, everything was wet. She pulled out the two dresses that comprised her wardrobe—it was the most lavish wardrobe she had ever possessed—the bag of bread that remained from her provisions—it was now useless—the two books, her shoes, her white gloves. Carefully, she opened the books, spread them in a patch of sun to dry, touched the water-logged pages with anxiety.

She lifted her face to the warm Southern sun, found fresh confidence there. She shucked away the sodden pantaloons, the camisole, draped them across the rhododendron bushes that grew here in wild, colorful abundance, reached for the two dresses, her gloves, similarly draped these across other bushes. She set the shoes in a garden of sunlight. Quickly, the summer sun would dry everything.

Eulalie settled herself on the sandy soil, for the present unself-conscious about her nudity because it was hardly likely that she would be disturbed in this wilderness. The birds sang, whizzed about, carried on their friendships and their battles and their lovemaking as though she were not there. Ashore, drying out, relaxing, Eulalie became conscious of hunger. She glanced about curiosuly, spied a berry bush close at hand, inspected it cautiously. She sampled a berry. It was edible. She picked a handful to appease her hunger.

Eulalie's clothes dried swiftly in the hot sun, as she had anticipated. She smoothed the soft cotton as best she could, slipped into the undergarments, then the quiet gray frock. With her belongings packed away in the carpetbag, she sought a protective corner under the bushes, lest someone should finally invade this wilderness and see her. In the shadows of the rhododendron, she lay reading the orations on liberty given her by the Quaker schoolmaster.

At dark, Eulalie knew it was time to move on. She felt a growing discomfort in the pit of her stomach from the lack of food. Maw had long ago taught her not to overeat of the berries that grew in such abundance this time of year. She scanned the sky, searching for the North Star. There, follow the North Star—it would take her to Maryland. She knew that, from Maryland, she would cross over into Pennsylvania, a free state.

By night, she traveled through the woods, moving with nervous haste, starting at any unexpected sound—a twig breaking underfoot, an animal scampering nearby, an unexpected cry. She was impatient to put distance between herself and the beach on which she had landed. At the sight of a chimney billowing smoke from a cookstove into the dark sky, she veered to the west, not able to breathe comfortably until she was beyond sight of the smoke-belching chimney.

Finally, exhausted, she stopped to sleep. She awoke an hour later, with the first color of dawn streaking across the sky. Immediately, she was aware of the gnawing hunger pangs that would be only partially alleviated by berries she might find here in the woods.

Her concept of distance was unknowledgeable. How far to Pennsylvania? She knew, from the studies with David that she must go through Maryland before she arrived at the free state. It might be many days, she realized with misgivings. Days of hiding out in the woods, nights of running. Now there was the problem of food. She couldn't hide another day without food to sustain her.

Her bright, quick mind alert to this new obstacle to escape, Eulalie considered the possibilities open to her. She opened the carpetbag, pulled forth the Free Papers the Quaker schoolmaster had forged for her. Luckily, the papers had been swathed in her clothing—the water of Chesapeake Bay had not touched them. She would have to think her way out, Eulalie realized, even while she trembled at the prospect of making a bravura stand with the Free Papers.

The decision made, Eulalie sought for a spring in which to wash. She found a trickle of a brook instead and swooped up handfuls of cool water to splash on her face. She made an effort to smooth her hair, then inspected her clothes, which hardly looked as though they belonged to a runaway slave. All right, she was ready. She began to walk with fresh purpose, her shoes in one hand.

Eulalie walked for miles in seemingly endless wilderness. Now a new anxiety was taking root in her. Would she find a house, people? Her hunger was growing. She was tempted to overeat of the berries, but resolutely kept away. She could not let herself be sick. With exhaustion blending with panic in her, she spied a house just ahead.

It was a neat brick house with a free-standing chimney and a look of minor prosperity about it. To Eulalie it appeared prosperity. The small-paned windows shone in the morning sunlight. Behind the house were a series of outbuildings, their condition showing little respect on the part of their owners. In the distance, Eulalie saw two men working in the fields.

She hesitated at the back door, her heart pounding. She could hear the woman of the house talking to the children, exhorting them to eat breakfast. Eulalie took a deep breath, knocked. She couldn't go on, she knew—not without food.

Someone was walking across the kitchen floor to the back door. The door swung wide, exposing Eulalie to the agonizingly tantalized aromas of a country breakfast. A heavy woman with ruddy face and sharp eyes stood in the doorway; she was obviously surprised at the appearance of a caller at this hour of the morning.

"What do you want, girl?" the woman demanded suspiciously.

"I be lookin' for a job," Eulalie stammered. "I work good aroun' the house."

Without saying a word to Eulalie, the woman pushed past her to call to a man in the fields.

"Ernst!" she yelled. "Ernst, come over here!"

Now, the woman turned to inspect Eulalie.

"You look like you been walkin' a piece. Hungry?"

"Yes'm," Eulalie admitted, trying not to stare at the table laden with platters of ham and eggs, hominy grits, fluffy, hot biscuits.

"Take yourself a plate and fill it up," the woman ordered, pointing to the cupboard where dishes sat in neat piles. She hesitated a moment. "You can sit at the table with the children."

Silently, quickly, trying not to appear as awkward as she felt, Eulalie took a plate, filled it, sat down to eat. The children watched with avid but friendly curiosity. She ate with her best manners, as learned from careful observance of the Woodstock table. The children whispered among themselves and giggled, yet Eulalie was aware that there was delight in the arrival of someone new in their daily lives.

"Ernst, she says she wants a job workin' around the house," the woman said complacently. "I could use some help, if she can do a day's work."

The man, tall and slightly stooped from the years of tilling the soil, stared quizzically.

"I work hard," Eulalie said eagerly, forgetting the savory plate before her. "I do everything like you say."

"You a runaway slave?" he demanded. "We don't take to them none." His faded blue eyes were cold with disdain.

"I be free," she said with a look of pride, playing the scene as she had planned it. "My Pa bought me, gave me my Free Papers. I show you." She stumbled to her feet, reached for the carpetbag nearby. "Here," she said, handing over the papers.

They seemed impressed by the papers. Hope spiraled in Eulalie. She *had* to hope. If they did not believe her, what would she do? Break out of the house? Run? Her heart pounding, she watched the man and his wife peruse the papers. Only the man could read. He was reading now to his wife.

"What you doin', walking this way?" the woman asked when her husband was done with the reading.

"My Pa be a white man," Eulalie said with dramatic simplicity. "I be the spittin' image of him. He don't wan' me aroun'. He buy me, give me the papers, send me out part ways from home, tell me to walk till I find me a job. I old enough to work, he say." She waited, breathless, fearful, watching the couple before her.

"You sit around doin' nothin', you go out quick," the farmer warned. "You do your work, we pay you—" he squinted in thought, "two dollars every month." He exchanged a trriumphant glance with his wife. Obviously, they were pleased with this situation. "We got a room off the barn. You can fix it up, sleep out there. You eat what we eat. You wanna take the job?"

"Yessuh!" Eulalie's eyes shone.

She would be done with the running for a while. She could stay here until the ads stopped in the newspapers—and she had some money to help her get up to Pennsylvania—and then to New York and Missis Henderson.

Eulalie fitted easily into the Schmidt family routine. She put in a long, hard day's work, which—to Eulalie—was no more arduous than back at The Willows, and for which she would be receiving two dollars every month. She cleaned, scrubbed, washed clothes, looked after the younger children, for whom she developed a genuine affection. Only the oldest son, Carl, disturbed her.

Carl was seventeen, a tall, muscular replica of his father. He was prone to furtive, hungry looks in Eulalie's direction. Sometimes at night, lying on her narrow bed in the lean-to that was her bedroom, Eulalie heard Carl moving about outside. Hastily, she would turn off the kerosene lamp, shove her book or newspaper—she read whatever came to hand—under the bed and lie in darkness, ears tuned uneasily to the sounds of Carl's feet. Whenever her lamp was off, he usually returned to the house.

Fall arrived, and the Schmidt family was busy bringing in the cotton. Some days, Eulalie too was ordered out into the fields to help. Carl was too tired after a day of picking cotton to roam about at night. Eulalie was relieved. Optimistically, Eulalie considered this a crisis passed. She was not yet ready to leave the Schmidt farm. When she had twenty dollars stuffed under the pallet on which she slept, she would leave. The money that David had given her, she kept in a cloth bag attached to a cord which she wore constantly about her neck as though it was a good-luck talisman.

Winter moved in. Eulalie shivered, those nights, in the badly constructed lean-to, which offered little protection against the cold. The weather in Virginia was more severe than what she had known in Georgia. Grudgingly, Helga Schmidt gave Eulalie a cast-off coat that was many sizes too large. The coat served, at night, to supplement the meager, worn-thin blankets that the farmer's wife had given Eulalie with the arrival of frost. A rag was nailed across the glassless opening that pretended to be a window in a futile effort to keep out the cold.

Again, Eulalie was conscious of long, furtive glances from the tall, somber-eyed Carl. His mother too, Eulalie realized, was aware of Carl's interest—and disturbed about it. Eulalie hoped Helga Schmidt would talk to her son. Instead, she became more harsh, more criitcal of Eulalie.

Christmas Day, Eulalie shared the huge Christmas dinner with the Schmidt family. The elder Schmidts relaxed and were almost jovial. After dinner, Eulalie sang for the children, who found this their increasingly favored amusement. Singing the songs Maw had taught her, the plantation songs, she was painfully conscious of Carl's continuing presence, his no longer furtive stares. His parents had gone off to make Christmas calls on neighboring farmers. Carl was in charge.

At dusk, Ernst and Helga reutrned. They brought with them a bottle of cherry brandy, which Ernst poured into three tumblers for himself, his wife, and his son.

Eulalie slipped out of the house into the cold night that carried a threat of snow. Shivering in the ridiculously over-large coat, Eulalie hurried across the cold earth to her shabby accommodations. Christmas was past. She was glad. Christmas made her think about Maw, about the big to-do at the plantation. More and more, she ached to be with Seraphina, to know the cozy warmth of her mother, the kindliness, even the resignation to life. Yet Eulalie knew she would never accept the kind of existence she had known in the past, even the one she knew now. This was but a way station on the road to living.

Eulalie spread her coat across the narrow bed, went to the pretense of a window to secure the rag across the gaping opening—at least to a point where less of the coldness invaded. Satisfied that she had done her best, she moved to turn off the lamp because Helga Schmidt had suddenly become parsimonious about the amount of kerosene Eulalie used. Tonight, she was in no mood to read anyway. She would lie in bed and think about Maw,

Eulalie decided nostalgically—and how it was going to be, someday.

Eulalie was half-dozing off despite the cold when she snapped into wakefulness because someone was tugging at the door. She had the latch on good, she told herself.

"Who there?" she asked fearfully, yet deep inside, Eulalie knew.

"Carl." His voice was thick with excitement. That cherry brandy inside him, Eulalie guessed. "Open up."

"No," she refused calmly. "Go away." She huddled, fully alert beneath the covers. They couldn't hear him, up at the house, not with that wind blowing up outside.

"Come on, Eulalie, open up," Carl wheedled. "Hey, I got a present for you." The children had made presents for her—there had been none from the parents. "Aw, honey, don't be like that." He was keeping his voice low, fearful of being heard up at the house.

"No!" She waited, tense, fearful. "Carl, go away!"

He stopped banging on the door. For a few moments, she believed he had capitulated and was returning to the house—until she saw his fist drive through the rag at the window. She sat up, shaking, her eyes wide. She leaned over for the lamp, turned it on.

"Carl Schmidt, you get out of here," she ordered, her voice rising perilously.

Carl was nonchalantly climbing through the window with a wide smile of satisfaction on his face.

"Now why you bein' so mean to Carl?" he crooned, coming towards her. "That ain't friendly like, 'specially on Christmas night."

"Your Pa'll kill you, he know you here," Eulalie warned shakily.

"Nobody's goin' tell him," Carl said craftily. "He's out in the kitchen with that bottle of cherry brandy. He won't be goin' anywhere, exceptin' maybe to bed. If he can make it there," Carl chuckled.

Eulalie swung her face away from him when he leaned towards her; the cherry brandy had been potent. Her throat was tight. It was happening all over again!

"Get away from me," she tried again, her breathing labored. "Carl, go away—"

His mouth came down, bruising hard on hers. Her hands shoved ineffectually at his muscular body, which was heavy upon her now. She heard the sound of the soft cotton of her dress being ripped down the front. His rough, farmer's hand was beneath her camisole, fumbling towards her breast.

His mouth left hers, his breathing hot upon her.

"No!" she cried out, her voice anguished. "No!"

"Shut up," he ordered thickly. "Shut up, or I'll kill you!"

He pinned her to the bed, with one hand at her breast, pinching until she cried out, while the other hand moved beneath her skirt. Eulalie gritted her teeth in frustration, eyes shut tight, her body tense with revulsion, while he had his way with her.

He lay upon her, triumphant that he had been successful despite the liquor, reluctant to leave her.

"You varmint!" Ernst Schmidt's voice was deep with fury when it shattered the heavy silence. "You git off her, you hear me? Git off!"

"Pa!" Scared, Carl leaped to his feet, and clumsily tried to conceal himself before his father's contemptuous eyes.

"I told your Ma you was hankerin' after that girl! I told you plenty times, Carl—I don't want you with them colored gals!"

Sick inside, Eulalie pulled the covers about her disarray. Her eyes were fastened on the tall, slightly stooped form of Ernst Schmidt swinging over the opening to stand before his son. His face was ruddy with rage.

"What does it matter, Pa?" Carl tried to brazen out his adventure. "Ever'body has got to have a taste of black gal before they's through. And it ain't like she never had it before," he wound up with triumph. "I got in, no trouble t'all."

Eulalie saw the sudden, unexpected flash of desire in the older man's eyes when they turned to her. Fleetingly, they lingered on her, then returned to Carl.

"You git yourself back to the house," his father ordered. "If I catch you layin' with this one again, I'll break your back. Now run!"

Cowed, Carl ran. His father stood there, arms akimbo, chuckling as his son beat a hasty retreat. Fearful, Eulalie waited. Was he goin' to send her packin'? she asked herself. It wasn't her fault. It was him, Carl!

"We don't say nothin' 'bout this to Carl's Ma," Ernst said slowly, his sharp eyes staring at Eulalie. "All right?"

"Yessuh," she agreed cautiously. Why didn't he go? Why was he hangin' aroun' this way? She was conscious of her ripped bodice beneath the sheltering covers, the pantaloons that lay on the floor. She saw his eyes roam to the disarray of the white pantaloons; she saw the glint of passion there, the working of his mouth as he visualized.

"Don't hold it agin' the boy," Ernst said with an unexpected show of good humor, yet Eulalie was frightened. "When he sees a pretty piece like you, it's natural he gits riled up." He ran his tongue about his lips as he walked towards Eulalie. " 'Course, a boy that age don't know nothin'. It takes a man to make a pretty thing like you happy."

He hovered above Eulalie, his faded blue eyes heated, his breathing accelerated.

"No," she whispered intensely when his hand reached to pull the covers away from her. "No!" She felt sick inside. Not again!

"You relax, honey," he coaxed thickly. He was not as drunk as his son had hinted. "I got a nice little present for you." He laughed uproariously as he reached for Eulalie's hand and brought it up to his body. "There now, how's that for a Christmas gift? I'll bet you ain't had nothin' like that in a long time."

"Leave me be," she said, her voice uneven, her eyes ablaze.

"You be nice to Ernst," he ordered. "Otherwise, I might forget myself and go over to the courthouse in town to ask 'em about them Free Papers of your'n." He smiled with nasty satisfaction at Eulalie's reaction of shock. "You wouldn't be wantin' that to happen, would you?"

"No." She was pale, her eyes terrified, the word wrenched from her bloodless lips.

He thrust aside the covers, stared greedily at the bared, golden breasts. He reached to tweak a nipple—not as rough as his son had been, but Eulalie bit at her lip while tears stung her eyelids. When was it goin' to end, this usin' her body this way?

Her skirt was high above her hips, his mouth slobbering at her breast. For a while, she hoped he wouldn't be able, with the liquor in him. She lay there, quiescent, eyes shut, stinging from the salt of her tears, waiting for him to abandon his clumsy attempts. And then suddenly, the roughness of him was tearing into her. He grunted and groaned above her while he strained to achieve his climax.

"Don't be dead wood," he complained. "Gimme some help, girl!"

She tried to close her ears to the raucous sound of pleasure that finally burst from him; she hated her body, for receiving the flow of his passion. Go way, old man!

Eulalie lay sleepless far into the night, debating about running away. Yet daylight seemed to change the whole complexion of her relationship with the older male members of the household. At breakfast, Carl was sullen, chastened. His father pretended that nothing had happened in the night. Moving about in the Schmidt kitchen, Eulalie felt herself encased in unreality, yet to Carl and his father it seemed almost as though nothing had happened.

Eulalie knew better than to say anything to Helga Schmidt. For what use? She wanted to stay here till spring, Eulalie told herself with determination. In the spring, it would be easier to move about—and she would have some money. The pile of dollar bills beneath the pallet was growing.

January moved along uneventfully into February. She told herself it was the long, cold winter that was making her so tired, making her hate to get up in the morning. By the middle of February, she dreaded walking into the kitchen, preparing the lavish country breakfasts. The

Missis was looking at her sharply sometimes, Eulalie thought, without comprehending.

It was the middle of February, Eulalie realized, staring at the calendar as she hovered over the cookstove frying up the thick slabs of ham. Suddenly, waves of nausea swept over her. She was white, trembling. She turned away from the stove, prepared to run for the outdoors. She turned, and there was Helga Schmidt gazing intently at her.

"You be sick, girl?" Helga shot at her.

"Jes' for a minute," Eulalie stammered, closing her eyes fleetingly, fighting down the rebellion in her stomach. "I be all right now," she gasped.

"Get out to your room," Helga lashed at her. "You get out there and I'll be with you in a minute."

"Yes'm," Eulalie whispered, running in her haste without her coat. What had she done wrong now? Why she be sick this way in the mornin'? Was the Missis goin' to purge her? She felt sick again at the prospect of that. Maw used to purge her every spring even though Missis tried to say it do no good.

Eulalie stood inside the lean-to; she was cold now, unhappy, uncertain. She stared as the door swung wide and Helga Schmidt strode into the small room.

"Who did it to you, girl?" Helga demanded furiously. "Which one of them varmints did it?"

Eulalie's eyes widened in shock.

"I not know what you mean—"

"Who put that baby in your belly!" the woman spat back. "Which one of 'em?"

"Me pregnant?" Eulalie's eyes dilated. Again her stomach churned.

"Don't you know you missed your time?" the woman demanded contemptuously. Eulalie's mind tried to cope with this, all the time ricocheting with the ugliness the woman had put into words. "Don't you know the mornin' sickness is a sign you be with child?"

"I not know," Eulalie said humbly. She was rocked by this confrontation with her condition. "I not know—" Her arms moved about her breasts, each hand clutching at the other arm. She moved back and forth in an ageless movement of anguish. "Oh, Missis, what I do?"

"Which one give you the baby?" Helga Schmidt rasped. "Which one?"

"I not know," Eulalie said simply, her eyes eloquent. "Both take."

Helga Schmidt took a deep, shuddering breath. "When?"

"Christmas night." Eulalie lower her eyes, her face hot with remembrance. "First the boy, then—then the Massa. He—he say I not talk."

"You no-good tramp!" the woman shrieked. "Comin' into my house, leadin' them both on!" Her hand slapped out at Eulalie's face with such force that Eulalie staggered. "You get outta here—we don't want the likes of you around!" Helga's eyes fastened on the pallet. She strode across to pick it up, her eyes smug when they lighted on the small packet of dollars.

"They's mine!" Eulalie's voice rose in shrill indignation when she realized Helga's intent.

"No more, they ain't!" Helga reached for the bills, shoved them down towards her mountainous breasts. Again her hand swung out, this time caught Eulalie by the side of the head. "I'm givin' you twenty minutes to pick yourself up and get out of here—before we hitch up the horses and drive into town to tell 'em we've got ourselves a runaway slave out at the farm! Now, you get outta here, girl!"

14

Eulalie walked with compulsive swiftness, the road hard and cold beneath her feet, the carpetbag clutched tightly in one hand. Running. Again, she was running. Incongruously, she wore the dainty shoes, the immaculate white gloves the peddler had given her, all those months ago.

She had to find a job again, Eulalie warned herself sternly. Maybe the woman be wrong about the baby. Maybe nothin' in her belly but the early spring sickness that come sometime. Don' think about the baby—think about findin' a job.

Eulalie frowned, concentrating on the newness on the horizon. In the distance, she saw the cluster of houses that made up the small town to which the Schmidts traveled once a month to buy provisions. Despite her anguish, her fears, Eulalie found her mind sharp-edged, instinctively groping for the answers she needed.

The Schmidts wouldn't be comin' into town for another three weeks, Eulalie told herself. Find a job in town, hope nobody ask questions, pray she pass for white. With a little more money, she could—maybe—buy a railroad ticket to take her up to Philadelphia. Into a free state. Like the peddler say, you be bold and you get 'way with a lot. She be bold. 'Course, since they pass that Fugitive Slave Law up in Washington, no state be real safe for a runaway slave. A slave could be sent back if somebody grabbed holt and showed she was wanted—even if she be in a free state. But she not want to go to Canada where it be real safe. She want to go to New York where someday David come, like he say.

Eulalie slowed down, her body aching, her feet burning from the miles she had walked without realizing it. She started, swung her head about at the sound of horses' hoofs in the distance. Somebody was coming down the road! In panic, she scurried off into the bushes.

Not until the wagon was barely twenty feet from where she concealed herself in the underbrush, did Eulalie realize she had lost one of her shoes in the dash to hiding. Now, desire to retrieve the lost shoe battled with her sense of what was the safe thing to do. Wistfully torn, she gazed at the dainty shoe lying on the dusty road.

On impulse, Eulalie darted from the underbrush into the road and grabbed for the shoe before the team of horses could trample upon it.

"Whoa-a-a!" The horses were pulled to an abrupt halt, while Eulalie sprinted for cover. "Girl!" a woman's voice called out peremptorily. "Why are you hiding there in the bushes? Come out here!"

Her heart pounding, her eyes widened in astonishment, Eulalie slowly emerged. A woman, alone on the wagon. Eulalie had thought there were more folks there. She should have run, she scolded herself silently—but there was only the one woman on the wagon. She hesitated, the shoe in one hand, the carpetbag in the other, poised for flight.

Unexpectedly, the woman smiled, as though aware that she had terrified Eulalie.

"I'll ride you into town," the woman offered. "No need for you to hop around like a scared rabbit. Come on, climb aboard."

Awkwardly, Eulalie scrambled up to the buckboard. The woman was nice, kind of painted-up, but pretty. Eulalie ducked her head self-consciously, intent on putting on her treasured shoe.

"What's a sweet young thing like you doin', on the road all alone?" The woman's voice was deep, pleasant. "It's over two miles into town."

"I be lookin' for a job," Eulalie said softly. Talk right, she exhorted herself. Maybe the lady think she be—she was—white. "I had a job, workin' at a farm, but—" She reddened, stammered, "They—they sent me away—"

"Menfolks took too much of a likin' to you, I'll bet," the woman guessed, smiling cynically. "It's hard on a pretty girl who's left alone to make her own way in the world. Always some man with ideas."

"You need a girl to work for you?" Eulalie asked softly, emboldened by the woman's friendliness.

"Well, I might," the woman said slowly. "Why don't we talk about it when we get to my house?"

"All right," Eulalie accepted happily. "I work hard—you see." She smiled. It was a dazzling, appealing smile.

"My name's Millie Long. What's yours?"

"Eulalie. Eulalie Washington." That was Maw's name—so it was hers, too.

"Look, honey, don't get upset," Millie said with gentle caution, "but if you're runnin' away from some slave-owner, let's stop right here on the road and fix you up before we head into town. We don't want no questions asked."

"Me—I got Free Papers," Eulalie said staunchly, red staining the golden cheeks again.

The woman pulled the horses to a stop, dug into her bag, turned to Eulalie.

"Eulalie, we won't go around trustin' those Free Papers of yours," she soothed, "though in a pinch I know a couple judges in the country who're owin' me favors. Right now, let's fix you up, so nobody gets ideas."

Eulalie sat still, solemn, while Millie dug into a jar and then smoothed a pale substance about Eulalie's face, down into her neck, all the way to the bodice of her dress. Then there was a heavy application of powder. Not like rice powder. What actresses wore on the stage, Millie explained. Finally, Millie straightened up and surveyed her efforts with satisfaction.

"All right, we can drive into town now. You just make sure not to talk too much till we figure out what we're gonna say about you. From now on," she said vigorously, a glint in her eyes, "you're workin' for Millie Long."

They rode the rest of the way into town in near silence. At intervals Millie made caustic comments about the masculine sex in general, and her absentee husband specifically. Eulalie gathered he'd walked out one morning and never showed up again.

Millie Long's house was at the edge of town. It was a two-story, neatly painted frame building with all the window drapes closed tightly, even in the bright of daylight. Back at the plantation, Missis keep the drapes shut that way, Eulalie thought, on hot days when she want to keep out the sun. But this was cold February.

Millie drove the wagon into the barn. She was making an obvious effort to put Eulalie at her ease while the two of them walked to the back door of the house. A tall, angular woman with unsmiling eyes was in the kitchen scrubbing a skillet. She looked up at Millie, then settled her eyes on Eulalie in a long, piercing stare.

"Agnes, Eulalie here is goin' to be stayin' with us." Millie's eyes sternly warned Agnes against any nastiness. Instinctively, Eulalie guessed that Agnes suspected she wasn't white and that she had only contempt for black folks. "You fix up somethin' to eat and bring it into the parlor. Where's Lem?"

"Where would he be this time of day?" Agnes scoffed, with a veiled surliness. "Sleepin'."

"You bring the food into the parlor," Millie said sharply. "I spent all mornin' talking' business with the judge, without him puttin' out anything to eat. Come on, Eulalie." She turned away from Agnes. "Let's go on inside, where it's warm."

The parlor was tiny, with three walls flanked by sofas. A small piano was wedged in at an angle beside the fireplace. A funny kind of room, Eulalie thought, staring curiously at the paintings that hung over the sofas. Dancin' ladies, she guessed—not wearin' much clothes.

"Tell me about your last job," Millie coaxed, dropping onto the end of the sofa that faced the fireplace. She patted the spot beside her in a friendly command for Eulalie to join her.

"I cleaned the house and washed the clothes and took care of the kids. I work hard, ma'am." Her eyes were earnest, clinging to Millie Long's sympathetic face. "I work maybe fifteen hours every day—I—I'm strong." She was speaking carefully, knowing it was urgent that she leave the old manner of speaking behind her. David said she could. Lots of times, with him, she talked good.

"It must have been lonely. A pretty girl like you stuck away on a farm that way." Millie's eyes were bright, probing.

"Yes ma'am." Eulalie's eyes sought the floor in sudden confusion.

"The menfolk give you a hard time?" Millie's voice was a caress.

"Yes ma'am."

"That's all men think about, what they can do with a woman." Disgust laced Millie's voice. "I been around long enough to know. Who was it after you, honey? The father or the kids?"

"Two of them—the father and the boy—" Her eyes slowly lifted themselves from the floor, to meet Millie's in mute misery.

"You mean they took you? Both of them?"

"Yessum." Anguish broke through Eulalie's fragile facade of control. "I—I didn't want to do it with 'em. I told them! They make me—"

"Eulalie—" Millie spoke very quietly. "Are you pregnant?"

"I—I think so." Eulalie's voice was barely audible. "I—I was feelin' sick this mornin'—and Missis Schmidt asked me some questions—" Eulalie halted. "She say I'm pregnant."

"You want to get rid of the kid, Eulalie?"

Eulalie stared in astonishment, a strange relief catapulting through her as she realized what Millie Long was saying. She remembered things that happened on the plantation, how she told herself—back there—if she ever got the Massa's baby in her belly, she make Maw take it away.

"Yes," she whispered. Then more strongly, "Yes."

"It'll be safe," Millie soothed, "you don't have to worry. I'll have the doctor do it. I'll send Agnes for him. He knows all about these things. Afterwards, you rest up for a day or two, and you'll be good as new."

"It hurt?" She didn't *care* if it hurt. Jes' take away this baby that didn't belong in her belly.

"It'll hurt less than havin' it," Millie promised, her eyes bitter. "Don't you know—all men bring with them is pain."

Agnes came in with a tray of savory food and an injured air of being put upon because her employer was sharing a meal with a colored gal.

"Agnes, you tell Lem to hitch up the wagon and drive over to Dr. Logan. You tell Doc I want him over here today, to take care of one of my girls."

"He'll be here Friday mornin' anyhow," Agnes pointed out.

"I don't want him Friday mornin'—I want him now." Millie's face was tight with annoyance. "You go tell Lem to get outta that bed and drive over for Doc."

"This'll be your room, Eulalie," Millie said, opening the door to a small, narrow room with a wide bed, a washstand, and a straight chair. It looked as though it might have once been part of another room. Millie walked over to pull the drapes wide, to allow the late winter sunlight to enter the room. "It's small, but it's comforable."

The bedspread was worn, but it was clean and pretty. A faded rug covered the floor. The washstand had a big, mahogany-framed mirror that shone. There was an odd stillness about the entire house that communicated itself to Eulalie, as though it were waiting for a signal to come alive. Now, the silence was broken by the sound of a wagon arriving.

"That'll be Doc," Millie guessed, staring out of the

window to confirm this. She squinted, straining for a look at the newest arrival. "Yeah, that's him. Now, Eulalie, no call to be nervous," she soothed because suddenly, Eulalie was trembling. "You take off your undergarments to save the doctor time when he gets up here. Just the pantaloons," she stipulated gently because Eulalie looked so stricken. "Then stretch out on the bed. I'll fetch Doc."

Eulalie waited for Millie to leave. She closed the door. Her hands were unsteady when she stepped out of the worn-thin pantaloons, neatly folded them, put them beside the washstand. She hesitated a moment before she lay down on the wide, feather bed. Her heart was pounding.

She wasn't scared of bein' hurt, Eulalie told herself proudly. She been hurt. In that ugly way. She recoiled, knowing what the doctor must do. Feeling shamed at this other kind of invasion. She lay stiff, tense, hearing Millie talking to the doctor while they climbed the stairs.

Eulalie bit at her lower lip when the door opened and the doctor walked inside. He looked like a nice man, she tried to calm herself. Short, heavy, with a too-ready smile, as though it were important to please everybody.

"So this is my patient," he said jovially, striding to the bed. His eyes moved over Eulalie—not in a medical fashion. A man's look. His hand dropped to her belly, palpated without disturbing her modestly arranged dress. "How long?"

"I—I'm not sure." Pride compelled her to speak her best. "Maybe three or four weeks since I miss."

"Good," he encouraged. "The sooner we get in there, the better. Millie, you'll have to help me."

"I done it before," Millie reminded cheerfully. "I told Agnes to bring up plenty hot water. I know how you be about washin' your hands all the time."

Agnes came in, even while Millie spoke about her. With an air of disdain, she poured water into the wash basin and left the room, closing the door loudly behind her. Dr. Logan took off his jacket, rolled up his sleeves. Millie was suddenly at the side of the bed, pulling Eulalie's skirt high above the small belly. Eulalie gritted her teeth, her face hot.

"You're not scared, Eulalie?" Dr. Logan asked genially,

but his eyes watched her. "It's harder when the girl gets hysterical."

"I'm not scared," Eulalie insisted shakily.

"Sorry I don't have any of that fancy anesthesia they got in the big city," he apologized. What did he mean, Eulalie wondered—anesthesia?

"I could get a few shots in her," Millie offered, her face compassionate.

"No!" Eulalie said urgently. Whatever was goin' to happen to her, she wanted to know about it.

Dr. Logan walked to the bed, carrying the wash basin with him. He set it down on the floor at the foot of the bed. Eulalie shut her eyes tightly, humiliated at lying this way before him, all exposed to her waist. And with Millie looking on. Eulalie started when his hand began to explore.

"Relax, girl," he ordered, faintly sharp. "I have to see how far along you are." She lay still, trying to pretend she was unaware of probing fingers. "Not bad," he reported with satisfaction. "Like you said, about seven weeks."

"You got enough light, Doc?" Millie asked.

"Plenty," he said opening his case, reaching inside. Instantly, Eulalie shut her eyes again. "Millie, you'll have to hold her legs."

Eulalie's mind darted to Maw. Why couldn't Maw be here with her, helpin' her? Did this doctor know how to do it? Was she going' to die? Not yet! Oh, not yet! She wanted to be somebody before she died. A lady livin' like Missy lived, better even. Wearin' beautiful clothes, goin' to all kinds of places, learnin' everything.

She was conscious now of Millie's hands positioning and holding her legs so that the knees were bent. Conscious of a sharp, painful intrusion. Involuntarily, a cry broke from her. Like she was bein' pumped up, she thought fearfully.

"Easy, honey—" Millie's voice soothed while Millie's hands gripped tightly. "Relax, like Doc said."

Eulalie felt herself breaking out in a cold sweat. Her hands clutched at the sides of the bed. She bit at her pale lips to keep back the sounds. What was he doin' in her? Her stomach was on fire. If Millie hadn't held on to her legs that way, she would have doubled with pain.

"Take it easy, girl, take it easy," Dr. Logan soothed. "We'll stop for a few minutes."

She lay there, panting, conscious of his hand smoothing her hair in comfort. Millie's hands never lessened their grip on her legs. Then came the scraping again; it brought forth an anguished whimper. Now Eulalie abandoned herself to pain. How much more? When would it be over?

"No!" Eulalie cried out. "No more. Please, no more!"

"Almost over, honey," Millie crooned. "Just a little more—Doc's got to get it all out. Then no more trouble."

A hand soothed her forehead. The scraping stopped, but the cramps were bad. She was conscious of cotton being wadded and thrust within her. It was over. No more baby. The doctor moved away from the bed. He was talking with Millie by the window. The words were barely coherent because Eulalie still battled with pain.

"What's the matter, Millie? Don't you teach your girls to take care of themselves?" the doctor was reproaching. "Third one in the last five months."

"Doc, my girls don't get knocked up here in the house," Millie protested. "It's what they do on the outside. And this one ain't one of my girls. Not yet—"

Slowly, the realization of her whereabouts pierced Eulalie's consciousness. This was a fancy house where white men paid for their pleasures. She stiffened with shock. Perspiration broke out on her forehead.

"Make sure she takes it easy for a day or two. Don't let her take on anybody for ten days anyhow. After that, she'll be okay."

Eulalie moved quietly about the house those first two weeks. Millie had insisted she stay in bed until late the second day, then brought her into the kitchen to help Agnes. Agnes was polite because she knew better than to cross Millie, who obviously wanted to keep Eulalie working in the house.

Eulalie fell into a pattern. She worked about the house during the day, scurrying to the seclusion of her room at nightfall when the raucous evening existence in the house commenced. She heard the piano playing, too loudly, downstairs, the ribald laughter of the men, the giggles of the girls, the walking up and down the halls, the sounds of bought passion being enacted in rooms on either side of her. She lay in the darkness and studied her words, fearing she had slipped back in these weeks of panic. Safety could depend upon her passing for white. Miss Millie said she could be high-born Spanish or Mexican—so long as she didn't give herself away talkin' like black. She repeated over and over again from memory favored poems from the book David had given her, orations from the book that had been a gift from the Quaker schoolmaster. Until eventually, cradled by poetry and the eloquence on liberty, she would fall into troubled sleep.

The other girls regarded Eulalie with frank curiosity and a certain mistrust. They were all older than she, Eulalie realized. They wore paint on their faces and wandered around the house in lacy, see-through garments that made her vaguely uncomfortable because white ladies were not supposed to be like that. But they were not regular white ladies, she kept telling herself—they were whores.

Eulalie was always the first one in the kitchen in the morning. The girls slept into the afternoon. Eulalie boiled the coffee, so it would be ready for Agnes and Millie and Lem whenever they showed up. She relished the morning solitude in the kitchen with its cozy warmth, its windows pleasantly steamed up, protecting her—it seemed—from a hostile outside world.

Coming into the kitchen this morning, Eulalie looked at the calendar Miss Millie kept hanging on the wall. Friday again. Her third Friday here. Each Friday—just before the doctor came to look over the girls—Miss Millie gave her fifty cents for herself. Miss Millie was the finest lady that ever lived, Eulalie thought with adoration—even if she did keep this fancy house. Look how Miss Millie give her money every week, be so friendly—look how Miss Millie help her get shed of the baby. Even now she shivered, thinking how it might have been if she hadn't met Miss Millie there on the road that day.

At unexpected, startling moments, she thought about the baby that had been aborted. You did that with a man, she thought with fresh understanding of the miracle of life, and sometimes a baby grew. She did it with David, but nothin' happened—it was the wrong time, like Maw said about breedin'. If it had been David's baby in her belly, would she have got shed of it? No, she decided violently! And was shocked at this reaction in her.

Eulalie put up the coffee so that it would be ready for the others when they came into the kitchen. Why did she have this funny feeling? She had a real room of her own, plenty to eat, fifty cents every week to keep—and Miss Millie was always givin' her clothes. But she didn't want to spend all her life cleanin' up folks' houses, washin' for them, and all—that's why she had this feelin' in her.

The girls in the house talked about New York, how wonderful it was. There was goin' to be a World's Fair there this year, the first one ever in the United States. She and David had read about having them in Europe, Eulalie remembered vaguely. How did you get to New York from here? It was a long ways off. It would take a pow'ful lot of money to get there. A lot of fifty-cent pieces. But David's Cousin Madeline—Missis Henderson—lived in New York. That was where David would go when he went to New York. That was where she had to go. Missis Henderson would help her—she knew that.

"Good-morning, Eulalie." Millie's cheerful, faintly husky voice broke into her introspection. "Do I smell fresh coffee boiling?"

"Yes ma'am." Smiling, Eulalie went over to the pot, poured a cup.

"Sit down and have coffee with me," Millie commanded good-humoredly. "I want to talk to you, honey."

Self-conscious, slightly uneasy, Eulalie complied. Had she been doin' somethin' wrong? Wasn't Miss Millie pleased with her no more? But Miss Millie was reachin' in her pocket to give her the fifty-cent piece right this minute.

"Eulalie, you're a mighty pretty girl," Millie said softly. "It seems to me a terrible waste, havin' you cleanin' and cookin'. Some of my customers would be right happy to pay fifty cents to be with a girl like you. For maybe fifteen minutes," she said pointedly, handing over the

fifty-cent piece, for which Eulalie worked a whole week.
" 'Course, you split that down the middle with me," Millie
said with candor. "But on good nights you could have
yourself three, maybe four customers a night. That's a nice
piece of change at the end of the week. And you're not
the kind to run into town and blow all that money on
some crazy man or on drinkin' and carousin'." She watched
Eulalie intently.

Color flooded Eulalie's face.

"I—I couldn't, Miss Millie."

"Eulalie, let's talk frankly." Millie smiled persuasively,
leaning across the table. "You ain't a virgin—you don't
have to worry about losin' it. And those fellows at the
farm, and the others, back wherever you ran away from—
they took what they wanted, didn't they? And they didn't
give you nothin'! Except one of them, along the road
gave you that baby. So I say, when you make a man pay
for usin' you, you're gettin' the laugh on them. You're
givin' them nothin'—and they're payin'."

"I don't want nothin' like that no more," Eulalie whispered, her cheeks hot. "No, Miss Millie."

"Honey, what have you got here? Scared even to leave
the house, to go into town. At night, with only the lamps
on, and you painted up, no man's gonna know you ain't
white. He's not goin' to ask questions." Her laughter was
harsh in the quietness of the kitchen. "You work plenty,
save up your money, and you can buy your way to New
York." Eulalie started. "That's where you belong, Eulalie.
Why, I hear tell there's more than half a million folks
there. When there's that many folks millin' around, they're
too busy to be askin' questions. In a city like New York,
you find lots of Mexican and Spanish girls—they'll take
you for that, for sure, the nice way you talk and all."

"I mean to go to New York," Eulalie admitted, lifting
her head high in determination. "But not like that, Miss
Millie. I couldn't do it."

"You think about it," Millie coaxed. "You change your
mind, you let me know."

More and more work was shifted to Eulalie's young
shoulders when Agnes realized she accepted it without

remonstrances. The drabness of Eulalie's existence, the monotony of being indoors constantly began to foment restlessness in her. But it would be a long time before she could leave, Eulalie warned herself. She wasn't takin' chances the way she'd been. When she left here, she would travel in the right way—like white folks. By coach and boat, and maybe on the railroad train. She was learnin', she thought with defiant certainty. You listened to everything folks said around you—and you learned.

By the end of her first month, Eulalie felt as though she had been in the house for a year. The girls ignored her now. Occasionally, she was conscious of a contempt on their part. She was fascinated, though, by the way they lived as she listened to the stories told about the kitchen by Agnes and Millie. She knew which whore was keeping a card shark in town, which one spent her free time—and all her money—trying to beat the gambling tables, which one had a pretty little sister living in a boarding house in town and going to school there—though, from snide remarks she overheard in the halls, Eulalie gathered some did not believe the girl was the little sister, and so the whore's motives hardly seemed so admirable.

Eulalie lay in her bed, the room dark, listening with distaste to the evening sounds, the thumping of the piano, the raucous voices. What was Maw doin' back home? Was the Massa takin' it out on Maw for her runnin' off? Someday, she'd send for Maw, get her away from the plantation. She'd do anything, Eulalie told herself intensely, to bring Maw up No'th, to be with her.

Eulalie started at the faint tap on the door. It was opening!

"It's me, Eulalie," Millie said in a quick, reassuring whisper. She closed the door, found the lamp, lit it. Eulalie half-sat up in bed, terrified, thinking only that somebody was on her trail. Somebody read an ad about her, was coming to take her back for the reward. "Honey——" Millie came over to sit at the edge of the bed, "we're havin' one of the best nights ever. I've got this handsome young fellow downstairs just pantin' to spend his money. But he says he don't want no old crows."

"Your girls not old," Eulalie objected defensively. Her heart pounded. She read Millie's mind.

"Eulalie, this is the judge's son—if he gets ornery, he'll go into town and have his old man close me up. He's in that kinda mood. I paraded half the girls before him, and he ain't havin' none of 'em. I know he won't like the others." Millie was visibly upset. It was real, Eulalie was certain. "Honey, I helped you out when you were in trouble. Now I'm asking you to help me."

Eulalie's eyes darkened in rejection. Yet she knew she could not turn Miss Millie down. Not after what Miss Millie had done for her.

"Just—just this once?" Eulalie stammered, her insides turning over. It was worse when you got paid for it, she thought, sickened.

"Just this once, honey," Millie purred. "And he'll pay a dollar. That's fifty cents for you." Millie smiled brilliantly, knowing she had won. "Now, you make out like you're crazy about it, you hear? Give him plenty of action."

"Yes ma'am." Eulalie's throat was dry, her eyes fearful.

"Remember, you're not *givin'* him nothin'," Millie said, a glint in her eyes. "He payin'."

Eulalie waited while Millie went out to bring her one of the filmy garments the whores wore. Docilely, she took off her clothes, changed into the wrapper, sat still while Millie painted her face.

"There, you look fine," Millie said with satisfaction. "I'll bring him up."

Eulalie sat on the edge of the bed—staring without seeing, hearing the sounds on either side of her room, and knowing the same sounds would be coming from this room in a few minutes. She wasn't goin' to be knocked up this time—Miss Millie taught her 'bout that. She had to do this for Miss Millie after all Miss Millie done for her.

The door opened. A man came in. Tall, young, swaggering. Eulalie closed her eyes when he grabbed at her. This room would never be the same again after tonight. Nothin' had really changed, had it? Except this time, the man was payin'.

15

It was an unexpectedly cold, drab April day when the Woodstock carriage turned in the lane that led up to The Willows. Cindy gazed out at the midafternoon grayness with a petulant frown of distaste which was not lost on her father.

"Weren't you over there in London long enough?" he demanded with jovial reproach. "Why, you should have come back home last June!"

"Papa, you wouldn't have wanted me to come back in all that heat." The guileless green eyes managed to chide and adore simultaneously. Cindy knew the potency of the look. "How many times in my life are you going to let me go off to London that way?" Fleetingly, her eyes went opaque while her mind banished the knowledge that she had been shipped off to London in disgrace. "And there's the World's Fair coming to New York this summer, and I'm missing it." She pouted, a slender finger stroking the rough, stubby ones of her father. "I wrote Mama to let me stop off to visit with the New York cousins before I came on home."

"You've seen enough for one young lady." His eyes could not conceal their satisfaction, though, at the modishly turned-out daughter before him. "Cost me so much I turned sick to think about it. Every time I got a letter from you, I had to send you more money for clothes." His eyes went somber. "And it's been a bad year at The Willows." He glanced at his watch, scowled, leaned forward. "Aristotle, you make those horses move. I'm expecting a business caller any minute now."

"Oh, Papa, business even on the day I'm coming home?" Cindy flirted provocatively with her father.

"With your expensive taste I have to make some money," he reminded, good humor returning. "Bradford Taylor—you know the Taylor plantation, about ten miles to the south—he has a stud he wants to sell. But never mind that—tell me about the house out there in Sussex. You know how proud your Mama is about her sisters in England."

"They were just horrid the last few months I was over there." She forgot her earlier intimation that her father was dragging her back from a veritable ball. Green eyes smoldered with resentment. "Just expecting me to sit around the house all the time, never going down to London any more—when it was less than an hour by carriage."

"What about all the young men you were meeting?" he demanded joshingly. "You kept writing about all the fine parties." George Woodstock narrowly scrutinized his daughter, anxiety for her showing through. "Your mother kept thinking you'd find yourself a husband over there."

"Papa, you wouldn't want me to marry an Englishman!" She pretended hurt. "And live all the way over there?"

"You know I've been pining away for you, since the day you left," her father chuckled.

"How's Mama and David?" Cindy leaned forward to gaze out the window. Cold as it was, Mama was out on the portico waiting to welcome her. Leave it to Mama to do a fool thing like that.

"Mama's the same as she always was," George said with

sardonic humor. "David—well, the older he gets, the less I understand him."

The carriage pulled up before the portico. Margaret Woodstock, tears in her eyes, moved swiftly to embrace her daughter. David, looking self-conscious, taller, more handsome, came forward to kiss his sister. Then Cindy was swooped up to Seraphina's capacious bosom.

"Oh, my beautiful li'l' baby done come home," Seraphina crooned richly. "This house don' be de same wit' yo' gone, Missy."

"I brought back the mail, Margaret," her husband said, his eyes focusing on the lane because a carriage was turning in. "A letter for you from Cousin Madeline in New York."

"It's raw outside." Margaret looked at the envelope for an instant, folded it over in her hands. "Let's go into the house. Seraphina, bring us hot chocolate in the drawing room."

"Aristotle, you get your lazy body down from there and bring Missy's luggage into the house," George bellowed. "I'll be in directly, Margaret. I think that's Bradford Taylor showing up now. He'll be staying for the night, Margaret," he called sharply as his wife and children moved into the foyer.

"I was expecting that, George," his wife threw over her shoulder. "I haven't forgotten how to be a good hostess."

The house looked less elegant, Cindy decided. Maybe she had been in England too long, seeing all those marvelous houses. And Mama wasn't spending money as freely as she used to, with Papa crying all the time about the bad crops. How was she going to stand it, tied down to The Willows again? She would go stark, raving mad!

"Cindy, darling, I'm so glad you had such a wonderful time in England." Margaret dropped an arm about her daughter as they turned into the drawing room with David trailing behind them. "I want to hear about every minute."

"I told Papa," she began in an aggrieved tone, "it wasn't very nice, the last few months. Almost like I was a prisoner, the way they kept me in the country."

"Why, Cindy, that doesn't sound like your aunts," Margaret reproached, a nervous glint showing in her eyes.

"Well, they did!" Cindy didn't mention that Kathy had snitched about her sneaking out to meet John Seymour. They were practically engaged—until after that night. The sullen, pink mouth tightened. He was so shocked when she said she wanted to do it with him before they got married. Oh, he wanted to do it lots of times—after that night. He just wasn't interested in marrying her any more. "You could just die, sitting around out there in Sussex with nothing to do." She allowed Mama to draw her down on the sofa beside her where the blazing fire in the tall, marble-topped fireplace could send its warmth out to comfort them. "What's Cousin Madeline writing you about?" she asked curiously. "She isn't coming down for another visit, is she?"

"I doubt that," Margaret began vaguely, pulling at the envelope. "You want the stamp, David?"

"I don't care." David stared down into the fireplace, looking as though he'd like to take off.

"Papa's business company is here," Cindy said, listening to the sounds in the foyer.

"Well now, we can talk business later, Bradford," George Woodstock said with the expansive Southern charm he was known to siphon out when the results seemed to merit it. "Let's go into the drawing room and have something to drink. You had a long, cold drive over here."

The two men sauntered into the drawing room. Cindy was chattering vivaciously with her mother and David, putting on a performance for Bradford Taylor. Oh, he was old, she realized with disappointment. Almost as old as Papa.

"Bradford, you wouldn't recognize my little girl, Cindy," George introduced fatuously. "She just came back from a year in London, a full grown young lady."

"A beautiful young lady," Bradford said with the expected gallantry, yet Cindy suspected he was not really impressed. "London must have been exciting for you."

"For a while." Cindy was cool, annoyed that Taylor had

not been smitten by her charms. "Have you ever been there?" A faint note of superiority crept into her voice.

"No, I haven't." Taylor sat on the chair that faced the sofa. "I like New York personally, when I can get away from the plantation. Though one of these days," he said with a narrow look of dedication, "I hope to spend some time in Paris. I understand that's about the wickedest city in the world. Even more so than New York."

"Why, Mr. Taylor," Margaret rebuked, "what kind of an impression of yourself are you trying to give us?"

"Mama's cousin lives in New York," Cindy drawled. "I doubt that she's very wicked."

"What did Madeline have to say for herself?" George demanded, his voice laced with sarcasm. He was pouring generous shots of bourbon, the glint of amusement in his eyes telling Cindy he realized her mother was watching and suffering. Mama's drinking was in secret.

"I haven't read it yet, George." Her eyes fastened to the bourbon, the tip of her tongue delicately moving about her lower lip.

"Read it, Margaret," he ordered humorously. "Let Bradford here know the latest word from the city. You said something about going up soon, Bradford," he reminded his guest.

"At intervals, when the pressure gets heavy at the plantation, I go away for a few weeks," Bradford conceded. "Remember, I run the place practically on my own."

"Time you got married, raised a family," George joshed. "That fine, big house, with nobody but you rattling around in it."

Cindy's eyes widened. Her face colored. Her eyes sought David's, seeking sympathy for this covert affront. Did Papa think she would be interested in marrying Mr. Taylor? That old man? Was Papa so nervous about getting her married? She was only nineteen.

"I wouldn't be wishing myself on any nice young lady," Bradford hedged with a show of amusement. "I work hard, play hard. With luck, I'll come up one of these days with a substantial overseer. Then I can go traveling about, enjoying life."

"Oh, my goodness!" Margaret's voice was shocked as her eyes scanned the letter spread across the silken pink of her frock. "How could Madeline!"

"What's the matter, Margaret?" Her husband looked mildly annoyed at the outburst.

"It's Madeline," Margaret said. "Mr. Taylor, please excuse me for dragging in personal matters this way—but Cousin Madeline moved up to New York when she was just a baby. She's developed some strange ideas."

"Get to the point, Margaret!" George's smile was ironic.

"Her husband built her a beauiful brownstone house on Fifth Avenue. That's one of the nicest places to live in New York City—"

"I know," Taylor said indulgently.

Margaret took a breath.

"What do you think Madeline did right after they moved into the house seven weeks ago? She invited this—this colored family for supper. To visit them *socially*. Even in New York, respectable white folks don't do that. Now, nobody else will set foot in their house. They've been absolutely ostracized! Her husband is so moritfied, he can hardly go down to the office and face his business associates, I gather. He's sending Madeline to Paris, to live for a year."

"Paris!" Cindy sat up, envy shining on her face. Why was David looking so upset, she wondered in the back of her mind? Had he grown so attached to Cousin Madeline when she was down here?

"They're closing up that beautiful house, and he's going to live at the Metropolitan Hotel while Cousin Madeline is in Paris. I suppose, until things blow over," Margaret wound up, breathless from the effort of explanation.

Mama was changing, Cindy thought. Mama used to take up for the colored folks all the time. Oh, Mama believed in keeping them in their place—but look how she used to keep Eulalie around the house all the time. Letting her learn to read and write and do arithmetic and all.

Giving her airs. Something had happened, these months she had been gone, Cindy guessed with an inner triumph. It was going to be fun to find out what happened.

Seraphina came into the drawing room, heavy of body but still graceful, as she carried the highly polished silver tray with its hot-chocolate service and lady fingers on the Woodstock's finest china.

"Don't give Mr. Taylor nor me any of that bilge," George warned Seraphina. "We're helping ourselves from the bar."

"Seraphina," Cindy said, her voice a velvet drawl, "I brought you a present from London."

"Thankee, Missy."

Seraphina shot a sharp glance in the direction of their guest. Had Seraphina guessed Papa had ideas about Mr. Taylor and her? Seraphina wouldn't like that, Cindy decided with righteous satisfaction.

This wasn't the old Seraphina, Cindy decided. Had Papa been carrying on with the slaves again? What about Alexander? Was he still around? Not that Alexander was going to be any good to anybody after what Papa did to him. How did it feel to be like that?

"I bought something for Eulalie too," Cindy improvised, at a momentary lull in the conversation. She watched Seraphina for that familiar look of adoration which had been strangely lacking since her initial warm welcome. "Tell her, Seraphina—"

"Don't mention that black bitch's name in this house!" A vein throbbed angrily in George Woodstock's forehead. "Your mother makes over her like she's quality, and what happens? The bitch runs off!"

"George," Margaret Woodstock tried to intervene, embarrased by the outburst.

"Cost me about two thousand, I'd say," George went on, ignoring his wife. Cindy listened avidly—so that was why Seraphina was behaving so strangely. "The same night, I lost the best stud on the plantation, plus three other field hands. You can't trust those black bastards, I tell you! You can't trust a damn one of them!"

Seraphina, stricken, had fled to the kitchen.

The house was quiet, except for the low hum of male voices in the library downstairs. Papa and Bradford Taylor, bargaining for that stud Taylor wanted to sell so he would have cash to run up to New York and live it up wild. Did Papa really think she would marry somebody as old as that?

Still, it nagged at her that Bradford Taylor had not succumbed to her charms. He would be different, she guessed smugly, if they were alone in his bedroom. She knew how to make him different. A secretive, complacent smile touched her mouth. John Seymour just about jumped out the window. But he didn't want to marry her any more.

Cindy tossed back the covers, reached for her wrapper, walked across to the crackling fire that would probably last until dawn. Papa was downstairs, talking with Bradford Taylor. Mama would be drinking in her room. What about David? How did he stand it around here? Curiosity spiraled in her. Had he taken himself a black wench?

On impulse, Cindy left her room, went down the carpeted corridor to David's room. En route, she passed her mother's door, hesitated fleetingly. Seraphina was with Mama. It must be awful to be a slave and have to listen to Papa carry on that way. She had never thought before about how slaves feel—maybe she never really thought they *could* feel. Papa always said their nervous systems were different from white folks'. But even now, all this time afterward, she could remember how Alexander felt— that time in the fields, when she reached out to touch him, there.

Cindy knocked lightly at David's door.

"David?"

"What do you want?" David's voice was startled. But he wasn't sleeping.

"Can I come in?"

"All right."

Cindy opened the door, walked in, carefully closed it behind her. David's bed was turned down, but he had not been in it. The sheets were unwrinkled, the blankets undisturbed.

"I didn't feel like being by myself," Cindy said with deceptive sweetness. "Can I stay a while and talk to you?"

"All right." David walked from the window, where he had been staring into the night, to take one of the two chairs flanking the fireplace. His eyes were curious when they rested on Cindy.

"Was it bad?" she asked. "When Eulalie and the others ran away like that?"

"He carried on like the devil!" David said violently. "He made it hell for everybody at The Willows!" David never used to swear. To Cindy, this brought his new maturity into flattering focus.

"I don't know why Papa behaves the way he does." Covertly, she watched David. "I mean—he can do anything he wants, and it's all right." Her eyes were suddenly jeweled with excitement. "David, why did Eulalie run away? Was Papa chasing after her?"

David's cheeks were flushed, his eyes angry.

"What do you know about those things?"

"Oh, David," she reproached. "How can you grow up in this house and not know? Ever since I was five or six, I guess, I knew about the black gals Papa took into his room. Maybe I didn't know what he did with them then, but I learned fast enough." Her eyes glittered with remembrance. "I was about eleven the night I opened the door to his room because I heard those funny sounds. They were on the floor, both of them naked. Papa was on top of her—"

"Shut up!" David lashed out, his voice furious but low. "How can you talk like that about your own father?"

"I hated him then." Cindy ignored his reproach. " I went to bed and cried myself to sleep. I hated every nigger wench he took. I knew about every one of them. When did Eulalie join the parade?"

"I don't want to talk about it." He turned his face from Cindy.

"I knew sooner or later Papa would get her," Cindy said softly. "Maybe that's one of the reasons I hated her.

But of course I hated her before then," she went on matter-of-factly.

"Why?" David's attention was drawn compulsively to her.

"Oh, the way Mama took her on for a little pet. How old was I then? I guess no more than six or seven, but I remembered. Mama kept Eulalie in her room all the time then, to have somebody to talk to when she was lonely at nights, she used to say. She wasn't going to wake one of *us* up and disturb *our* sleep," Cindy reminded. "But I hated that Eulalie then, and I hated her when she started the lessons with you. It seemed like she was always getting between me and somebody that belonged to me." Her eyes were bright when they returned to David. "How did she like it, Miss High-and-Mighty, when Papa used her like any other black wench about the place?"

"I didn't say that," David countered, reddening.

"You don't have to," Cindy threw back at him with triumph. "I know. That was one of the reasons she ran away. I always knew she would someday. I don't blame her," Cindy wound up honestly. "Only I guess it just about broke Seraphina's heart. She'll never run away. Not even to go to Eulalie. She'll spend the rest of her life making up to Papa because her baby ran off that way."

"Go back to your room, Cindy." David was unfamiliarly brusque. "I want to go to sleep."

"David—" Cindy's voice was caressingly soft. "What about Eulalie and you? Did you ever do it with her?"

"Get out!" David's voice rose traitorously to the edge of hysteria. "Get out of here before I tell Mama how you've been talking!"

"You won't do that." Cindy smiled securely.

"How do you know?" David challenged.

"Because you don't like to start trouble. You're like Mama. All bursting with ideals and principles. I'm like Papa. I take what I want. When I can get away with it," she amended. "Eulalie's the smartest one of us all. She got out of here."

"Why did you come back?" David demanded savagely.

"I had to, for now," Cindy stated calmly. "Aunt Sara

and the girls were making it miserable for me, and Papa threatened not to send another penny for new clothes. I had to come home." She shrugged wryly. "But I won't be staying here, David. I'll get away again. And this time, I won't be coming back. You'll have Mama and Papa and The Willows all for yourself, for the rest of your life. You'll never get away, David!"

16

Eulalie came awake slowly, aware of the noontime spring sun infiltrating the drapes drawn tightly at the windows. She opened her eyes. Instantly, her mind was drenched with her surroundings. She had lived in an aura of unreality these past three weeks. Yet within that unreality, her mind grappled with reality.

Millie was lying to her about the split. Right off, Eulalie grasped that when one of the customers left her a tip with a telling remark. She even suspected Millie had lied about the judge's son, that the crisis had been contrived. But she was seeing more money than she had ever seen in her whole life. She envisioned New York ahead of her in the foreseeable future. Her money was safely hidden where she was sure neither Millie nor any curious girl might look—pinned into a bag she had attached to the top of the drapes.

Eulalie lay still, her mind active. Sometimes you did things because it was the only way to get some place, she reasoned. You didn't like doin' it, but what happened after made it wo'th your while doin'. Every man that came into her room was buyin' her another piece along the way to New York. Millie was right about some things.

Eulalie stiffened to attention. What was goin' on out in the hall? The girls fightin' again, she realized with distaste. No, it was Millie, battlin' with somebody. Iris. It was Iris out in the hall with Millie.

"I don't care!" Iris's voice rose stridently. "That fancy little nigger has taken on Del Mattox four times in the last two weeks. He's the only one around here who leaves somethin' extra for the girl! How come she's the only one who gets him?"

"Del Mattox asks for her, that's why!" Millie shot back. "You don't like it around here, you get out! Eulalie's the best girl I ever had. She acts like quality, even when she's givin' a man a good time."

Eulalie lay still, her heart pounding, listening to the screeching out in the hall. Lem had come forward now to separate the two women. He was herding Iris—his voice loud with recriminations—back to her own room.

Was Iris goin' to start trouble for her? Iris called her *nigger*. Iris was mad enough to drive into town and talk about the runaway slave playin' everybody for a fool back at the house. She wasn't ready to leave yet! Eulalie fought down panic and forced herself to think. She needed money to live on, once she got to New York. She heard that a maid up there could get as much as six dollars a month plus her keep. But you didn't fin' a job like that right away.

Eulalie's door swung open. Millie came into the room, her face working nervously.

"You hear the ruckus out there?"

"I heard." Eulalie's voice was low, fearful. She knew why Millie was staring at her now. Wonderin' how many of the others suspected she wasn't white.

"Honey, you're the best girl I ever had. I don't want to see you go. But that Iris is gonna start trouble for both of us. Under that new law, it's treason to hide a runaway slave—" Millie's eyes were somber. "Now I know you ain't been spendin' your money," Millie picked up vigorously. "You got enough to buy your way up to New York. Best place for you, Eulalie. I told you that, right in the beginnin'."

"When do I have to go?" The words were barely audible.

"Honey, it's for your sake too," Millie said. "You pack up and I'll have Lem drive you across the county to the stagecoach station. You get dressed, put away your money where nobody's gonna rob you. And this time, you don't look like you're runnin', you hear?" Millie exhorted, her eyes holding Eulalie's. You go part ways by coach, then take the boat from Portsmouth to Baltimore—" She looked sharply because Eulalie cringed, remembering the last time she was aboard the boat en route from Portsmouth to Baltimore. "Eulalie, you listenin' to me?"

"Yes, ma'am." Eulalie managed to sound calm. "I take the boat to Baltimore."

"From Baltimore, you take the railroad to Philadelphia. I'm not sure exactly, but from there—" Millie frowned in thought. "I believe you can get a boat from Philadelphia to New York. Leastways, you find a stagecoach goin' there. You ask, understand? And bluff it all the way. With your fine features, and that way of carryin' your head high, you can pull it off, Eulalie. You can bluff as good as anybody."

"Yes, ma'am." She had to, Eulalie reminded herself. She had no way to go, but ahead.

Lem, laconic but sympathetic, drove her across the county to the place where she could pick up a stage. She had to wait until well in the afternoon for the stagecoach. Relief filled her when she was finally able to climb aboard. Nobody looked suspiciously at her, yet she was tense, watchful. It was still slave country. Eulalie knew that New York had acquired a reputation for taking kindly to runaway slaves. She concentrated her thoughts in this direction all the way to Portsmouth.

Eulalie went aboard the night boat for Baltimore, feeling as though a thousand years had passed since the last time she had walked up a similar gangplank with the

Quaker couple. It was a month less than a year. She walked with her head high, her eyes polite but uncommunicative. She was proud of the way she carried herself through the steamboat tea, the assignment of berths. Her roommate was snoring before Eulalie was ready to retire. Still, Eulalie felt self-conscious, recalling with sharp clarity the night swim ashore which had been necessitated by that other roommate and her companion.

The steamship journey was uneventful. Along with the other passengers, she disembarked in Baltimore. Polite inquiries guided her to the railroad. She was shocked at the amount of money she had to pay for her ticket on the train. But by two-thirty this afternoon, she was told, she would be in Philadelphia.

Eulalie took her place, at the direction of a kindly conductor, in a separate car reserved for women. Most of the women in the car traveled with children. Eulalie was able to relax. The women were all too busy to notice her. Eulalie's mind raced ahead now to her arrival in New York. Twice, to reassure herself, she opened the carpetbag to make sure that Missis Henderson's address was safely tucked away. David said, go to her. Missis Henderson was a good woman—she would help.

At the Susquehanna River, the passengers had to disembark to take a steamboat across. On the other side of the river, they climbed aboard the railroad carriages again. Eulalie watched the passing scenery with intense interest, marveling at the spring display of flowers and trees along the banks of the Brandywine, as they approached Wilmington. Beyond Wilmington, they traveled through flat, low meadows skirting the Delaware. Far less picturesque than the earlier scenery, Eulalie thought. When they crossed the Schuylkill, over a bridge that brought alarm to Eulalie, she realized they were close to their destination. The woman across the way had just pointed this out to her children as a landmark that was scarcely a mile from Philadelphia.

Late in the afternoon, in Philadelphia, Eulalie was able to acquire passage on a coach going up to New Jersey, the next hurdle to be crossed. She handed over another sizable chunk of her nest egg, shocked at its dwindling state. But she was in a free state, she reminded herself with satisfaction. She was close to New York City.

The coach stopped at dusk to allow the passengers to put up at an inn for the night. Eulalie shared a room with two elderly sisters who left her strictly alone. In the morning, the passengers ate breakfast in a dining room of the inn, then resumed their journey. At Jersey City Eulalie's stagecoach trip was completed. Her heart pounded when she realized only a short ferry ride across the river separated her from New York. She was here!

Wearing her white gloves and the peddler's shoes, Cindy's dress and the coat that Millie had given her in a rush of sentiment at her departure, her hair demurely arranged around the golden oval of her face, Eulalie walked in awe, carpetbag clutched in one hand. Terrified and bedazzled simultaneously.

This was Fifth Avenue, this display of grandiose brownstone mansions, all of which looked like duplicates of the other. Her heart pounding, Eulalie watched for the neat numbers that identified each house. There, she was coming close, she realized—the house here was only a few numbers above that of her destination. Missis Henderson's!

Eulalie quickened her steps, her eyes watching avidly. And then she saw the number—and for a few moments she stared without understanding at the boarded-up windows of the elegant brownstone. Her eyes darkened with alarm when the significance of the boarded-up windows broke through to her. Still, she mounted the stoop, reached for the brass knocker, though she knew that no one was going to reply. Madeline Henderson had closed up her beautiful house and disappeared into nowhere.

Eulalie stood before the door, trying to assimilate the knowledge that Mrs. Henderson was not here to help her. Again, she was on her own. Confidence ran away on scared, swift feet, leaving her shattered. She turned around, stared at the strange sights that moments ago had been exhilarating.

She would have to find a job by herself, Eulalie exhorted inwardly. Other folks did it. Why couldn't she? Lifting her head with a show of optimism that was not mirrored within, Eulalie walked down the stoop and looked about her. She would just walk up to the other houses along here and ask if they wanted somebody to clean or help with the children. No, say she's lookin' for a maid job, Eulalie emphasized, her mind pulling forth bits of conversation she had heard in the railroad carriage. The ladies there talked about their maids.

At door after door, Eulalie was rebuffed—sometimes politely, more often with annoyance or arrogance. Nervousness was infiltrating her. Maybe she'd try another street, she decided. She walked west to what was obviously an important thoroughfare. She glanced up at the street sign. Broadway.

She felt herself pushed along by the throngs of people rushing along the sidewalks. She was fascinated by the masses of humanity on the street, the incessant surge of white-topped, guadily painted, horse-drawn omnibuses that moved densely along the wide avenue, the hackney coaches that vied for space. How did you ever cross this street? Eulalie shuddered, vowing to remain on this side.

"Sweet potatoes. Git yo' hot sweet potatoes," a rich Negro voice chanted at the corner, and Eulalie realized she was hungry.

She halted before the vendor, found a coin, exchanged it for a butter-drenched sweet potato.

"Thankee, Missy," the woman said, nodding her head respectfully, making Eulalie homesick for Maw.

The woman thought she was white, Eulalie told herself with satisfaction while she dug into the succulent sweet potato. If she could fool a black woman, then she ought not have too much trouble foolin' white ones. It was a comforting realization. Still, she had to find herself a job. Quick, Eulalie warned herself, optimism taking flight again. Her money was practically gone.

Resolutely, Eulalie made inquiries at stores and in the restaurants. Nobody wanted help. She walked endlessly and, in her desperation, made the dangerous crossing to the other side of the street. Day was merging into dusk.

Gaslight from restaurants and bars and the elegant hotels spilled onto the scurrying crowds on the sidewalks. Uptown traffic along Broadway reached its peak as fine horses tried to maneuver their elegant carriages through the maze of vehicles carrying home the gentlemen who had finished their business for the day.

Eulalie was conscious again of growing hunger. Only a few coins remained in her carpetbag. Night was approaching. Where would she sleep? Panic closed in on her. It was a glorious, mad carnival, here on the streets of New York—but the time had arrived to go home for the night. Eulalie had no home.

"Corn. Hot corn," a young white girl chanted in a singsong fashion. "Buy your hot corn, straight out of the pot!"

Eulalie hesitated. The corn was tempting. She needed the respite from panic as well as a concrete objective. She reached into the carpet for one of the few remaining coins and handed it over to the girl. The corn was hot, savory. Eulalie ate with relish, momentarily at peace.

"Say, Miss, don't stand still on the street that way," a masculine voice chided her good-humoredly. "This here is Broadway, you know!"

"I'm sorry." Eulalie stammered, frightened at a personal confrontation with a New Yorker even while she yearned for this.

"You new in the city?" The man squinted at her appraisingly, fell into step beside her. He appeared friendly, interested. He didn't look at her in the way that the men back at Millie's house had looked at her. She felt reassured.

"I just came here today." She took a final, delicate bite of the corn, dropped the husk at the curb. Talk to the man like she was any white girl arrivin' in the city, Eulalie reminded herself. Bluff your way, Millie said. "I never saw anything like it."

"From the South?" He made it a gentle rib.

"Ever since I can remember, we lived in Virginia," Eulalie told him, trying to sound casual. "But I was born in Mexico." The improvisation protected the gold of her skin. She could see him accepting this.

"And you ran away from home to see the big city." He chuckled knowingly, with sympathy. "How old are you? Fifteen? Sixteen?"

"Sixteen," she said. Not yet, but it sounded more grown-up. She waited, eyes liquid amber, praying for a word from him that would give her direction. "I'm lookin' for a job," she said finally, desperation edging her voice. "I can clean real good and take care of children. You know anybody needs a maid?"

"Not right off," he said thoughtfully, "but why don't you come along home with me and talk to my old lady? She's full of ideas."

They turned off Broadway at the corner, the man politely holding Eulalie's arm, carrying the carpetbag for her. Like she was a white lady. Eulalie looked up to read the street sign. Worth Street.

"We're going to Five Points," the man explained. "That's where me and the missis live."

The streets, the alleys, were lined by low, clapboard houses, decaying tenements that cried out for repairs—but to Eulalie, it was beautiful. In comparison to the slave huts on the plantation, this was beautiful though the inner life was sordid. Often a whole family lived in one room—ate, slept, entertained there. Five Points was the most degraded, dangerous section of all New York. Here lived the hoodlums, the thieves, the murderers, the prostitutes. To Eulalie, it was the city, the beginning of living for her.

"This is the Points," the man said vigorously. Covertly, he inspected her. Watching for a reaction.

She was wordless, her face enigmatic. She was learning that this was the safest way to meet an unfamiliar situation. Eulalie gazed at the second-hand shops, the grocery stores, the pawnshops that were strategically placed on the street corners. In the center of Five Points was an open area of almost an acre. Eulalie squinted at a sign. Paradise Square. With a growing awareness, Eulalie realized this was a misnomer.

"This way," he said, his hand protectively at her elbow, yet misgivings were forming in Eulalie.

Barefoot half-naked children roamed about the streets though it was growing dark. They played in the gutters, competing with the pigs for scraps of food. This was not the New York Eulalie had envisioned, and it was grotesquely unlike the New York a few blocks away.

"We turn off here," the man said, prodding Eulalie across the street.

Why hadn't she stayed on Broadway, Eulalie asked herself with growing unease. She felt safer there. But it was night. She couldn't keepin walkin' up and down until mornin'. She had to have a place to sleep. Where did you find lodgin' in a city like this? Not in the fancy hotels back on Broadway!

"Right here," her escort said with a touch of pride, pointing to a low, red-brick-fronted house that was run down, dreary, half its windows broken. Still, it was less blatantly decaying than the houses on either side.

They walked into the narrow hallway that led to the upper floors. The gaslight was so meager that Eulalie had to squint to see the steps. Laboriously, they made their way up the narrow, winding stairs to the top floor. Eulalie's companion slid a key into the door, turned it, opened the door.

The room inside appeared overcrowded with furniture only because it was so small. A double bed usurped most of the space. A slovenly blonde, her eyes cloudy from drinking, sat at the table used for eating—the soiled dishes from a meal still remained there, beside a whisky bottle. Once, Eulalie guessed, the blonde must have been beautiful—before the features became bloated, the body too heavy.

"Flo, baby," the man said, caution undercoating his elaborately affectionate approach, "I brung home a young lady to visit with us."

"So?" But Flo looked up, seeming to become sober. She leaned forward, the bulbous breasts all but flopping out of her bodice. "She a nigger?" Curiosity rather than contempt in her voice.

"Mexican," he said, sounding hurt. "This is my missis— Flo. Call me Biff—everybody does."

"My name's Eulalie—" She stopped herself from adding Washington. That was no Mexican name. What was? She sought one in her mind frantically until she realized that Biff had offered no second name himself and obviously expected none from her.

"Eulalie's lookin' for a job," Biff was telling Flo. "Before we talk business, you rustle up some grub for her," he ordered, growingly expansive. "She looks hungry."

"Are you?" Flo demanded, staring sharply.

"Yes ma'am." All she had eaten today was the sweet potato and the ear of corn.

"Biff, you sure she ain't no nigger?" Flo pursued. "If she's a nigger, you send her down to Carmine Street, you hear—where all them nigger shacks are."

"Flo, shut up!" His slack mouth was compressed in rage. "I told ya, didn't I? She's Mexican!"

"You may have a hard time convincin' some folks of that," Flo warned with a snide smile. But she was moving her bulk from the chair to waddle over to prepare food for Eulalie.

"You fix her up with paint and powder, nobody's askin' questions," Biff pointed out.

Eulalie shot into alertness, her body tensing. Paint and powder meant somethin' she didn't care to think about. A maid's job, she'd told him. That was what she was lookin' for! All the big houses in New York—they had to have maids to take care of 'em!

Flo was busy with the food. Now she moved about to face Eulalie.

"Come on over to the table and sit down. We don't eat fancy, but it's fillin'." She turned to her husband. "Where you puttin' her up? I told you before, I ain't havin' anybody sleepin' in my room."

"Annie's away for a few days. She can use Annie's room down in the cellar. If they handle themselves right, they can both use it. Put in another cot."

Eulalie ignored the plate of food Flo was setting before her even though her stomach was rumbling with hunger.

"What kinda job?" Eulalie asked, her throat tightening.

"Honey, the kind of job a pretty little thing like you can handle with no trouble." Biff smiled broadly, displaying the browned stumps of four missing teeth. "I do all the work. All you hafta do is entertain the customers. I pay you half of everything that comes in."

"No." Eulalie pushed back her chair, forgetting the food.

"What do you mean, no?" Flo demanded belligerently.

"I'm not a whore." Eulalie struggled to conceal her trembling. "I be a cleanin' girl, or nurse for children." For a while, she had been a whore, Eulalie admitted inwardly, sickened in remembrance. She had to do that to get the money to come here. But she was here. No more bein' used in that ugly way. "You didn't say that kind of job," she accused Biff. She was trying to ignore the food before her, the savory aroma of coffee boiling.

"Eulalie, who do you think is gonna give you that kind of job here?" he asked derisively. "New York's just swarmin' with Irish girls lookin' for jobs. How you gonna stand up beside them—a Mexican girl that lotsa folks are gonna take for nigger." He stared hard, doubts arising in his own mind, now.

"I'll look," she bluffed, head high, stumbling to her feet, reaching for her carpetbag.

"You won't get far." Unexpectedly, compassion softened Flo's bloated face. "You go outside on the Points, this hour of the night, somebody's gonna throw you on your back. You could be dead tomorrow. You won't get a block from here. If it ain't some drunk, it'll be the metropolitans—" She grinned at Eulalie's incomprehension. "The cops, honey. You ain't got a mackerel workin' for you, the cops pick you right off the street at night, throw you in a cell." Again, Flo grinned at Eulalie's look of incomprehension. "A mackerel, a pimp, the man who brings you customers. Now you go out there on the Points tonight, you're gonna be lyin' dead or in jail."

Eulalie gazed from Flo to Biff, unsure of the veracity

of what Flo was saying. She shuddered, remembering the unsavory faces she had seen on the way about the Points en route to the house. She could believe it was worth her life to go out there alone. And she could not let herself be thrown in jail—where they might ask questions. A runaway slave could be sent back, even from New York.

"Now you eat your supper, love," Flo crooned, sensing victory before Eulalie herself was aware of capitulation. "After you eat, Biff'll take you downstairs to your room. Annie's got some things down there you can wear. You fix yourself up pretty, and old Biff'll go lookin'. You'll make out real good," she promised with a satisfied smile. "Just do like Biff says, and you'll be havin' no trouble at all."

17

Eulalie hated the filthy cellar-room ten feet below the street that she shared with Annie. The two cots were sagging and vermin-infected despite Eulalie's and Annie's efforts at eliminating them. The sheets, grudgingly supplied by Flo, were rotting from the many washings undertaken by the girls themselves. Flo expected the bed linens to be used until the customers complained. Eulalie had won a meager triumph in being allowed an extra sheet to hang between the two cots for privacy during "business hours."

Eulalie had arrived at an uneasy philosophy. At the plantation, she had to do what the Massa wanted whenever he wanted—and got nothing for it. Here, she was doing the same thing—and being paid. This was the situation in which she must remain until she smartened up sufficiently to find a more palatable way of earning a living and until she saved enough for Maw's eventual escape. She was learning to play the game, to give nothing of herself except her body—to remove herself mentally and emotionally from the scene.

She sat, tailor-fashion on her cot, dreaming about Maw. She suspected that the night was over for her, that dawn must be breaking outside, but it was impossible to know in this windowless, unventilated room. Sometimes, like now, with the perspiration rolling down her throat and between her small, high breasts, Eulalie thought nostalgically of the open fields, the pungent scent of magnolia and honeysuckle and roses. June was a month of glory in Georgia. But in Georgia she was a slave—not for an instant would she ever forget that.

The door opened. Annie strolled in. Her eyes were warm and secretive.

"Biff wasn't lookin' for me, was he now?" Annie asked anxiously.

"No. I think he won't be bringin' any more tonight."

"Oh, I'm beat," Annie complained, yet there was a look of jubilation in her eyes. Eulalie guessed that it must be that sailor who had come to Annie as a "client"—as Biff liked to refer to the paying customers. Annie got stars in her eyes with the sailor. If it wasn't for Biff, Annie wouldn't take money from him. "Since Biff picked up that kid—that René—looks like we never stop."

"Annie—" Eulalie hesitated, wanting to ask the questions that plagued at her these weeks, yet fearful. "Annie, I don't think Biff plays right with us about the money."

Annie threw her head back and guffawed.

"You just findin' that out?" Annie mocked. "Look, Biff rents these holes from Mr. Astor—the old man died, I mean his son—and he pays two dollars month, maybe. Then he charges us *twenty*. He's got that slob servin' bilge to us for food every day and chargin' us like we was livin' at the St. Nicholas Hotel! And on top of that," she wound up with bitter triumph, "he plays crooked on the take. So what can we do about it?"

"It's not right," Eulalie insisted stubbornly, her eyes flashing.

"What are we gonna do about it?" Annie demanded. "No jobs outside with all the Irish comin' here to grab everything off." Her mouth tightened with hostility. "At least, we're eatin', we're not sleepin' in the gutters or up in the fields. Maybe we could get jobs on the farms for our keep," she admitted candidly, "but no money from them farmers, so what would be the use?"

"Biff's a thief," Eulalie said intensely. "He's stealin' from us every night."

Annie stifled a yawn.

"So we can't do nothin' about it." Her eyes softened. "Unless we find somebody who wants to marry us—" Her sailor, Annie was thinking. "To hell!" Annie returned to reality and reached over to turn off the kerosene lamp.

Who would want to marry a whore? Eulalie asked herself somberly. But she wasn't goin' to stay a whore. She had lots to learn, but like David always said, she was quick, she picked up things fast. Like tomorrow. Her eyes glistened with anticipation. She'd been readin' the newspapers regular, and she knew all about the banks. Tomorrow, she was takin' what money she had saved and puttin' it in the bank where none of the thieves on the Points could get their dirty hands on it. As long as she could sign her name, she could open a bank account. She could do more than that—she could write as good as anybody. Better than Cindy.

She wished there was some way she could write a letter to David, so he could tell Maw she was all right. But if she wrote a letter, somebody beside David would see it. And they'd find out she was in New York. She wished there was some way she could get somebody to mail a letter from Canada for her. To let Maw know she was all right. Always, there was this unrest in her because Maw didn't know, because the Massa might be takin' it out on Maw since she ran away.

Annie was already stretched out on her cot, clothes shucked off because of the unbearable heat of the night— the cellar was without a window to offer relief. In a minute, Annie would be snoring. But Eulalie was fully awake, as usual at this hour of the night, her mind assimilating what she had learned during the day.

Every day she devoured *The New York Herald,* which cost only a penny and which was loaded with all kinds of information—including the addresses of the more affluent prostitutes. Once a week she allowed herself the luxury of buying *The Evening Post,* which she was coming to realize was a more dignified, a more intellectual newspaper. She was brushed with awe when she discovered Mr. Bryant, the editor who wrote about the corruption of New York politics, was the poet who had written *Thanatopsis,* which she and David had memorized for Mr. Jefferson.

Eulalie fell asleep despite the discomfort in the cellar room and woke—as always—well before Annie. None of Biff's girls rose until well in the afternoon when the first meal of the day was served. Eulalie made a point of providing for herself by saving bread from the night meal. She wrapped it well and hid it beneath her pillow. So far, the rats had not attacked her cache.

Eulalie dressed quickly, worked with earnest concentration on the delicate application of cream and powder to tone down the gold of her skin. By night, this was unnecessary; in the brightness of the day, Eulalie was uneasy without this subterfuge, particularly with all the talk that circulated around New York about the city being such a nest of slave pirates. She was fearful not only of being labeled a slave and held for a possible reward, but also of being plucked from the street to be shipped off on a clipper laden with "black ivory," as slave cargo was called.

Satisfied at last with her appearance, she ate the bread that constituted her morning meal and hurried from the humid, dank room, up the stairs into the noonday sunlight. She walked with determined swiftness past the lodging houses where derelicts found a place to sleep for ten cents a night—men and women crowded into tiers of bunks, were filed away until the next day—past the run-down houses already spewing out their litters of half-naked children—intent on her destination. She was going to walk into the grandeur of the bank and hand over what money Biff had turned over to her at the end of each night and which she had, thus far, worn sewed into a rag about her neck. She trusted no one in the Points.

The bank she had chosen from the ads in *The Evening Post* was on Broadway. Her heart pounded as she entered the grand, high-ceilinged edifice. She gazed about uncertainly. Aware of a curious gaze in her direction, Eulalie lifted her head high, smiled distantly, walked across to the man who was staring at her. It was easy, she thought with inner triumph, demurely listening to his polite reply to her question—easy, when you make out you was—you *were*—as good as anybody else.

With glory in her heart, Eulalie strolled from the bank. Oh, what Maw would say if she knew her baby had money in the bank! Maw wouldn't believe it at first! It had taken her two years to come this far, but it was worth it.

Eulalie walked north, relishing the presence of the shops, the hotels, the theaters, the fast pace, the look of constant change of which she was becoming aware. One day soon, she promised herself—when she had built up the nerve—she was going over to Purdy's Theater on the Bowery to see that play she read about in the newspapers and saw advertised on the bulletin-wagons. *Uncle Tom's Cabin*. It was a play about slaves. And since last year, colored folks were bein' admitted inside the theater in a part of the house that was set up for them. For twenty-five cents admission. But she wasn' goin' to sit in the colored section, Eulalie reminded herself. Sit with *white* folks. Fleetingly, guilt brushed her, that she might be slighting her own.

Eulalie walked with a purposeful air because that was the way everybody seemed to walk along Broadway. Daily, she walked this way straight up to Lafayette Place—past the huge, white-marbled St. Nicholas Hotel which cost more than a million dollars and had rooms for almost eight hundred guests plus a heating plant that brought hot air into every room. Annie had been in the St. Nicholas once and talked about it with extravagant imagery.

Above the St. Nicholas, Eulalie slowed down to enjoy the view of the gigantic brownstone building that was the Metropolitan Hotel, which had—in addition to its fancy heating system—the elegant sky parlors high over Broadway where guests could sit and watch the view below. Further up Broadway, Eulalie again slowed down. She was approaching the famous department store, A. T. Stewart's; it was six stories tall and, like the St. Nicholas, faced with white marble. The cynosure of Eulalie's eyes were its fifteen enormous plate-glass show-windows. Already, though it was just past noon, a line-up of carriages sat out front while their ladies shopped inside. Not far beyond was the John Taylor Ice Cream Saloon where ladies could go in unaccompanied by a male escort, which caused considerable eyebrow-lifting among New Yorkers.

Eulalie enjoyed this self-planned orientation into New York life. Each day for weeks now, she walked up Broadway, then shot off in various directions to see the miracles that were on display for New York inhabitants and visitors. Invariably, she continued on Broadway to Lafayette Place because at Lafayette Place was one of the sites of the city—the Astor Library, set up, Eulalie had learned, from a fund left for this purpose by John Jacob Astor as a memorial to himself. It was the same John Jacob Astor who had collected his rents from his tenants with such tenacity that legends of his greed were multitudinous.

Today, with the knowledge that she had walked into the bank and accomplished her mission, Eulalie felt a surge of daring. Maybe today she would walk into that fine building—it was supposed to be a public library which anybody could enter. She would go into one of those reading rooms and sit down—like a fine lady—and read.

Her pulse was racing when she arrived before the Astor Library. There was supposed to be a hundred-thousand books inside—the largest collection in the world! As she entered, she was faintly breathless with expectancy. She had never seen so many books before—on every side, they climbed up to the high ceilings.

Eulalie, striving for an air of composure, found her way into a reading room, went to a shelf, scanned its contents, pulled down a book, took it to a table. She was trembling when her hands flipped the book wide. She leaned forward with an earnest air and began to read the words before her.

Eulalie developed a pattern of living that was to sustain her through the summer, the winter, and into the spring. She lived the ugly, dirty existence in the Points in the shadows of the night, refraining from becoming involved in the squabbling that took place among the other girls. She was intent only on putting into the bank each week whatever money she had saved in the past days and on spending her waking hours in the reading rooms of the Astor Library where a kindly librarian, impressed by her determined daily presence, prescribed a course of study for her, which she followed with religious fervor. She was watching her speech with a growing awareness of inflections until Annie taunted her with playing the snob.

In April, Annie confided that she was leaving. Annie was terrified of letting Biff know that she was running off with her sailor. Biff's temper—particularly when he had been at the bottle—was notoriously bad.

"Look," Annie said matter-of-factly, "maybe my lad will marry me, maybe he won't. His ship's in harbor, and he can get me aboard. He's tired of sailin', and he wants to settle down near Montreal. That's in Canada." Annie preened slightly. "So tonight, he's comin' like he always does—so Biff won't think anything. And afterwards, he's gonna wait for me over by the old brewery."

"Annie—" Eulalie's eyes shone with excitement. "Would you mail a letter for me from Canada? It's to this boy back home—he collects stamps. He'd be so pleased to have a stamp from Canada. I'll give you the money," she added eagerly.

"Okay," Annie agreed, her eyes wise. "You write the letter. I'll mail it."

"I'll go right over to buy the paper and an envelope." So Annie guessed now. A lot of times, she'd thought Annie was suspicious. But it didn't matter if Annie believed her story—just let her mail the letter. Maw would *know* she was all right. David would get the letter, and he'd make sure to tell Maw. It didn't matter if the others at The Willows found out—in Canada a slave was safe. If they thought she was in Canada, they wouldn't think about putting any more ads in the newspapers for her return.

Seated at a table in the reading room at the Astor Library, Eulalie wrote the letter to David. She was tempted to say much, but fought off the temptation. Just say what have to be said, she ordered herself sternly. She signed the letter, "Your friend, Eulalie." So many times, lying with those faceless men, Eulalie remembered David.

Eulalie and Annie believed themselves to be free for the night when Annie slipped away to meet her sailor. Eulalie kept the lamp burning because of an unexpected reluctance to be alone in the dark hovel. When she was—at last—about to turn down the lamp, René showed at the door with two men in tow.

"Annie's not here," she nervously told the slight, delicately featured boy who went soliciting customers for Biff's girls. At the same time, she ushered the unshaven, short, stocky man who had been the first into the room behind the curtained area.

"I'll go see if we got another girl," René said timorously. The other man was big, pot-bellied, and bellicose at the prospect of waiting. "You stay here—" Eulalie was certain that if she had not moved between the boy and the man then, he would have hit René.

"I don't wanna wait!" The big man's voice soared drunkenly, his breath hot and fetid on Eulalie.

"Call Biff," Eulalie ordered quickly, her eyes urging René to be cautious. "Go on—"

"Come on, honey, I ain't got all night—" Eulalie's client complained. "I give him the money already."

"Wait over there," Eulalie told the other man self-consciously as she nodded towards Annie's side of the curtained area. "René'll bring a girl."

He grinned drunkenly, suddenly aware that he would be on the other side of the washed-thin sheet while the earlier customer collected his due. Eulalie gritted her teeth and allowed herself to be brought down to the bed as she willed her mind to ignore the physical invasion. Sickened, she realized the drunk had climbed atop the other cot to look down upon the scene of passion. She fought down a surge of nausea while her body received the rough, impatient thrusts from the man above her while the voyeur leered above the curtain and uttered obscene exhortations. No matter how many times, she thought with painful frustration, she would always feel sick this way.

The man above her grunted, became still, then swaggered to his feet. Why didn't René come back? *Why didn't he?* Then, just as the first arrival strutted out of the room and the waiting man moved menacingly towards her, Biff stalked into the room with René at his heels. Biff took one sharp look at the waiting client and began to shout.

"No, you don't!" Biff yelled belligerently. "You get outta here. I ain't havin' you give the clap to my best girls. Go on, I know about you—I told you to stay outta here!"

The big man muttered ugly retorts, but he was leaving, obviously wary of tangling with Biff who had "protection" from the Mets. Eulalie trembled, realizing the portent of Biff's accusation.

Now Biff turned his wrath on Eulalie and René.

"Where's Annie? Where's she runnin' at this hour of the night? Layin' out in the street with somebody, keepin' the money from me!"

"I don't know where Annie is!" Eulalie said strongly, contempt rising in her for Biff, for the whole ugly situation in which she found herself.

Biff turned to René and cuffed him till the boy staggered. Fury captured Eulalie.

"You take your hands off him!" Her voice rose stridently. "You hit him again, I'll walk right out of here!"

Her eyes clashed with Biff's. She sensed his backing down even before he spoke.

"So what you gettin' so worked up over? It might make a man outta him if he gets pushed around a little. It don't look to me like he'll ever be a man," he said with nasty insinuation, "not the way he don't even look at the girls when they're right in front of him the way they are. All right now," he demanded, ignoring René, "where's Annie?"

"Annie went out," Eulalie said calmly. "I don't know where. She didn't say." By now maybe Annie was on the boat with Eulalie's letter.

After her defense of René, Eulalie discovered him sleeping nightly at her door on a ragged mat that served as a bed. He spoke little, but he was always underfoot when he wasn't darting about the Points soliciting customers for Biff's girls. Finally, Eulalie took him inside her

Julie Ellis

room to sleep on Annie's cot since no replacement had been brought in for Annie.

Gradually, René told Eulalie about himself. His parents, who were French, had gone out to California in search of gold. He was slight, small for his age. They feared he would be a burden. They left him behind. He lived, like other vagrant children in the Points, in the gutter—for months until Flo brought him home, fed him, cleaned him up, and turned him over to Biff. He slept in hallways of the house Biff rented and ate at the communal table. Occasionally, Biff tossed him a coin.

Eulalie lived with a sense of waiting. The nights—the parade of men—were unreal. Only the days, now with René as her companion, were real. She began to teach René, as she had been taught, finding pleasure in her ability to do this. René, in turn, began to teach her fragments of French.

Eulalie and René moved about New York as though they were a pair of young Marco Polos. They luxuriated in the wonders they observed; extravagantly they imagined the lives that existed behind the magical doors which they could not enter. Neither Eulalie nor René was aware of the curious glances they collected as they wandered about the city. The fragile-appearing, patrician-featured dark beauty and the esthetic-faced slight boy—he was almost as dark as Eulalie—with flashing Gallic eyes. Passers-by considered them a remarkably handsome sister and brother.

During the hot summer months, Eulalie and René continued the daily pilgrimage to the Astor Library. René was enamored of the fine books of paintings and was happy to stare for hours at the replicas of masterpieces. The World's Fair, which President Franklin Pierce himself came all the way from Washington D.C. to open in July, was a fascinating project to Eulalie and René. New Yorkers were loath to visit the World's Fair in 1853 in this long hot summer when the temperature was soaring to a record one hundred degrees in the shade. In one day, two hundred thirty New Yorkers died from the heat. But Eulalie and René, seeking the shade whenever possible, walked all the way up to Forty-Second Street and Fifth Avenue to observe the Crystal Palace, which housed New

206

York's first World's Fair. The horse-drawn street cars were barred to Negroes. Eulalie preferred to walk rather than expose herself to the possible humiliation of being refused admittance. Besides, street cars were expensive. Eulalie hoarded what little money remained for her after Biff deducted rent and board from her earnings.

The Crystal Palace, a replica of the Crystal Palace in London, was a huge building shaped like a Greek cross and made—except for the floors—entirely of iron and glass. It was topped with a translucent, Moorish dome. Directly behind it was the Latting Tower and Ice Cream Parlor. The tower rose three hundred and fifty feet into the air. A steam elevator lifted passengers to the top where they could view the city and the neighboring countryside. Eulalie and René eschewed this expensive sightseeing to enjoy their view of the city from atop the tall walls of the Croton Reservoir. The structure, reminiscent of an Egyptian temple, provided a wide promenade where they could stroll and gaze upon the sweeping views without paying a fee.

The summer faded into autumn. Eulalie was fascinated by the front-page stories about the Women's Rights Convention, which met for two days at the Broadway Tabernacle on Worth Street. Women like Miss Susan B. Anthony, Miss Lucy Stone, and Quakeress Lucretia Mott attended. Not only were the ladies asking for the right to vote—they wanted women to be fully equal to men. An exhilarated Eulalie, with a dubious René in tow, stood outside the Tabernacle while the Mets poured inside after a free-for-all broke out in the gallery. One of the ladies— somebody said she was Miss Lucy Stone—wore a new costume, a short skirt above long, baggy bloomers. Eulalie thought wistfully of Madeline Henderson, who certainly would have been here at the Broadway Tabernacle if she had not closed up her New York house.

Winter arrived, with Eulalie parting with some of her precious money to buy René a coat to protect him from the rigorous New York winter. The other girls snickered when he appeared in such luxurious trappings. Like other New Yorkers, Eulalie and René watched the trotters exercised on Third Avenue regularly. On afternoons when the snow was packed hard underfoot, they enjoyed the colorful sights of bell-jangling sleighs racing up the avenue. On mild days, they traveled to the waterfront to see the clippers that sailed to the far corners of the world—to Java, India, Shanghai, Sumatra—to bring back exotic cargoes. The shipyards were hard put to build sufficient clippers to meet the demands for sea transportation, especially since so many folks were going off to California to look for gold.

Eulalie thought constantly about Maw and about how long it would take to bring her mother out of the slave state and to New York. She knew there were ways. Expensive ways. She was restless—the money was coming in so slowly. She hated Biff for his thieving ways, yet felt herself as yet unready to move out of this phase of her life.

Compulsively, she traveled from time to time to the Negro huts on Carmine Street, promising herself that Maw would never have to live here. Yet she was drawn there, knowing that with René at her heels she passed for white.

As always on a day when she was making a trip to the bank, Eulalie arose with a sense of exhilaration. René was already awake. He made it his business each morning to fetch fresh water for them to drink with their private meal. They dispensed with this rapidly, hurried out of the small, dark room, up the stairs into the bright spring sunlight. René half-danced beside her as they crossed the Points and headed for Broadway. René adored these moments within the august, high-ceilinged bank.

Eulalie yearned to take some of the money out of her account to go over to A. T. Stewart's and buy herself a pretty dress. Today was special. It was exactly a year ago that she crossed the ferry from Jersey City into New York. Had Annie mailed the letter to David? This question plagued her constantly. She had no way of knowing whether David had received the letter or not. Was Maw all right? Had Mister Woodstock been hard on her because Eulalie had run away?

"Let's go walk past the Astor House," Eulalie said, a plan fomenting in her mind, but about which she remained silent—because it was such a terrifying step to take. "And up past the St. Nicholas and the Metropolitan."

"I looked in the windows once," René said with a roguish glow on his pixie face. "At the Metropolitan! They have fancy balls every week, and the people dance and drink champagne."

Eulalie gazed at him, astonishment churning together with reproach and concern.

"René, what were you doin'? Biff didn't tell you to go up there!" Biff operated right within the Points. Anything five blocks removed was foreign territory to Biff and Flo.

"I went lookin' anyhow," René said airily.

"You be careful," Eulalie warned. "Don't go lookin' for trouble with Biff." Biff had connections with the Mets here in the Points—she wondered if those connections existed outside the area. More and more, she suspected this was not true.

Eulalie and René walked up Broadway past the elegant hotels which so enthralled Eulalie. For a little while, she could imagine herself living within such grandeur. Even Cindy would be impressed, she told herself with satisfaction. Then the pair began to weave in and out of the side streets—a departure from their routine. Eulalie was interested today in looking at the less pretentious, smaller hotels. She had heard things lately about the girls that lived in these hotels. They gave themselves airs, but their business was no different from that transacted by the prostitutes in the Points. Their mackerels were fancier than Biff and his boys. Their money was better, Eulalie guessed wisely. She tucked this knowledge away in her file cabinet of a mind for later usage. Tonight she would lie in her bed and think about those girls.

It was the end of May, and it was hot. Eulalie stood at her door and waited for René to come home. It was nearly dawn, and René was late. Where was he? She stood in the dank, evil-smelling hallway that customers were apt to use as a latrine, and watched anxiously for René.

Eulalie grew tired of standing, went back into the room, leaving the door ajar to court a breath of fresh air.

At last she heard René coming down the stairs. His quick, light step sounded somewhat subdued tonight. If Eulalie had not been so tired, the sound of his feet on the stairs would have alerted her.

"You're late," she scolded, meeting him at the door. "I was gettin' worried." You sometimes hear terrible stories about boys wanderin' around the Points late in the night, she remembered.

"I couldn't help it," René mumbled, his voice sounding odd.

René moved into the semidarkness of the room. Eulalie's eyes sharpened as they settled on René's face. She moved forward, to turn the lamp higher. She blanched.

"René, what happened?" she demanded, fury building in her, even as she imagined what had happened. René's mouth was swollen, one eye already half-shut. "Did Biff do that?"

"It was a slow night." René hung his head. "Biff wouldn't listen to me. I tried, honest I did. But he'd been hittin' the bottle"—René gestured expressively.

Eulalie's hand reached out to settle on René's slight shoulder. She was trembling.

"René," she whispered with quiet determination. "We're gettin' out of here. Tonight." All these months she had lived in an aura of waiting. The waiting was over. "He won't touch you again!"

"Where are we goin'?" It never entered René's mind to protest. Wherever Eulalie went, he would go.

"Never you mind," Eulalie said, already reaching beneath the cot for her carpetbag. She fought against apprehensions that rose to undermine her determination. She wasn't goin' to be scared of Biff. So he had connections here in the Points—he was nobody outside. They were goin' away from here. Biff couldn't stop them—not once they were out of the area where his Mets could throw her in jail if they wanted. "We'll have to wait a while," she decided cautiously. If Biff was drinkin', he'd soon be out cold—nothin' would wake him till tomorrow. "Half an hour," Eulalie decreed with a new recklessness. "Then we're leavin' the Points. And we won't be comin' back, René!"

18

Eulalie and René left the windowless cellar-room when the first streaks of dawn brushed the sky. They knew they would never return to the ignominious hovel. They walked swiftly, a look of urgency on their young faces—fearful of being accosted before they were safely beyond the narrow confines of the Points. They crossed Paradise Square, headed west through the filthy streets, the alleys, towards Broadway. They walked in silence, René clutching tightly at the carpetbag that contained Eulalie's and his meager belongings.

A drunk staggered towards them, murmured obscenely. Eulalie reached for René's hand, walked staunchly forward. A pair of Mets loomed into view—they only traveled in pairs in the Points. Eulalie lunged towards a doorway, dragging René with her. The Mets sauntered into a grog shop. Eulalie and René deserted the doorway to hurry on their way.

They turned north along Broadway where a few stragglers moved along the street, even at this hour.

"It's all right," Eulalie said quietly, taking a deep breath. "It's all right now."

"Where are we goin'?" René asked, his dark eyes somber, yet trustful.

"Where are we *going*," Eulalie corrected. Leaving the Points behind them emphasized, to her, the necessity for bettering themselves. "You hear the man up in the library every day. We have to talk like him, if we're going to live like quality." Suddenly, her smile was brilliant.

"Eulalie, you going crazy," René said solemnly.

"You do what I say, René—and everything'll be just fine," Eulalie promised. She pulled René with her to gaze into a store window because a passer-by was eying them curiously. They couldn't just walk up and down Broadway until the bank opened, her mind acknowledged as she grappled with this immediate problem. "The bank won't open for maybe four hours," she said slowly.

"We going to the bank today?" René was making a conscious, though imperfect, effort to speak as Eulalie instructed. Both Eulalie and he had a natural ear for inflections.

"We have to take out money, don't we?" she said airily. "So we can go to a hotel and give the man a week's rent and move in."

René was shocked.

"Eulalie, you taking money out of the bank?"

"We have to," Eulalie said slowly. Besides bringing Maw North, it was for something like this that she had been saving so painstakingly this whole year. "I know I said I never would. But this is—is setting us up in business, René. We won't have to share with Biff no more. I've been thinking about this a long time—how we handle it," she went on with a simple dignity for an undignified situation. "It'll take too long working for Biff to get the money to bring Maw up here—" Eulalie started, her face growing hot. Close as she was with René, she had never talked to him about Maw. But now, looking into his eyes, she realized he knew, knew and didn't care because he was her friend. David had been her friend—and he hadn't cared. Her eyes grew wistful, remembering all that David had been to her. "I hear talk about men who go down and bring folks out," Eulalie went on briskly. "I aim to bring out my Maw."

"The bank won't be opening for a long time," René said. "We can't keep walking all that time. Let's go over to the ferry station and sit on the benches for a spell."

"All right," Eulalie accepted. She was glad he knew about Maw.

Eulalie maintained a surface calm, yet inwardly she churned with unease. Biff wouldn't come running after René and her, would he? Right from the beginning, Flo had thought she was colored—even Biff had his suspicions. Would they turn her in for being a runaway slave? Thinking about this, she could feel herself turning cold. But Biff never moved off the Points, Eulalie reminded herself with a stern effort at rationalization. He wasn't going to come chasing after her. There was always a new girl showing up to take the place of one who ran away.

Eulalie and René left Broadway and walked through the nearly empty streets to the ferry station. They rested themselves, walked again to Broadway, and took time this morning—emboldened as they were by the lack of traffic and the close of business—to explore the wonderous show-windows of the A. T. Stewart department store.

"The bank'll be opening soon," Eulalie said with satisfaction, noting that Broadway was beginning to show signs of its normal morning-rush activity. "Let's walk down there, René."

"Tout de suite," René chirped, his pixie face alive with a glow of adventure, now that Five Points was hours behind them.

With a polite smile, Eulalie went into the bank when it opened. Her heart pounded with the newness of what lay ahead of her. For an instant, panic touched her. Suppose the man refused to give her the money? But it was hers. He had to give it to her. Not all. She'd leave enough so she still belonged here in the bank. And she'd bring more, each week—if things worked out the way she planned.

"You're going shopping," the man joked gallantly,

familiar with the young pair who waited patiently for him to count out the bills. "You be careful now, young lady."

"I will." Eulalie smiled. She had worn Cindy's dress a lot, but it still looked nice, she thought complacently. That was what happened when you bought good things. She was proud too of the elegant, often-washed white gloves. She wore the gloves this morning despite the warmth. Millie had been so right when she talked about bluffing.

They left the bank and walked out into the bright morning sunlight. René's eyes turned inquiringly to Eulalie's face.

"We're going to rent ourselves a hotel room," she said with quiet triumph. "For my brother and me. Eulalie and René Cartier," she emphasized, giving the surname the French pronunciation. She had read at the Astor Library about Jacques Cartier. René had taught her how to say the name. She relished the musicality of the French inflection. "And then, René, I'm going into one of those little shops where I can buy a dress—" She took a deep breath, envisioning this activity. "A fancy dress. This evening, I'll walk along Broadway, up and down in front of the big hotels—and if a gentleman looks at me, you go over and talk to him."

"I will, I will!" René sang avidly. "You tell me what to say." Instinctively, René realized his approach in this instance would be different from what he had used on the Points.

"First," Eulalie decreed, "we go into a hotel to rent us a room."

Asking about a room in the hotel, Eulalie made a point of holding money in her hand to make it clear that she could cope with the munificence of their accommodations. The man behind the counter gazed sharply from Eulalie to René and back to Eulalie again. He was not certain of the situation with which he was being confronted. Eulalie's frock was worn but once had been of fine quality. She bore herself like a lady. The boy was shabby, yet appeared genteel.

The clerk shrugged. Maybe they knew what kind of hotel into which they were moving—perhaps they did not.

He conceded that there was a vacancy. Watching for her reaction, he mentioned the rent. Eulalie fought against flinching and simply pulled forth extra bills to hand over to the clerk.

When her eyes met those of the clerk, Eulalie smiled faintly as though the money were of no import. Yet alarm seeped through her at the amount of money it was necessary to relinquish. So much, for one little room! For only a week. She made a point of not looking at René, guessing he would be as rocked as she was.

"We expect to be here a while," Eulalie said politely. "We're not sure just how long we'll be staying."

Annie and the other girls had told her about the fancy money some of the whores in the parlor-houses received. They had to pay a lot of money for their room and board—sometimes as much as a hundred dollars a week. But a bright girl could sometimes make two hundred dollars in one night. Eulalie realized she was not on the threshold of such affluence. This small side-street hotel could hardly compare to the grand brownstone houses further uptown that offered the quintessence of sexual diversions. But she ought to be able to make out good, Eulalie told herself with a surge of optimism while the clerk led them up the stairs to the room that René and she were to share.

The room was small, but there was a window, a carpet on the floor, a chair. The two small beds wore neat, clean covers. To Eulalie, she and René were walking into luxury.

"It'll do," Eulalie said politely to the clerk, and he moved to withdraw from the room. "Thank you."

In a burst of exuberance, when the door closed behind the clerk, René threw himself on the bed, grinning jubilantly.

"Eulalie, you can do anything," he sang out. "You got us in here!"

Eulalie sat at the edge of the other bed, touched the mattress experimentally. It was a long way from the moss mattress she had shared with Maw and the comforter in which she had wrapped herself in the kitchen at the big house. She was going to work so hard, she told herself resolutely, to save up enough money and find the folks who could bring Maw out of slavery. With Maw behind her, she could go any place in the world. Maw, René, and Eulalie.

With René as her escort, Eulalie left the hotel and went looking for a shop. She wouldn't try on the dress in the shop, Eulalie decided self-consciously. She'd die if the ladies in the shop saw her undergarments—the way they had holes and patches. She'd pick out a dress, buy it, and take it back to the hotel to try it on.

Eulalie bypassed the elegant shops with their gowns from Paris, knowing this was far beyond her range. She was searching for a modest one. She lingered at the window of one such shop, torn by indecision, fumbling for the courage to face the austere saleswomen inside.

"Let's go in," René ordered impatiently, dragging her by the hand. "You got the money to pay."

Again Eulalie was stunned by the amount of money she had to hand over for what she chose. It was the least expensive one in the shop, and only coins remained from her bankroll when the transaction was consummated. To eat tomorrow, she would have to earn money tonight.

Early in the evening, gowned in the becoming cambric dress, deftly cut to highlight her exquisite shoulders and her small, high breasts, her skin creamed and dusted with a pale powder that toned down the golden glints of her skin, Eulalie was ready to set forth on her first independent venture. Her heart pounded. As usual, distaste welled in her throat for what lay ahead of her. But every man she brought to the hotel room would carry Maw that much closer to freedom.

She strolled slowly in front of the white-marbled St. Nicholas Hotel and moved among the crowd of hotel loungers that spilled over into the sidewalk at this time of the evening. Not far behind her hovered René, who had been carefully rehearsed in what was to be done. From the corner of her eye, she saw him dart towards a man, exchange words. She smiled faintly. The man was nodding. Eulalie Cartier was launched.

Staying at the hotel was expensive, yet Eulalie was pleased because the money which she took to the bank each Friday was many times what she had previously taken in a whole month. Most of her clients were transient businessmen from the St. Nicholas. But when they returned to the city on fresh business, they looked for René's now familiar figure outside the hotel.

Eulalie and René continued their daytime pilgrimages to the Astor Library. Once, in a burst of extravagance, when the Crystal Palace was opened as a permanent exhibit, René and she went inside the august doors to walk with awe before the displays of the finest collection of paintings and sculpture ever assembled in the United States, to marvel at the model elevated-railway that carried passengers inside the House of Glass. Eulalie stared reverently at the Sèvres china, which was even more beautiful than Missis Margaret's best china back at The Willows, the Gobelin tapestries, the armor from the Tower of London which Cindy once wrote about in her letters home. There were nuggets and bars of pure gold from the gold fields of California as well as the famous Marochetti statue of George Washington.

For days, René rhapsodized, dreamed about, the fine paintings Eulalie and he had seen in the Crystal Palace. On impulse, Eulalie sought out a store that sold art supplies, then brought René paints and drawing paper. His joy brought rare tears to her eyes. Obediently, each day, she sat for him while he painted—and discarded with disapproval—endless portraits of her.

The compulsion to bring Maw to freedom monopolized her waking thoughts. She eavesdropped on conversations, read the newspapers omnivorously. She was beginning to understand the crosscurrents of feeling on slavery among the people who lived in New York.

The New York merchants were against the abolitionists and on the side of the slave-owners because they did business with the Southerners. Millions of dollars were due to the merchants from the Southerners. With the South deprived of its unpaid slave-labor, New York businessmen considered themselves hovering on the brink of bankruptcy. They would fight with any means at their command to maintain the institution of slavery.

The New York Anti-Slavery Society was struggling heroically against fearful odds. Eulalie know about the meetings that were frequently disrupted by angry New Yorkers. Yet the society continued its fight. New York City had become an important link in the Underground Railroad. And late in the summer of 1854, Eulalie made her contact with a man reputed to be able to bring Maw out of slavery.

Calvin Rutledge was a Virginian who had no stomach for slavery. He was handsome, daring, and accepted as a Southern gentlemen by those who were unaware of his true allegiance. He took pleasure in the sorties he made into slave territory to help runaways to safety. This was his way of life.

Traveling, as always, with René, Eulalie went to Calvin Rutledge's current lodgings, which of necessity changed frequently. Amber eyes alight with fervor, she told him of her own escape and of her inflammatory determination to bring her mother into freedom.

"It'll take money, girl," he warned gently. "I don't do it alone—I have to buy along the way. Help comes high sometimes."

"I have money." She spilled the contents of her purse onto the table before Mr. Rutledge. "And I'll have more by the time you bring Maw out. I'll put it into the bank for you." Her eyes clung to his face. "As I get it, I'll put it into the bank."

"If this isn't enough, you'll pay me more when I return," he said with a courtly bow. "But there's no guarantee I'll be successful." His eyes were somber, momentarily haunted. "Many times I am—but there have been failures. It could be—tragic." His eyes eloquently said what he was reluctant to frame into words.

"Maw will take that chance," Eulalie said urgently. She

thought about the huts, about the Massa and his temper, about the floggings—that Maw might have encountered because of her own escape, about being a piece of property supposedly without a soul. "Better to die in freedom, Mr. Rutledge, than live down there!" Her eyes burned with contempt.

Eulalie and René left Mr. Rutledge's lodgings. Not until Maw walked into the hotel room, all in one piece, Eulalie thought with inner agony, would she have another night's sleep. She sickened as she considered the hazards of escape, which would be harder for Maw than it had been for her. Still, despite her fears, joy surfaced because with Mr. Rutledge's help Maw had a fair chance of making it.

"Mr. Rutledge," René said with quiet respect. "He's a gentleman."

19

Coverless, Margaret Woodstock lay sprawled across the wide bed on this humid morning in late August. Her nightdress lay rumpled high above her legs, all that remained beautiful of the once exquisite Margaret Woodstock. One hand, which revealed its age, rested at the opened neckline of the nightdress caressing a blue-veined breast that half-spilled upon the pillow.

Margaret resolutely kept her eyes shut, though she heard Seraphina moving about the room. She wasn't ready yet to cope with another day, she told herself defiantly. These two weeks that Madeline had again been down here at The Willows had been a trial for her, the way she had to watch herself all the time. She would die rather than let Madeline go back and say Cousin Margaret had taken to the bottle. But Madeline wasn't going back home. She was going back to Paris and taking Cindy with her.

"Missy," Seraphina crooned softly. "Wake up, Missy." It touched Margaret, the way Seraphina had taken to calling her Missy in private, like she was her little baby.

"Me brung yo' tea. Breakfas' be served downstairs in a little while."

Margaret opened her eyes.

"Seraphina, do I *have* to go down to breakfast?" she asked petulantly, allowing herself to be propped up against a bank of pillows. She reached greedily for the tea, which she knew was laced with bourbon. Oh, good, she thought, sipping slowly, feeling herself relaxing already, although there was hardly time for the bourbon to soothe her nerves. "Good, Seraphina."

Seraphina was almost herself again, she decided complacently, ever since David got Eulalie's letter from Canada. George nearly had a stroke when he walked into the drawing room and saw David reading that letter. To George it was adding insult to injury for Eulalie to flaunt herself that way. But Seraphina felt better. Secretly, Margaret was glad Eulalie wrote. An ironic smile touched her thin mouth. It was because of *her* that Eulalie was able to write.

"Me bring fresh water and wash you down, Missy— make cool. Den yo' go downstairs."

"Seraphina, I don't really feel up to going down to breakfast."

"Now honey, yo' got guests in de house," Seraphina reminded, a look of firmness about her face.

"It was quite a party last night, wasn't it?" Margaret smiled in satisfaction. When it came to giving a party, she had *carte blanche* about spending money—George liked to let the neighbors know how well they could entertain. "I'm sure Cindy will remember last night for a long time, even if she is going to live in Paris."

Margaret lay back against the pillows while Seraphina moved quietly out of the room. She had hoped—just for a while, these past few days—that maybe Cindy would be interested in that gentleman from Roanoke who was down here studying specimens for his book on horticulture. What a handsome, dashing man he was! Something unfamiliar stirred in her when she thought about Calvin Rutledge. The feeling embarrassed her.

Cindy just wasn't ready to settle down in marriage,

Margaret told herself as she tried to push from her mind the recurrent accusations George threw in her face about *her* daughter, the ugly insinuations that forced her to confide in Madeline, to seek advice from her more worldly cousin.

"I'll kill her before I'll let her mess around with the blacks!" George yelled, looking capable of doing that, the night she wrote the letter begging Madeline to help her with Cindy. George was so insanely jealous of Cindy that he put the wrong meanings into things—not that Cindy was without guilt, Margaret admitted in this moment of truth. At times, her heart pounded with concern when she saw those dark, secretive looks on Cindy's face. When Cindy was a week late for her time, last month, she was in agony, certain Cindy was pregnant. You couldn't watch her, not every single minute. Now, George's words echoed in her mind. "Every time I turn around, I see something that turns me sick! That daughter of yours—she's got a taste for black meat!"

"Your daughter, too," she had thrown back at George. "It runs in the family!" For a moment, she thought he would slap her. But he hadn't, she remembered with vindictive satisfaction—he'd just turned livid and stamped out of the room.

It still got on her nerves, the way he brought the black wenches into the house. Was Aphrodite pregnant? She had that look about her face. Was it George, or her own man, Tony? That was a handsome buck, that Tony, after the years of being a gangling, skinny black kid. Cindy thought so, too. Well, she wouldn't have to worry about *that* any more, Margaret thought with relief. Cindy would be in Paris.

She would have to compose herself for the day ahead. There was Mr. Rutledge, who had stayed overnight at George's invitation. And then there was Bradford Taylor. It would have been absurd for him to ride all the way back to his plantation at that hour of the night, especially since he and Madeline had been talking about Paris until it was practically daylight.

It was Cindy's last morning at home, she realized sentimentally. This afternoon, Aristotle would drive Cindy and Madeline over to Columbus to take the railroad. They were on their way to New York where they would board the ship for Paris. It was going to be terrible to have Cindy all the way across the ocean again.

Madeline was going to live permanently in Paris. Her husband was reopening their lovely brownstone in New York for himself, with the understanding that Madeline remain in Paris where she couldn't embarrass him with her strange ways. He was just loaded down with money—he didn't care how much Madeline spent. And Cindy adored Madeline, Margaret reassured herself. Cindy would be fine with her.

George always said the niggers had no feelings; after all, they have a different nervous system from white folks —but Seraphina had become a shadow of herself when Eulalie ran off that way. She was humiliated—and scared. George would have flogged her, sold her to anybody who put up a bid, if I hadn't put my foot down, Margaret thought. Without Seraphina, I couldn't have stayed in this house.

Oh, it was hot! She mopped ineffectually at her forehead with a small, sodden handkerchief. Again, in her anxiety to get Cindy married off, her mind moved to Mr. Rutledge. He was a fine, handsome Southern gentleman; but all he cared about, she told herself wistfully, was that book he was writing. Why, he spent hours yesterday roaming about the fields looking for new specimens he could describe in that book of his. He said he'd probably be going back up to Roanoke tomorrow or the next day. They wouldn't see him again, once he left The Willows today. Cindy and he would have made such a beautiful couple.

The door opened. Seraphina walked in with a basin of fresh water and a towel—she used her ample rump to shut the door behind her.

"Me git yo' all freshen up and yo' go down to de table," Seraphina soothed. "Me tell that lazy Venus git de buffet set up de way yo' lak."

Margaret lay back, giving herself up to Seraphina's

large, gentle hands. The house was going to be so empty again without Cindy—but a less tortured place in which to live. David. What were they going to do about David? It terrified her sometimes, the hostility between David and George. David wanted so much to go off to college. He had a right to go to college, he was so bright. They could afford it if George sold off a slave or two—somebody that didn't have family connections, she added conscientiously. David was too grown up for tutors any more—he was ready for college. The last tutor told them that. If it had been Cindy, George wouldn't have thought twice about selling a slave.

Seraphina finished bathing Margaret, then helped her into a dainty, fresh cambric morning-dress and brought her the small box of powder as well as her comb and brush to complete her toilette. Seraphina was cajoled into bringing a second bourbon-laced cup of coffee. That surprised Margaret because normally this effort was futile. Seraphina was pampering her this morning because she was feeling good about the party last night, Margaret decided. There was a special bond between Seraphina and her—both of them with their little girls off in strange parts of the world.

In a few hours, Cindy would be out of this house. When would she see her again? George talked, vaguely, about the two of them going off to Paris next year—or was that just bragging in front of Mr. Taylor? When did she and George ever go anywhere together?

Margaret went downstairs, her fixed hostess-smile on her face. Madeline was already at the breakfast table, and Venus was tempting her with various platters from the buffet.

"Margaret, how cool you look," Madeline greeted her affectionately. "However do you manage it in this heat?"

"I move as little as possible," Margaret said with ironic humor. "Madeline—" Her eyes were grateful, serious. "I do want to thank you for taking on Cindy this way. I didn't know where else to turn."

"I'll be glad to have her with me," Madeline said lightly. "You need someone of your own, living over there the way I do. Not that I would have it any other way," she picked up vigorously. "I couldn't live in my husband's world."

"Good morning, ladies." Calvin Rutledge, smiling broadly, strode in through the French doors that opened out onto a side portico. "I've been out walking for hours. Mrs. Woodstock, you have such marvelous flora around this plantation that I'm tempted to sell my place in Roanoke and try to find something close by."

"Come join us for breakfast, Mr. Rutledge." Margaret was spilling over with Southern charm. "We would so love to have you for a permanent neighbor." She flirted lightly with him, feeling the years roll back, knowing this was only table talk, yet enjoying it. "It's going to be so lonely here, with Madeline leaving with Cindy. And David talking about going off to college next month."

"Is he doing any more than talking about it?" Madeline asked dryly. Margaret shot her a glance that pleaded for discretion.

Out in the kitchen, china crashed to the floor. Seraphina's voice rose loudly in sharp rebuke. That was unusual for Seraphina, who normally chastised in low tones, recoiling from the sounds of wrath. Margaret plunged into compulsive small talk that at the same time embarrassed her because she could hear herself chattering inanely.

David joined them at the table, taking his place quietly beside his mother. Minutes later, George and Bradford Taylor strolled into the dining room. They were already engrossed in heated discussion about the state of the Southern plantations.

"I tell you, George," Bradford picked up, after the amenities had been satisfied, "it's going to be a lot worse here in the South before it gets any better. I'm not talking only about the cotton crops, mind you—" He paused, to consider what Venus was offering for breakfast.

"We'd be a whole lot better off if we paid some attention to the soil," David burst in recklessly. "We wear out the earth by putting in cotton year after year."

"You may have something there, young man." Bradford

Taylor looked at him with respect. "You going to take up agriculture at college?"

"I want to." David shot a wary glance at his father.

"Isn't there an agricultural college, right here in Georgia?" Taylor asked.

"It's a school for orphans," David explained. An undercurrent of excitement coated his voice. "But there's the Philadelphia Agricultural Society—and a school in Maine that teaches agriculture—" His eyes moved compulsively, again, to his father.

"The boy has to learn to run the plantation," George said brusquely. "I can hire all the help I need to worry about the crops. It's the over-all picture David has to learn to handle."

"I wouldn't shortchange the lad on his ideas about taking up agriculture in college." Surprisingly, Bradford Taylor was intervening in David's behalf. "The time is coming when that earth out there won't turn out another cotton crop, no matter how we sweat—and we'll need men with education to tell us what we have to do."

"As long as we have slaves to put in the seed, we'll have cotton crops." George, annoyed at this pessimism, gestured angrily to Venus to refill his coffee cup.

"Venus, bring in a fresh pot of coffee," Margaret ordered quietly. Everybody seemed to have a good appetite this morning, despite the party last night.

"I can tell you right now," Bradford offered, "once I find myself an overseer who can handle my place, I'm doing what the ladies here are doing." He smiled gallantly at Madeline and Cindy. "I'm taking myself off to Paris for six months or a year."

"Don't wait too long, Mr. Taylor." Cindy's eyes were a blatant invitation. "We would love to see you visiting us in Paris, wouldn't we, Cousin Madeline?"

Why did Cindy lean forward that way, so that everybody at the table could almost see her breasts? Even her father and her brother. Margaret sighed. Why couldn't Cindy learn that you didn't throw yourself at a man?— especially not at Bradford Taylor, who made it plain he wasn't interested in being annexed as a husband.

"Conditions down here are not heartening." Bradford conceded. He waited until Venus had sashayed out to the kitchen—with a tantalizing undulation of her hips that was offered for the benefit of any interested male. "I don't like what's happening, what with these uprisings and the increasing number of runaways."

"We have to show 'em who's boss!" George's eyes bristled with anger. "You walk out there, and they know there's a flogging waiting anyone who acts up, they won't be acting up. That's what I keep telling David." His eyes clashed nastily with his son's. "You have to be a man to run a plantation. Like this morning—" He smiled with a secretive relish. "There's a black working out there in the fields since sunup—he knows he's getting his flogging when I've finished with my breakfast. And he's going to put in a hard morning's work before he gets it—and after he mends in the hospital down at the quarters, he'll be working harder than ever—because he knows there'll be another flogging if he don't."

Margaret stared unhappily at her plate. George disgusted Mr. Rutledge. Couldn't he see that? No gentleman liked to hear that kind of talk at the breakfast table. But then, she knew long ago that George Woodstock wasn't a gentleman.

"David," his father demanded, "you coming out with me while I flog that nigger? Maybe you'd like to put a hand in for me?"

"No, sir!" David flushed from his throat all the way up to his hairline. "I don't take to flogging any humans."

David's eyes were defiant, accusing. Margaret felt herself breaking out in a cold sweat. Dear God, don't let George start up a nasty scene! Not with strangers here at the table. And then—quite unexpectedly—George chuckled, pushed back his chair, and rose to his feet.

"You'll change your mind, boy, when you're running this plantation! Now, if you-all will excuse me, I've got a flogging to attend to."

Standing before a long, narrow window in her bedroom, Margaret fanned herself, opened her wrapper with a querulous frown. Not a leaf stirred out there tonight. She walked across the room to the bourbon bottle on the mantel. Empty. She should have remembered to bring up another. Now she'd have to walk downstairs, pick the lock on the cabinet, the way she had learned to do, and bring herself up a fresh bottle. Why did George enjoy humiliating her this way, making her pick the lock like a common thief? A year ago, he started that.

Margaret walked out into the hallway, down the wide staircase, conscious of the strange stillness in the house tonight—more than normally apparent because of the festivities last night. She wished now that she had not let David go off to visit the Butler boys for a few days. She had let him go because of the flogging incident this morning. He was so upset. George was off somewhere. This hour of the night the slaves were all in bed in their quarters. George wasn't bringing that Aphrodite into the house tonight. He was probably tired after the party last night and driving all the way to Columbus this afternoon with Cindy and Madeline—to see them off personally that way.

She walked to the liquor cabinet in the library. Heard the night sounds that were no sounds at all because they were so familiar. Felt suffocated by the heavy scents of the flowering shrubs and the still-blooming trees. Only silence from the slave quarters. The flogging had insured that.

Because she was unstrung, impatient, she found it difficult to pick the lock tonight. Finally, the door opened for her. She withdrew her fresh bottle of bourbon, closed the door, hurried back upstairs to her own room. She was going to miss having Cindy home. She wished, again, that she had not allowed David to go over to the Butlers. The house was so big. She was so alone.

Margaret poured bourbon into an iced-tea tumbler. Her hand trembled in her anxiety to lift the glass to her mouth. She walked to the window, which was thrown wide in tonight's heat. Moonlight splashed across the landscape. She lifted the glass to her mouth with both hands. And then, suddenly, her hands froze, the bourbon forgotten. Fading blue eyes dilated in disbelief as they probed the bizarre tableau below.

George! George was pinioned between two slaves while a third lifted a whip into the air and brought it down upon George Woodstock's bloated white body. His cry, as the leather cut into delicate flesh, pierced the night. The glass fell from her nerveless fingers.

"No cry out, Missis!" a harsh, masculine, Negroid voice rapped out sharply. "Let him do!"

Margaret tore her gaze away from her husband's body cringing beneath the lashes. She stared at the tall, muscular, near-naked black buck that hovered in her bedroom door. Perspiration shone on his face, his bare chest, his arms.

"Tony!" She paled, dazed by the unexpected happenings.

"Let him do!" Tony commanded, lifting his hand to display the knife he held. "No stop—"

In a state of shock, of utter unreality, Margaret pulled her eyes away from Tony to focus on the scene below. Moonlight bathed the face of the man with the whip. It was Alexander. Alexander flogging George! This couldn't be happening. Not here at The Willows! At other plantations—but not here!

Margaret turned again to Tony. Her mouth opened. No words came out. She felt as though her breath were being snuffed out. Her chest hurt. Tony moved forward menacingly, the knife lifted eloquently high in his hand. He stalked closer to her. Margaret, instinctively backing up, felt the windowsill at the base of her spine.

"Watch!" Tony ordered, his face glistening with satisfaction.

Like Tony, Margaret turned again to the drama being enacted below.

George cried out in rage, in pain, in frustration, each time the leather cut into unaccustomed white flesh. But Alexander was discarding the whip now. He pulled a knife from his waist. With the other hand, he shucked away George's trousers while the other two men held the master between them.

"Oh, my God!" Margaret's voice rose perilously.

Alexander dropped to his knees. The knife moved towards its quarry. For a moment, Alexander's hand obscured the view. How long had Alexander waited for this moment? The knife was *there*. She shuddered at George's high, shrill scream, as the knife severed the skin.

"He'll bleed to death! You have to do something!" Margaret hovered at the edge of hysteria, hearing George's voice, three years back, when he came into the house that hot June morning after flogging Alexander—"and then, Margaret, then I cut off his big black nuts!" "Tony, do something!"

"No, Missis," Tony refused softly. "Alexander fix, de way Massa fix him. But Massa no bother yo' no mo'. No bother my woman."

Margaret pulled her gaze away from the three blacks and the white below. Two men, two eunuchs. George Woodstock would never again bring a black wench to his bed.

"Why?" Margaret whispered. "Why?" But she knew why.

Her eyes clashed with Tony's. An odd excitement took root in her. Her heart pounded. They were not mistress and slave at this moment. Male and female. Tony was staring at her as though she were a woman, not an aging ruin. No man had ever looked at her in that way—not since she married George, all those years ago.

"Yo' be glad," Tony said. His eyes fastened on Margaret's half-exposed milk-white breasts. "No pester yo' no mo'."

"Put away the knife," she whispered, shutting out the sounds of her husband's anguish below. "Please—"

Tony dropped the knife to a table, moved the huge black body towards hers.

"Pretty," he whispered. "Pretty."

Nobody had called her pretty in such a long time. Had it ever happened? Once, she was supposed to be beautiful. Her heart pounded, but she wasn't afraid. Not the least little bit. How big he was, how strong! George had used his woman, and now he was going to use her! She quivered when his black hand touched the blue-veined white breast.

"Me real man," he boasted, gripping her by the shoulders now, pushing her back towards the bed. "Black bettuh than white—you see!"

The feather mattress received her weight. His blackness hovered above her while his hands tore away the wrapper, the fragile nightdress beneath. He didn't see her as an old woman. His dark eyes smoldered with passion. To him she was beautiful. He touched her skin with awe.

"Don't hurt me," she whispered, but she wasn't afraid.

"Me make you feel like woman," he boasted.

She closed her eyes, her mouth parting in excitement when his maleness invaded her. Passion rippled over her in waves. Tonight, she was a woman. She was desired for what she was. With George, she had been a receptacle for his passion—valued mainly for the money she had brought with her.

A low cry escaped her. Her white hands closed in about the black back. Poor George.

20

Each evening at dusk, Eulalie and René left their hotel to parade before the grandiose hotels along Broadway. It rarely took longer than half an hour for René to signal that Eulalie had a suitor. In a burst of bravado, she ordered René to raise her fee, met not a single rebuff, raised it again with a like reaction. She could have been almost happy if her mind were not plagued with concern for Maw. She had arrived at a fatalistic acceptance of her profession—her body was the means by which she and René lived, and it was the way she was bringing Maw out of slavery.

In the small, modest hotel-room late in the afternoon, Eulalie sat on one narrow bed, slim legs gracefully folded beneath her. She was motionless, silent. René concentrated on his current painting of her. Painting Eulalie's portrait had become an obsession with him. At first, she had been shocked when René asked her to pose for him without her clothes. But she realized that from René this was a compliment. He found true beauty in her body.

"You moved," René reproached.

"I'm sorry," she apologized with the faint smile that was so effective with the gentlemen from the hotels, and resumed her ordered position.

"You're worrying about your Mama," René said softly, as usual attuned to her moods.

"It's been so long, René." She stared somberly into space. "We went to Mr. Rutledge at the end of August. It's three weeks since then."

"These things take time, Eulalie," René soothed. "You trust him. He's a real gentleman."

"I know." She nodded somberly. "We'd best get out of here. It's almost dark. Put away the paints for today. I'll dress."

It meant nothing to René to have her walk around him without her clothes on. To René, she was beautiful, the way a statue was beautiful. What would she have done if she hadn't found René that way? To Eulalie, René was the young brother she had never had. She had grown to love him fiercely, protectively.

They left the hotel and joined the promenade on Broadway. Eulalie relished the air of gaiety, the evening excitement of the city, even while she mentally rejected the way in which she earned her livelihood. For half an hour, walking along Broadway, she could pretend she was a lady—until René signaled her that it was time to return to the hotel.

Tonight René snared a customer right away. Eulalie catalogued the bold yet friendly way the stocky, ruddy-faced man in his forties was surveying her. He would talk a lot, but he would be quick, and he would not argue about the money. She saw him bend towards René, say something. What did he want? René was disconcerted. Eulalie frowned uneasily as she watched René approach her.

"Eulalie—" René looked at her apprehensively. "He wants to take you to supper first." He turned to look at the waiting man, who appeared amused at René's uncertainty.

Eulalie shot a covert, searching glance at the man.

"All right, René," she accepted quietly. "You go back to the hotel, wait there till I come."

"Eulalie, you sure it's all right?" René frowned, his dark eyes questioning.

"It's all right," she said firmly. She was certain he was not one of the Mets preparing to throw her into jail. That almost never happened. Not here on Broadway.

Immediately, Eulalie knew that she could relax with Bill Marchand. Nothing horrendous was going to happen to her. He was loud-mouthed, rough in his speech, yet she sensed a goodness in him that put her at ease. He treated her like a lady, she decided with satisfaction when they were seated at a table in the hotel dining room—and Eulalie struggled to conceal her awe at such august surroundings.

"I never been to New York before," Bill Marchand announced expansively when he had ordered for the two of them and the waiter had withdrawn from their table. "I had to come here on business. We got ourselves a silver mine—my partner and me—out in Nevada?"

"What's it like in Nevada?" Eulalie asked with genuine interest. She knew, vaguely, where Nevada was.

"God's country," he said solemnly. "My part of it. The land rolls towards the mountain ranges. In the spring, peach trees dot the sky with their flowers. Squat juniper and nut pine everywhere—and the kind of sunsets and sunrises you don't see nowhere else. And, of course, there's that silver," he reminded humorously. "Everybody got the gold fever out there—they don't wanna believe about the silver. The Mexicans keep yelling, '*Mucho plata*,' but nobody listens. They think they're so much better than the Mexicans—they can't be bothered being friendly with them folks." He grinned broadly. "Except my partner and me, and them Grosh brothers."

"Who are the Grosh brothers?" Eulalie asked shyly. She liked a man who was friendly with folks, even if they were dark-skinned Mexicans. It was a new experience to sit across a table with a man this way and have him talk with her. Only René ever talked with her. And David. The other men just cared about what happened on the bed in the darkened hotel room.

"The way them Grosh brothers are going, they'll hit the biggest silver vein anybody ever saw. I guess maybe they're a-sitting on a whole mountain of silver. Oh, I'm not complaining," he said quickly. "My partner and me are doing all right." He chuckled reminiscently. "I'm here in the city to finance our mines. Got some good connections through my partner. That'll keep me in New York five or six weeks." He leaned forward, his keen brown eyes pleased with what he saw. "I figure I need a pretty little thing like you to keep me company while I'm here, make up for them long, empty nights out there."

Eulalie was glad that her table manners were so good. Better than Mr. Marchand's, she noted without braggadocio. Slowly, through supper, she began to relax sufficiently to enjoy the elegance of her surroundings. She watched the parade of courses with wonder. Turtle soup, lamb with mint sauce, salmon with peas and asparagus, a roasted chicken, champagne—which she drank sparingly and which seemed to have no effect at all on Bill Marchand.

After supper, he took her, not back to her own room but upstairs to his hotel suite.

"Like it?" he demanded with pride, showing off the parlor, the chamber, the dressing room.

"It's beautiful," she conceded self-consciously. No matter how many men, there was always this moment when her mind must do battle against her emotions.

"All right, you stay here," he ordered jovially. "Till I get done with my business and have to go back out there to Nevada. Oh, you can go off during the day to see your friends," he gibed good-humoredly. "I don't care about what you do during the daytime, so long as you're here in the evening to keep me company. Every night, over there on the mantel," he pointed to the marble-faced fireplace, "you'll find one of these for yourself." He pulled out a bill. "Now you think that's gonna be enough to keep you happy?"

"Yes, sir," she stammered, never expecting such munificence, momentarily thrown into confusion by its evidence.

"Don't you *sir* me," Bill Marchand roared, his eyes crinkled with laughter. "I don't want to be respected—I want to be made happy!" He walked over to a lamp, turned it down, moved to the next. "Now show me how good you are, Eulalie Cartier."

Bill Marchand was a strange man, Eulalie decided. Good-humored, loud-mouthed, occasionally given to outrageous boasting. But each morning after a heated night of romping beneath the covers, he started off, quiet, cautious, to do business with those men downtown who were going to help him and his partner finance their silver mine. And nobody was going to put anything over on Bill Marchand, Eulalie guessed with respect.

Marchand made it clear that he was pleased with her. He took her shopping at A. T. Stewart's, which she would never have dared enter alone. He showed her silks from Lyons, dresses and gloves from Paris, exquisite English cambrics and wools, Irish linens, carpets from Brussels. He bought her more clothes than she ever thought of owning. René was ecstatic over their acquisition, fondling the fine materials with reverence.

On the surface, Eulalie maintained a charming aura of serenity. Bill never suspected the anguish, the gnawing anxiety, that lurked beneath her gentle smile—there was still no word from Maw. Nor from Mr. Rutledge. Nothing. Only this terrifying silence.

On impulse, Bill took her dining at Delmonico's, where only the rich and the socially elite of New York were permitted to dine. One of the men with whom he met during the day—he had an eye on the potential fortune to be amassed in Nevada—had arranged for their admittance to Delmonico's, Bill confided snugly.

Eulalie held her head high as she and Bill were ushered, without waiting, to their table at Delmonico's. Eyes wandered, with curiosity and amusement, towards Eulalie and Bill. He was in his stubbornly Western attire, and she in the modish Paris gown bought in A. T. Stewart's—it would have delighted even Cindy Woodstock.

"A visitor from Spain, probably," a male voice murmured with admiration. "The Spanish women have that pride of bearing, you know."

Bill winked, hearing the comment. Seated at the table, he reached across to hold her hand with a possessive pride. But Eulalie realized that Bill's business would soon be transacted and that she would soon be parading along Broadway after dusk. She sat stiffly, self-conscious in such grandiose surroundings. Bill knew they were shocking some of the folks—he enjoyed that, didn't he? Did they know she was Bill's fancy woman?

The weeks were speeding past as Eulalie's apprehension for Maw's welfare grew to disquieting proportions. René tried to comfort her. Once, Eulalie—with René as her escort—went down to Carmine Street to walk among the squalid Negro shacks. There was a compulsive need in her to move among the familiarly dark faces, as though she were bringing herself closer to Maw by this action. Yet, instantly, Eulalie realized they looked upon René and her as intruders, sightseers curious about the "niggers." It was an upsetting realization. She belonged in neither world.

Lying in bed with Eulalie on Sunday night, Bill announced to Eulalie that they were going to a costume ball the coming Saturday evening.

"The way I hear it told," Bill drawled, "this here is not the *avenoodles* like my friends."

"What's that?" Eulalie asked, ever curious about the unfamiliar.

"Avenoodles?" he chuckled. "Why, them's the Fifth Avenue Noodles, folks that struck it rich in gold or made a killing here in cotton. They got the money to buy them Fifth Avenue houses, but not to get themselves invited into the real New York society."

"Bill, what are we going for then?" Eulalie recoiled from the prospect of snubbing.

"Well, I kinda like to see how them fancy families live. I hear they don't take to costume balls much—this is taking real nerve to give one now. It appears that, back thirteen or fourteen years ago, there was this big scandal when Mr. Henry Brevoort gave a costume ball in his new mansion on Fifth Avenue. A pair of his guests—he was a captain from the South—were secretly engaged against their families' wishes. Still in their costumes, they left the ball and went off and got married. That put the costume balls into sad disrepute," he mocked. "But this here lady decided she wasn't going to be happy without giving this ball Saturday evening."

"Bill, you really want to go?"

Eulalie cringed before the prospect of moving among such august strangers. In the dim gaslight of Bill's hotel suite, in the concert saloons and the restaurants to which he regularly took her, she felt that the theatrical make-up she wore was effective. But a costume ball! Perhaps the lights would be bright. Perhaps some of those folks would look hard and decide she was not Spanish or French— though she had adopted a studied habit, self-conscious but determined, of dropping a French phrase here and there. She always did it loudly enough so that diners at neighboring tables would hear. Every day, when she and René took their never-missed stroll up to the Astor Library, they spoke only in French. She was going to speak French as fluently as René someday, she had promised herself.

"Come now, Eulalie—" Bill brought her back to the moment, "I think we can have ourselves a real fine time at that costume ball." His eyes twinkled; his mouth curled in a wide grin. "I'm getting the tickets that'll take us inside through my contacts. It's at one of them brownstone mansions uptown on Washington Place. We'll have to get ourselves set with costumes—I'm calling in a dressmaker to make you the prettiest costume of any lady that shows up at that ball! It's gotta be in the fashion of the French court in the period of Louis the Fifteenth."

"*Louis Quinze*," Eulalie extracted from her file-cabinet mind.

Bill beamed admiringly.

"Now, where the hell do you come by all this fancy

information?" Her dropping French phrases from time to time, had amused him.

"I learned French from my grandmother," she improvised. "A little bit."

"What else do you know about this French king?"

"Well, I think he was the one who had a—a friend named Madame de Pompadour—and then there was Madame Du Barry." Eulalie colored faintly, remembering the relationship between the king and the two ladies.

"All right!" Bill thumped his thigh with one large, work-worn hand. "You're going to that ball as Madame Du Barry."

For the balance of the week, Eulalie was alternately enthralled by and terrified of the coming ball. Every day, the modiste came to the hotel and carried on dramatically about Bill's demands for the gown, which changed with lightning rapidity and which she swore she would never be able to execute in time for the ball. If the modiste harbored any suspicions about Eulalie's antecedents—she saw Eulalie stripped down to her undergarments in the candid daylight—she kept these discreetly to herself.

On the night of the costume ball, René was practically beside himself with excitement. He swore that he would creep up to the windows of the splendid mansion and look inside to see Eulalie amid such glory. Eulalie herself—in her ivory-colored satin court-costume and powdered wig— was nervous when the carriage deposited Bill and her before the imposing residence. She gazed with awe at the mansard roof, at the Corinthian columns, pilasters that flanked the main entrance through which the guests were now entering. On Bill's arm, she walked up the stoop and smiled loftily as Bill showed his invitation to the costumed doorman.

Eulalie battled to conceal her excitement at being inside this elegant mansion which had been refurnished, at fantastic expense, in the *Louis Quinze* period especially for this evening's affair. The costumes the ladies wore were awesome, their jewels blinding. The servants wore wigs and uniforms that reflected the Versailles Court. The male guests wore self-conscious smiles, like Bill, at finding themselves in satin breeches and silk hose.

Bill leaned towards Eulalie and whispered, "Honey, you see that old lady over there? I'll bet she's carrying around thirty-five thousand in diamonds on her!" He chuckled knowingly. "Her husband can afford it. He owns a fleet of clipper ships."

But Eulalie was not looking at the lady wearing thirty-five thousand in diamonds. Her eyes were fastened to a tall, handsome young man in satin breeches and silk hose. Her heart pounded. He was older than David, but the features were so similar that Eulalie found it impossible to remove her gaze from him.

The strange young man was talking politely to an elderly woman in ornate costume. Seeming to feel the weight of Eulalie's gaze, he turned to look in her direction. His eyes clung compulsively. Eulalie's mouth went dry. And then, she felt Bill's hand at her arm.

"Honey, look—but don't get ideas," Bill warned gently. "That there is one of the Sanders' sons—I mean, *the* Sanders family. I been meeting them in the line of business. They're so much society, you prick 'em with a pin, they'll bleed blue."

"I wasn't looking," Eulalie protested, the telltale pink at her throat betraying her.

"Come on," Bill ordered. "Let's go over and try some society vittles before they start up with the dancing."

When the dancing commenced, Bill made a point of drawing Eulalie away from the activity. He was embarrassed about taking his silk-stockinged legs through the intricacies of the polkas and the schottisches. For Eulalie, it was sufficient to view the splendor of the ladies' gowns against the authentic setting provided for this occasion.

At regular intervals, Eulalie's eyes sought out the handsome young man who had appeared quite taken with her earlier. He was doing a schottische now with a haughty young lady who seemed to be unbending before his charms.

"Oh, Gilbert, you say such terrible things," the young

lady giggled when they pranced within hearing distance of Eulalie and Bill.

Gilbert. His name was Gilbert Sanders.

Eulalie was simultaneously disappointed and relieved when Bill decided, fairly early in the evening, that he had had enough of these society festivities.

"Let's go home, get outta these clothes, and have ourselves some supper in bed," he decided. "I don't want to waste too much time on these things. I'll have to be leaving for Nevada in another two or three weeks. I been stalling my partner as it is," he admitted humorously.

Eulalie felt a tightening in her throat when she considered Bill's imminent departure. She would have to go back on the street again. She would never touch the money that she had been putting regularly into the bank—that was to take care of Maw when she got here.

Eulalie's mind returned recurrently to Gilbert Sanders. He was so like David that she trembled in remembrance. Would she ever see Gilbert Sanders again? All the society ladies were probably throwing themselves right at his head. He was that handsome.

In the morning, Bill had gone off already to those daily conferences of his with the wizards of finance when Eulalie awoke earlier than usual. Again, she remembered what he had said last night about going back to Nevada in two or three weeks. She was going to miss this fine hotel-apartment with the funny little metal things—Bill called them registers—through which hot air was piped on the cool days that arrived now and then, like this morning. Maw would just not believe a room being heated this way!

It was October already. What about Maw? Why didn't she hear from Mr. Rutledge, hear *something* about Maw? She told him she would give him more money when he came back—he wasn't worried about that. She got out of bed and dressed quickly before taking a lingering look at the ivory-colored satin costume that Bill—with a rare show of practicality—was selling to a theatrical costumer. This morning, there was an odd urgency in her to get back to the small hotel-room where she would soon be spending her nights.

Wearing her faint, protective smile, Eulalie walked through the lobby with her head high. Nobody asked questions about her—nobody cared as long as Mr. Marchand paid his bills. The outside air was crisp, autumnal, the sunlight brilliant. Eulalie walked with compulsive swiftness.

At her own hotel, she hurried inside the entrance, crossed the lobby to the stairs. Some intuition telling her that today would be unlike other days in this hotel. She walked quietly up the dimly lit, narrow stairs, conscious that most of the hotel guests—who plied a profession similar to her own—were asleep at this hour.

She knocked lightly, impatient for René to admit her. The door opened wide. She moved inside. Her eyes fell on the thinner-than-remembered, older-than-remembered woman who sat at the edge of one narrow bed.

"Maw!" Eulalie fell to her knees before Seraphina. "Oh, Maw!"

21

Eulalie was beside herself with joy at having Maw safely with her. Mr. Rutledge had supplied Seraphina with Free Papers that were substantially better than those Eulalie had received from her Quaker benefactors. Mr. Rutledge, after all, was a Virginia gentleman belonging to a well-known family of slave owners.

Seraphina had made her escape, she reported, along with Alexander, Tony, and two other bucks unknown to Eulalie. The trip had been fraught with near-disasters.

"Us had some trouble up one river," Seraphina said simply. "Some buckshot hit me in de laig. Dat's how come me limp."

"Oh, Maw—" Eulalie's eyes were anguished.

"Don' matter—me make free." Seraphina's eyes were serenely triumphant. "Alexander take de others one way, Massa Rutledge, he take me where me can stay till well again. Then Massa Rutledge bring me up here with some other niggers. Them other niggers go on to Canada. Me got mah baby here." Her eyes were warm with love.

"Maw, I've got·some money in the bank. For us."
Pride was overshadowed by humiliation. She lowered her
eyes. "I couldn't find a job, working at cleaning or taking
care of children. I asked lots of places. Other girls had
come and got all the jobs, it seemed like—white girls. I—
I bring home money regularly. Maw—I entertain white
gentlemen," she said softly. "René goes out and brings
them to me."

Seraphina's eyes were sad, wise, compassionate.

"Baby, us does what us has to do to stay alive in dis
worl'. Yo' don' need hol' your head down in shame.
Eulalie, you be a lady de way yo' handle yo' self."
Seraphina's voice rang with assurance.

"I'm learning, Maw," Eulalie said passionately, "All
kinds of things. René is even teaching me to talk French!"

"Yo' know what's the mattah with dat boy?" Seraphina
shook her head mockingly. "All skin 'n' bones. Me hafta
fatten dat boy up if he's goin' out workin'!"

"Maw, we'll get a nice place to live," Eulalie decided
recklessly. A place where Maw could cook for them and
watch over them. She couldn't bring the clients here, not
with Maw in the room, and she couldn't turn Maw out
into the streets at night. They would get themselves one
of those family apartments in a cheap building. Not on
Carmine Street, nor up in Shantytown where all the poor
Irish lived. Somewhere close to the hotel. "There's the
money in the bank—and I'm making out real good. The
gentlemen like me—" For an unwary instant, Eulalie's
eyes betrayed her distaste for the gentlemen.

"When, Eulalie?" René pushed, his eyes alight. He
was thinking he would have more room for his painting,
Eulalie guessed with sympathy. "Let's go look today!"

"Maw, you hungry?" Eulalie asked solicitously. "René
can go downstairs and bring you up something nice to
eat."

"Me ate," Seraphina said with dignity. "That Massa
Rutledge, he feed me good, like me white folks. And he
say, tell Eulalie, no more money—yo' give him·plenty."

"Then let's go out and look for a place to live," Eulalie
decided, relieved that the obligation to Mr. Rutledge was

complete. Her eyes glowed with a new *joie de vivre*. Maw was *here!* "Right now—"

Maw hesitated, her eyes concerned. Eulalie stared at her anxiously.

"Honey, we make like yo' the little missy—me yo' nigger."

"Maw!" Discomfort welled up in Eulalie, staining her cheeks with color.

"Like yo' be now, baby, yo' pass for white," Maw pointed out gently. "Bes' dat way, even up No'th."

"I pass at night," Eulalie corrected with an alien bluntness. "In the daytime with the sun shining bright, I don't know. Even with the powder and all, I'm not sure." Now, in the same room with Maw, guilt tugged at her. "Maw, is it wrong to pass for white?"

"Yo' Paw be white," Maw said. "Yo' be either way yo' want to be."

"I don't want to play at being white." Eulalie's eyes flashed disdainfully, pride pricking at her. "It's just easier that way. My papers wouldn't be worth anything at all if somebody came up and said, 'you're a runaway slave.' I have to try to pass."

"Honey, maybe Canada be safer fo' us all," Maw said, her eyes searching Eulalie's.

Eulalie was silent for a moment.

"Nobody's advertising for me—it's been too long for Mr. Woodstock to bother about that. I'm safe enough," Eulalie summed up determinedly. She couldn't leave New York. Someday, David was coming up here. She knew he would. "I sent that letter to David, making everybody think I was up in Canada. They did, didn't they?"

"Sho' did, baby." Maw confirmed, smiling.

"That wasn't why I sent the letter," Eulalie said quickly. "I wanted you to know I was all right—I knew David would tell you."

"Massa David, he give me dat lettuh." Seraphina fished into her bosom, brought forth the tattered sheet of paper. "Me cain't read, but me keep."

Tears stung Eulalie's eyes.

"Let's go looking for a place to live," she said softly. "A place fit for my Maw."

Together, Seraphina, René, and Eulalie left the hotel, ignoring the curious glances from the man behind the counter. Let him think anything he liked, Eulalie told herself defiantly. Maw had papers saying she was freed by Mr. Rutledge. But deep within her, Eulalie realized the man behind the counter was seeing Eulalie's golden skin in a new light. But that was none of his business—she paid the rent, that was all that mattered.

Eulalie guided the other two to a row of lodgings where she was certain the rents were in keeping with what she could afford to pay. She would hold the hotel room for business—and Maw and René and she would live in the new place.

"Here," Eulalie said expectantly, spying a sign in a window. "Let's go inside and see. And Maw," she said sternly, "if it's not nice, we don't take it. We'll go looking some place else."

Eulalie walked into the building, beckoning Maw and René to follow her. She knocked on the indicated door. A man, unkept and unshaven, opened the door.

"I saw the sign about the rooms in the window," Eulalie said. "How big a place is it, and how much does it cost?"

"Two rooms," the man said slowly. His eyes moved from Eulalie, to Maw, back to Eulalie again. His eyes went opaque. "But it won't do no good to look. We don't take niggers in here!"

Eulalie, Maw, and René walked back out into the autumn sunlight that no longer seemed so bright. Eulalie reached for Maw's hand, held it tightly in hers. She walked with her head high, her face taut with anger.

"Eulalie, de man, he mean me," Maw said gently.

"He meant both of us," Eulalie insisted.

"He meant all three of us," René contributed with determined cheerfulness. "I'm as dark as Eulalie." Guilt by association disturbed René not at all.

"Baby, don' yo' be all upset," Maw urged. "Folks be folks, in de South or in de No'th. Not ever'body likes niggers—yo' know dat."

"Some of them are scared blacks will beat them to the job—and that they'll work for less money," Eulalie said bitterly. "I listen to them talk sometimes."

"Let's go look some place else," René suggested. "Not everybody feels like that."

"Eulalie, yo' can leave me where de colored folks stay," Maw offered somberly. "Dey must have some place like dat."

"Maw, you're not going to live on Carmine Street," Eulalie insisted intensely. "We're staying together." She squinted in concentration. Maybe Bill could help. He was leaving very soon anyhow. If he got mad, finding out she wasn't white, she would be out that much money—but it was worth the gamble. "I'm going to talk to my friend tonight," she picked up with a show of enthusiasm. "He knows something about everything. And today, Maw, we're going to show you the kind of sights you never saw before!"

The trio spent much of the day in walking about New York until Seraphina admitted to being exhausted. They returned to the hotel room with the tacit understanding that the three of them would share this for now. No questions asked here, Eulalie guessed with her growing young cynicism. They would turn the other way as long as she paid her rent—exhorbitant as she had learned it was.

At twilight, Eulalie stood before Bill's door, knocking lightly. She could hear his robust baritone inside. It must have been a good day for him.

"Well, I was wondering when you were getting back," he drawled, slapping her affectionately across the rump. "I got good news, from the business standpoint—all the financing we need is set. But I'm gonna have to be leaving by the end of the week. Got a telegram from my partner— he's raising all hell about me getting back out there."

"I'm glad you got the money," Eulalie said softly. "I'm sorry you're leaving so soon—"

"We'll have some hell-raising to do before I get outta town," he said, his eyes kindling as they rested on Eulalie, recognizing that their time together was to be short. "Come here, honey—"

Afterwards, when they were dressing to go down to the hotel dining room to have their dinner, Bill inspected Eulalie with a quizzical gaze.

"Something's bothering you," he reproached and grinned. "I figure it's more than me going back to Nevada."

"It's nothing." She hesitated, hoping he would probe.

"It's something," he corrected. "Come on, Eulalie, tell old Bill what's eating at you."

"My Maw's just come up from the South," Eulalie confided quietly. Bill had never asked her about her folks, and she had never volunteered any information before now. She took a deep breath, then met Bill's eyes squarely. "Maw—she's not white. We went looking for a place to live—they said they didn't want niggers." Her eyes were overbright, faintly defiant.

"You don't have to look at me that way, young lady," he chided mildly. "I don't pick my friends by the color of their skin. My best friend—next to my partner—is a Mexican four shades darker'n you." He chuckled. " 'Course, if you get technical, he can claim to be pure Caucasian. Ain't that a fancy word?" An unfamiliar sarcasm undercoated his voice.

"I don't want to take Maw down to Carmine Street," Eulalie said earnestly. "Maybe I can rent another room for Maw at the hotel, but she won't be happy where she can't cook and take care of René and me." Eulalie smiled. "René's not my brother, but Maw's adopted him already."

"I got an idea honey," Bill said thoughtfully. "Before I go downtown tomorrow to sign all them papers the lawyers are drawing up, you and me are going looking for that family apartment you're hankering for." His eyes crinkled in amusement. "You can't go in the real cheap places, because they think just one way. We go looking somewhere more expensive. Now don't get in an uproar," he ordered. "I'm paying the first six months' rent for you—I can handle that easy enough. After that, I figure you'll be able to handle it yourself, a bright little thing like you. We're going looking for a place for a young lady and her brother, the family of my partner back in Nevada.

You're being looked after by an old family retainer. Now I think that's respectable enough for anybody. And Eulalie—" His eyes crinkled in laughter. "With all the shopping we been doing at A. T. Stewart's, don't you tell me you can't carry off that part!"

"Bill, you're a real gentleman," Eulalie said softly, her eyes shining.

"I know a lotta folks who might disagree with you," he chortled. "Now, you finish prettying up your face, and let's go over to Delmonico's and have ourselves some fun. They're still lettin' us in there," he wound up ebulliently.

Eulalie and Bill were just leaving Delmonico's after a gourmet dinner that awed even Bill, when Eulalie found herself face to face with Gilbert Sanders. He was escorting the same haughty young lady with whom he had danced repeatedly at the costume ball. For an electric instant, Eulalie's eyes communicated with his. She was trembling when Bill prodded her past the other couple.

As Bill had prophesied, they encountered no difficulty in renting an apartment in the more expensive area. Bill's explanation was accepted without question. He made a disparaging remark about the condition of a chair and the parlor rug, and immediately he was assured these would be replaced before the new tenants moved in at the end of the week. Behind the obsequious manager's back, Bill winked at Eulalie.

Bill's last week in town sped past for Eulalie and him. He was intent on taking in every sight he had missed thus far, yet Eulalie sensed in him an eagerness to return to his Nevada. She knew she would never see Bill Marchand again.

Bill left New York, by railroad, on the same day that Eulalie moved with Maw and René into the new apartment—she was keeping the hotel room for business. Nobody in the apartment building was to realize that Eulalie was anything but what she pretended to be. Yet she realized the hazards of the situation, even while she attemped to rout them from her mind.

Maw, enthralled with the apartment, was determined

to play her role to perfection. Eulalie discovered an inexpensive modiste and ordered two elegant uniforms made to fit Maw; she also gave strict orders to leave material to be let out when Maw regained her ample proportions.

Daringly, Eulalie decided upon a new approach to her profession. She would no longer parade up and down Broadway with the other "cruisers." She would go, with René, into one of the more refined concert-saloons where ladies were admitted free and gentlemen were charged twenty-five cents. René was shooting up handsomely—he could pass for eighteen. René and she would go into the saloon, presumably for entertainment, and René would make certain that interested-appearing gentlemen would know the price of her favors.

The first night, Eulalie was nervous. She need not have been. She had a delicate beauty that stood out in these surroundings. René was bright, quick. A contact was quickly made. The fee, upped again in deference to the high rent of the apartment, caused not a ripple of discontent. Eulalie was learning her value on the marketplace.

By the end of the first week. Eulalie moved with superb aloofness among the crowds that frequented the concert saloon of her choice. She sat at a small table with René, pretending interest in the "turns" being offered onstage. Eulalie ordered nothing—René was permitted a glass of wine which was chalked up to operating expenses. The waiter girls moved about in their very short skirts, their bare legs rising above tall, tasseled red boots, in what was virtually a uniform. The girls distracted René not at all. Sometimes, he looked wistfully at one of the handsome young men.

On an extravagant impulse—with the money in the bank and the paid-up rent on the apartment to back her up—Eulalie decided to visit the most expensive and most refined concert saloon in New York. She and René went uptown, all the way up to Broadway and Twenty-third Street, to try their luck at the Louvre.

The Louvre overlooked Madison Square, which was nearly surrounded by the fashionable new mansions occupied by respected society families. The Louvre itself occupied almost a whole city block and was considered one of the sights of New York.

Eulalie walked in with René, knowing the pair of them always attracted attention. She was immediately impressed by the glittering crystal chandeliers, the gold and emerald paneled walls, and the tall marble columns. The waitresses were the prettiest Eulalie had seen. It was obvious their favors would be highly sought.

Eulalie knew that the Louvre was famous for the beautiful, expensive demimondaines who frequented its rooms when they were seeking fresh liaisons. Glancing about, she was conscious of the sharp competition and momentarily assaulted by dismay at having invaded such exalted quarters.

"Wait, Eulalie," René said importantly when they were hardly seated at a table. "There is someone already."

René moved with slim grace across the floor. Eulalie quickened. She recognized the young man who was displaying an avid interest in her—and above whom René now hovered in whispered conversation. Gilbert Sanders!

Confusion overtook Eulalie. She fought down an impulse to flee. Gilbert Sanders had seen her at the costume ball. He thought she was a young lady of quality. Now he knew. He was rising to his feet, following René to their table. But she had wanted to meet Gilbert Sanders under such different circumstances!

"I've looked all over New York for you," Gilbert Sanders chided. "I haven't been able to sleep nights, thinking about you—"

"So now you have found me." Eulalie smiled brilliantly.

He knew what she was, but it did not matter, Eulalie told herself passionately. Now she understood how Annie felt about her sailor—about not wanting to take money from him.

22

From their first hours together, Eulalie was infatuated by Gilbert Sanders. This was David several years older—David's lean handsomeness, David's gentle voice, except for the absence of the velvet Southern accent. Eulalie existed in a world of unreality, waiting for the hours she would spend in Gilbert's company.

Gilbert Sanders lived with his family in a fashionable brownstone mansion overlooking Madison Square. But, like other gentlemen of means and no legal attachments, he maintained an apartment discreetly removed from his home. This was Eulalie's domain. Daily, at the appointed hour, she would leave Maw and René to hurry to the apartment, to be there when Gilbert arrived from his father's downtown offices.

Gilbert took her to dinner—at the dining rooms favored by out-of-town visitors rather than by New York society families. He took her for sleigh rides up Third Avenue when snows began to blanket the city. They would go into Wintergreen's in the growing suburb of

Yorkville, up in the East Eighties, for sherry flips and hot buttered rum. He took her to Harry Hill's Concert Saloon because he was fascinated by the well-known sports figures who frequented the place—along with the judges, politicians, criminals, and prostitutes.

Regularly, Eulalie gazed with wistful interest at the Astor Place Opera House and the elegant Broadway Theatre. She longed to go to the theater with Gilbert and then to supper afterwards at Delmonico's. She remembered with recurrent unrest that, at Delmonico's, she had encountered Gilbert with the imperious young lady of the costume ball—the young lady with society connections.

Eulalie had convinced herself that she and Gilbert were lovers in the true sense of the word. There were nights when she ignored the money he conscientiously deposited on the mantel for her—and he argued with her not to leave this behind. They would have a voluble argument about this and usually wind up in bed again.

Winter was waning. Signs of spring pushed to the fore when Eulalie and Gilbert drove about the countryside now. He talked about picnicking in Jones's Woods, up above Fifty-ninth Street. Tonight, letting herself in the modest parlor-and-chamber apartment, Eulalie promised herself she would coax Gilbert into taking her to the theater—to see that new actor, Edwin Booth, about whom everybody was talking.

Eulalie stood at the window, watching the gas-lit street for Gilbert's arrival. Mentally, she was thoroughly aware why Gilbert never took her to the theaters, to the opera—which he professed bored him to death—or to Delmonico's for supper. He might encounter his family or friends at any of these places. Emotionally, she refused to accept this because, to her, she and Gilbert were all the famous lovers of history and literature.

Eulalie started at the sound of the door opening and swung about with the usual, welcoming smile. She knew the effectiveness of this smile.

"I was watching for you," she complained. "I didn't see you alight from a carriage."

"I walked," Gilbert explained, drawing her close, his eyes appreciative. "Hungry?"

"Famished," she said. "I'm always famished." Her eyes shone because, to Gilbert, she was beautiful and desirable.

"Where shall we go?"

"Delmonico's." Her smile was brilliant, determined.

Gilbert's eyes went opaque.

"That stuffy place?"

"It's the finest place in all New York," she reminded him spiritedly, watching his eyes closely.

"I don't want to share you with all those other men," Gilbert said. "They'll make me jealous, the way they'll stare at you."

"Oh, David, nobody but you," she whispered intensely—and felt Gilbert stiffen. *Why had she said that?*

"Who's David?" Gilbert demanded without loosening his hold.

"A little boy I knew when I was a child," Eulalie stammered. "I was talking about him with somebody before I came over. He must have been in my mind." Oh, what was the matter with her, to do a thing like that?

"See how jealous I am?" Gilbert mocked. "Even of a little boy."

His mouth was reaching for hers. She felt his hand, hot on her breast. She went limp against him, in the fashion that she had learned would stoke his passion. Gilbert was not like all those other, ugly men. Gilbert was David. She loved him!

After they had made love, Eulalie and Gilbert lay across the wide bed. He smoked one of his "paper cigars," a box of which a friend had brought back for him from Turkey. He seemed preoccupied. Eulalie made light conversation that required no response. She was waiting for him to talk. At last, his eyes, his smile, told her Gilbert was with her again. Her face lighted.

"Tomorrow night we'll go to the theater," he promised grandly. "And afterwards, we'll go out to supper." He had not said, we'll go to Delmonico's for supper, Eulalie acknowledged. Still, it was a triumph. "What about now?" he pursued. "I seem to recall your saying you were famished."

"I am," she insisted effervescently. "Let's go this minute!"

"You'd be a sensation," Gilbert laughed. "Walking into a restaurant without clothes!"

Eulalie moved through the evening in an aura of delicious unreality, intoxicated with the knowledge that tomorrow she would be at the theater with Gilbert. What would they see? There was Shakespeare in repertory, wasn't there? Oh, it didn't matter. Anything would be marvelous!

Gilbert put her into a carriage and sent her home. She sat, tense with impatience, on the edge of the seat, fretting to tell Maw and René that tomorrow evening she was going to the theater with Gilbert Sanders.

René's dark eyes were hostile, arrogant, when she told them her news.

"So he's taking you to the theater," René shrugged. "Why is that so important?"

"He's not ashamed to be seen with me at a place like that," Eulalie shot back, candid as always with René and Maw. "His *friends* come to the theater."

Maw sighed unhappily. Eulalie looked at her with a defensive lift of her head.

"Eulalie, baby," Maw said compassionately, "yo' be gettin' bad ideas. Massa Gilbert—him want only to pleasure yo'."

"I know that!" Eulalie's voice rose to a shrill pitch. "But he's taking me to the theater—like I was a young lady who belonged in society. I made him promise to take me!"

Again, her eyes clashed with René's. A chill brushed her. She knew why René looked at her that way. He was jealous because she lay with Gilbert. He wished to be Gilbert's lover. She had seen the way he had looked at Gilbert, the few times the three of them were together. She kept telling herself René was not like that, yet she read this recognition even in Maw's eyes. René did not care about girls. He craved men.

Eulalie went to bed, conscious that Maw lay sleepless beside her. Maw knew how she felt about Gilbert. That scared Maw. Sometimes, it scared her. Determinedly, she shut her eyes and willed herself to sleep.

She awoke to the savory aromas of food cooking. Maw tiptoed about the apartment, letting her sleep much of the day. For all these months now with Gilbert, she had abandoned the hours of reading at the Astor Library with René; with reluctance, she still posed for him. Only Gilbert monopolized her thoughts every waking moment.

Eulalie ate with a lusty display of relish because Maw enjoyed that. René was already on his way to see the paintings on display at Barnum's Museum, Maw reported. René kept talking about finding himself a job, Eulalie remembered uneasily. So far, he had not come up with anything. In the deep recesses of her mind, she knew that René would be working with her again. For the present, she refused to face this certainty.

She dressed with elaborate care for her first evening at the theater in Gilbert's company. She chose the most elegant of the gowns Bill had bought for her and spent hours on preparing her face and hair. Looking at Maw, she knew she was beautiful. Gilbert would not be ashamed of her tonight.

Tonight, Gilbert was in his rooms before she arrived. He was extravagant in his praise for her gown and her appearance, but speedily proceeded to divest her of the gown so that they might make love. He enjoyed the way she responded, she told herself with pleasure. Never before, to anyone else, had she given of herself in bed. Except that one precious time with David. Why must David keep coming into her mind? David was at The Willows. Gilbert was here. She lay in his arms.

Gilbert helped her to dress again. They found a carriage downstairs and rode off to the theater. Eulalie's heart was pounding when Gilbert helped her down from the carriage and walked with her across the sidewalk to the theater lobby, milling now with elegantly gowned ladies and their escorts. Eulalie smiled with low-keyed triumph. She was going to the theater with Gilbert Sanders. She felt as though she had crossed a formidable barrier.

She was fascinated by the performance onstage. Now, she resolved to read all of Shakespeare, to devour the plays as she had devoured the American and English novels. She remembered, guiltily, that she had ignored René's offer to translate for her the new novel by that French writer, George Sand. Covertly, she glanced about at the splendiferous assemblage in the darkened theater. It was a long, long way from the slave hut at The Willows.

Eulalie glowed with the excitement of her first attendance at the theater. She hardly noticed that Gilbert seemed in a hurry to depart. They walked out into the cool May evening and Gilbert signaled for a carriage from the line-up waiting for theater patrons who did not have their own carriages standing by. On the sidewalk, in the shadows, hovered clusters of onlookers avid for a view of those august personages who had attended the performance.

Gil helped her into the carriage. Smiling slightly, she gazed out at the sightseers. The carriage swept forward, just as her eyes lighted on a slight male figure at the curb. Her pulse raced. David! It could only be David!

She sat tense, shaking inwardly, half-listening to what Gilbert was saying. David here in New York.

"Eulalie, I didn't want to spoil the evening for you," Gilbert's voice dragged her back to reality. "But I have to go to my parents' house for some family gathering. I'm having the carriage drop me off, then he'll take you on to your place."

"Oh, Gil." She managed the expected pout of disappointment. "But then, it was such a wonderful evening."

Gilbert chuckled.

"Personally, I prefer the turns over at the concert saloons," he admitted. "Shakespeare isn't exactly my sort of thing."

Dutifully, Eulalie accepted his decorous good-night kiss before he alighted from the carriage. Her heart pounding, she waited for the carriage to turn the corner before she leaned forward to communicate with the driver.

"Please go back to the theater," she ordered urgently. "I've left something behind."

It had to be David watching the crowds leave the theater. He said that someday he would come to New York. It didn't matter that Cousin Madeline wasn't here—he had come! Oh, hurry, she prayed silently. Let him still be there.

"Shall I wait, Miss?" the driver asked solicitously when he pulled up before the now-darkened theater.

"No," Eulalie said quickly, descending to the curb.

She walked slowly, up and down the block, around the corner, her eyes earnestly searching the street for someone who might be David. No one. No one at all. A man sidled towards her, murmured a blunt invitation. Head high, eyes cold, she walked away, looking for a carriage to take her home.

When Eulalie arrived at the apartment, Maw and René were drinking tea. Instantly, Eulalie sensed that both were disturbed.

"Baby, a man brung a letter fo' yo'," Maw said quietly before Eulalie could probe. "Dis heah—" She picked up a square white envelope that rested on the table.

"Who's it from?" Eulalie demanded, extending a hand. For a fleeting instant, she thought it was from David, and her heart sang. But it couldn't be from David—he wouldn't know where to find her. David thought she was in Canada.

Eulalie ripped open the envelope and read the printed card inside. The scribbled note across the bottom said, "Eulalie, I'm sorry—I couldn't bring myself to tell you."

It was the formal announcement of the engagement of Miss Rowena Edwards to Mr. Gilbert J. Sanders III.

Eulalie was silent, refusing to talk with Maw and René about Gilbert. She hurt with the shame of repudiation. All the time, he knew he was going to marry that girl. She felt humiliated because she had pretended that it was something different with Gilbert and her, that she was not just a girl he had picked up in a concert saloon to satisfy his lust.

Eulalie said nothing to Maw about being so certain she had seen David. Maw would never believe this could happen. Eulalie wandered aimlessly about the city alone—refusing René's company. Knowing Maw was distraught, that René too was upset for her.

She stared into strange faces on the streets in the meager hope that she would find David. At last, she realized the futility of these daily sorties. Perhaps it had not been David at all—only something deep in her mind. Perhaps now, in searching for David, she was running away from the memory of Gilbert. That whole, final anguished evening was jumbled together in her mind, with David and Gilbert sometimes blending into one.

When René tried to coax her back into their old existence, Eulalie was furious with him. She refused to resume the old way of life, one day each week going to the bank to withdraw money with the regularity with which she used to deposit it. The paid-up rent period was past. Her money was ebbing away with a speed that alarmed Maw and René. They watched in shocked silence—afraid, Eulalie subconsciously realized, to tangle with her.

Listless, she moved about the apartment like a pale wraith through the whole month of June. Rarely did she go out.

Today she awoke, late as usual, aware that the usual cooking aromas were absent. Maw was not home. She went out into the parlor where René was painting to ask about Maw.

"She's out looking for a job," René said, dark eyes accusing.

"Why?" Eulalie was shocked.

"Because we need the money," René said brusquely. "We can't stay in this fancy place on what I'm making."

"I don't want Maw working," Eulalie said strongly.

René's eyes brightened. "She's got enough to do here, taking care of us."

"You tell her that when she comes home," René said cheerfully. "I've got to be going."

"Where?"

"To work," René said jauntily and hurried off.

Eulalie walked to the window and stared out into the overcast early-July dusk. It was humid, uncomfortably so, with rain appearing imminent. Where was Maw? Where was René working? Questions suddenly bombarded her. She had been thinking only of herself these past weeks!

Maw was out looking for a job. René was working, earning little. She couldn't take a maid's job if she found one. What would she make? If she were lucky, she'd have six dollars a month, over her board and room. That wouldn't help much, to pay the rent here and take care of Maw. *She didn't want Maw working.*

The door opened. Maw came in, her face looking tired.

"Maw—" Her voice was rich with tenderness. "René says you're looking for a job."

"Me cain't find," Maw admitted, dark eyes unhappy. "Me don' talk nice, like yo'. Me cain't read, nor write—"

"Maw, I don't want you going out to work," Eulalie said firmly, reaching for her mother's hand. "It's going to be all right again, I promise." She hesitated a moment. "Maw, where's René working?"

"That concert saloon near the Bowery." Maw hesitated. "Eulalie, me worry 'bout dat boy. He come home, he got paint on his face."

Eulalie stared in shock. She knew about the concert saloons near the Bowery where some of the waitresses were really boys, in girls' short skirts and red-tasseled boots. She knew why the boys were there in the saloon and recoiled from the thought of René's being one of *them.*

"I'll be back soon," Eulalie said. "I'm going over there to bring René home."

Eulalie and René resumed their habit of going to a concert saloon each evening, though Eulalie paled in refusal when René suggested going uptown to the Louvre again. René appeared happy now. Eulalie posed for him for long periods each day. They were again on their schedule of reading at the Astor Place Library. Eulalie was becoming almost fluent in French—to Seraphina's everlasting astonishment. René had taken on the task of smoothing out Seraphina's own speech, to which she submitted with pride and affection.

Summer merged into autumn, and then it was winter again. Eulalie churned with a new restlessness. She found it a growing effort to mask her contempt for the men who bought her nightly favors. This was retrogressing. Eulalie was determined to rise in the world. René talked grandly about going to Paris some day to study painting. Eulalie envisioned herself as a famous courtesan in France, moving about with famous people, perhaps even royalty.

New York wore an air of festivity, with the arrival of the Christmas season. And ten days before Christmas, Eulalie read in the newspapers about the splashy society-wedding of Miss Rowena Edwards and Mr. Gilbert J. Sanders III. She read the items slowly, digesting each word, visualizing the wedding, the splendid reception—and then she ripped the pages into small shreds, promising herself never to think about Gilbert Sanders again.

Eulalie steeled herself to do what she realized was most likely to be productive. The night after Gilbert's wedding, she told René that they would go that evening to the Louvre.

She felt sick inside when she walked into the plush concert saloon where her liaison with Gilbert Sanders was born. She had given herself to him. Money couldn't buy that. Never again, she swore with inner heat. There was only one way to play this game.

She and René seated themselves in the large drinking hall across from the mirrored bar where Eulalie was shown off to best advantage. They talked in the light gay manner they knew to be most effective. All the while, René scanned the male faces as he searched for a new customer for Eulalie.

"I'll be right back," he said confidently, pushing back his chair, rising to his feet.

"No," Eulalie ordered, smiling brilliantly. "Leave me alone for a while."

She watched a slender, dapper man with waxed mustache and expensively tailored clothes saunter casually in her direction. Instinctively, she sensed that this would not be an affair for one evening. Not if she handled herself properly. She lifted her eyes in delicate invitation.

"Permit me to introduce myself," the tall, suave gentleman drawled. "I am Carter Douglas, of New York, London, and Paris."

23

Eulalie quickly comprehended that Carter Douglas was a far more complex man than any she had ever known. With him, she was moving into a strange world that was simultaneously fascinating and ego-destroying. Compared to those who peopled Carter Douglas' existence, Eulalie was untried, unsophisticated, unknowledgeable. Eulalie vowed to rectify this situation.

Two nights after their meeting at the Louvre, Eulalie was installed in Carter Douglas' hotel suite. He escorted her to extravagant suppers with his business associates, whom she guessed were important personages in the world of finance. She graced business luncheons, sitting between Carter and his associates like a beautiful, silent fixture—but one with mental antennas gathering in information.

Carter did something with railroad and mining stocks, Eulalie gathered. He had come East from San Francisco with a bundle which he was proceeding to build into a fortune. Carter harbored only contempt for the fashionable society of New York, the "upper tendom," about which he made ironically amusing remarks from time to time—though he was not averse to business-socializing with the menfolk. Curiously, he spoke with high respect about the new Bohemia in New York.

Eulalie and Carter attended the theater regularly. He spoke eloquently about the great French actress, Rachel, whom he professed to have seen in Paris and who had recently appeared in New York in *Adrienne Lecouvreur,* creating such a furor that puddings, ice creams, coiffeurs, and gaiters were named after her. He had seen Laura Keene—a favorite of Eulalie's—in many roles, and he seemed enchanted by Jean Davenport, who had brazenly presented *Camille*. This play about a lady of loose morals had been written by the younger Alexandre Dumas and had already been a sensation in Paris. Eulalie listened avidly to every word Carter uttered, though she guessed there were colorful embellishments on the truth at regular intervals.

New Year's Eve, Carter was host to a champagne supper for his business associates and young ladies who were obviously not their wives. Eulalie, with a faint smile and an air of reticence, was his hostess. A week later, he escorted Eulalie to a new after-theater supper spot, about which he made provocative remarks while they were en route. He wore a look of smug, secretive anticipation, but Eulalie was disappointed—at first—when they walked downstairs to a cellar restaurant. The noises from Broadway above them and the roar of the horse-drawn omnibuses richocheted through the unpretentious room.

Once they were seated, Eulalie noticed the private alcove at the far end of the cellar where chairs flanked a single, long table. All the seats were occupied now by a vivacious gathering. There was a quality about the diners in the alcove, which captured and held Eulalie's attention. These, she was certain, were the people who had drawn Carter into the modest quarters of Charlie Pfaff's cellar restaurant.

Absorbing the atmosphere, Eulalie sat back while

Carter ordered. A commanding man at the head of the long table in the alcove was reading poetry aloud; the others were hanging attentively to his words. At intervals, some of the lines were audible to the other, less segregated diners—shocking the unwary and impressionable.

"Who is he?" Eulalie's gaze clung compulsively to the poetry-reader with the grizzled beard. He wore no tie, his hairy chest exposed by his unbuttoned shirt.

"His name is Walt Whitman," Carter explained, pleased that Eulalie was drawn to the man. "He's had a book of poetry recently published, called *Leaves of Grass. The Saturday Press* calls him one of the greats."

"What's *The Saturday Press?*" Eulalie asked with flowering curiosity. She was an omnivorous reader of newspapers—this one she had missed. In the back of her mind registered the knowledge that, for all his grandiose talk about business and Wall Street, Carter yearned to be part of the artistic world. He told her he had been stage manager for an acting company in San Francisco—she had not known whether to believe him or not.

"*The Saturday Press* is a fairly new literary weekly," Carter explained, "catering to the Bohemians. One of these days I might send in a contribution myself," he said offhandedly.

"Do you write?" Eulalie pressed.

"When I find time," he hedged. He looked at Eulalie, appraisingly. "You know what I like about you, Eulalie," he drawled. "In addition to the obvious—" He nodded with mock deference. "You have a mind. You listen. You assimilate. And you don't chatter. That's a blessing in a woman, second only to beauty. Of course, beauty is wasted on a woman who isn't passionate."

His eyes rested on her with speculation. Was he wondering about the passion she displayed in bed? Couldn't a man as keen as Carter Douglas know that it was simulated, a commodity he bought? Some things, no man could ever be sure about, she decided with satisfaction.

Their supper arrived. Eulalie was hardly aware of what she was eating. For the first time, she was listening with only half a mind to what Carter was saying. The assemblage at the long table in the alcove was all-absorbing. These were the people who wrote books, published magazines, acted on the stage. She knew, without his saying so, that Carter plotted to become part of that inner circle.

When they returned to Carter's suite, he was unusually taciturn while she changed into one of the diaphanous wrappers which he fancied. She waited, as always, for his lead. But she blanched when he walked to a commode, pulled forth a leather riding crop, and ripped it through the air. His eyes, fastened to her, were inscrutable.

"You look frightened," he said detachedly.

"What are you doing with that?" Her gaze was riveted to the leather length in his hand. Her voice was unsteady. Suddenly, she was back at The Willows trying to shut out the cries of a slave being flogged.

"Did you know that in Paris, there are houses where men—and women—are flogged to arouse their passions? Rather different from the poor devils who are flogged in the South." His eyes narrowed. He smiled faintly. "Have you ever been whipped, Eulalie?"

"Why should I have been?" Amber eyes blazed in defiance. Her stomach churned. *What did Carter mean?* What did he know about her?

"Interesting, to note a woman's reaction to this sort of thing." With a sharp, unexpected movement, he raised his arm. The leather rent the air, just grazing Eulalie's shoulder.

"Stop it!" Her voice soared in fury. "Stop it!"

"Make me," Carter dared her. "Make me, Eulalie!"

He raised the whip again, his face daring her to rush him. She lunged towards his arm. They struggled. She gained control of the whip. Later, she realized this had been a deliberate concession. Her body reacted independently of her mind. She swung the leather across Carter's shoulders, across his back, as he bent forward, gritting his teeth to contain the sounds of pain. And then, as suddenly as she had leaped to flog him, Eulalie dropped the whip, fell to her knees, sobbing uncontrollably.

Carter lifted her bodily, carried her to the bed, and took her with a passion that was towering in its intensity—and to which she reacted without pretense.

"I hurt you," she whispered when they lay back exhausted from their efforts. "Oh, Carter, how could I?"

"I wanted to know what you would do," he said with relish. "It was worth it." She knew he had goaded her to whet his passion. How many other women had flogged Carter Douglas?

"Your shoulders—your back—" Her voice was deep with shame. Now, she felt degraded.

"We'll take care of the cuts later," he promised. His hand fondled her breasts. His eyes were opaque. "Anyone ever beat you, Eulalie?" he asked casually. "Back home?"

"No." She stiffened, guessing that he knew.

"But you saw others beaten." He paused. "Other slaves. How did you get away? Tell me about it, Eulalie." He was growing passionate again, thinking about this.

"How did you know?" she whispered.

"The powder and the creams might fool the others," Carter gibed. "In dim gaslight, in the heat of passion. But I have this deep curiosity about people. I must know all the whys."

"You—you won't tell anyone?" Her pride stung because she had been found out.

"I'm on your side, girl," he chortled. "Whatever you can put over on this world, that's to your advantage." His eyes narrowed in contemplation. "Eulalie, if I had the time—and you had the inclination—I could make an actress of you."

"You mean, like Laura Keene?" Excitement chilled Eulalie.

"Like Eulalie Cartier," he corrected. "You have it in you to be anything you want to be." Passion subsided. He rose briskly from the bed now. "Come, I have creams to fix these wounds. They're beginning to throb devilishly"

"Carter, what were you before?" she asked curiously. Somehow, the flogging, the moments of reciprocal passion, had destroyed any wall that had existed between Carter and her. Eulalie felt an equality with him that was exhilarating. Carter had come far—so had she. And there was far, yet, to go. For both of them. Would both of them make it? Would she? "Carter, what have you done in this world?"

"My dear girl," he said with a secretive satisfaction in his eyes, "there's little that I haven't done in this world, except murder and steal." Now humor lit his eyes. "And stealing is a matter of semantics."

Eulalie settled into a stimulating pattern of living. She was learning to handle herself with new poise as she sopped up learning with her customary spongelike absorbency. There was sufficient money to send René for sketching and painting lessons, to inundate Maw with the sweets she adored, to take reassuring amounts to the bank again. Carter, with practiced charm, penetrated the inner circle of Bohemia. He was in his glory—New York was his city, he declaimed. He carried a copy of *Harper's Magazine* and professed to be indignant about its complaint against the city—"New York is notoriously the largest and least loved of any of our great cities. Why should it be loved as a city? It is never the same city, for a dozen years altogether." Carter compared New York, lyrically, to San Francisco, Chicago, Boston, Philadelphia. He said that the changes New York displayed were duplicated in Paris—and everybody was in awe of that French city.

The months whirled past. A new year arrived—1857. Eulalie reveled in the new associations. She had become a petted darling of Bohemia—of which Ada Clare was queen—because she was so appreciative of artistic talents, was such an avid listener, and so *simpático* with these dazzling young rebels who mocked conventions and scandalized the more sedate New Yorkers.

When Eulalie heard about Ada Clare's love affair with the famous pianist, Louis Moreau Gottschalk, who was the friend of Chopin and Berlioz, she impulsively coaxed Carter into allowing her to take piano lessons. A piano was moved into the suite to allow her to practice daily. Carter encouraged her to sing to him each evening in her charming, melodic but untrained voice.

It was a make-believe world, and Eulalie told herself— later—that she should have expected it to explode. In that year of 1857, Eulalie was very conscious of the controversy over slavery. Carter explained to her how the money manipulators in New York City controlled every phase of the cotton trade, all the way from the plantation to the final product. He showed Eulalie editorials in *The New York Evening Post,* whose writers claimed that "the City of New York belongs almost as much to the South as to the North."

The London Times asked James D. B. DeBow, a well-known New Orleans magazine editor, what he believed New York would be like if slavery were abolished, and he wrote: "The ships would rot at her docks; grass would grow in Wall Street and Broadway, and the glory of New York, like that of Babylon and Rome, would be numbered with the things of the past."

In the early months of 1857, the market began a steady decline. Too many railroad companies had set themselves up in business. Companies were failing. Gold shares were dropping along with banks and other issues. The Crimean War was keeping European money out of America. By July, rails were sliding to dangerous levels. In early August, the Ohio Insurance Company failed. A major panic gripped Wall Street.

Carter rushed to the hotel on the eve of the Ohio Life Insurance Company's announcement of failure and told Eulalie they were moving immediately to Jersey City. She asked no questions, yet made it clear that wherever she went, Maw and René also went. Carter appeared distressed, harassed, but determined to salvage himself. From careful studied remarks, Eulalie gathered that Carter had utilized the holocaust to his advantage, but in some fashion that did not meet with legal approval. In Jersey City, he could not be extradited.

Carter found a modest hotel in Jersey City, set up Eulalie, Seraphina, and René on one floor and himself on another. René made regular ferry-trips across the river to New York at Carter's bidding. Eulalie sensed that this day-to-day existence would be short-lived. After three weeks of being a Jerseyite, Carter announced his intentions.

"Eulalie, it's all arranged," he said with relish. "We leave next week for Europe. First stop, Liverpool."

"Carter!" Her eyes were bright with astonishment, yet misgivings flooded her. A strange country now!

"All of us," Carter said grandly. "The whole entourage."

Carter enjoyed traveling with Maw and René, Eulalie had come to understand—this was his retinue of servants, it appeared to outsiders.

"We'll have to go back to New York," she reminded.

"We'll go in time to board the ship. It's the S.S. Pacific —one of the American Collins Line. They assure me we'll make the crossing in ten days!"

They boarded the ship on a gray early-September afternoon. Despite Eulalie's soothing consolation, Maw was full of gloomy prophecies about the possibilities of the ship's sinking. Even René, always so ebullient and ready for new experiences, was quiet, respectful.

The crossing was rough, for which Eulalie was partially grateful. She had reason enough to remain in her stateroom with Maw while René shared one with Carter. He played at being his valet which Carter enjoyed and René loathed. Maw spent much of her time on her knees, praying that the ship would make it to their destination.

Eulalie had thought that Liverpool was to be their new home. It was a stopover. They traveled by train to London. Eulalie wistfully tried to coax Carter to remain in London for sightseeing, but he was intent on arriving at their ultimate destination.

"We'll take a boat to Monaco," Carter outlined briskly, his restiveness now apparent. "It's on the French Riviera— a tiny country built on terraced bluffs high above the

Mediterranean. Marvelous views. You'll love the place," he promised.

Before they arrived at their hotel in Monte Carlo, Eulalie realized—with grave misgivings—what the deep attraction in this tiny principality was. In Monte Carlo was the new gambling casino that was drawing an international assemblage.

The carriage deposited them at their hotel. They were assigned rooms. Carter glistened with anticipation.

"Dress," he ordered Eulalie crisply en route to his own room at the far end of the corridor from the suite harboring the others. "We'll go to the casino!"

Eulalie admitted to being impressed by the grandeur of the gambling rooms and by the fine gowns of the ladies moving about the tables. Yet, knowing Carter, she was concerned. What would happen if he went through his bankroll? They would be stranded in a foreign country.

In the beginning, Carter was in high spirits. His luck was good. He credited this to Eulalie's presence beside him at the tables. Then, his luck began to change—slowly, at first. Then he was dropping huge sums at the table; he was becoming surly and rough with Eulalie.

Maw was sharp-eyed, nervous, conscious of Eulalie's unease. René was enthralled with the scenery and spent long hours high on the bluffs with his easel. Eulalie felt as though disaster were about to descend momentarily. She had no way of knowing the extent of Carter's bankroll, but his losses were the talk of the casino.

At the end of their first month there, Carter was silent, tight-lipped, spending every waking hour at the tables. Eulalie heard the manager ask, politely, when Carter planned on settling his bill. Carter was arrogant and insulting to the manager.

That same night, Carter tried to cash a check at the casino. He was refused. His face white with rage, he stalked from the casino with Eulalie at his heels. Together, they went upstairs to his room. These nights, when Carter took her, it was as though in fury, as though he were using her body to vent his anger on circumstances. She bore faint bruises from his roughness, which she tried to conceal from Maw.

Carter went to the door, locked it, crossed to a table to pour himself a drink.

"I'm flat," he said bluntly. "Not a franc left." His eyes turned canny, resting on Eulalie. "What about you?" he mocked. "You must have money! Look at the way I've thrown it at you." He moved closer. "Where's your money, Eulalie?"

"I don't have any," she lied, red spots staining her cheeks. Before they left Jersey City, she had gone into New York to withdraw her bankroll, which Maw wore tucked in her ample bosom. Carter was not losing *her* money at the gambling tables! She harbored only contempt for such activity. "I've spent it—on Maw, René—" Her slim, golden hands gestured eloquently.

"I don't believe you!" His voice was harsh. "Come on, Eulalie, where is it? With the old lady?" He poured himself a drink, watching her closely.

"I spent everything," Eulalie insisted. "I have these things," she offered nervously, fingering the trifles of jewelry she had bought herself.

"Junk." He stared contemptuously at the fake jewelry, swigged down his drink, poured another. "You're lying to me, Eulalie!"

"I'm not!" She lifted her head high in defiance, bracing herself for the blow she saw coming.

She staggered beneath the slap across her cheek, trembled with a mixture of fury and alarm. He captured her by the upper arm, pulled her in close.

"Where's the money? You've got it stashed away somewhere—either on you or that nigger Maw of yours!"

"No!" she screamed at him. "No, no, no!"

He ripped her dress from neckline to waist, then fumbled about her breasts as though expecting bills to be concealed there somewhere.

"I want that money, Eulalie!" he roared, slapping her again across the face, thrusting her onto the bed, hovering abover her now—not in passion but in panic.

She closed her eyes, gritted her teeth, waiting for him

to stop flailing her with blows. She hurt, but no amount of hurt would bring her to turn over to Carter Douglas the money she'd saved so assiduously—to be thrown away at the gambling tables. Finally, muttering vilifications, intent on pouring himself another drink, he staggered away from the bed.

Eulalie waited. He had not eaten all day. He had been drinking heavily. Soon he would fall into a stupor. When his head fell forward, when she knew he was no longer aware of her presence in the room. Eulalie rushed for the door, self-consciously clutching her torn bodice. He would sleep for hours, she was certain. She had much to do before he awoke.

Maw and René asked no questions when they saw her bruised body. René's face went red; he clenched and unclenched his hands in helpless fury while Maw, moving about the rooms, packed their luggage.

"René, go downstairs and pay the bill," Eulalie ordered, calm now and in complete control of the situation. "Tell them we're leaving right away."

"Where are we going?" René asked, taking the bills Eulalie counted out.

"To Paris, René," she said, a lilt in her voice. "To Paris!"

24

Eulalie, René, and Seraphina arrived in Paris on a chill, drizzling early-October evening. Eulalie's exhilaration at being in Paris was only slightly checked by her realization that paying the hotel bill in Monte Carlo—for Carter as well as her own trio—plus their fare to Paris had cut sharply into her bankroll. Instinct told her that Frenchmen would be as receptive to her charms as American men. René was joyous at returning to the land of his childhood, shadowy in his memory through the years.

With a coachman as their guide, they were traveling through the ancient, narrow, twisting streets in search of lodgings.

"No more lanterns!" Memory spilled over to drench René. "I remember lanterns on every street corner! And one in between. By midnight, the candle would burn out. Mama used to say it was worth your life to go out at night!" On impulse, he leaned forward to question the coachman, who—to their pleased astonishment—spoke a fairly comprehensible English.

"Ah, Monsieur, Paris is now lighted by 13,910 gas jets!"

the coachman boasted. "Every jet is made of porcelain, which is pierced by thirty tiny holes. Not until dawn is the gas turned off. Paris has become *la ville-lumière*."

René leaned back, for the moment thoroughly pleased with the world. Then he leaned forward to whisper to Eulalie.

"You talk French only," he exhorted. "Except with Maw and me."

"I will," Eulalie promised. She struggled, though, to ignore the incipient self-consciousness seeded in her by this necessity to tangle with a foreign language. In Monte Carlo, she had spoken French. Only brief phrases, at the gambling table, true—but no one had laughed. There were the years behind her of having French drummed into her mind by René—but here, they were among a nation of French people. To survive, she considered realistically, she must speak the language. Eulalie shrugged her golden shoulders, smiled with insouciance. "Another country, another language—*ce n'est rien*."

Eulalie leaned forward, inspecting the rows of four- and five-story houses, most of them with dormered roofs that transformed garrets into living accommodations, as attested by the curtained windows. Questions shot through Eulalie's mind about the cost of these seemingly modest rooms, about the possibility of entertaining gentlemen in such quarters with impunity. First, they must get settled, she summed up—then they would find their way.

"Ici," the driver announced importantly, pulling to a stop before an aging house with mansard roof and flowerpot-laden windowsills. "I will speak with Madame for you."

Eulalie discovered in the process of their settling on accommodations that, on the first floors of the Paris houses, lived the rich in the midst of awesome luxury. The judges and the well-to-do merchants, lived on the second floors. Above them, on the third, lived those confined to limited incomes, pensions, and actresses who were developing a following in the theaters. The higher the floors, the less affluent the tenant, with the garret apartments inhabited by the shop-girls, art students, and struggling would-be writers and musicians.

Eulalie installed her family in rooms that looked down upon the roofs of Paris. Where the rents were cheapest and she was confident no questions would be asked about the guests she would bring up the narrow, winding stairs. Not until later did Eulalie come to realize that the tiny rooms hovering beneath the roofs were sweatboxes in summer and iceboxes in winter. But moving in, she told herself they would not be staying in such mean quarters for long.

With her native ability for languages, Eulalie found herself adapting easily though she was frequenting the grosser types of cafes to rebuild her shaky confidence in these new surroundings. She was quick to understand that, here in Paris, with her golden skin, her accented French, her patrician good looks, she was an exotic. How, then, to capitalize on this? What were the steps to take her into more exalted levels? Eulalie did not push herself. There was time.

Eulalie discovered that there was money enough now—with Maw's talents, despite language barriers, at bargaining in the markets and with their modest rent—to send René to an art school where the fees were low and paid daily. René lived an existence of highs and lows, one moment transported to ecstasy at being able to study seriously, and the next plunged into despair at his lack of knowledge.

"God, Eulalie, I know so little!" he would rant, stalking about the tiny room. "How will I ever learn enough? It's all been wrong. Everything!" he would cry out dramatically, banging his fists against a table.

"You'll learn," Eulalie said calmly. "Pay attention, work hard—listen, René. Listen to everything."

Gradually, Eulalie worked to develop a complete new facade. With René's help, she circulated rumors about herself. She was an Eurasian born of a French father and a Hindu mother. René was her half-brother born of their father's legal marriage. Seraphina was an ex-slave stranded by her owners in Europe years earlier and hired to raise the pair of them when his mother died and their father returned to the Hindu mistress in the Far East.

Eulalie, in changing her name to Liani Cartier, found a

strange satisfaction in her new exotic background. The French seemed unconcerned about the shade of one's complexion. Eulalie embellished her story to include hints that René and she had been educated in England. She assiduously cultivated an English art-student friend of René's with the intent of acquiring an authentic British flavor for her English speech.

After several months, Eulalie was sufficiently confident—and affluent—to move into more spacious quarters on a lower floor in the section preferred by the artists, the writers, the demimondaines of Paris. There was the family apartment, ruled over by Seraphina, plus the studio room where Eulalie entertained her gentlemen.

René was deeply involved in his art-student world, studying at the studios much of each day and arguing techniques with other students far into the night. Eulalie no longer required his attendance when she went out in the evenings. She walked, with her superb carriage and an air of faint detachment, into the cafes frequented by men with fuller purses and deeper generosity in paying for favors.

On a dare to herself one day, she walked alone into the Frères Provençaux, the most expensive restaurant in all Paris. She sat down and waited to be served. This was a business investment, she considered realistically. She glanced about with pleasure, found herself fascinated by a man at a nearby table—a huge man, probably standing six-foot three in his stocking feet, with crinkly Negroid hair and blue eyes—and a tableful of fashionable women obviously hanging on to his every word.

"Mademoiselle." The man's voice startled her, so intrigued was she by the man at the other table. "So beautiful a young lady should not be alone. May I join you?"

"Who is that?" she inquired with a radiant smile to reassure the gold-chained, jewel-fobbed gentleman with the sword cane that he was welcome. But her interest was focused on the magnetic man of Negro blood.

"Why, that is Alexandre Dumas," her new companion drawled, seating himself at her table.

"The writer?" Eulalie glowed. "That play, *Camille?*" Carter had talked over and over again about the play, about Jean Davenport's performance—though he was sure it could not be compared to that of Rachel. "I hear it is a marvelous play!"

"This is the father," the elegantly turned-out gentleman explained with a slight smile of superiority. "Alexandre Dumas Pére. You must know of him. He turns out novels and plays the way a secretary turns out letters! *The Count of Monte Cristo, The Three Musketeers, Twenty Years After.* Perhaps—" he moved in more closely, "perhaps you would do me the honor of attending Dumas' new play tonight at the Theatre National. Frédéric Lemâitre is appearing in it."

Eulalie, thereafter, no longer frequented the cafes in the less fashionable sections of Paris. Her favors were bought by men with more finesse as well as more francs. Liani Cartier, the Eurasian beauty with a handsome young brother who was an artist, became known about Paris.

A year rolled by, and then another. René was moving ahead. He talked with fierce dedication about his painting. He was fascinated by a painter a few years older than himself—Edouard Manet, who favored strong and harsh contrasts and argued that the whole claim of traditional art to have discovered the proper way to represent nature was wrong.

René continued to use Eulalie as his model whenever her schedule permitted this. When he first began to show his nudes of her to fellow art-students, she had been embarrassed. Now he talked ebulliently about someday having a one-man show featuring his paintings of Eulalie.

"It won't be at the Louvre," he mocked in high good humor. And as always, Eulalie flinched at the reminder of her nights of association with another, less illustrious Louvre where she met Gilbert Sanders. "A shack somewhere, at the edge of Paris—" René's eyes glittered. "But it will be my show."

"When you're ready," Eulalie conceded indulgently, knowing it would be years before René himself permitted this public display of his efforts.

René was moving ahead. Eulalie felt herself standing

still. Restlessness was building in her. Surely, life could offer more than this. Recurrently, her thoughts turned to David. If she had remained in New York, would she have found him? She was certain it had been David in front of the theater that last night with Gilbert. Why hadn't she stayed in New York, instead of running off with Carter that way? Yet, running with Carter had ultimately brought her to Paris—how could she consider living anywhere else? In Paris, everything was possible.

In her restlessness, Eulalie found herself drawn into René's world of students, artists, musicians, yet she withheld herself—in this overwrought atmosphere—from any of the typical emotional entanglements. René, she noted with satisfaction, was so engrossed with his painting that he never looked upon a fellow artist in the way that had sometimes alarmed her. There was such a world here in Paris; but René, Eulalie reassured herself, was not part of it.

Late in the spring, when Eulalie fell in love with Paris all over again, she allowed René to take her along with him to a *bal masqué* on a night when her current "protector" was engaged in family obligations. René's friend, Henri, had entrée to the *bal*.

"It will be a marvelous evening," Henri promised effervescently as the three of them—elaborately costumed and masked—stepped down from the hired carriage in front of an imposing private residence which belonged to a patron of the arts whose name was illustrious in French society.

Eulalie lifted her eyebrows in candid approval. When René and Henry coaxed her to attend this masquerade, she had expected it to take place in a modest house on some side street where there would be much gaiety but little signs of opulence. At the door, Henri knocked importantly. A liveried doorman admitted them.

The *bal masqué* was at its height. The noise that greeted them was deafening, with the orchestra hard-put to make itself heard above the lively chatter, the laughter, the tinkling of glasses. Mirrors, glittering on every wall, highlighted the preponderance of gas-lit chandeliers and tranformed the colorful costumes of the crowd into garish murals.

Some of the costumes worn by the ladies were extremely daring as well as strikingly attractive. Models, Eulalie assumed, from whom such daring was expected. One such costume particularly drew her attention. The girl was small, delicately blonde, with her breasts half-spilling from the white satin court-gown. She was dancing with a young, black giant, lifting her skirts high as they cavorted in the schottische, which had been forbidden at court balls by Empress Eugénie, who considered the schottische vulgar. At intervals, the girl reached for one dark hand, brought it to the hollow between her breasts. Beneath her half-mask, her smile was provocative.

Eulalie avoided any romantic entanglements at the *bal*, feeling herself something of an onlooker and sending pleading gestures for rescue to René or Henri when an overly amorous suiter hovered over her. Again and again, Eulalie found her gaze returning compulsively to the small, masked blonde. While much of the assemblage was persuaded to engage in the lengthy cotillion, the blonde and her black companion took themselves off into a corner where the girl hoisted her skirts to her hips and lifted her legs high in an eye-catching can-can that quickly brought a circle of admirers about her.

The party was growing more raucous. The cotillion was abandoned by most of the throng; only the orchestra diligently following this course. The amorous scenes were growing numerous, overt. Eulalie was embarrassed by the public display of what she felt was suitable only for the bedroom.

Someone hoisted the uninhibited blonde atop a table. A crowd surrounded her in high approval. Perspiration glistened about her throat as she lifted her legs in the provocative can-can; she obviously relished the vocal encouragement, the looks of male heat fastened upon her—because there was nothing beneath the white satin court-gown except white velvet skin. She tugged at the shoulders of her gown without slowing the tempo of her dancing until the bodice displayed. her breasts completely, the nipples stiff in dusky circles. She danced with a frenzy that seemed a substitute for the sex act, as though she were about to move to orgasm with every male encircling her.

"René," Eulalie called, thrusting aside the drunken courtier who was whispering obscene suggestions into her ear. "René, please, I'd like to leave."

"I'll get Henri," René agreed readily, amused—but not aroused—by the perspiring efforts of the half-nude blonde atop the table.

"Henri," Eulalie heard Renè say briskly when he had pushed his way through the overheated crowd that surrounded the can-can dancer, "Henri, it's time to leave."

René resolutely tugged at Henri, who was remonstrating at this early departure. But the two were pushing their way through the crowd to where Eulalie waited.

"Henri!" The girl atop the table had stopped dancing. "Henri, wait!"

Male arms hoisted the girl down from the table and laughingly patted her on her rump as she danced forward after Henri.

"Henri, why are you leaving so early?" the girl demanded in heavily accented French. Eulalie realized she was an American.

"We have another *bal masqué* to attend tonight," Henri explained in English, which he relished practicing at every opportunity. "Besides," he gibed, his eyes traveling beyond her to the young black giant watching them with narrowed eyes, "you're quite busy."

"Jean is a wonderful animal, isn't he?" The green eyes glowed sensuously. "But tomorrow night—" The liquid, Southern voice startled Eulalie. "Come to another party." Her eyes traveled past Henri, to Eulalie and René, "Bring your friends. My cousin has a salon, you know— every Sunday evening. Some of the most exciting people in Paris come."

The girl reached to pull off her mask, as she moved in seductively towards Henri. Eulalie was transfixed. She felt the blood draining from her face. Her stomach tied itself into knots. Cindy! Cindy Woodstock!

25

Cindy's eyes moved with supercilious disdain over the thinning crowd, whose attention she could no longer hold with her seminude prancing. They were divided now into small groups and pairs, raucously involved in their own erotic diversions. The more fastidious guests had long since departed.

"I've had enough," Cindy said petulantly. "Let's go to your studio, Jean."

"As you wish." Jean's dark face wore an ironic smile. "Let's go for our coats."

His arm about her waist—she barely came to his shoulder—they threaded their way through the dying embers of the *bal*, to the door. Jean signaled to a passing carriage and helped Cindy inside.

"Who was the girl with Henri?" Cindy asked. "Do you know her?"

"René's half-sister," Jean explained. "I don't know her—I know of her. Henri finds her fascinating, but

she's far too expensive for him," he reported humorously.

Cindy squinted thoughtfully.

"She looks familiar—I can't imagine why."

"All dark skins look alike to you," he mocked.

"You don't," she shot back, her mouth parting in a
reminiscent smile. "You're special, Jean." For now, he
was special. Her hand moved to caress his thigh.

"Because I have a beard and speak French," he gibed.
"Or don't you really care, so long as I'm a black man?"

She pulled away, the green eyes sulky.

"Stop saying those things, Jean! You make me furious."

"And when you're furious," he reminded, moving towards her in the darkness of the carriage, "you want to
make love."

"Here?" she demanded, astonished at his overtures.
Excitement rose in her as she considered this. With the
carriage clattering through the dark Paris streets, with
dawn minutes away? "You wouldn't dare!" Oh, but he was
passionate! It was exhilarating for her to have this power
of arousal over this black giant who talked with such
pride of the freedom of his native country. But for a ship's
destination three generations ago, he might have been a
slave at The Willows.

"Why wouldn't I dare?" Jean challenged with relish.
"It's at least ten minutes till we reach the studio."

"Suppose something happened?" she demanded while
Jean moved beneath the satin folds of her costume to her
satin-white skin. "Suppose a wheel came off the carriage—" She felt his hot breath upon her as he hovered
above her. Her throat was dry with anticipation. "Suppose
the horses ran away and the carriage spilled over—" Her
hands clutched at his shoulders, her body reacting like a
street bitch in heat. "And we were dumped into the gutter—like this."

"Somebody would throw a blanket across us," Jean
guessed. "To provide the privacy such an act deserves."
But he continued the performance Cindy expected.

Jean swore in his colorful, Haitian-tinted French when
the carriage pulled up before the ancient building that

housed his studio, before Cindy and he were prepared to descend.

"Drive around the block," Jean called out, while Cindy laughed in low excitement, moving beneath his massive blackness.

"Jean," he asked, "how would I do as a whore?"

"You'd make a fortune," he chuckled, his eyes appraising her in the faint spill of gaslight from the street. "You considering abandoning your amateur status?"

"Would I do as well as that slut we saw with Henri tonight?" she demanded. Why did that girl persist to plague at her?

"One way to find out," he taunted.

Caught up in merriment, pleased by the unorthodox setting for their passion, Cindy and Jean left the carriage and climbed the mountain of stairs that led up to his studio.

"Pose for me," Jean commanded when they were inside the studio. "It will be light in an hour."

"I'll pose in an hour," she promised, finding a savage pleasure in the larger-than-life nude on which Jean had been working since she first undertook to pay his studio rent. Her mind returned again to the girl at the *bal*. She had seen girls at The Willows with that same dancer's grace. "The girl you said was René's half-sister," Cindy pursued, "she's Haitian, too?"

"René is white, Liani is Eurasian. Her mother came from one of the Asian countries." A hint of laughter lighted his dark eyes. "Since when have you become so interested in women?"

"Never me," Cindy shot back smugly. Sometimes, she wondered about Mama—and that Amelia. "Haven't I proved myself, you black giant?" She dropped onto the bed that served as a couch as well.

"There is a decadence about you," Jean said carefully, "that could turn in any direction. I have an intuition that says, before you are through, you will have tried everything."

"Not women," Cindy said firmly. Some of the contrived merriment left her eyes. "Jean, get me something to drink."

Why did Jean say that, about a decadence in her? Why did she sometimes have these strange feelings—like running through the dark, alone and lost? Why did that Eurasian girl—*was* she Eurasian?—make her think of home?

Someday, she would have to go home. Madeline kept throwing Bradford at her, old as he was. Bradford was back from Georgia—she would see him tomorrow night. Sometimes, she wondered about Bradford. Was he interested in boys? There was something secretive about him. How convenient it could be for both of them, married and with separate interests. Explore that.

"Your drink," Jean said, handing her the goblet of wine. His eyes were amused because Cindy had no stomach for drinking—two glasses of wine and she was on her way out.

"I'm not getting drunk tonight," she promised, green eyes glistening with pleasure as they rested on Jean—six feet three, black, and handsome. Only one drunk in the family, she thought with uneasy nostalgia. Not that she blamed Mama, the way Papa carried on with the black bitches. Not that he was doing any more of that, not after what Alexander did to him. Why didn't Mama get smart, take herself a big, black buck? How could Mama live like that? "Why get drunk?" Cindy picked up brightly because Jean was inspecting her with one of those odd, speculative glances that unsettled her sometimes. There was a look of arrogance, now and then, that brought her back up. For all his blackness, Jean considered himself a king among men. "When I'm drunk, I don't actually know what's going on, do I?" Her hand reached out to touch him. Her mouth parted in a satisfied smile at his instantaneous reaction.

"As long as I don't get drunk," Jean stipulated, hovering before her. "If I drink too much, I'll be useless to you."

"Suppose I were black?" Cindy questioned, sprawling catlike across the bed-masquerading-as-couch. "Would I do this to you?"

"Possibly," he evaded. "If I were white, would I arouse you this way?" He took the empty glass from her hand.

"No," she said with candor, stretching languorously while he freed her of the white satin court-gown. "I have what Papa calls a taste for black meat. That's inherited." The green eyes darkened with bitterness. "Plus the pattern was set for me by Papa. Watching him throw himself into all those black gals back at the plantation. I was jealous of them. I wanted it to be me." Her laughter was unpretty. "I lusted for Papa!"

"Not now," he reminded complacently, his massive black hands moving about the satin-white nakedness of her.

"Not now," Cindy concurred, watching him through slitted eyes. "Papa is useless," she told him. There, she shocked him. "Back at the plantation, there was a small uprising. A buck castrated him. That was when he had the first stroke."

"So you carry on for Papa," Jean mocked, his hands moving about her whiteness. "Why do you stay here in Paris? Why don't you go home?"

"You know why I don't go home," Cindy told him. "So I can pay your studio rent." Ah, he was furious with her! "Jean, come back," she commanded, her simulated arousal becoming real now. "You know I love to make you angry!"

"One day you'll go too far," he warned.

"How far is too far?" Cindy challenged. "Jean, kiss me. Here—" She touched a nipple. "And here—and here—and here—"

Maybe she could go home with Bradford Taylor, Cindy considered while her body responded to the amorous pursuit of Jean's mouth. He had no family, but he did have that big plantation—and he had ways of going off by himself at intervals. There was room on that big plantation for them to indulge their whims. She was tired, so tired of running.

26

The realization that the blonde at the *bal masqué* was Cindy Woodstock threw Eulalie into mental chaos for a while. Cindy would not recognize her, Eulalie finally forced herself to acknowledge. If she did, it hardly mattered here in Paris. Yet, Eulalie's agitation was difficult to assuage. She saw concern in Maw's eyes though Maw asked no questions.

Eulalie had been thrown into the arena of memory. Her heart pounded when she considered the evening's festivities at Madeline Henderson's salon. It had to be Madeline Henderson. Eulalie remembered herself walking up the stoop of that elegant brownstone, unable to accept the terrifying fact that Madeline Henderson was not in New York. All through the agony of escape, she had clung to the belief that David's Cousin Madeline would be in New York to help her. Now, she was fearful of walking into that salon tonight—yet she knew that nothing on earth could keep her from attending.

Don't tell Maw about Cindy, Eulalie exhorted herself.

Maw would be terribly upset. Maw had settled down into this new life and gloried in their affluence though Eulalie continued to make a point of never discussing her gentlemen with Maw. Maw knew, of course, that Eulalie was kept by a series of admirers who contributed generously to their way of life. But that life was sternly separated from the activities at the comfortable apartment over which Maw affectionately ruled. No names were mentioned, no details of the liaisons.

"Henri likes you very much," René teased, when they were preparing to leave for Madame Henderson's salon. "I think he is developing romantic ideas about you."

"Henri knows better." Eulalie smiled serenely. Henri was familiar with her life.

"You really want to go tonight, Eulalie?" René was watching her with covert curiosity.

"Why not?" Eulalie shrugged, her amber eyes opaque.

Her admirer was at his country house for the weekend. She suspected that this liaison would end shortly—he was running into too many family problems. But there was always a successor to be annexed, before Eulalie would begin to feel a financial pinch.

"That girl," René asked keenly. "The one who invited us tonight. She talks strange—like a Southerner."

"Yes," Eulalie acknowledged and forced a stiff smile. "So she's a Southerner."

René was concerned that she might feel hostility towards this Southern white girl. He had no way of knowing all she felt towards Cindy Woodstock. That last night, she had awakened in a cold sweat. She was dreaming of herself back at The Willows, fourteen again, cornered across a bed by Cindy's father in the heat of animal passion. Everything, the whole kaleidoscopic maze of the years past, had assaulted her in the darkness of the night. She had awakened, drained, exhausted.

"Henri says she's kicking up her heels for that black man," René contributed casually. "He's an artist from Haiti. Henri says she pays the rent for his studio. Before him, there was another Haitian—an ex-slave who was part of a bad uprising in the islands."

"Henri is an awful gossip," Eulalie retorted. "Let's go. It should be an amusing evening."

Madeline Henderson had grown more sophisticated through the years. A true cosmopolite now, she dressed superbly, entertained lavishly. Exiled from home, she had established herself here in style. Eulalie recognized some of the faces about the elegant drawing room. René and Henri whispered well-known names to her as the trio moved from group to group. Eulalie's smile was fixed, self-conscious, though she was confident neither Madeline Henderson nor Cindy recognized her. After all these years —and the changes wrought in Eulalie—how could they recognize her?

Eulalie was captured by an effete dancer from the ballet, who rhapsodized about her grace while his eyes made silent, unacknowledged advances to René. On the surface, Eulalie lavished her absorbed attention on the dancer because the pair of them stood closely enough to Cindy and her graying gentleman companion, who was also from the South, for Eulalie to hear what was being said by them. Eulalie's eyes were overbright, her ears straining to hear every word, even while she appeared to be listening avidly to the dancer.

"Bradford, I don't know why you just don't get rid of the plantation and stay over here," Cindy pouted. "But tell me, how did you find Papa and Mama? You did go over to The Willows to visit with them one day while you were back? You promised."

"George is doing as well as you can expect a man to do, who's survived two massive strokes. He's confined to his bed, of course," her companion reported calmly. "Your mother has rallied rather wonderfully." His smile was ironic. He must have known about the drinking. "Of course, my sympathies really lie with David caught in a bind that way."

Eulalie's heart pounded. She repositioned herself, so as not to miss a word. The dancer was unaware of her efforts.

"It's a shame David had to leave college and go back home when he was doing so well," Cindy acknowledged though she hardly sounded concerned for her brother.

"And how he ever let Mama push him into marrying that silly Annette Butler, I'll never know."

Eulalie's face grew tense with the effort to reveal nothing of what she was feeling. David had been at college! Perhaps in New York. Why hadn't she looked more earnestly for him? She *had* looked—but not enough. Why hadn't she stayed in New York? But David was married now. To one of the Butler girls. What else had she expected? What could there ever be for David Woodstock and her? Except a few moments of infinite beauty—which she remembered even now.

Eulalie responded with the gentle smile, the slight air of hauteur that had become her trademark when the gentleman with Cindy broke away to approach her. The effete dancer was discouraged at René's departure and had politely excused himself.

"Bradford Taylor, from the United States," he introduced himself gallantly. Cindy was darting across the room to the entrance where the black giant named Jean hovered uncertainly; he was probably here for the first time.

"Liani Cartier," Eulalie introduced herself, "from Paris, London, and New Delhi." Her eyes frankly challenged him to ignore her golden skin. "My father was French, my mother Hindu." From the corner of her eyes, she watched Madeline, whose gaze was fastened to Cindy. Madeline was upset. Familiar with Cindy's propensity for blacks, she was naturally upset.

"A charming combination." Taylor approved of her explanation of her background, but his eyes were appraising, weighing, arriving at a decision. "I've always found Indian women fascinating."

Before a week was past, Eulalie was installed in a lavishly furnished apartment on the Rue de Rivoli. She knew the affair with Bradford Taylor would not last more than two or three months because he would have to go back to check on activities at his plantation, Taylor Place. But it pleased her vanity to find Mr. Bradford Taylor of Georgia squandering such vast sums of money on her by catering to her whims.

As the weeks sped past with her monopolizing much of Bradford's attention, Eulalie was conscious that Cindy herself was deeply involved with several artists, all of whom flaunted a skin that hardly belonged to the Caucasian race. Still, there were times when Eulalie suspected Cindy of throwing herself at Bradford. Did Cindy dream of marriage to a white gentleman when she constantly traveled about Paris in the company of black men?

Bradford was aging. His tastes in bed leaned towards the esoteric. But Eulalie found him generous, usually considerate, most attentive. She was astonished one night towards the end of his stay in Paris—he was already regretfully hinting to Eulalie that this trip must soon be curtailed—to hear him make a disparaging remark to her, over dinner, about the complexion of the men most favored by Cindy.

"I'm of mixed blood," Eulalie reminded him, head high, eyes flashing. "I told you—my father was French, my mother Hindu. Do you consider yourself degraded for having indulged yourself with me?" she mocked.

"Liani," he reproached, "don't talk about yourself in the same breath as Cindy's blacks. So they've come from Haiti or some such islands and give themselves airs—they're niggers, the same as any I have working down South on my plantation." He leaned forward, reaching for her hand, his eyes growing amorous. "You could travel anywhere in the South, and they would know you for a lady of good blood." He lifted a hand to signal the waiter. He was ready to go back to the apartment on Rue de Rivoli and play at his esoteric love-making.

So brown skin was acceptable in the dear old South, Eulalie considered with sardonic humor. They wouldn't ask for her Free Papers. Yet she doubted that Bradford Taylor would invite her to join him on his return trip to Georgia, despite this show of approval. He paid for her favors—paid extravagantly. It suited his sense of humor to call her a lady of good blood.

"I'm going to miss you," Bradford said quietly in the privacy of the carriage when they were en route to the apartment. "You don't know how dull it can be back there in that big house of mine. Nobody there except the house slaves."

"Tell me about it," Eulalie commanded. She was in an odd mood tonight and impatient to hear Bradford Taylor talk about his life at Taylor Place, which was a scant twenty miles from The Willows. What black wenches warmed his bed on cold nights? He didn't have to pay for having his will back there. Was it really so different—a slave wench or Liani Cartier, who was fast becoming one of the most expensive demimondaines in Paris?

In the apartment, Eulalie went immediately to her chamber to change into one of the costly costumes in which Bradford preferred her in the privacy of their rooms. He was in the parlor now, pouring himself a drink from the crystal decanter he had bought personally for the apartment. Even in a furnished apartment, there must be the Bradford Taylor touch.

Eulalie went to the window and gazed out into the night. Why did it upset her that way when Bradford talked about Cindy's "niggers"? Did she have any illusions about how he felt about black people? It was just as well that he was going back to the States, to Georgia. She would stop seeing Cindy and Madeline Henderson. It would be better that way. Her nerves were raw from the constant resurgence of old memories.

"Liani—" His peremptory voice commanded her attention, when she appeared in the doorway.

"Yes?" Amber eyes, faintly mocking, her smile brilliant, she walked towards him. "Yes, Bradford?"

It was fantastic, the way she could make this old man believe she was on fire for him. She made them all believe that! The knowledge of this lifted her above their contemptuous use of her body and transformed her into a disdainful onlooker, even while she played her passionate role. She was the deceiver—and for being that, she was paid generously. As Eulalie Washington at The Willows, she received only pain.

"I'm going to miss this," Bradford murmured, bringing her down to the bed. His eyes were aroused, his hands impatient. "I'll lie awake nights down there and remember you, Liani."

"You won't," she challenged. "You'll find someone else."

"A black wench from the fields?" he asked with sardonic humor. His voice deepening because he held the golden breasts in his hands.

"Cindy Woodstock?" she taunted him, remembering the sly efforts of Madeline to bring Cindy and Bradford together despite the disparity of their ages. Madeline was concerned for Cindy's future—it shone from her. "She'll be going home." Cindy kept saying that, but she wouldn't be going home.

"Do you think I'd ever involve myself with Cindy?" Bradford flashed back. "She's looking for a husband so she can spend her days lying with the blacks on the plantation—when she tires of Paris, or when Madeline can't bear the strain any more. I swear, Madeline lives in daily terror of Cindy's coming home to say she's pregnant with some black bastard!"

"If Cindy were ever pregnant, she would know what to do," Eulalie countered.

"All Cindy cares about is having some black man stuff himself into her," Bradford said with flagrant disgust. "She's not happy until some big black thing is driving her into spasms!"

"What about you?" With the weight of Bradford hovering above, Eulalie was dangerously calm. "It's all right for you to push yourself into a black girl!"

"Shut up, Liani," he ordered scowling. "What's the matter with you tonight?"

But Eulalie had no intention of being shut up.

"You're no different from Cindy Woodstock!" she shot at him from between clenched teeth. "Both of you taking your pleasure with blacks!"

"Oh, for God's sake! Are you jealous of some ignorant slaves back on my plantation?"

"No!" Too overwrought now to backtrack, Eulalie spat at him. "I'm talking about you and me. I'm black, Bradford! Did you honestly believe that story, about my being half-French, half-Hindu? I'm black, do you hear? A nigger! My Maw brought me to The Willows when I was still in her belly! I grew up there with Cindy and David. I'm an escaped slave, Bradford. Eulalie Washington, born of Seraphina Washington—and some white stud who took her at his will!"

Suddenly, Bradford was on his feet. He was staring at her, his eyes sick, his face ashen. For a moment, Eulalie feared he was about to have a stroke.

"You were born at The Willows—a slave?" His voice trembled.

"I ran away." Eulalie crouched on the bed in defiance. "I made free, Bradford—and now my favors come high. Nobody throws me across the bed any more, the way George Woodstock threw me, the way some white animal threw my mother on her back—and then sold her when she was pregnant because he didn't want his issue moving about the plantation to mock him! You're no different from Cindy Woodstock, Bradford—you're both paying for what you could take back in Georgia for nothing!"

Bradford straightened his disheveled clothes and put on his jacket with shaking hands while Eulalie crouched half-naked on the bed, her amber eyes blazing with a generation's contempt. All the rage, all the pent-up hostility towards Cindy's and Bradford's world, exploded in her now.

"The rent is paid up here for the rest of the month." His words emerged from between bloodless lips. He tossed the key to her. It hit the bed, fell to the floor. "I won't be back."

Bradford Taylor's eyes were anguished when they rested on her. She saw something else there—at this moment undecipherable—in his final glance before he strode from the apartment on the Rue de Rivoli. She heard the door slam. She was alone.

Eulalie returned to the less fashionable—though comfortable and spacious—apartment where Maw liked to sit at a window and watch the Parisian life flowing past.

Maw's dusky face brightened at Eulalie's arrival. She never knew when Eulalie would be home. Yet Eulalie knew, whenever she walked into the apartment, that these were the hours when Maw came fully alive. Each time, it was as though she had been away for just an hour. Maw preferred to know nothing about that other life.

Eulalie and Maw sat long over coffee, talking about little nothings, about Maw's minor concerns or gripes about René, whom Maw adored and spoiled and worried over as though he were her own. Early, Eulalie retired to the smallest bedroom, which was hers, with the expectation of falling into exhausted sleep. Instead, she tossed fretfully until dawn, her mind assaulted by replays of the scene with Bradford Taylor. Why had she behaved like that? After all these years, why did she react so violently to the white Southern attitude towards the "nigger"?

Half-asleep, yet conscious of noonday sun creeping between the drapes, she heard René burst into the parlor.

"Eulalie home?" he was demanding excitedly. What was he doing home, instead of being at the studio?

"She be home," Maw said. "Sleepin'."

"Eulalie!" René called. "Eulalie, get up."

Eulalie sat up in bed, trying to clear her mind. René was stalking to her side to shove the morning newspapers beneath her gaze.

"Bradford Taylor," René pointed to the headline, his voice harsh with shock. "He killed himself!"

"Oh, my God!" Eulalie clutched at the newspaper, feeling the blood drain from her face while she struggled to translate the lurid account before her. Bradford Taylor had shot himself early this morning—the police were certain it was suicide.

"Who say?" Maw's voice was unfamiliarly high. "Who kill hisself?"

"Eulalie's last gentleman," René explained delicately. "Mr. Bradford Taylor."

"My fault!" Eulalie's voice broke with remorse. "Last

night, I told him who I was—it turned him sick, to know he'd been fooled that way. He couldn't stand that!"

"No, baby, no!" Maw moaned, tears streaming down her face as she rocked back and forth. "His'n own fault, baby. Massa Bradford Taylor—he been takin' his pleasure with his own daughter!"

27

"Eulalie, honey," Maw coaxed gently, "you gotta talk to the lawyer man."

"No," Eulalie reiterated, shaking her head. "I don't want to see him."

"Baby, he's out there in the parlor. He say he's gotta talk to you. He bin here three times already. It's—it's about your Paw's will."

Eulalie lifted her head, her eyes glistening with scorn.

"My Paw? My gentleman, you mean!"

"Eulalie, we done talk a lot about that," Maw said sadly. "You cain't go on sittin' alone in your room, day after day this way. What happened—it's all done. We cain't keep cryin' over what's past. Now, you make yourself real purty, and you go out there and talk to that lawyer man," Maw said firmly. "If there be somethin' comin' to you, I wants you to have it."

"All right." Eulalie was too sapped of energy to argue any more. What difference did it make? Bradford must have left her some conscience money in his will—so she would take it for Maw.

It was a matter of pride with Eulalie to look her best when she emerged from the bed chamber to consult with Bradford Taylor's lawyer. She smiled faintly at the surprised look of admiration and respect with which the lawyer greeted her in their initial exchange.

"Miss Cartier," he explained carefully, "Mr. Taylor awakened me in the middle of the night to draw up this new will. He made certain that every legal detail was correct, that there could be no questioning of his bequest. Duplicates of all legal papers were made up to be signed by him, for me to forward to his attorney in the United States."

"And then he went to his hotel and put the bullet through his head," Eulalie said softly, shutting her eyes. Because an incestuous relationship was too painful for him to bear. She felt sickened each time she remembered—yet, Eulalie realized detachedly, *she* did not want to die.

"Miss Cartier—" The lawyer made a valiant effort to be businesslike, "Mr. Taylor had no immediate family— only cousins in the Southwest. There will be no contesting of the will. Everything is yours." Eulalie stared in open-mouthed shock. She had expected a small bequest. Everything, the lawyer said. Taylor Place? The plantation? The lawyer cleared his throat self-consciously. "You will, of course, have to apply to the Georgia courts to take over your inheritance. A mere formality." His eyes were curious. How much had Bradford told the lawyers? Everything, Eulalie guessed—the knowledge shone from his eyes. "As Liani Cartier," he pursued smoothly. "I doubt that you will encounter any racial difficulties, even in the deplorable conditions of the South."

Eulalie's heart pounded. Go back to Georgia as Liani Cartier? See David. Claim the plantation. *Her* plantation. Her head spun with the drama of what lay behind and ahead of her. She could go back—and nobody would guess. She could carry it off!

"When—when shall I leave?" Her eyes glowed now.

"She cain't go," Maw intruded, her voice rich with terror. "Honey, you know you cain't!"

"I can go back, Maw," Eulalie said quietly. "It'll be all right. I'll stay just long enough to take care of the legal things and then come back to Paris." What would people think when they saw her down there? What would they say about the Eurasian stranger who inherited Taylor Place? She lifted her head defiantly. What did it matter? Bradford—her Paw—had made a legal will.

The lawyer coughed nervously.

"Mr. Taylor told me he was leaving the country quite unexpectedly—this explained his requirements for my services in the evening hours. I had no idea of the tragedy that was to take place. Mr. Taylor was sometimes unconventional in his demands—I had no idea," he reiterated, fumbling in his pocket. "This belonged to Mr. Taylor's mother—he cherished it highly. The painting inside is of her."

Eulalie put out a hand to accept the tiny parcel, pushed aside the tissue, pulled forth a diamond-chip-encrusted locket on a gold chain. Her hands were unsteady when she opened the locket to inspect the hand-painted miniature inside. The lovely Southern beauty in her teens was an ivory replica of Eulalie, Eulalie's grandmother, on her father's side.

In late June, 1859, with many Southern plantation owners still struggling to recover from the Panic of 1857 and with unhappy rumblings of trouble between the North and South reaching a fever pitch, Eulalie arrived in Georgia. Maw and René remained in Paris. Eulalie was met by a carriage, as arranged by a telegram the attorney sent to the presumably highly efficient overseer who managed Taylor Place.

She sat back in the carriage for the long drive to the plantation and listened to the polite, uneasy reports of Mr. Ashton, the overseer. Mr. Ashton had been informed by the attorney that Liani Cartier, the new owner of Taylor Place was Eurasian, and he had made it equally clear that she was not to be confused with the blacks. To enhance the illusion that she was Eurasian, Eulalie had gowned herself in the colorful attire of a high-born Hindu lady and spoke with the carefully cultivated British accent which she had acquired from an art-student friend of René's some time past.

She listened to Mr. Ashton with a quiet smile, while her heart pounded because she knew that David, a scant twenty miles from Taylor Place, had no inkling of her arrival. He knew about Bradford's death. Mr. Ashton must have dropped some hints about the new owner. It was probably reverberating about the whole county! It wasn't likely that her new neighbors would be making social calls—not knowing about her complexion. How would she arrange to see David? There had to be a way. For what other real reason had she come back here? She could have dispatched a lawyer with the right to act for her. But David was here.

"Of course," Mr. Ashton was saying ruefully, "conditions are not at their best on the plantation just now. Not for the past two years. Mr. Taylor was aware of this. I do my best to bring in a good crop. We sold some slaves in the spring—the money was deposited to Mr. Taylor's account." Much of which money, Eulalie thought wryly, had been spent on her and for Bradford's high living in Paris. She still thought of him as Bradford.

"I'll probably sell the plantation," she told Ashton quietly. He was concerned about that, wasn't he? Worried about his future. Concerned about taking orders from a brown-skinned lady. "I don't hold with the institution of slavery," she said with slight disdain. "I couldn't bear to profit from such labor."

"It's all a matter of upbringing, ma'am," Mr. Ashton said with a deferential smile. "I thought you might be thinking of selling. I took the liberty of discussing this with Mr. Butler, who might be interested in buying—at the right price. He's been talking about a plantation for his youngest son."

"I have no intention of being cheated," Eulalie assured

him, her eyes cool. "I've been appraised of the value of the plantation. When I'm settled in, you may approach Mr. Butler about coming over to Taylor Place to talk about a possible sale."

"I'll take care of that, ma'am," he promised politely.

Eulalie sat stiffly erect when the carriage turned in the lane that led up to the big house, her house now. There must be much anxiety, much talk, in the slave quarters about the new Missy. They were in for a shock when they saw her skin. How many would guess the truth?

No, the slaves would never know—except, perhaps, an especially bright one. Her whole facade was excellent. She was the Eurasian lady who had captivated the Massa—and inherited his estate. Did they wonder why Bradford killed himself? The neighbors must wonder about that. Nobody would ever know except Maw and her, and of course René.

Eulalie tried to concentrate on the elegant white mansion that rose tall among the magnolia trees. The house slaves, hearing the carriage approach, were gathered in excited clusters on the portico. Her house. Her slaves. Her smile was ironic as she listened to Mr. Ashton enumerate the slaves on the estate and discuss their particular functions—as though this stranger from Europe could not possibly understand the operations of a Southern plantation.

At first, Eulalie had told Maw she would go back home and free every slave on the plantation—and then she would sell the house and the land and bring back the money. Maw, startling her, had warned her that many of the slaves would be terrified of having their freedom. And the French attorney, to whom she had imparted her thinking about the slaves, was briskly realistic.

"Mademoiselle," he said frankly, "do not concern yourself for their freedom. The Northern states will assure this for you within the next year or two. Everywhere, you hear about this. There will be a war—and there will be no more slavery. Sell, Mademoiselle Cartier. Let the buyer take the loss!"

Eulalie made a point of keeping Mr. Butler waiting over a week before she allowed Ashton to arrange an appointment for Butler to come calling with his son. All that time, she churned with restlessness because she could devise no excuse to call on David at The Willows. She didn't dare call on him, she acknowledged, despite the bravado she had displayed to herself on the ship crossing the Atlantic. Somehow, through Mr. Butler, she must contrive to meet David. Perhaps she would be invited, socially, to Mr. Butler's plantation—and David would be there. She refused to consider that he would be there with his wife.

Ashton was delighted when she finally consented to see Butler. He was anxious for this sale to be consummated. Young Butler would need a strong overseer—Ashton was confident of retaining his job.

Eulalie moved graciously about the slave quarters, a replica of the quarters at The Willows. She enjoyed the admiration her appearance evoked, their gentle astonishment that her skin was golden. She made discreet inquiries about Ashton. If he were a hard overseer, she would never sell without a stipulation that he be removed. Ashton, however, was an overseer for whom the slaves had respect. He was a fair man. Their lot, as slaves, was no better than it had been all those years ago when Eulalie was growing into adolescence at The Willows—yet there was a new hope everywhere. Eulalie felt the undercurrents; she overheard unguarded remarks. The slaves themselves felt that freedom was no longer a dream. A new day was coming. Not only for Liani Cartier, born Eulalie Washington—but for all slaves.

Eulalie pushed aside guilt and contemplated the sale of Taylor Place. She herself went over, in detail, all the figures about the property. Bradford's local attorney—whose disapproval of Eulalie as heiress to Bradford's estate crept through from time to time—was efficient in the execution of his obligations and pushed through the legal technicalities with all possible speed.

Eulalie arranged the meeting with Mr. Butler and his

son for a midafternoon during the first week in July. A humid heat had settled over the plantation. Eulalie had forgotten the near-tropic climate of this part of the South. She moved about languidly through the uncomfortable days and nights before the meeting. Her mind was constantly beset with intrigues that might bring David and her together. It would be bad taste to give a ball when Bradford was dead. Could she invite her neighbors, the Woodstocks, to come to dinner? George Woodstock was paralyzed—he would be unable to attend. What about his wife? Would Margaret Woodstock leave her husband to come to dinner to hear about their old friend, Bradford Taylor, who died so tragically?

Eulalie shivered, envisioned Mrs. Woodstock with David and his wife—the girl she hated without knowing because she lay with David—walking into the splendor of this huge house to be entertained at dinner. How could she sit through dinner, across the table from David, without giving herself away? Yet, she had come here with the express determination of seeing David. She would not leave until she had seen him.

Eulalie was nervous when she waited in the elegant drawing room for Mr. Butler and his son to arrive. She had dressed with care in the native Eastern dress that was so becoming to her slight figure. Mr. Ashton, out on the portico, was waiting to bring them in. Eulalie rose to her feet, moved restlessly about the room. She went to the small, inlaid table that she remembered Bradford buying in Paris and shipping back to this house. In the small drawer beneath the table top were the two volumes of orations of freedom given to her by the Quaker schoolmaster, and the slim book of Shelley's poems given to her by David.

She pulled open the volume of Shelley, forcing herself to become absorbed in the familiar words before her. There, the horses were pulling up before the portico. She snapped the book shut, returned it to the drawer. Mr. Butler and his son were arriving—she could hear the genial sound of masculine voices coming into the foyer now. She walked across the room to stand there beside the marble fireplace surrounded by Bradford's splendid antiques; she knew the dramatic, exotic picture she offered her visitors.

The ebony-skinned, statuesque Juno was bringing the guests into the drawing room. Juno was abject in her admiration for Eulalie, particularly since being gifted with a pair of jeweled earrings and necklace to match. She wore them even in sleep.

"Miss Cartier," Mr. Ashton began expansively, "May I introduce these gentlemen—"

Eulalie heard not one word of the introductions. The guests included the senior Mr. Butler, the youngest Mr. Butler—and Mr. Butler's young son-in-law. Eulalie's pulse raced. She fought to retain her poise. David. David was here before her; he was hardly changed at all, but he was taller and filled out. The same quiet, serious eyes, the same lean handsomeness.

"Mr. Butler," she said politely, extending her hand to the older Butler while she gestured to Ashton to seat the younger men. "How nice of you to come." She turned to Juno, who hovered avidly in the doorway. "Juno, bring some glasses and ice for the gentlemen's drinks."

Eulalie sat on the sofa with the elder Mr. Butler beside her. Ashton stood at the fireplace, anxiously watching them, hoping this meeting would go well. The Butler son, for whom the plantation would be bought—if the sale were consummated—was staring broadly. David looked ill-at-ease. He was making an effort not to gaze overtly at her. David couldn't believe this was Eulalie— he must be thinking, Eulalie realized, the slim, Eastern-garbed girl before him is a double come to haunt him.

"Now, let's dispense with the chit-chat," the elder Mr. Butler ordered in high good-humor after the drinks were served and small talk indulged in for the requisite few minutes. "My boy here is getting himself married in the fall—when this infernal hot weather is over." He mopped his florid face with a white cotton handkerchief. "We might be interested in buying this place if the price is right."

"I've considered selling it," Eulalie said quietly. David

was here. So close, she could take five steps and touch him. "I'd like to hear what you have in mind, Mr. Butler—and then think about it a while." She couldn't leave, not right away. Not after seeing David.

Butler shot a reproachful glance at Ashton, as though the overseer had led him astray.

"What Miss Cartier means," Ashton interpreted nervously, "is that she would like to hear other offers before jumping into a sale." He looked upset, though, at Eulalie's lack of enthusiasm for a speedy sale.

"Young lady, you won't be hearing a better offer than mine," Butler said vigorously. "These are bad days in the South. Money is hard to come by. I'll pay you cash on the line, no notes."

Eulalie managed to carry on her share of the conversation—in the British accent that seemed to impress the Butlers—without making any definite commitments. She hedged at being pinned down, but promised Mr. Butler a detailed breakdown on the assets of the plantation. Even the furniture would be sold, she said, except for the small inlaid table near the window—which Mr. Taylor and she had shopped for together.

As soon as Eulalie mentioned Bradford's name, she was conscious of the undercurrent of excitement that ricocheted about the room. They were all curious about Bradford's death, about her position in his life. They were doomed to disappointment. She would say nothing except what she wished to say.

Her eyes oblique, Eulalie rose from the sofa, walked across to the small, inlaid table, and brushed the top affectionately with one graceful hand.

"I have a deep affection for this table," she explained while she reached into the drawer to pull out the slim, worn volume of Shelley. "It is—how do you call it?— my good-luck talisman."

Her eyes focused on David. She saw him stare steadily at the book in her hand, saw him whiten, touch his lower lip with the tip of his tongue. He raised his eyes to meet hers. He knew! David knew!

28

Eulalie had an early, solitary dinner on the portico at the side of the house where the breeze from the river afforded some light relief from the heat. Immediately after dinner, she sent the house slaves back to the quarters. She went to her room to discard the Eastern dress for one of her stylish Paris gowns. She touched perfume delicately behind her ears and at her throat, all the while listening carefully for sounds on the road that led to the house.

Was she wrong? Would David ignore the invitation in her eyes? Could he not come back to the house, knowing who she was? She stiffened to attention. A carriage! A carriage was coming up the road. She ran from her room, down the wide, curved stairway to the foyer and hurried out on to the portico. David. It was David.

"I couldn't believe it," he said softly, reaching for her hand. "I saw you—and I couldn't believe it until you brought out the volume of Shelley."

"You were in New York," she said breathlessly. "May,

four years ago. I saw you in front of a theater. I came back—I tried to find you, but you were gone."

"I was studying agriculture at a school in Philadelphia—I went to New York to see the sights," he explained. "We thought you were in Canda. I hoped things were going well for you."

"It was bad for a while," she conceded. She smiled in bitter memory. "I saw Cindy in Paris—and your Cousin Madeline. They didn't know me."

"How could they?" His eyes chided gently.

"Come inside," Eulalie invited. Don't let him ask about Bradford. She didn't want to talk about that—nor even to think about it. "Let's have champagne for this reunion."

Her eyes were liquid fire when they met his. He was married to one of the pallid Butler girls, whom his mother had pushed upon him. Don't think about that now. Think about David and Eulalie. Together. Alone in this house. Her eyes became bolder, flagrantly inviting. She saw the answering excitement in his eyes.

In the drawing room, Eulalie flirted lightly with David while she poured from the waiting bottle of champagne.

"You knew I'd come," he murmured.

"I prayed you would."

They took the bottle of champagne along with them when they went upstairs to Eulalie's room. He took her first with gentleness, then with towering passion that was matched in her. They lay back against the silken sheets dampened by the perspiration of their heated bodies, and he rested himself upon an elbow to gaze upon her golden nakedness.

"I wish I could stay the night." His smile was rueful.

"Stay," she coaxed, her eyes eloquent. Don't think about his wife and that other life that laid claims on him. Think about now, these nights she could salvage for David and herself. "David, stay—"

She smiled with brilliant satisfaction when he emitted a low, anguished oath at the touch of her hand. He would stay.

Eulalie stalled Mr. Butler about the sale of the plantation. At the same time, she cannily let it be clear that she preferred to talk business with his astute young son-in-law, which gave David and her a legitimate opportunity to be together. And then there were the long nights when David left The Willows to come to the empty, big house where Eulalie waited for him. Did his wife wonder where he was? Did she care? Did she suspect he was lying with some black wench, in the tradition of the South?

David talked to her seriously and in full detail about the problems at The Willows and his efforts to keep his head above water. He also talked about the condition of his father, who was practically helpless, and about the new sobriety of his mother and her devotion to his father. He spoke not at all about his own young wife.

René wrote a long, reproachful letter demanding her instant return to Paris. Maw was upset. He was disturbed. Why didn't she come home? Eulalie wrote, promising to leave within two weeks. It must come to an end—yet how could she let this happen?

At first, Eulalie pretended to dismiss the suspicion that she was pregnant. Yet, she watched eagerly for the telltale signs. Subconsciously, she had plotted to conceive. The small, high, golden breasts were faintly full now. She could touch them and know their fullness. She yawned at the slightest provocation. She had none of the sickness that had attacked her during that first, unwanted pregnancy, yet there was a queasiness in the morning that she welcomed because it confirmed her suspicions. At last, the calendar told her she was right.

Eulalie spilled over with happiness. David's child. This child she would have. Yet the knowledge of her pregnancy increased her reluctance to leave David. She trembled with a new hope. David hated the plantation, the worn-out earth. Would he come with her to Paris? Mr. Butler had pushed his price high—higher than even Mr. Ashton had anticipated. David and she could buy a house outside Paris. David could experiment with his agricultural theories. Would he come with her?

She waited for him with impatience, that day when she determined to take David back to Paris with her. She and David with their unborn son! Eulalie was certain it would be a boy. Already, she felt maternal. Her breasts tingled. She touched them tenderly, imagining David's son suckling there.

She breathed a sigh of relief when the slaves left the house for the night. Did any of them guess about David? Did they talk among themselves? Did they pass the word to the slaves on the Butler plantation? Eager for David to arrive, she roamed restlessly about the house. She wouldn't tell him about the baby—not until they were on their way to Paris.

She heard the horses' hoofs kicking up the dry summer clay. She ran to the door to welcome him. There was a new lilt to her voice when she spoke to him tonight.

"You look about fifteen tonight," he teased while they walked, arm and arm, upstairs to her room.

"David, I'm accepting Butler's offer," she told him, watching his face. There, he was upset—he knew this meant she must be leaving. "David—" She sounded breathless, as though she was just that instant hitting on the idea. "David, why don't you go back with me? You'll love Paris. I'll have money enough from the sale to buy a fabulous place outside of Paris. You'll be able to try out all your theories there."

"Your money," David reminded. Yet there was anticipation in his eyes.

"Our money," she corrected. "Oh, David, I'd never have got away except for you. Whatever I have is yours, too."

"The overseer we have now is fairly competent," he said slowly, battling in his mind. "He can manage the place. But, Eulalie, how can I?" He shook his head in frustration.

"David, think of us!" She pulled him to her. "Oh, David, come back with me."

"You know I want to, Eulalie." His voice was deep with intensity. "But I have responsibilities. I can't think only of myself."

"Don't say no," she begged. "David, think about it."

He'd said nothing of his wife, she rejoiced inwardly when they lay across Eulalie's bed, resting after spent passion. So, there was no love between him and his wife—only a sense of responsibility, which she would have expected of David. His mother had pushed him into that marriage so there would be a son to inherit The Willows. Cindy would never give them a child—Margaret Woodstock must know that. Oh, how glad she was to carry David's child in her belly! But she wouldn't tell him. Not yet. The certainty was growing in her that David would not allow her to leave alone.

Eulalie went ahead with the sale of the property, conferring with the lawyers, doing whatever was necessary to speed up the transaction. All the while, she watched David, saw the agony in him, the tearing apart brought on by his innate sense of responsibility versus his love for her.

The night before the final papers were to be signed, David came to her. They would leave together. Tomorrow night, while the Woodstocks and the Butlers slept, they would ride across the state to the railroad line that would take them North. David had made his decision.

Eulalie was gay, charming, as she sat in the lawyer's office with the clutter of men involved in the transaction. She even flirted a little—with everybody except David. And then it was over—and Bradford Taylor's inheritance had been transformed into American cash, which Eulalie would take back with her to Paris.

"That's a lot of money for you to have lying around the house," the elder Butler quipped. "Why don't you come over and stay with us for the night?" His wife would not appreciate that, Eulalie laughed inwardly.

"I'll be fine," Eulalie insisted. "I'll keep a pair of slaves down in the kitchen tonight to make sure." She wouldn't, of course. Tonight—much later—she and David would be riding through the darkness to a new life.

Eulalie returned to Taylor Place with the knowledge that tonight she was a guest in that house—until such time as David came for her and they left. She had an early dinner, then dismissed the house slaves. Presumably, she would not be leaving until the end of the week.

She was waiting on the portico when David rode up to the steps.

"Last night in the house," she greeted him effervescently. Not even a whole night—just until David felt it was late enough for them to ride undisturbed.

What did his wife think when he left her bed all these nights? Or was Annette Woodstock too fragile to share her bed with her husband? Did they sleep separately, like George and Margaret Woodstock?

"Let's go inside," David said, his arm closing in about her waist.

Tonight, there was a new intensity in him that should have forewarned her. After they had made love, she lay against the pillows with his head on her breast and talked fervently about her beloved Paris. And then David lifted his head from her breast, propped himself upon an elbow, and gazed down upon her. Looking into his eyes, Eulalie felt a faint stirring of unease. A coldness closed in about her, even before he began to talk.

"Eulalie, how am I going to tell you?" His eyes were agonized, his voice miserable.

"Tell me what, David?" But she knew it was something bad.

"All our plans—it's no good, Eulalie." He closed his eyes for a moment, then shook his head. "This morning, Annette called me to her room." So they didn't sleep together. "She—she told me she's pregnant, Eulalie." He took a deep breath and forced himself to go on. "I can't walk out now, not on my child."

His untainted, *white* child, Eulalie gibed at herself in bitterness. She had never had a chance with David Woodstock. Deep inside, hadn't she known something would arise to stop them? But it wasn't his wife, she thought with meager triumph. His child stood between them.

She would not be completely the loser, Eulalie told herself sternly. She too was carrying David Woodstock's child, the child she had deliberately conceived in love. David's son, about whom he would never know.

"No, David," she said with painful quietness. "You can't walk out on your child."

Eulalie walked out on the portico for the last time. The hot July air was drenched with the scent of honeysuckle and roses, and a house slave was singing at the window as she polished the glass to a glistening splendor for the new owners. How many Southerners, like David, believed that the days of the old South were numbered? How long before slavery vanished into the history books? What would David tell his son about the institution of slavery?

The carriage rolled up before the house. Only Juno came out to hover solicitously over her as she prepared to leave. Juno, wearing the outrageous earrings Eulalie had given her. The other slaves kept an admiring distance from her. Didn't they suspect at all?

The horses came to a noisy stop. Juno and the driver transferred Eulalie's luggage from the portico to the carriage. Eulalie lifted her skirts, daintily climbed into the carriage. The driver lifted his whip.

"Wait!" she called out imperiously, suddenly descending without help, running into the house again to the small, inlaid table which she had not bothered after all to take back with her to Paris. She fumbled inside the drawer, pulled forth the two books. The orations of freedom and the slender volume of poetry. Now, she headed back for the carriage. Juno hovered mournfully at the steps. "Juno, can you read?" she asked.

"Me?" Juno looked startled. Then she grinned. "No read, but someday me learn," she said, eyes solemn.

Eulalie smiled brilliantly.

"Here," she said to Juno, handing over the book of orations on freedom. "Learn to read this."

Eulalie climbed into the carriage, the book of poems gripped tightly between her hands. She refused to acknowledge the tears that spilled over. David's book—and David's son growing here in her belly—that would be enough. Eulalie lifted her head proudly. It would be enough.

Romantic Fiction

If you like novels of passion and daring adventure that take you to the very heart of human drama, these are the books for you.

☐ AFTER—Anderson   Q2279   1.50
☐ THE DANCE OF LOVE—Dodson   23110-0   1.75
☐ A GIFT OF ONYX—Kettle   23206-9   1.50
☐ TARA'S HEALING—Giles   23012-0   1.50
☐ THE DEFIANT DESIRE—Klem   13741-4   1.75
☐ LOVE'S TRIUMPHANT HEART—Ashton   13771-6   1.75
☐ MAJORCA—Dodson   13740-6   1.75

Buy them at your local bookstores or use this handy coupon for ordering: